P9-AGH-724

REUNION

BRUCE SIMONIAN

TATE PUBLISHING
AND **ENTERPRISES**, LLC

Reunion
Copyright © 2013 by Bruce Simonian. All rights reserved.

No part of this publication may be reproduced, stored in a retrieval system or transmitted in any way by any means, electronic, mechanical, photocopy, recording or otherwise without the prior permission of the author except as provided by USA copyright law.

This novel is a work of fiction. Names, descriptions, entities, and incidents included in the story are products of the author's imagination. Any resemblance to actual persons, events, and entities is entirely coincidental.

The opinions expressed by the author are not necessarily those of Tate Publishing, LLC.

Published by Tate Publishing & Enterprises, LLC
127 E. Trade Center Terrace | Mustang, Oklahoma 73064 USA
1.888.361.9473 | www.tatepublishing.com

Tate Publishing is committed to excellence in the publishing industry. The company reflects the philosophy established by the founders, based on Psalm 68:11,
"The Lord gave the word and great was the company of those who published it."

Book design copyright © 2013 by Tate Publishing, LLC. All rights reserved.
Cover design by Allen Jomoc
Interior design by Deborah Toling

Published in the United States of America

ISBN: 978-1-62746-854-1
1. Fiction / General
2. Fiction / Contemporary Women
14.10.17

Dedication

This novel is based on a true story. It is dedicated to those families. It reaffirms hope and love and that life can be stranger than fiction.

Acknowledgments

I would like to thank my wife Suzanne for her unwavering support and enthusiasm in writing this novel, my first book. I love you dearly.

I would also like to thank my children, Dusty, Daniel, Taylor, Frank, Gina, and Johnny. They make life worth living to the fullest.

Kat Terrey, for her inspiration and valuable input.

Dale Brown, for being a mentor and friend.

Kris Kozar, for helping me navigate the process.

Chapter 1

Raley's Supermarket, South Reno

Taylor doubled over as the bottle crashed to the floor, her curly brown hair touching the tile. Two shoppers, an elderly man picking out salad dressing and a mother with her little boy sitting in the cart, stopped frozen with hesitation in the aisle a few feet away.

"Mommy, look, that girl's praying."

"Sssshhh," the mother said, gesturing with her finger against her lips.

"Honey, don't move." "Someone help us here," Gina carefully brushed away splintered glass and brown liquid looking around for assistance.

The balsamic vinaigrette smelled like ammonia. The shoppers didn't move. Broken glass dripped off a nearby shelf.

Taylor's breathing was strained and shallow. "Mom, I feel sick to my stomach."

Gina stood nervously, pulling her short hair with her eyes wide open. A tall young man, wearing a gray apron, came running down from a display where he'd been stacking bags of chips and bent over Taylor. "What is going on? How can I help? Should I call an ambulance? I know CPR." The eager young teenager leaned over them, waiting for an answer, his long hair a curtain over his face. His hands twitched at his sides.

"Please just help us up. I'm sorry about the mess. My daughter had radiation this morning, and she's feeling weak and nauseous. She said she was feeling okay earlier. I should have taken her straight home."

She stepped back as the boy came forward. He helped Taylor up, gently grabbing her elbow and lifting her to her feet.

"Young man…"

"It's Adam…"

"Adam, we need to be careful, she bruises easily," Gina said, moving Taylor back a step.

Taylor looked up through dilated eyes. "I feel so sick, Mom. Please take me home."

"Don't worry about a thing. I'll clean this up. You get your daughter home," Adam said, rubbing his hands together. "Give me your grocery list and I'll get the things you need. I get off work in twenty minutes, and I'd be happy to drop them off."

"That is so nice of you," Gina pulled out a piece of paper from her purse. "It's a gray house with white trim." She said while she wrote down her address. "My white Lexus will be in the driveway. Here's the list and the address, and please let me pay you for the bottle we broke as well." Gina pulled a plastic produce bag down from a roll over the lettuce and stuffed it in her pocket while she helped her daughter negotiate the aisles. Taylor was pale and her lips were almost blue.

Gina clicked open the doors on the Lexus and helped Taylor swing her legs into the passenger seat. Her knees were stained a light brown and smelled from the balsamic.

"Sit up a sec so I can get your seat belt on," she said softly. "Lean against the door. I'll put the window down."

Taylor didn't say a thing, but moved as directed, pressing her pale olive skin against the door. "The fresh air feels good," she said, taking short breaths.

"It should help ease the nausea." Gina watched as Taylor fought the urge to vomit. "I'll get you in bed and then I'll, I'll…" She took a look at Taylor. "I hope you don't get sick, honey. I…"

———*∞*———

Adam wiped his hands off with a rag, pulled on a pair of pale white latex gloves, cleaned up the broken glass and vinegar. Gina had scribbled the list on the back of an envelope. He looked it over, got a shopping cart, and started gathering the items. Low-fat 2 percent milk, whole-wheat bread, eggs, the balsamic, olive oil, crackers, chicken, tri-tip, oranges, apples, bananas, broccoli and spinach. He packed each bag carefully and then placed them in the back seat of his Mustang. He drove down the highway toward the end of town, listening to a tune by Frank Tarantino.

Taylor had been diagnosed with stage 3 lymphoma three weeks earlier. She got radiation and chemotherapy twice a week, but the cancer continued to progress. Dr. Lippert, her attending physician, met Taylor at Renown Hospital each day when she was scheduled for radiation or chemo. He was the best oncologist in the area.

"Taylor, you're young, you're strong, you'll be fine. Keep a positive attitude about this thing and you'll beat it," the doctor said that afternoon. "I know you're tired, but that's okay. You'll get better."

At fourteen, she did have the strength to combat this terrorist in her body, but her body was waning. Taylor's thinning hair hung in ringlets over her shoulders. Because of the pain and loss of energy, she carried herself hunched over so she appeared older than her years. However, despite the fatigue, she still smiled.

"How are you feeling, Taylor?" people would ask.

"Slightly better than fabulous," she replied, flashing a wide smile.

She edged her way out of the car and stumbled up the walkway against the wind into the house. Looking at the ground,

Taylor kept her hands wrapped around her stomach, knees and head bent. Sally from next door was out watering her flowers and looked over. Her horse hung his head over the wooden fence with its ears up. They watched Taylor as she made her way into the house. Once inside the entry, she kicked her sandals off and staggered down the hallway to her bedroom. She peeled her clothes off, leaving a trail, crawled into her bed, and pulled the sheets over her head.

"Honey, here's a glass of cold water and a bowl in case you get sick. There's a towel next to it here on the nightstand," Gina said, tucking a blanket around her.

Outside, the wind pounded its fists against the house trying to shake the color from the paint and the grain from the exposed wood. Leaves flew in swirls, stopped, caught their breath and attacked again.

"Do you want your pajamas or are you okay in your underwear?"

"I'm okay," Taylor moaned against her pillow.

"Call me if you need me," Gina said softly as she quietly left the room.

The drapes were drawn together in front of a window that gazed over a garden of daffodils and tulips. The room reflected amber on its walls and ceiling as the noon sun tried to push through the heavy curtains. The wind continued to groan outside, rattling the closed panes. Taylor was a still lump under the covers, her shallow breathing the only sign of life. Gina walked silently down the hall to the den, lowered herself into the brown leather armchair near the window, and put her head in her hands.

A short time later, Adam pulled up outside, parked his car and pressed hard against the wind as he walked up to the front door with two bags of groceries. On the porch, there was a small bench with a pot of daisies and petunias shaking in the strong breeze. He stared at them as he rang the bell.

Gina heard the bell, tossed her hair back and wiped her eyes with the heel her hand. She adjusted her pants and slowly got up. Opening the door, she was staring directly into the sun as the wind whipped her hair around her face like brown feathers.

"Hi, I ah, I've got your groceries," he said, looking down at her, extending his arms with the bags.

Squinting in the bright light, she struggled to focus. "Oh, thank you, I really appreciate the help," Gina dabbed her eyes again.

Adam stood motionless in the whirl of the wind, and then turned to go back for the remaining bags. The screen door banged against the house as he returned. He knocked on the open door and stepped inside. "Hello, ma'am. I've got your other groceries." The room was a dark chamber. Missy, a docile white pit bull, lay quietly by the sliding door. She raised her head, checked him out, and then went back to her nap. The shades were pulled down tight. Not a book or magazine appeared out of place. A multi-colored area rug lay across a dark hardwood floor in front of the sofa. Limp flowers lay over the edge of a glass vase on the coffee table. The wind slammed the door open against the interior wall as Gina reappeared from the kitchen.

"Ooo, that scared me. I don't like the wind." She froze in mid-step. "Adam, you are so kind. How much do I owe you?" Gina walked over to a small mahogany desk in the entry hall. She located some cash and her checkbook in the center drawer among some pencils, pens, and stamps. She took a deep breath and sat down.

"It's $41.50 including the broken bottle," he replied, walking up and handing her the receipt. The ink was faded. She held it up, checking the items to see what he bought. Her writing was illegible as she struggled with the pen to fill out the check.

"This wind is horrible today. Thanks again, this is for your help," Gina said, handing him the check and a ten-dollar bill.

"Oh, you don't have to do that," Adam said, raising his hands in protest, still holding the groceries.

"Please take it," Gina replied, leaning forward, pushing the check with the bill into his shirt pocket and grabbing the bags. "I hope these handles don't tear off."

"I can help you carry those to the kitchen."

"No, I'll be fine."

"Well, okay, thanks then. I hope your daughter is okay. I hope she gets better soon. I should have picked a purple flower for her. I'll remember flowers the next time."

"Thanks, she'll be fine." She slowly closed the door, her eyes following him to his car.

The Mustang roared to life, and then it was gone.

The house was quiet, except for the relentless gusts outside. Gina walked back to the kitchen and began putting things away. She paused for a moment, pulling her short hair back taunt staring out into the backyard. It slipped back through her fingers strand by strand as she sighed. She looked around the corner and down the hall. She had left the bedroom door open a little so she could hear Taylor if she needed anything.

"Taylor, are you okay in there?" No reply.

She put the fruit in a large wooden bowl decorated with painted flowers they brought back from a trip to Puerto Vallarta a year earlier. She stared at it now, recalling the fun they had walking up and down the cobbled streets looking at art, listening to music, and trying different foods. They took a picture of their feet in the sand with the ocean in the background. It hung in Taylor's room over her bed. Gina took another deep breath and slowly let the air out. She filled the hanging, metal, webbed baskets with the vegetables. She used to enjoy arranging the fruit and vegetables as though they were art, adding to the ambiance of the kitchen. Since Taylor began her treatments, those simple little things had drifted away.

"Taylor, what would you like for dinner?" Gina asked, knowing there would be no answer. She continued, "We've got chicken or hamburgers. I can make steamed broccoli or squash. *This is so difficult,* she said quietly to herself, selecting a vegetable from each bin. "Taylor, can you hear me?" she said so softly she barely heard the words as they left her mouth. "Just a little salt and pepper, I'll cut up the leftovers for sandwiches and lunch tomorrow." Her cheeks became red as she rubbed the tears with the back of her hands. "Please eat, honey." There was no answer.

Taylor had radiation on Wednesdays and chemo on Fridays. It gave Gina and Taylor time to recover over the weekend and get ready for work and school. Thursdays were the toughest. Wednesday nights were a sleepless ordeal and both would be dead tired come morning. "Thank heaven, it's Friday," Gina said as she finished preparing the food.

Saturday morning, Taylor walked into her mother's room as she was getting up. "I want to be a doctor like you, Mom. I want to help young children," she said, twisting her curls with her fingers as she spoke.

"The work is emotionally tough, but the rewards are beyond measure, honey. You have so much empathy, compassion and understanding. Children need those things when they are sick. They are the best prescription for an illness. There is so much going on that youngsters can't comprehend. I think you'd be an awesome doctor," Gina said, walking over and taking Taylor in her arms." I love you so much."

"I love you too, Mom," she said, returning the embrace.

"Would you like to go shopping today? Macy's is having a sale."

"I'm tired, but that sounds like so much fun. Yes, let's go." Taylor said, walking back to her room and getting dressed.

"It's so refreshing in here." Gina touched Taylor's elbow as they entered the mall. "Let's go to Seventh Heaven, they're having a special on scarves, two for the price of one."

"I want to try on some jeans first. We can do scarves on the way out," Taylor said, leading her mother towards Macy's.

"Mom, look, these are awesome," Taylor said, pulling out a pair bejeweled with the knees missing.

"Taylor, only half the jeans are there. Look, there are holes in the butt and they're ripped on the sides."

"Mom, that's the look now. I'm gonna try 'em on. Tell me what you think when I come out," she said, heading to a fitting room.

She returned moments later, spinning in front of the large mirror in the aisle. "Mom, these are awesome."

"Yes, and they're thirty percent off," Gina said, throwing her arms in the air spinning with her. "I think that's because so much of the fabric is missing."

"Oh, Mom, be serious."

"They do look good on you," Gina said, dropping her arms. "Anything would."

"I know," she said smiling, looking over her shoulder in the mirror. "When I get better, let's go back to Mexico or Lake Powell. I heard it's beautiful there."

"It's the lower part of the Grand Canyon. I'd like to see that. Maybe hike down to the bottom."

"Like, take a mule ride?" Taylor asked, walking back into the fitting room.

"Sure, and they have rafting too. We could do all sort of things," Gina said, talking over the café doors.

"Maybe, I'll meet a guy like Brad Pitt. You know, get married have kids. I want all boys, though," Taylor chuckled.

"You can't just choose."

"Sure I can. Why not? It's just a dream," Taylor said, returning with the pants over her arm.

"You're too funny. Why, of course, anything else you'd like to try on?"

"No, that's it," Taylor replied.

"You two are so cute," a customer said as she walked by. "Have a wonderful day."

"Thanks, you too," Taylor followed her mother to the check-out stand.

"Taylor, are you going to get up?" Gina asked, poking her head in the bedroom Sunday morning.

"I feel so weak. I want to lie in bed for a while. I still feel nauseous from the radiation," Taylor said with her head buried in the pillow.

"Your Gramma will be here shortly. I've got leave for work in an hour or so," Gina walked up to her bed. "Are you sure I can't get you something? Crackers, a soda?"

"No, Mom. Is she spending the whole week again?"

"Yes, is that okay? She could stay longer, but she likes to be back for church on Sunday. She misses your grandpa too."

"Mom, Grandpa doesn't like me, does he? He never comes down here, and he's always so grumpy."

"Don't talk like that. He loves you. He just doesn't know how to show it sometimes."

"Mom, do you miss Daniel? I do...where's Missy?"

"She's lying by the door. Yes, I miss Daniel very much," Gina said, turning her head away and looking outside. A gaggle of quail pecked away in the front yard. "It's hard to believe he's gone."

"Missy. Here, girl. Missy," Taylor called.

"I'll get her for you. I'll be right back." Gina walked out to the living room where Missy rested against the sliding glass door. "Shane, where are you?" Gina said, looking into the backyard, taking a deep breath and exhaling. "Come, Missy, let's go see Taylor."

Chapter 2

Fifteen years earlier, the baseball field at Incline High School. It's Friday afternoon, the last week of school before graduation.

"Move over, we need to get to our seats," Maria said as she and Gina helped each other up the bleachers just behind the dugout fence. They looked over at third base and pounded their feet. "Come on, boys, beat 'em bad."

"Hey, Dusty, Chip, up here. Woohoo!' Gina yelled through her megaphone, rubbing shoulders with Maria.

"Team Incline, team Incline," the crowd chanted as they stomped their feet.

"Gina, you can be our secret weapon against the other teams," JT shouted. "Hey, Shane, what do you think?"

"Leave her alone," Shane shouted back, walking out to the field. "We don't need a secret weapon to beat these guys. We have Hard-Hitting Chip Sinder here at the plate and Dangerous Dusty Morgan over there at second," he said, catching their attention as he tossed the ball in.

"Thanks, Shane. We do what we can though, haven't missed a game yet," Gina said, laughing

"Shane's talking a bunch of smack again." Maria leaned over toward Gina. "They're all good and undefeated. Just wait, they won't be beat this season by anyone."

"Baseball is Shane's ticket to a great university. He has offers from ASU and Cal-Berkeley. I'm so excited for him," Gina said, watching Shane warm up. "He throws in the mid-eighties and he has a good ERA."

"Earned run average," Shane's father said, elaborating as he and Suzanne, Shane's mother found seats to the girls. "Coach said it's around 4.3, not bad for a high school pitcher. He's built like a pitcher too, six feet two inches, one hundred and eighty pounds and it's all muscle."

"Oh, I know, and his brown hair and eyes are nice too." Gina blushed.

"Go for two," Chip yelled as he threw a fastball to Dusty covering at second.

Dusty tagged the imaginary runner at second and fired the ball to first. Nick looked down at the ball in his mitt and tossed it back to Shane on the mound. Walking back to the screen, Chip pulled off his mask and cap and brushed the perspiration off his short blonde hair. He bent down and swept the dust off the plate with his mitt. Dusty adjusted the bandana under his cap and pushed his mirrored aviator shades back up on his nose. It was a very hot day and the shade from a departing sun was hours away.

"Let's get some more infield practice before they bat," Nick said, looking at Shane.

Coach Pacini walked out to the mound. "JT, you and Jake work on your release to first. Nick, throw them some balls before the game starts," Coach said, pointing at the players. "Kyle, I'm going to run to the restroom," he said as Kyle came in from left field to get some water. "Have Tommy hit you some more flies so you get used to the sun in your eyes." He walked toward the green cinderblock building a short distance away.

Shane scrunched his mouth and dipped his head in agreement. Shane threw a two-finger fastball over the plate to Chip and stepped out of the way as Chip fired a grounder to Jake at short. Jake took it on one hop and threw a strike to Nick. There was a loud crack as it hit his mitt. Nick in turn threw a hard grounder to JT near third. He dug it out of the dirt and threw it high and wide to first. Nick jumped as high as he could, stretching toward right field and snagged it before it got away.

"I thought I pulled a hamstring. I'm tall, but I'm not that tall, JT," Nick joked. "You released the ball too late. It has to leave…"

"I know," JT replied. "I just got distracted by that girl in the bleachers over there winking at Shane."

"I heard that, you creeper," Gina said, smiling.

Shane stepped back on the mound and began a tirade of cheers. "Remember what Yogi Berra said, 'It ain't over till it's over.' Now, get your rears in gear. Dig deeper! Let's get it. Get tough."

Pacini pulled a pack of Marlboro's out of his small utility bag. He grabbed one cigarette and packed it against his palm. He lit up as soon as he disappeared into the facility. A small trail of smoke filtered out from the window over the sink. Looking over at the green building, Tommy saw a faint sign of the burning tobacco and could hear Coach coughing after each deep inhale.

"Coach ought to quit smoking," Kyle said to Chip who was leaning against the cyclone fencing behind home plate. "He used to be such a super athlete. It's a shame."

"He ain't no quitter," Chip replied, laughing. "Anyway, he can't run anymore, so what's the point?"

"True," Kyle said, turning back around toward the field.

"All right, batter up!" The umpire walked onto the field tossing a new baseball in play.

Frank adjusted his chest protector and mask as he took his position behind Chip. The boys tossed the practice balls in and Chip handed them to the umpire for his inspection. The umpire rolled them over to the dugout as the other team trotted in from the field.

"Look at his face," Jake said." The ump looks like he's trying to take a dump."

"That's why he's so miserable. He's all backed up," Chip added.

"Dag nabbit, young kids today have no respect for their elders," JT said, mimicking the umpire.

"I wish we could find someone else to call the pitches." Jake loaded a handful of sunflower seeds in his hand. "The strike zone is two inches high and four inches wide when Shane's throwin' and it's huge when we're at bat. It is not fair at all. I don't know what pitches to hit and which ones to take," Jake said, looking at Coach Pacini as he returned to the dugout.

"Don't worry about him. Just play ball the best you can. Frank's tough calls keep your game tight."

Jake shrugged his shoulders and rubbed his bare knuckles hard against his mitt. "Prick."

Three up and three down, the Vikings returned to their dugout. Then, it was the Highlander's turn to try to score some runs. It was the bottom of the first inning.

"Batter up," Frank yelled again, lowering his mask and crouching behind the catcher. "Let's go."

Chip walked up to the plate. "Chew a breath mint," Chip said under his breath. "What crawled in your mouth and died?" He mumbled.

Chip dared not look over his shoulder. He glanced toward Coach Pacini at third in the coach's box. His head was damp with perspiration.

"Come on, Chip, send it over the fence. Get a hit! Come on now! Wait for your pitch," the crowd yelled as the first pitch smacked into the catcher's mitt. Shane looked over his shoulder at his mom and dad and Gina. Gina winked when she saw him.

Chip flexed his knees, rolled the bat front to back, and then cocked his front foot, holding the bat off his shoulder. The pitch sailed by him waist high over the center of the plate.

"Strike!" the umpire bellowed. Shane stood up and pressed his face against the dugout fence as Chip stepped out of the batter's box.

"What?" Pacini was busy giving Chip signs. "Got it, Coach." Chip nodded and stepped back in. The sun was high and intense. Chip took a deep breath. A bead of perspiration dripped down behind his left ear. He wiped it away with his shoulder.

Bill grabbed hold of the metal bleachers with both hands, tense with excitement. "Let me know if we yell too loud," Bill said, leaning over toward Gina and Maria. Suzanne glanced at Bill and smiled.

"Ball one," the umpired yelled as he stood up.

"Good eye, Chip," Shane's mother shouted. Shane looked back at her.

"Hey, you, up at the screen shooting video, move your head," Bill said, raising his Highlander cap as Ralph, Chip's dad turned around. "You're blocking my view." Ralph waved him off with his free hand.

"Bill, nice t-shirt. I used to have one just like it and then my dad got a job," Ralph said, laughing.

Bill stood up and pulled his worn Highlander shirt away from his chest. "I'm proud to wear this, you should get one. At least we have caps."

"I don't need a cap. I'm not bald like you. Atta boy," he said softly as Chip took another ball.

"Good eye," Bill yelled. "Wait for your pitch." He took a sip of his beer, hidden in a brown paper bag.

"Wait for a good one," Chip's mom said, raising her voice to match Bill's.

"And the wind up and the pitch," the announcer broadcasted, finally getting the microphone working, as the pitcher tossed a curve ball down and in. Chip connected hard, hitting a line drive between short and third down the left field line. Coach Pacini waved Chip around first and held him up at second. The crowd stood up and cheered as Chip slipped his gloves back into his pocket and tossed his ankle protector into Jake who was coaching first base.

"Yeah!" Jake yelled as he caught the equipment and threw it over toward the dugout. The umpire jumped out of the way.

Chip readjusted his cap and helmet and wiped the sweat off his forehead with his forearm. "Come on, hit the snot out of it Shane."

The boys leaned against the fence from in the dugout, fingers holding onto the wire, their faces focused on Shane as he left the on-deck circle heading toward the plate. Gina intertwined her hands nervously.

"Come on, Shane, knock it out. Bring 'im home. Come on," Gina yelled.

Maria joined in as the crowd started to chant. "Shane, Shane, Shane!"

"Low and inside," came the voice from the speakers. "Ball one." Shane stepped out of the batter's box, adjusted the Velcro on his gloves, looked to Pacini for a sign, and stepped back in.

"Low and outside," the announcer blared over the loudspeakers.

The umpire held up two fingers. Shane dug his cleats into the dirt, twisting for traction. Leaning back, bat at the ready, he swung at the next pitch. He sent the ball back to the screen.

"Foul ball, two balls, and one strike," said the announcer.

"The next one's yours," shouted Gina, sitting on her hands and bouncing up and down. Shane looked up at her and winked. Gina smiled as he turned his head back around.

The next pitch was a changeup, moving slightly right to left and down. Shane hit the ball, fully extending his arms toward left center. Crack! Shane took off running, carrying the bat and then tossing it aside near first base. The ball dropped between the fielders in left and center and bounced to the warning path coming to rest against the fence. Chip scored easily. The ball came in as Shane rounded second on his way to third. The shortstop cut it off and threw high and wide toward home. Shane slid past the catcher's feet and stopped in cloud of dust beyond the plate. The catcher came down with the ball near the screen too faraway to make a play. The crowd was on its feet cheering. Chip was waiting for him. He reached over and helped Shane up giving him a high five with his free hand. Shane brushed the dust off and turned toward the stands.

"Atta boy, Shane," his dad yelled while Suzanne clapped until her hands were red and swollen.

"I love you, Shane," Gina shouted amongst the roar of the crowd.

Shane looked up at the bleachers and smiled. He gathered his helmet off the ground, brushed off his shirt again, and headed back to the dugout. After the high fives and fist bumps, the boys settled down. "He knew just where to put it. The pitcher didn't fool him for a minute with that changeup, an in-the-park homerun. That's my boy," Bill boasted, taking a sip of his beer.

Suzanne stood, shaking her head in agreement. The game concluded in the evening shadows near suppertime. The final score was seven to two, Shane's team defeating the Vikings. After showering, Coach Pacini had a few words to say in the locker room as the boys were dressing.

"You played well today." The players pulled on their shirts, pants, and shoes, hardly paying any attention.

"Shane, listen up, you too, Dusty," Pacini said. "I think we could have done better in the outfield. Tom and Kyle, you were a little slow out there."

"I'm missing a sock. Who stole my sock?" JT asked.

"JT, I'm trying to talk here. I'll be done in a moment. Some of you and I know you know who you are, need to spend more time at batting practice. Ned, make sure you use the cutoff man.

Ned, I'm talking to you. Your arm is not as strong as you think it is. There was great fielding at the bases, and Jake, you were on it at shortstop. The bottom line is you all played an excellent game."

Jake turned around, pulling his t-shirt over his thick blonde hair. "Thanks, Coach."

"Shane, you were excellent on the mound and got a nice hit. There were two scouts in the stands watching you this afternoon. I would have shared that with you sooner, but I wanted you to keep your mind on the game."

"Thanks, Coach. I saw 'em," Shane replied.

"Men, go home, get your homework done and get a good night's rest. We have practice tomorrow after school. We also need to get ready for Saturday's game against Whitel. We have practice at ten o'clock, and the game starts at one."

"It's game night, Coach. Homework? Really?" The team said as they gathered their things.

"It is still a school night, academics first."

"Let's go get pizza!" a few of the players shouted.

Bill, Suzanne, Gina, and Maria were waiting by the exit door for Shane when he came out of the locker room. "That was a great game. They hit well, they fielded, they..." Bill started to say.

"Shane looked awesome on the mound," Suzanne said, still beaming.

"He sure did. His..." Gina said, trying to speak.

"I think the scouts were impressed," Suzanne added.

"Excellent game, son," his dad said as he saw Shane appear. "Your arm won the game. We should ice it when you get home for a while and then protect it," Bill added, extending his hand to shake Shane's. Suzanne wrapped her arms around his neck and gave him a kiss on the cheek.

"I love you, son," Suzanne whispered in his ear. She stepped back and looked at him from bottom to top. "I can just see you in a major league uniform, blue and white stripes...Go Yankees!"

"Let me take a picture of all of you," Maria said, pulling out her camera. "Stand over here in front of the Highlander banner." She directed and then took the pose. "One more and we're done. Look at me and smile. Really, Shane, now be serious. No rabbit ears and smile."

She lifted up her large handbag and dropped the camera in while searching for lip gloss. Gina slipped her hand in Shane's, rubbing her shoulder up against his, searching for his eyes. His hair was still wet and his t-shirt had water spots where he hadn't toweled off. He looked down at Gina as Maria was talking.

"Gina, do you want some gloss?" Maria asked before putting the lipstick away.

"No thanks, Shane'll just kiss it off," Gina replied, looking at Shane and blinking her eyes.

"The guys want to go out for pizza. Gina, would you and Maria like to come?" Shane asked.

"I'd love to, but I need to study for our geometry test tomorrow," Gina replied.

"I've got homework and I have to study as well," Maria chimed in.

"Wow, I thought pizza with a couple of hot girls like you was a done deal," Shane said, joking.

"Our finals are important," Gina said. "Don't take it so personal, you handsome hunk of muscle." Listening, Suzanne laughed as she and Bill walked to their car and left.

"Well, I guess we'll take a rain check then," Shane said, feeling disappointed.

Shane kissed Gina tenderly good night and gave Maria a quick hug as he unlocked the Jetta. He tossed his gym bag in the backseat. The interior was hot from the afternoon heat. He turned on the AC and lowered all the windows. Shane selected a CD. Paula Cole was shaking the dash as he pulled away from the curb, singing, "*Where have all the cowboys gone…*" "To do their homework," he answered under his breath.

It was close to 7:00 when Bill and Suzanne arrived at their small home on Wendy Lane. Beige with white trim, it had a one-car garage and a patchy green lawn surrounded by a split rail fence. A walkway of gray quartzite led from the street to the front door. Bill parked their blue Sentra near the garage and walked around to open Suzanne's door. Bill picked up the newspaper in the driveway, and Suzanne opened the mailbox, pulling out the day's delivery. He opened the front door for her and stepped aside.

"Thank you, honey," she said, leafing through the mail as they entered the house. Bill headed toward his favorite armchair in the living room.

Handing him a cold beer, "I can put the news on or the ball game if you want. I'll have dinner ready shortly. I just have to steam the vegetables. The meat is done. Would you like to clean up or shower before it's served?" Bill grabbed the paper and sat down, sipping his drink.

"I'll wait until later. I just want to sit for a bit," he replied. "I really enjoyed Shane's game this afternoon."

"Yeah, that's what you said, so did I."

Bill's hands were dried and cracked from doing construction. Suzanne massaged his shoulders, working from his back up through his neck while the vegetables boiled. Then she slowly massaged moisturizing cream into his palms and fingers. He put his head back and closed his eyes.

"Honey, that feels so good. Thank you," Bill said, barely moving his lips. Suzanne went back to the stove.

"Mom, I'm starving," Shane confessed, as he entered the kitchen.

"Dinner's ready," Suzanne announced, dishing up fresh steamed vegetables, a spinach salad, and curried chicken. "Here's your plate." She handed one to Shane. "Wait, this one is for your dad." Arms and elbows on the table and faces in their plates, they didn't say a word until the first few bites were gone. Suzanne stood back and smiled, then quietly sat, pulling her chair up between the two of them and setting her plate down. "How's the house coming, Bill?"

"I spent the day crawling on my stomach, connecting ducting and strapping loose drain pipe. There were only eighteen inches of clearance between the joists and the powdery dirt. I got lucky, there were no dead mice or snakes, but I felt like Charles Bronson when he was digging the tunnel in the *Great Escape*. I still have a couple of things to tie up with the plumbing in the kitchen and that should be it. I found the water line for the icemaker lying under the house so I reinstalled that, but the rest of the copper line under the sink was still six inches short. Anyway, I have to get an extension, so I'll get that hooked up tomorrow. I changed out the orifices on the new stove from natural gas to propane. My eyes are getting so bad I could barely read the markings on the parts. I left a bottle of Silver Oak cabernet on the counter as a house-warming gift. I wanted to do something a little special for the new owners. It's good karma."

"That was nice of you," Suzanne said, taking a bite of salad.

"Is there another Coors in the fridge?" Bill asked, wiping his mouth.

Shane got up, got another scoop of rice, a piece of chicken, and grabbed a beer for his dad. "I got an A on my American history test. I was a little nervous because Chip said the test was going to be tough. He took it first period, and he barely finished in time. The essay questions were so long, I started to get writer's cramp. I have a geometry test tomorrow. Can't wait until this is over and it's summer, yes, sir," he said, handing Bill his beer and sitting back down. "Boy, I just have a couple more tests and I'm done."

"If you get your studying done, let's go hit some balls," Bill offered. "I understand it's been a long day so let me know how you feel."

"Sure, Pops, I'll let you know. I have to study a bunch of math problems. I have most of it down, so now it's just reviewing the material."

"Shane, we're excited about the prospect of you attending Berkeley or Arizona State, and at the same time, we are sad that you will be leaving and be so far away. We'll come and visit as often as we can, but it won't be the same. Do you have your applications in?" Suzanne asked, getting up from the table.

"Yes, I do. I'm just waiting for them to contact me now." Shane finished his dinner and went to his bedroom to study.

"Bill, do you mind helping me dry the dishes?" Suzanne asked.

"Why, it'd be my pleasure, darlin'," Bill said, tipping his imaginary hat.

Suzanne chuckled and tossed him a dishtowel. Bill leaned over and gave her a soft kiss on the neck, grabbed a plate out of the dish tray, wiped it, and put it up in the cabinet by the sink. Suzanne smiled. "I love you, honey."

"So there were a couple of scouts at the game. Pacini said they were from the Diamond Backs. They didn't speak to Shane at all. I wonder what they thought of his playing ability?" Bill asked reflectively.

"Maybe they were just getting a little more insight, information, or whatever. Heck who knows?" Suzanne said. "Bill, I'm going to miss him if he goes."

"Me too, but we'll be fine, so will Shane," Bill said, still holding the dishtowel. He wrapped his arms around Suzanne and held her, his head against hers while she finished the last dish. "Let's take a shower while Shane is busy with his schoolwork," Bill whispered in her ear. "We need to practice just being with each other." He pulled Suzanne down the hall to their bedroom, their shadows disappearing into the dark silence.

Chapter 3

The sound of a lone bird chirping woke Suzanne early. Opening one eye to check the time, she rolled over and snuggled up against Bill as he slept. He opened his lids slightly at his wife's touch and then closed them again. They laid there until the heat of their bodies became uncomfortable. Suzanne gave Bill a kiss on his ear as she pulled the covers back and got out of bed.

"Rise and shine, sleepyhead." Bill didn't move, groaning as the cold air met his skin.

She put on her pink bathrobe and slippers and made her way to the kitchen, yawning and stretching down the hall past Shane's room. She peered in and he was still fast asleep, mouth wide open. She closed the door quietly and rubbed her eyes.

The early light from a pale blue sky bathed the breakfast room in soft yellow as Suzanne washed out the pot and prepared to make coffee. Staring out the window, she noticed a neighbor walking his dog and waved. She opened the pantry cabinet and got out the Bisquick, found a bowl and milk and eggs out of the fridge. She started humming as she mixed the ingredients into pancake batter. A little vanilla, some cinnamon, powdered sugar, sliced bananas, some cut-up strawberries, and she was ready to go. *Now if the boys would just get up,* she thought impatiently. She poured herself a cup of coffee in a large mug, pulled up a chair at the table, and started leafing through a magazine. At that moment, Bill appeared.

"Mornin', hon, whatcha doin'?" he asked, pouring a cup and looking at the food prepared on the counter. "Looks like pancakes."

"Are you hungry? I'll make you some, and Shane can eat when he gets up," she said, looking up as he stood there a bit groggy.

"What time does Shane have to be up?"

"Practice starts at ten so I'll get him up in a little while," she said, spreading out small circles of batter on the griddle.

Bill poured a generous amount of maple syrup over his pancakes and then added pieces of strawberry and banana. Suzanne joined him with a small stack of her own. They sat quietly until they finished. A short time later, she woke Shane, and he seized the moment to take a shower. She set down a plate of pancakes covered with bananas, strawberries, and powdered sugar for him as he strolled into the kitchen, his hair still wet. He didn't say a word as he smothered the pile of food in butter and maple syrup. Suzanne set a glass of orange juice in front him.

"Good morning, sleep well?" she asked. "You went to bed and were snoring in no time. I hope you're refreshed and ready to play some ball."

"Oh yeah," he continued to eat without looking up. He got up and headed to the sink to rinse his plate when his mother took it. He gave her a hug while she buried her head in his chest and hugged him with the plate in hand. "I love you, Mom."

"I love you too, honey."

Shane got to the ballpark around nine forty-five and suited up. Chip, Jake, and JT arrived in Jake's Ford F-150 flying the school flag. Jake dropped Chip and JT at the gym entrance and then he took off, slammed on the brakes, causing the oversized tires to slide. He proceeded to spin donuts and burn rubber until the coaches came running over from the ball field to put an end to the horseplay. The gas and rubber filled the parking lot with a pungent smell and smoke.

"Yeehaa, wooo wee," he exclaimed, as he hopped down out of the truck pushing the door closed behind him. "I've been wanting to do that since I was a freshman. They can't suspend me now," he said to his teammates, who had been standing just on the other side of the cyclone fence, cheering him on.

"No, but they could decide to not graduate you next week. That was a stupid stunt to pull," Coach Woodward said, coming up and standing chest to chest with Jake.

"He's got more hormones than brains, that kid," Coach Pacini said to Woodward.

"Get over there. You can burn off some of that energy taking six laps around the field while we stretch. Don't stand there looking at me. Go!" The coach said, folding his hand across his chest.

"I was just having fun. I wasn't doing any harm, Coach," Jake said, waving his hands. "I'm innocent."

Nick was still laughing when Jake trotted by to start his run. "I thought you'd flip that old truck of yours."

Shane laced up his shoes and joined the other boys as they walked out to the field. The air was still cool. They left their sweatshirts and jackets on as the sun continued to rise over the trees. The deep fragrance of pine grew as the morning heat evaporated the dew. The dampness kept the dust down while the infielders practiced and Shane warmed up on the mound. After a few minutes, the players started to shed the layers that kept them warm earlier. Jake ran the red dirt warning path in the outfield, down the base line, and around the backstop toward first, and then back out to right. He kicked the small piles of cut lawn in his path like tin cans. He looked over occasionally for sympathy, but no one was paying attention except Coach Pacini.

Counting Jake's laps silently, still steaming, he wanted a cigarette badly. He coughed in anticipation. He took a long deep breath, smelling the residual tobacco on his fingers like it was fine wine.

Chip's mom Diane brought snacks, setting up a serving table a short distance away from the bleachers. She spread orange wedges, energy bars, bottles of water, and oatmeal cookies out for the players. Jake came by as she was finishing up. Diane wore a green ski jacket and a knit hat to keep her ears warm. Her Highlanders sweatshirt was underneath. blue jeans, wool socks, and tennis shoes, she was ready for a day at the park.

"Help yourself, Jake," she said, waving her cold hand over the display of food and then stuffing it back in her jacket pocket.

"Ah, no thanks, not right now. Coach wants me to do some fielding. I'll come back later."

He knew the coach was watching, so he didn't want to make him any madder by taking a snack break while the rest of the team practiced. He smiled at Pacini, as though he knew what he expected and was happy to disappoint him. Pacini turned his head and continued working with JT at third.

The boys took a lunch break at around noon. Several of the team members helped themselves to Diane's snacks and took them out to the lawn in the center field. Although a little damp, the grass was soft to sit on and they could talk undisturbed by the coaches. JT laid back and pulled his ball cap over his eyes. Chip, Nick, and Jake discussed their plans for grad night.

"My dad's got a fifth of Sky Vodka and I'm pretty sure I can sneak some of that out of the house in my water bottle. They'll never know," Jake said confidently.

"I might be able to get some Crown Royal too," Nick added. "The folks have so many bottles of booze, I don't think they'll miss one or two. Anyway, my dad is trying to quit drinking, and I'll be doing him a favor by getting it out of the house."

"My brother said he'd buy up for us. I was going to have him get a case of Bud and a case of Sam Adams," Chip said, pushing his chest out.

"Who's going to drink all that beer?" JT said, overhearing the conversation. "Is that for everybody?"

"It's for whoever pays me for it," Chip replied. "The more money I get, the more beer I get. Simple."

"Shane. What are you and Gina doing tonight? Are you going to a movie?" Dusty asked. "I asked Maria out. I thought we could all drive down to Reno and find something to do. What do you think? How about dinner at Bertha Miranda's and movie?"

"You know, I was thinking about going bowling," Shane replied. "I haven't been in a while. Gina likes to bowl. How about that?"

"I'll ask Maria. Bowling, huh? The last time I went bowling, we still had to get up to change the channel on the TV. Seriously, Shane?" Dusty said, wrinkling his forehead.

"Whatever," Shane replied. "Gina's got church tomorrow so we can't stay out too late. We're probably going to grab a burrito or a salad at T's and then head over to Bowl Incline around eight. We may go to the movie. You guys can join us if you want."

The coach started waving the team in. The boys got up slowly, checking to make sure they got all of their garbage before heading toward the dugout. Pacini had the roster out and was making some final adjustments. He wanted to make sure everyone on the team had the opportunity to play in this final game. He would get his usual starters in first and then rotate the alternates in as soon as feasible. Tommy, Kyle, and Ned took off for the outfield and tossed fly balls back and forth as JT, Chip, Nick, Jake, Shane and Dusty warmed up in the infield. Parents and friends filtered into the bleachers. The normal concession stand was closed, so Diane was busy selling drinks and snacks to the spectators to support the team.

The Highlanders retreated to the dugout while Coaches Pacini and Woodward conferred with the refs, showing them the lineup and getting the guidelines for their calls. The Whitell Rangers took the field for their warm-up in the meantime. Their starting pitcher, number 14, Rollin Stanger, had a hard fastball, but was not consistent. The team had seen his slider, change-up, and curve. He worked the strike zone well. Coach Woodward discussed how to hit Stanger while the team watched and waited to take the field.

Pacini discussed which batters to look out for and where to set up to play them. "I want you guys to talk it up when you are up to bat and when you're out in the field. I want you to be aware of every pitch and literally be on your toes. Keep the energy high. Let's hear it!" Pacini raised his hands for a high ten all around. They huddled, from a low murmur to a loud burst, "Hoaaahhhhh, Highlanders!" The crowd joined in at the end to rock the stadium with volume and excitement.

Bill and Suzanne found two seats behind home plate. Mike and Lacy sat behind first base. Gina, Ally, and Maria found space between first and home, about four rows up from the field. They wore their Highlander caps and t-shirts. They spread out their cushioned green-and-yellow booster seats, grabbed bottled waters, and cheered their guys on.

"Watch his fast ball. He can't get it over the plate. I think if he gets it close, our team will crush it," Bill said to Suzanne, his hands taut on the metal bleachers. "I hope so. Dusty and Jake have been hitting well. Shane too."

Gina and Ally talked while Maria tried to get Dusty's attention in the dugout. "Dusty, hey, second base. Dusty!" He stuck his head out from around the wooden backboard and smiled.

"Hey," he said nonchalantly.

"Have a great game," Maria said with a huge smile.

"Thanks." Dusty stepped back in and sat down.

Whitell's coach got the players together for a meeting on the pitcher's mound, and then they noisily entered the dugout single file. The announcer called out the Highlander player's names as they made their way out to the field. "Playing left field and batting fourth, Tom Wellman, Playing center field and batting eighth, Kyle Ellison, Playing right field," and so on until every man was at his position. The crowd cheered and clapped as each man was introduced. "The starting pitcher for today's game is Shane Kaufmann, with a record of six wins and four losses." Shane warmed up, throwing a few fastballs. Chip threw the last pitch down to Dusty at second as the umpire yelled, "Batter up."

After eight scoreless innings, the Whitell Rangers had a runner on second with the top of the order up. Shane gave up eight hits, walked four batters, and the Rangers still weren't able to get a man across the plate. The Rangers' chance at a win rested on the next batter with two out. Number 24, Rubeschek, was a wiry boy with a wisp of brown hair hanging over his brow and a determined stare. Shane took the sign from Chip and sent a curve ball down and in for a strike. Two-four stepped back and took a sign from his third base coach. Shane looked in, nodded, looked back at second, and threw a fastball chest high that Rubeschek drilled past JT at third out toward the left field line. It landed just fair, bouncing on the warning path. Kyle played it off the wall on a dead run and fired into JT who threw into Chip covering the plate. The throw was late, and the Rangers got their first run. The Highlander's bleachers went quiet as the Whitell fans exploded in applause. Rubeschek ran to second on the throw to home. Shane hung his head as Chip threw him a new ball from the umpire. He turned toward the outfield, rubbing the ball in his glove, trying to compose himself. *Dang it*, he said to himself.

"Atta boy, Shane. It's okay. We still got final ups. Shake it off. Let's go now," the Highlander fans yelled as the boys reorganized themselves for the next batter. Looking down at the dirt, JT pounded his glove in frustration.

"Talk it up out there," Pacini yelled from the dugout. Number 22 was up. He got a hit in the first and another in the fourth. Shane was not going to give him anything good to hit as he looked in for his sign. He looked back at Rubeschek at second and threw it hard to Dusty covering second as 24 took a long lead toward third. Rubeschek made a diving leap back to second, but Shane's throw was right on the money as Dusty tagged his arm reaching for the bag. Bill, Suzanne, Gina, and the others stood and screamed in exhilaration. "Yeah, Yeah! All right, now we got 'em!" The crowd went wild.

———

The Highlanders exited the field as the Rangers got their gear and headed back out from the dugout. Kyle, Tom, and Nick ended the game unceremoniously, three up and three down with Nick swinging at a pitch that was low and away for the final out. The Highlander crowd shuffled out in muffled silence. The coaches congratulated the boys on a good game and a great season. Shane avoided all eyes as he slipped away, feeling totally responsible for the loss. Gina went looking for him before he went into the locker room, but he had hustled along fast enough to evade even her support. The boys tossed their dirty uniforms into a large laundry bin, showered, and got dressed.

Dusty slipped a clean red bandana over his head as he caught up to Shane. "Hey, great game, buddy. Wasn't your fault we lost. We played 'em real tough. They got lucky, was all."

"Yeah, but I threw a fat one that Rubeschek got a hold of. That guy may be small, but he's strong."

"Enough already. Hey, I'll talk to Maria. Maybe we'll see you guys at T's or at the movies." Dusty threw his backpack around his shoulder, gave Shane a fist pump, and got in his car.

Shane called Gina on his way home. "Hey, let's go to the movies. I'm too tired to bowl. Pick you up at six?"

"Are you okay?" she asked.

"Just a little tired, is all," Shane replied.

"The movies are fine. I'll see you at six, bye."

Suzanne and Bill were waiting for Shane when he got home. He tried to slip in unnoticed, but Suzanne saw him and gave him a big motherly hug as he came in the side door off the kitchen.

"Great game, son," Bill said, adding his hug to theirs. "You guys played great defense and got some nice hits. You just needed to link them together. Gosh, I can't believe the season is over."

"Can I fix you something?" Suzanne asked, untangling herself from the threesome. "I know you're hungry."

"Mom, I'm just gonna chill for a while. I'm supposed to pick Gina up at six."

"Where are you two going this evening?"

"We're going to grab some food at T's, and then go to a movie."

"Well, let me know if you need anything. Bill, would you like a cold beer while I'm up?" Suzanne asked.

"Sure, love," Bill said as he sat down heavily in his easy chair and clicked on the TV.

The hot sun and the excitement had worn them all out. Suzanne poured herself a cold glass of water and lay down on the sofa to read.

Chapter 4

Shane lay down for an hour and woke up disoriented. After he got his eyes to focus, he brushed his teeth and combed his hair. He put on a loose short-sleeved shirt and some clean jeans. He slid his feet into a pair of sandals and checked it all out in the hall mirror. He found his parents asleep with the movie still playing. Softly, he whispered, "Mom, Pops, I'm outta here. I'll be home by twelve. Can I take your car? Mine's out of gas."

"Sure, the keys are in the bowl by the front door," Bill replied, waking incoherently from his nap. Suzanne had fallen asleep with her book open on the sofa.

Shane closed the kitchen door quietly, got into his dad's car, readjusted the rearview mirror, and moved the seat back. He changed the music from classic rock to harder rock 'n' roll as he backed out of the driveway.

"Hey, I'm ready. Where are you? How long before you get here?" Gina asked.

"Be there in a sec." Shane was still on the phone when he pulled up. The right front tire screeched as it hit the curb. Gina's mom and dad were in the living room staring out the picture window.

As Shane bounded up the steps. "Good-bye, Mom, Dad, see you later," she said, opening and closing the door quickly behind her. "Let's get out of here. I'm ready to have some fun. How about you? Great game, honey. I tried to find you afterward, but you were gone," she said as he opened her car door.

He hustled around to the driver's door and jumped in, leaned over, and gave her a kiss while watching her parents watching him. He sat back up, smiled, and started the car. "Wow, you look amazing."

Gina had done her eyes in different hues and her mouth with a burgundy lip gloss. She had put on a short red dress and red sandals. "Thanks, just for you."

The parking lot was busy. Patrons were going into the various restaurants and the 7-11. Shane drove around for a few minutes, waiting for a car to leave. Gina talked to Maria on her cell phone, discussing the plans for the evening until they parked. At T's, the line of people waiting to order snaked out of the door and around the building. After fifteen minutes, Shane stood at the counter and ordered a burrito and a cucumber salad for Gina, some chips and guacamole.

"Shane." He grabbed their food when his name came over the speaker. They found a table outside and sat down in the cool evening air to eat.

"That was a tough game. I'm sorry you lost. It was so close until number 24 got that hit. Honey, he just got lucky, was all. I hope you're not bummed," Gina said, rubbing his arm as she spoke.

Shane smiled. "Nah, I'm okay."

"I talked to Maria. She and Dusty are going to drive down to Reno to see a movie at the mall. She'll see us tomorrow if we go to the beach," Gina said, putting her phone away and finishing her salad. Shane finished his burrito and the remaining chips. They cleared off the table, got up, and walked hand in hand next door to the theater.

The line at the theater wound its way out of the rotunda and out into the parking lot. Kyle and Ally were in line with Tom and Nick when they arrived.

"Hey, guys. What's happening?" Kyle said, moving over to let them in line.

"I'm getting some popcorn. Gina would you like anything?"

"Just some water," she replied. "I'm stuffed from dinner."

They found seats near the back of the theater. Shane finished most of the popcorn during the previews, and then ten minutes into the movie, he fell asleep. Gina put up the arm cup holder, letting him drift away against her as she silently cried when the young girl finally found her father. When the lights came on, she leaned over and shook Shane gently awake.

"Wow, did I sleep through the whole thing? Sorry." His popcorn bag still in his lap, he helped Gina up and followed her out of the theater as she related the sad but happy ending.

"Would you like to go down to beach for a swim in the moonlight?" Gina asked, dragging Shane to the Sentra. "It's still early and it feels warm out."

"Sure, I think there's a blanket and maybe some towels in the car. Do you want to walk down to Whale Beach? It's a short hike, and there'll be no one there. I'll run in and grab some bottled water and a snack from Sevi." Shane ran into the 7-11 and came back with a bag of M&M's and a large bottle of water.

They drove down East Shore a few miles. The moon was just coming over the eastern Sierras, its light filtering through the pines. They pulled up over the curb, partially onto the shoulder, and parked just inside the fog line. There were no other cars. It was quiet except for the sound of a few birds. They followed the trail down to the beach as it wound around fallen trees and rocks strategically placed to mark the path. They took their shoes off and went barefoot part of the way.

"Ooo, the dirt is cold," Gina said as they walked.

"We're almost there," Shane said, leading her with his hand.

It took a few more minutes, and then they were standing in the sand, watching the moon's shimmering path cross the lake. Whale rock lay silhouetted in motion against the silver line. The round granite monuments knelt in centuries-old water lines, bathing quietly in the night light. Shane tossed the blanket down on the sand and took off the backpack. He pulled out a couple of towels and laid them over a rock. Gina giggled, dropped her sandals, and pulled her dress off over her head. She reached behind her and slowly unhooked her bra. Then, she inched her thong panties down, dancing in the moon shadows, as Shane stood silently watching.

"Wow, you look beautiful."

She looked at Shane, "Come on, silly, don't be shy. Let's go for a dip. This is the prettiest night ever."

Shane unbuttoned his shirt, dropped his jeans and boxers. Gina took his hand. She guided him chest deep into the water, pulling him close to her glowing smooth white skin. He gently pulled her head toward him, stroking her long hair as they began to kiss. The cool embryonic water swirled around them. Aroused, Shane leaned against her, softly caressing her breasts. She reached down and stroked his firm desire as it pressed searching for her inner beauty in the sparkling lake water. He moved his hands down her sides over her narrow hips to her soft pubic hair, probing.

"I want you, Shane. You know, this will be the first time for both of us," Gina moaned in between long tongue-exploring kisses.

He led her from the water, spreading the blanket out with one hand as they collapsed entwined, kissing, exploring each other's bodies, gently touching, massaging.

"Am I hurting you? Let me know if you want me to stop. Are you okay?" His breathing became rapid. She released herself as a deep voluminous current moved through her in unison with his strokes. Exhausted with love, covered in perspiration and water, they lay limp, looking up at the moon's white affirmation.

"M&M?" Shane said playfully, handing Gina a green-colored piece of candy. "I didn't hurt you, did I?"

"That was wonderful. I only imagined what this moment would be like, the moon, the water, the rocks, and you," Gina said, taking a long drink of water and passing the bottle back to Shane. "Thank you for being gentle. I adore you so much."

Shane wrapped the blanket around them like a cocoon to warm them up. "Gina, I never thought that it would be so magical. Your body is as beautiful as your heart and smile." They held each other in silence, pressing their flesh together. Shane released his grip, still looking deep into her eyes. "We should head back. Our folks may get upset if we're late."

Shane untangled himself and stood up naked and vulnerable, the remaining perspiration on his torso reflecting in the light. Gina tucked her hands behind her head watching Shane while he toweled off and dressed.

"I don't want to move. Let's come back on grad night," Gina said, pulling her knees up to her chin as she sat up. "I would rather spend a romantic night here with you than go to Chip's party."

"Me too. Let's plan it."

She used the other towel to dry off and then gradually got her clothes on. Carrying their sandals, they slowly made their way back up the hill. Over their backs, a soap bubble moon continued to rise, floating over the lake. By the time they reached the car, it was eleven forty-five.

"Dang, I hope my dad doesn't ground me for getting home late," she said, tired from the hike back up the hill. They tossed their gear into the backseat of the Sentra and carefully made a U-turn going back home.

Under the moon's glow, they stealthily pulled up to the house. In the living room, she could see her father on the sofa, watching the TV in the dark.

"I had a great time," she said, barely waiting for the car to stop before getting out. Shane gave her hand a tender squeeze as she left.

"Me too." Shane gazed out of the car as her dad got up and let her in the front door. Her father watched Shane pull away before closing the door and turning off the porch light.

Shane always desired Gina, but he didn't realize she wanted him. He felt flattered, bewildered, calm, and anxious all at the same time.

His mother had given him condoms months earlier. "Here, take this just in case. I know how things can happen, and I want you two to be safe."

"My mom gave me some condoms. She wants us to be careful," Shane shared with Gina a few days later.

"Shane, someday, we may have sex, but not now, perhaps after we are married," Gina responded at the revelation.

What a paradox, he thought.

Chapter 5

Bill got up early and packed the boat for a day at the beach. He stowed the life jackets, ski rope, gloves, oar, sunblock, and towels up under the bow. He checked the tires and lights on the trailer. Suzanne was up by the time he went back in the house.

"Coffee? I was going to make some eggs. What do you want with 'em? Toast? Fruit? What should I pack in the cooler?" Suzanne asked.

"Coffee'd be great. How about if we scramble the eggs up with some veggies and ham? I'll help you cut up some fruit," Bill said. "Maybe some chips, sandwiches, waters for the beach."

"Oh, hey, Shane, good morning," Bill said as Shane walked into the kitchen, rubbing his eyes and opening the fridge.

"Hold on. I'm making eggs. There's milk and juice already on the counter. Grab a glass out of the cabinet. Your dad cut up some fruit. Add that to some yogurt and granola and then the eggs will be ready."

"How was the movie?" his mother asked.

"I told Dad I fell asleep right after it started. Gina loved it."

"It doesn't sound like you were very good company."

"Gina didn't mind. You know how she is."

Across town, Gina and her mother were getting ready for church. Her father went in early to set up the stage and pulpit for the sermon. Diane Bell, one of the parishioners, brought in bouquets of fresh flowers.

"Mom, I'm going to meet Shane at the beach after church. Is that okay?" she said, sharing the mirror, putting on her lipstick, and curling her eyelashes.

"That's fine. Who are you going with? Oh, and how was your evening?"

"Probably Maria and Ally, T's was T's. I had a salad and Shane had one of those huge burritos stuffed with tri-tip, rice, and beans," Gina replied. "The movie was so sad. Jessica, the main character, searched for her father her whole life and they were finally reunited at the end of the movie. I cried…"

"Please put on a different dress. That one is too revealing for church," her mother said, looking it over.

"Oh, Mom. You can't see anything."

"Your dad will not approve. It's too short and low cut. Put on that light green summer dress or the slacks you bought a couple of weeks ago," she said, applying hair spray, using her hand to help style.

Back at the Kaufmann's, Suzanne made sandwiches and filled the ice chest with sodas and water. Shane helped her load the heavy cooler into the boat.

"Pops, did you put soap in?"

"It's right next to the ski."

They arrived down at Ski Beach, and Richard, the attendant, directed them to pull into the Aspen Grove parking lot. He told them to line up and cross Lakeshore Boulevard when the other boats passed through the security checkpoint. One boat was ahead of them. William, the other attendant, walked up to Bill's window in a wide-brimmed hat and sunglasses.

"Shouldn't be but a few minutes' wait. It's actually been a little slow this morning. I thought more people would be up trying to get out on the lake early. It's going to be a beautiful day," William said, looking around.

"That's good news. I hope the lake stays flat for a while. I'd like to get in a ski before it gets lumpy. Shane is able to wakeboard when it gets rough, but for me, it's like skiing moguls."

"Okay, here you go. Have a great day. Janet will check your passes and get your wristbands on," William said, waving them on.

When they got to the ramp, Suzanne began to set up their spot on the beach. Bill and Shane brought over the towels and spread out a large blanket. They set the cooler in the shade next to the lawn and got the umbrella up. Bill backed the trailer down to the water just far enough to float the boat off. Shane turned the engine over and slowly backed it up. He idled out to the No Wake buoys to warm it up before sliding it up on the beach. He called Gina.

Gina and Lacy took their usual seats in the second pew on the aisle. The phone vibrated. She looked down as her mother gave her the look. She could feel the stare as she pushed the button to turn it off. Her mind drifted to the night before as she raised her head gazing absently out the stained glass windows. She began to perspire with guilt. Her mother couldn't possibly know, or could she? If she turned, would she see it her eyes? She wished she had worn the dress instead of the slacks. She crossed her legs and opened the hymnal at her side. She imagined Shane was still inside of her as she pressed her flesh against his. She felt vulnerable, naked before God.

"Are you all right? Put that phone away," her mother said inquisitively, noticing Gina's discomfort.

Gina slipped her phone back into her purse. "I'm fine. It's a little warm in here, don't you think?"

—◦◦◦—

Shane sat in the captain's seat with Suzanne next to him, watching Bill as he got his vest, gloves, and ski on. She got up and feathered the rope out and the boat moved slowly forward. Bill slid off the transom with the handle in his hand.

"Ooooh, it's chilly," Bill said as he adjusted his feet in the bindings.

"Say when," Shane said, watching him in the mirror.

"Hit it!" Bill yelled.

Shane pushed the handle forward full throttle. The bow lifted up momentarily and then leveled out as Bill rose out of the water. "Woohoo!" Suzanne hollered.

Bill adjusted his gloves, pulled his board shorts back down his thighs, and cut to the left of the wake. He stood still for a moment and then leaned over, cutting hard to the right slicing through the wake, skiing away from the rope. Extending his arm, he cut back hard to the left. Shane watched the ballet in the mirror as he drove on past Burnt Cedar Beach into Crystal Bay Cove. A multicolor crystal wall of water sparkling in the morning sun rose and fell with each turn. Bill could see the blue-green rocks below the clear fluid as he passed over. He pointed to Suzanne to look down at the water.

Bill made a sign that he was done and glided to a stop, releasing the rope, sinking up to his neck. Shane brought the boat around. Bill slid up on the transom and sat for a few moments getting his breath. "It's beautiful," he said, taking in the vibrant scenery around him.

"Atta way, Pops. Lookin' good."

"The water is so delicious this time of morning. I can't believe we live here," Bill said, looking over his shoulder at Suzanne and Shane. "Okay, Shane, get out there while it's still smooth," Bill said, peeling off the vest and gloves. "Hand me that towel there, thanks," he said, taking his turn in the captain's seat.

Shane stood on the swim deck, wedging his feet into the wakeboard bindings. He grabbed the gloves and vest. Suzanne handed him the rope and held the orange flag up.

"Wow. That's cold," he said, zipping up the wet vest.

Suzanne got up as he turned around and pushed him into the water, laughing.

"Thanks, Mom. I needed that."

Bill started the boat up and took the slack out of the line.

"Ready?" Bill asked.

"Go!" Shane shouted.

Shane popped right up and got himself all adjusted ready for the tow. Hopping up and down, he switched stance back and forth as he cut in and out of the wake, surfing it like a wave. Suzanne grinned. He cut hard left, doing a three-sixty, then cut hard right, tossing his head back as his body rotated backward over the wake landing on the down slope.

"Whew, Shane! Fantastic flip. Whew, whew!" Suzanne cheered.

Looking in the mirror, Bill gave him a thumbs-up. Shane rode all the way back to the boat ramp before letting go just outside the No Wake Zone. When the boat stopped, Suzanne stood up and dove over the side. "The water is so nice," she said, doing a sidestroke around the boat. "Bill, get in and swim with me." She kicked her legs behind the transom pushing the craft toward shore.

"Here I come," Bill said, diving off the bow.

Shane toweled off and idled the boat in while Suzanne and Bill swam together toward shore.

"There's a lot of people at the beach today," Suzanne said as she walked up to their picnic site.

I cannot wait to get out of here, Gina thought as she mouthed the words to the hymn without singing. There were throngs of people leaving the church ahead of them. By the time Lacy and Gina got outside where Mike was standing, it was late morning. He still had his pastoral robe on. With his thick white hair combed straight back and his piercing blue eyes, he looked almost like a saint.

"Gina, so nice to see you. You look so lovely this morning," Diane Bell said.

"Thank you, Mrs. Bell."

"Mike, we sure enjoyed your sermon, didn't we, Jim?" Diane asked rhetorically.

"Why, yes. It was very inspiring. I will make a point of keeping it with me. Diane, we must be going. The PGA is on. Tiger was two strokes up on Tom Kite, and I want to see how it stands now. It's going to be a close tournament."

"Hey, Gina. Are we going to the beach?" Maria asked, strolling up with Ally.

Gina looked at her mother with pleading eyes. "Can we leave now?"

"Let me say good-bye to your father and we'll go."

Gina took her clothes off as though they were on fire, leaving a trail across the bedroom floor, got into her thong bikini, and tied a sarong on in less than five minutes after arriving home. She ran to the 4 Runner, almost tripping in her sandals. She threw her purse in and headed across town to pick up Ally and Maria.

By the time they got to Incline Beach, the parking lot was full. Richard directed them to the overflow lot. With a sigh, she located a place back by Incline Creek. They ran up to the security checkpoint with their passes out and got their wristbands. Shane was just pulling up to the beach when they arrived at the volleyball court.

"Shane! Over here!" Gina yelled.

He helped his dad get the boat secured and then met the girls. "Shane, give me hug," Gina said, running up to Shane.

"What has gotten into her? I don't think I've seen her this excited in a long time," Maria said, holding some towels and her purse.

Shane walked over nonchalantly as Gina jumped into his arms.

"What'd you do? Buy her diamonds?" Ally said, backing up.

"I didn't think church would ever end. It was so hot in there, and Mom kept staring at me. Do you want to play some volleyball? I saw Chip and Kyle at church. They said they'd be down here as soon as they changed their clothes. Maybe we all can play," Gina said as she gave Shane a kiss.

"I can't do church at all. It's good to see you." Shane set Gina back on the sand. "Hi, Ally, Maria. How are you all this fine sunny day? Ready for some V ball? I'm ready. The sand feels great."

"We could play girls against the guys unless you're scared to lose," Ally said, strutting around, tossing her hair confidently. "We'll take it easy on you since you haven't played in a while."

"You can't even get it over the net when you serve. Sure, that'll be fun. We'll cream you," Shane said.

Suzanne and Bill lay out on their blanket and watched the kids organize the event. Bill grabbed a sandwich and a bottle of water.

"You want a sandwich or something, honey?" Bill asked.

"I'll take a carrot and I'll just share your water."

Chip and Kyle strolled up as Ally was spraying down the court.

"Hey, it's us against you guys, so warm up because we are going to stomp you," Maria said.

Kyle rolled his eyes. "Yep, I'm scared. Chip, maybe we should get another guy for our side."

Chip, Shane, and Kyle bounced the ball around while the girls warmed up on the other side of the net. JT came walking out of the shade of the aspens as they were about to begin.

"Got room for one more?" JT said, his tall frame a definite asset.

"They were just saying how they needed more help," Gina chimed in.

"I'll play," Suzanne said, bouncing up from her blanket. "I used to be on the volleyball team for four years in high school. We'll really work 'em now."

"Mom, they didn't have volleyball when you were in school. They had just invented the wheel."

Suzanne laughed, pulled her pink ball cap down on her head tight, and ran to the girl's side of the court, taking a position in the back corner. "Rally for serve. Let's go," she said, slapping her hands together.

JT took a position at the net as Gina sent a high lob over the net. Chip got it with a two-hand dig to Shane who set it to JT. JT jumped and hit it hard and down to Suzanne who barely got it out of the sand.

Gina got underneath it, ricocheting the ball out of bounds.

"Our serve. Nice try, Gina. Suzanne, nice dig," JT said, passing the ball back to Shane.

"Whoo, that knocked the wind out of me," Suzanne said, brushing herself off.

Shane tossed the ball high into the air and connected with it, driving right at Maria who had shifted into Gina's position at the back of the court. The ball slapped her arms as she dug it high to Suzanne. She got a good set to Ally, but Ally's attempt at a spike bounced off the top of the net and landed back on their side out of play.

"One. We got one point. Hey, Ally, we got one point," Chip said. "It's all over now. Look out. Anyone over there want an autograph? Signed picture?"

"You got lucky. We gave you one so you wouldn't cry," Maria retorted. "Hurry it up and serve."

The girls pulled up even at seven to seven. The sun was reaching its peak, making the sand and the players hot. Chip's return of serve from Ally hit the support pole and rolled down the slope into the water. Chip and Shane ran after it, diving into the cool water followed by the rest of the players. A big explosion of arms, hands, and feet splashed in between boats and jet skis.

"No swimming in the boating area," came the announcement from the lifeguard over the megaphone.

They all slowly exited, waving good-naturedly at the guard as they trudged back up to the court. JT found the hose and sprayed down the sand to cool off the court again.

"I have some sandwiches and snacks if you want to take a short lunch break."

"Suzanne, we brought some food, too. I'll bring it over. Can we sit on your blanket?" Ally said.

"Of course," she replied as Bill stood up shaking the sand off the towels and blanket.

"I have a huge hunk of salami, jack cheese, and french bread," JT added, grabbing his backpack. "I have a few Red Bulls here if anyone would like one too," Suzanne said.

Gina wound her arms around Shane and climbed on his back. Like her personal sherpa, he brought her over and set her down softly, holding her close for an extra second before letting her go.

"Oh, Shane," she whispered. "I love you so much."

Just a hint of wind shook the Aspen leaves behind them as they shared the food. Suzanne cut the sandwiches in half and Bill helped to pass them around.

"There's water and sodas in the cooler. Any takers?" Bill grabbed the fruit and veggies. "Carrots, oranges, apples, celery? JT, how about you?" Suzanne asked.

JT shook the sand and water out of his hair. "Sure, I'll have some orange. Thanks."

The wind came up midafternoon. Bill and Shane, with the other boys' help, pulled the boat out and loaded the truck back up.

"I've had chicken breasts marinating if any of you would like to join us for dinner. We're going to start barbecuing around six or so. I'm making rice and a vegetable salad," Suzanne said.

One by one, they each declined. JT lingered an extra moment, contemplating a home-cooked meal from one of the best cooks in the neighborhood before saying no.

"Can I take a rain check?" JT asked rhetorically as he left. "You make the best meals, Mrs. K."

"Ah, thanks, John. I appreciate that. We'll have you over soon. Say hello to your mom and dad for me."

Maria and Ally started the long walk back to Gina's car while she said good-bye to Shane. The leaves wrestled with the wind while they held each other in the shadows of the trees.

"Shane, it was so hard for me in church today. It was as though Mom could see right through me and somehow knew that we'd slept together last night. My dad too. I felt so guilty and wonderful at the same time."

"You're just imagining things. Everything is okay. I feel different today too. I feel so much closer to you. It's like, well, like, we're one person. Like our two lives became one energy. I feel so much a part of you now. Do you think that's weird? It's like we're on a higher plane of existence."

Gina listened while he talked, their lips almost touching. "You are such a romantic, my love. Call me later. Maria and Ally are waiting. I adore you," she said softly, slowly releasing her hands from his.

"Shane, there are people waiting to leave. We're blocking the whole exit ramp," Bill said, getting his attention.

Chapter 6

The last week of school was a slow farewell for the seniors. Each of the last four days passed as though they were a week long. Monday, Tuesday, and Wednesday were filled with remaining finals, reports, and yearbooks. After a glorious weekend of sports and warm beach days, it was difficult to walk into class and create the energy that the students needed to finish the school year off. They picked up the projects they made in art, wood shop, auto shop, science, and other classes. Gina's ceramic pieces were going to be on display at an art museum in Reno. She made a ceremonial mask decorated with feathers, a birdhouse, and a few eclectic pieces that were ornamental in nature. She and Anne Davis, her teacher, carefully wound bubble wrap around them for the trip over the hill.

Shane built a pine end table. He still needed to stain and finish it, but that would be a summer project at home. He loaded it in that backseat of the Jetta. Jake assembled a dark-blue Yamaha mini bike as his last semester project. He rode it home: no helmet, no lights, no worries.

"Be careful, Jake," Woodward said as he watched him try to pop a wheelie out of the driveway. He shook his head, "I hope you live to see another birthday!" he shouted after him.

The seniors were let out of class twenty minutes early and gathered around the courtyard signing each other's yearbooks. Gina took Shane's and sat in the shade of large vine maple to write:

I believe that it was fate that finally brought us together after growing up in this small village. That first kiss at the Junior Prom, and the lazy days at the beach during last summer brought me so close to you. The first time I lay my head on your chest, I heard your heart calling me. I adore you. You have been my rock and my teddy bear. I know we will always be in each other's heart, mind, and spirit. As we journey forward on our life's path, we must remember to dance when we have the chance, to laugh out loud, no matter where we are, and live every day as though it were our last. I will always love you.

Gina xoxoxo

Shane was busy signing books from his fellow team members, students, and friends he'd grown up with. He stacked them, putting Gina's on the bottom.

Yo, Chip, great year, dude! Hope all your dreams come true. You've been a great friend. I won't forget all the fun times we had together, Shane Kaufmann.

Ally, congratulations on graduating. Have an awesome summer. Good luck in college. You and Maria were a lot of fun to hang out with. Best wishes for great future, Shane.

Dusty, you are one of a kind. You always make laugh. Good luck in the future. I know life is going to be good to you. I hope I see you around, Shane.

By the time he was down to Gina's, his hand was tired. It did not feel like a time passage, but it was. He could not fathom what the future would bring for any of his friends. A few were going in the military, but there was no war currently, so that seemed to be a safe bet. Some were off to college, and others had no idea what they were going to do except have fun over the summer. He knew he was off to college somewhere, but made no definite plans yet. He sat staring at Gina's yearbook, her name printed on the cover in gold leaf. He flipped it open. He stared at the blank pages treading absently in a sea of blue.

Gina.

He paused for several moments after getting her name to paper.

Gina, I never imagined that we would be together. I cherished you from the moment I saw you walking down the hall to class. You were happy and full of life, and wow, so beautiful. I finally got the courage up to ask you to the prom. The first time I held you in my arms, I knew you were special. I could feel those warm beautiful brown eyes of yours pulling me into your world. I have never enjoyed being with someone as much as I do you. You are full of wonderful surprises: Whale Beach. You have brought me so much joy and happiness. You are my best friend and lover. No matter what the future holds for us, I will always love you,

Shane, June 13, 1997

Tuesday evening was the sports award program. The coaches, students, and faculty set up the gymnasium for the event. They pulled out the bleachers on one side of the auditorium and opened a few padded folding chairs for the principal, coaches, and some of the teachers. Coach Woodward was also the auto shop teacher. Mr. Porter, the tennis coach, taught chemistry and math. Next to the podium stood the American flag, the Nevada State flag, and the school colors. The parents, friends, and family sat on one side of the bleachers. The students sat on the other half.

After class ended, Shane wandered into the gym. He found a seat on the corner of a lower bleacher and sat down with his hands between his knees. It was quiet except for the rhythmic brushing of the custodian's mop at the far end near the locker rooms. So many memories hung from the walls; all of the records that were set and then broken, championship pennants from the year the school opened up including this year's golf and basketball teams. The list of names brought back faces and events forgotten in the chaos of class schedules and new sport contests. The hair rose up the back of his neck as he contemplated life after graduation. Four years, they went by so quickly. The future was uncertain and scary.

"I have a cramp, Coach. Can I get out of the pool?" Shane said to his swimming coach.

"You have to have a muscle to have a cramp, Kaufmann." Ah, freshman year. "If you are in the pool with four other people, it is guaranteed that one of them is urinating." *Thanks for the memories, Coach*, Shane thought laughing to himself. *I'll probably remember those for the rest of my life.* What a dumb thing to think about. Gosh, and golfing in the snow. What a nightmare that was. Only in Tahoe. Mike Blume, Grant Dennison, he read the names, wow, Jim Trilish. Those guys were all seniors when I was fourteen.

"Hey, Shane. You excited about tonight?" Mr. Woodward said, spying him as he entered from the locker room.

"I guess. Gosh, Coach. It went by so fast. It's weird. I mean the dance is almost over."

"Son, you're leaving, but you'll never be gone. You will remember these years the rest of your life. And heck, who knows, you may come back and teach here someday like I did," he said, crossing the floor.

"Yeah, maybe. You know, I'm all excited to leave this place, but I'm going to miss it, you, the other kids, and well, a few of the teachers too," Shane said, looking around the gym.

"That's normal. You know, son, it's hard for me too. The teachers and we coaches get close to you, and we know in just a short time you all will leave. It's important that you stay in touch. You know, stop by, say hello. You are always welcome here. Several past students still call, write, or send me e-mails. It means a lot to me and the other teachers. Anyway, I'll see you tonight. Remember, shirt and tie," Woodward said as he was leaving.

"Got it."

The eerie resonance of his footsteps and the shutting of the door caused Shane to stand up suddenly. He stuck his hands in his pockets and pushed the door open with his shoulder as he left.

———◦◦◦———

"Hi, honey. I made tacos for dinner. We have to be at the gym by six. Bill, I have two kinds of tortillas, flour and corn. Shane, do you need to shower? I ironed your shirt. Bill, do you have a black tie he can borrow? I laid your slacks out on the bed."

"Thanks, Mom. Yeah, I need a shower."

"I like flour. Here's a tie."

"Do you have a narrower one?"

"No, this is it. You're lucky I even have this. I haven't worn a tie since the Christmas party at the Chateau two years ago."

"It'll be fine. Thanks, Pops."

"Gina's on the phone."

"Thanks, Mom."

"Hey, you. I'm so excited. I heard you might get athlete of the year. Is that true?" Gina asked.

"I'm not sure. I heard that Chip might get it. I'm good with it either way. They are going to honor a lot of us this year. Most of the football team and baseball team are graduating this year. I can't wait to see you. We're having tacos for dinner. What are you having?"

"Pizza. Got a Lakeshore from New York Pizza where Dusty works. He had tonight off for the awards. We should go in there sometime so he can wait on us. Hey, more water, I want more cheese. I think he's cute."

"Cuter than me?"

"No, of course not, silly. I'll see you in the gym. We're going to go early so we get a close parking spot and good seats. I love you."

"Love you too," Shane replied.

Shane got dressed and his mother helped him with his tie. It took a few attempts before they got the right length and right knot. Bill stood and watched his son transform into a mature-looking adult.

"You look so nice and you're going to put on tennis shoes? Don't you have a nice pair of dress shoes you can wear?" Suzanne asked, looking him over.

"I do, but they're too small. I haven't worn them since that same Christmas party."

"I wish I'd known. We could of run down to the thrift store. Bill, you don't have any shoes he could wear, do you?"

"Shane, what else do you need? Socks? Belt? Cologne? I'll go check. I should have something that will fit those huge feet," he said, chuckling over his shoulder.

"How do I get salsa off a white shirt?"

"Really?" Suzanne said, putting her hands on her hips. "Really?"

"Sorry, it just fell out of the taco," Shane said, pulling the shirt away from his chest.

"Come here." Suzanne got a wet wash rag and blotted the red emulsion until it was a light pink. "That'll have to do."

"Here, try these on." Bill set the shoes on the counter with a pair of black socks.

"Thanks, Pops. I don't know what I'd do without you two."

"I don't either," Suzanne said, giving him a hug and a kiss as he tried on the shoes. "It looks like they fit. Nice. Are we ready? Any more surprises?"

Mike and Lacy found the seats they wanted four rows up and with a good view of the podium. Gina joined several of her friends in the student section. Katy, Kyle, Dusty, Jenna, and Ned were busy talking and greeting more of their friends as they arrived. Bill and Suzanne headed up to the back of the bleachers and almost missed Gina's mother and father in the shuffle. The shoes tramping up and down on the wooden bleachers were deafening.

"Hello. Nice to see you," Bill said, shaking Mike's hand before moving up further.

"Hi, Mike. Hi, Lacy," Suzanne said as she passed.

The noise bounced off the floor, the concrete, and brick walls. The staff took their seats and waited for Mrs. Kyper to start the festivities. She shuffled a few papers at the podium and adjusted herself, leaning into the microphone.

"Please stand for the pledge of allegiance."

The ROTC color guard brought forward the American flag, Nevada state flag, and the Highlander flag dressed in sharp military tradition. "Left face. March. About face, arms. Attention! I pledge allegiance to the flag…"

"Please take your seats and turn off your cell phones or put them on vibrate during the ceremony. We will start the certificates and awards with basketball, then track, volleyball, swimming, and baseball. Please save your applause until all of the team members have received their awards and recognition," Mrs. Kyper said, looking at all of the people.

When it was time for the baseball team, Coach Pacini walked up to the microphone, clasped his hands, and looked at his players. "I have had the privilege of working with these boys, most of them, since they were freshmen. Some never played baseball before starting high school or coming out for the team. This season we fell short of our goal: taking the state championship, but nonetheless, these young men showed their passion, strength, and courage. We had a great year. We saw excellent fielding, pitching, hitting, and base running. There were standout players in every game. Students and parents, Kyle Ellison, Tom Wellman, Nick Witty, Jake Monahan, Chip Sinder, Shane Kaufmann, Dusty Morgan, John Tarantino, and my assistant, Coach Woodward."

The boys stood in a single file, facing the audience; some wore slacks, khakis, blue jeans.

"Shane looks so much older and intellectual in his tie," Suzanne said to Bill

Bill took his camera out. "I think I am too far away. Yes, he sure looks handsome in my tie and shoes," he said as the camera flashed.

"Bill, you do too. We need to dress you up more often. Shane takes after his father." Suzanne said. "Seventeen, gosh, I remember bringing Shane home from the hospital, that little face tucked in a blanket, too small for the smallest car seat. Time has flown by, Bill." Her lip started to quiver.

"Don't these kids own a belt? For Pete's sake, I don't want to look at their underwear," Gene Sinder shared with the parents around him.

Diane rolled her eyes. "Gene, there's worse things to fret about. At least, they are not out doing drugs and getting girls pregnant. It's just a stage."

"My niece got her nose pierced and a tattoo on her back., Jack Morgan said, leaning in. "Dusty thinks it's foolish, thank God."

"They call that a *tramp stamp*. If that was my daughter, I don't know what I'd do. I'd have to kick her out of the house," Gene responded as Diane shook her head.

"Ssssh. Listen. Coach is talking," Mrs. Morgan said, quieting the group down.

"This award is for the most improved player. He didn't get to play a lot at the beginning of the season, but he came to every practice. He always was in a good mood and cheered the team on from the bench. He never played ball until this year, and his athletic ability and grasp for the game is stellar. And, he would add, that he looks great in uniform, John Tarantino, JT, please step forward."

JT nonchalantly took a step toward the podium, with his tall athletic frame, friendly brown eyes, and easygoing smile. The coaches shook his hand and handed him the plaque with his named engraved on it.

"Thank you," he said, looking up at the crowd, a bit embarrassed. He grinned, returning to his place among his peers.

"Although we didn't win every game, this next player exemplified team spirit and leadership above and beyond the norm. His pitching earned him sports scholarships from Arizona State University in Tempe and the University of California at Berkeley. He worked his tail off all season long and still was able maintain a 4.0 GPA. Selected by his teammates and his coaches, please stand for the Most Valuable Player and Male Athlete of the Year, Shane Kaufmann."

Suzanne stood up immediately, tears streaming down her face with Bill next to her and began to applaud their son. Bill quickly brought his camera up to his eye to record the moment. "No applause please," Mrs. Kyper said over the microphone, as the rest of the crowd came to their feet clapping and hooting with congratulations. "So much for rules."

"We love you, Shane," Gina, Maria, Ally and the others shouted above the noise.

His face flushed, Shane hung his head and lowered his eyes in the first moment. He slowly regained his composure, as his big broad smile greeted the teachers, players, coaches, students, and parents around him. With his hands folded in front of him, he walked toward Pacini's open hand and shook it. Coach put his hand on Shane's shoulder as he spoke into the mike.

"Thank you. This is quite an honor. I would not be up here if it weren't for my fellow teammates and our coaches. I'd like to thank my mom and dad for all their support and for always believing in me." Suzanne wiped her eyes with a tissue as he continued, "I also want to thank all my teachers for letting me out of class to play and helping me achieve my academic goals." Looking up at the students in the stands with misty eyes, he mouthed the words, "I love you, Gina."

He shook several more hands and then received his plaque from the coach. As he made his way back to his seat, his teammates slapped him on the back, congratulated him with high fives and fist pumps.

"Thank you all for coming," Mrs. Kyper said. "We'll see some of you again next year and the rest of you at graduation."

The crowd slowly departed and congregated out in the hall. It was hard to move. Family, friends, and faculty surrounded the athletes. Shane passed around his award, keeping a close eye on it while he talked.

"Shane, over here," Gina yelled through the throngs. Her short stature made it difficult for her to see. She waved her hands to get his attention, but he was inundated and unable to move. She squeezed through the people one by one until Shane was able to grasp her hand and pull her the last few feet. She held on to him with both hands.

"Wow, athlete of the year, you earned it. Congratulations," Mike said as he and Lacy pressed on toward the exit examining the plaque. "Are you coming with us or are you going with Shane?"

"I want to go with Shane," Gina replied.

"Well, call us later and let us know what you are doing." Her father's voice faded into the distance.

"The sun and fresh air feels so invigorating," Suzanne said to Bill as they stood waiting outside the auditorium for Shane. He arrived with Gina in tow.

"Do you want to walk down to Starbucks?" Shane asked Gina, taking a deep breath.

"Sure, that sounds like fun. I'd like to stretch my legs. We were sitting for a long time in there."

"Pops, here take the plaque, and we'll see you at home later," Shane said, turning to Gina. "I can't believe it's almost over, one more day."

"Shane, I'm so proud of you. What an awesome award. I am going to help Ally with the grad party set up. Do you want to help us?" Gina asked as they walked down the street.

"What time?"

"We're going to start tomorrow morning around ten. The tables and chairs are already set up, so all we are doing are the decorations," Gina said as they entered the coffee shop.

"Yeah, maybe. What kind of drink would you like? Do you want something to munch on too?"

Chapter 7

A few workers set the final chairs around large six-foot round tables while two men brought in the dance floor on dollies. They fit the four-foot squares together with small setscrews. The finished oak parquet floor measured twenty feet by twenty feet. They wiped it down, removing the dust and debris from the last event, and placed a DJ table draped in black near the exit doors at the far end of the room. Ally, Gina, Maria, and Kyle helped Bryn set up his turntables and computer electronics that he formatted to cover several years of music. Kyle met Chip as he pulled up with balloons and garlands to hang from the beams throughout the room. Shane and other volunteers arrived around ten. They got a ladder out of the storage room to hang a large mirrored disco ball above the dance floor. Bryn had the boys lay out the colored spotlights and synchronized them with his music, attaching them to the beams, walls, and pillars. Maria and her helpers spread out dark green tablecloths and draped the chairs in Highlander yellow. They used sugar pinecones sprayed yellow and green sprinkled with gold glitter for the centerpieces. Other workers set up tall cocktail tables around the room, which the girls covered in black linen. A large buffet table draped in dark green was set up at the east end in preparation for meat, salad, vegetables, sliced fruit, hors d'oeuvres, and bread. They set up separate areas in each adjacent corner for drinks and desert. By noon, the room was ready for the evening's event. Bryn, with his headphones on, was doing sound and light checks when they left.

It would be another three hours before graduation. Shane went home and took a nap. The rest of the group drove down to the beach for a dip in the lake and a bite to eat at the snack bar. They dragged a few white vinyl lounge chairs down over the hot sand close to the water's edge.

"Oh, wee, that's hot!" Ally said as she hopped around, setting up her chair.

They stripped as fast as possible and ran into the cool liquid to decompress and reenergize. Dripping with relief, they plopped down to relax before going home to get ready.

"Ahhh, I could sleep. I am so tired," Kyle said, pulling his baseball cap down over his eyes.

"Would you put some lotion on my back?" Maria asked Ally, passing her a dark bottle of oil.

Ally sprayed her back and then passed it to the others. Kyle didn't move. A cool breeze textured the lake and lifted the sand with an occasional gust.

Ally's mother called, "Where are you? You need to come home and get ready. Your aunt and uncle are here and would love to spend a little time with you before graduation."

"Be right there," Ally said, shaking her friends awake. "Hey, I've got to get home."

Grumbling, the rest of the group gathered their things and staggered back to their cars.

"See you all later," Kyle said, getting into his car.

Volunteers in lime green and white florescent striped vests directed a myriad of cars into proper parking spots around the school. Some drivers ignored the directors and drove in the wrong way, congesting traffic as they dropped people off. Police on the street kept people out of unsafe areas and off private property as they vied for other locations.

Inside, the stage was set in three tiers with a dark blue drape as a backdrop. Parents, friends, and family trickled into the auditorium dressed in evening gowns, suits, ties, shorts, sandals, blue jeans, and all matter of clothing in between. For some, it was a momentous occasion; for others, it was obligatory. Mothers carried flowers to honor their sons and daughters. Earlier, large groups of attendees reserved their folding chairs by placing programs on the seats. The superintendent, school officials, and faculty reserved the front row of chairs facing the podium. Two huge video screens presenting the Class of 1997 faced the audience on the left and right sides of the stage. A group of band members set up under the screen on the right up against the wall. A piano, a large bass drum, and music stands waited silently for the proceeding to begin. Several people chose the bleachers for a better view above the crowd. The custodians attached firm green plastic cushions to the hard wood planks to sit on.

"These cushions look soft, but they're hard as nails," Diane Sinder said as she got adjusted. "Over here!" She stood, waving her hands to attract her friend's attention. They exchanged handshakes and greetings as they situated themselves.

The band played a graduation march to indicate the beginning of the ceremony. A group of young ladies, fashionably dressed, held curved flowered arches over the aisle as the graduates entered the auditorium. Parents and friends cheered as the girls dressed in white gowns and caps walked in escorted by their male counterparts dressed in forest green all with gold tassels adorned with a gold '97 year pin. Cameras flashed and video recorded the moment while heads bobbed and weaved to get better perspectives. The faculty followed dressed in black robes with white sashes and black hats. Once the stage filled, the graduates sat in unison.

"Please stand for the national anthem," Principal Kyper said as the color guard entered through the promenade of flowers.

"To the left, march." Four students shoulder to shoulder walked in step. "Halt. About face…attention! Present arms," the unit commander ordered.

Two graduates came forward to sing the national anthem. Their voices moved through the air delicately, hitting the high notes with sustained accuracy and final applause. With the assembly still standing, Mrs. Kyper introduced the superintendant of schools, the Washoe County school board president, trustees, and faculty.

"This is the finest class I've had the privilege to know. These past four years have strengthened and shaped these students into the young adults that will someday be the leaders of our society and possibly our country. More than half of this class are honor recipients. This year's senior class president and valedictorian is Ally Aldridge."

Seated in the front row, she stood up and walked to the podium. "Thank you, Mrs. Kyper, faculty, parents, and friends. My professors and mentors taught me to surround myself with people that inspire me. These teachers, coaches, and friends will forever be in my mind as I move forward on my life's path. We must continue to seek new motivation and energy with our eyes wide open to all possibilities. Dreams, we all have dreams. However, we cannot fulfill them by simply sleeping and hoping they come true. We must take that first step through the door of opportunity to start the journey. As George Bernard Shaw once said, 'A life spent making mistakes is not only more honorable, but more useful than a life doing nothing.' I believe we should exhaust all roads until we find our life's direction. We have been given the support, the courage, and the knowledge these past four years that will be the foundation we will walk on into our future. We…" she continued.

A loud applause interspersed with whistles and hooting culminated the speech. Ally gathered her papers, whisked her tight black curls away from her face and over her shoulder. She returned to her seat.

"This is so exciting," Gina said, holding on to Ally's hand.

"The commencement will now begin," Mrs. Kyper broadcasted as the entire back row stood and walked in single file. A picture collage of each student appeared on the screens when their names were called. They included a baby picture, their senior portrait, and a candid shot. The crowd applauded and laughed at the slide shows. The students received their diplomas shaking hands or hugging Mrs. Kyper and then shaking hands with the superintendent before returning to their row.

"Shane James Kaufmann, National Honors Society, Advanced and Honors Diploma recipient." Shane crossed the floor in front of a sunset portrait taken at Sand Harbor and another of him wakeboarding, flashing a shaka sign. Suzanne, Mike, and Lacy stood to applaud. Bill went up to the front of the aisle, squeezing between other parents, to photograph Shane. He looked tall, proud, and distinguished as he took the parchment paper record of his achievement.

"Dustin Edward Morgan." Dusty had a black bandana under his hat as he strolled up to Mrs. Kyper without a care in the world. Dusty's snowboarding shot of him throwing a three-sixty off a lip at Alpine Meadows had the crowd cheering. Ed Morgan, on one knee, caught his son's infectious smile as he got his diploma. He and Bill returned to their seats having accomplished their photographic objective. After the whole row had received their diplomas, they remained standing, and then sat in unison as the second row stood.

"Kyle Nathan Ellison." A little shy, he kept his head down, eyes diverted, until summoned by his father to, "Look at the camera, son." Kyle's senior portrait on the large screen showed off his square jaw, deep-set eyes, and rugged frame set against the rocks and creek at Incline Beach. The second row mimicked the back row, standing until all had received their diplomas and sat as the first row stood. It was a striking exhibition.

"Ally Marie Aldridge, our Valedictorian, National Honors Society, Advanced and Honors Diploma recipient." Ally shared a euphoric smile as she crossed the stage. Her portrait pictured her nestled amongst fall Aspens bathed in various shades of yellow and orange decorated with glittering sunlight.

"Gina Kathleen Conrad, National Merit Scholar, National Honor Society, Advanced and Honors diploma recipient." The screens revealed a smiling young woman standing on a wooden slat bench at Ski Beach chasing the clouds with her arms, allowing the sun to shine through. Her senior picture was taken at Aspen Grove with the creek in the background and a full palette of colors hanging from the trees. Lacy, Suzanne, and Bill stood to congratulate her as she accepted her diploma.

"What a beautiful portrait. She is a gorgeous girl, Lacy," Suzanne said. Mike, like Bill, went down to the front of the aisle to take a video of her receiving her diploma. Norma Aldridge was next to him, motionless with tears in her eyes, trying to take a picture as Ally passed. The students stood and then sat down quietly when their row was complete.

"Please give a round of applause for the Class of 1997," Mrs. Kyper said, turning to her students. "And now, Shane Kaufmann, our Athlete of the Year."

Shane walked up to the mike, head held high, looking directly at his audience. "Thank you, Mrs. Kyper. I would like to thank my mom and dad, coaches, teachers, and mentors over these last four years for sticking by me, encouraging me, and keeping me on course. Education is the window into the future. It allows light in to help us grow and see beyond today, reaching for tomorrow." Suzanne and Bill sat holding hands, their heads leaning against one another as he spoke. "We stand here upon the shoulders of those who have passed before us, creating new paths, planting seeds today for the visions we have for our future. We are the next stewards of our planet. We leave here today as a collective positive energy moving forward, changing the world one idea at a time. In the words of Henry Shane Thoreau, 'Do not be too moral, you may cheat yourself out of much life. Aim above morality. Be not simply good; be good for something.'" Shane paused briefly as the crowd applauded. "We carry the torch, lit by years of history, to improve this world, spreading education, understanding, and compassion. We now, having met the requirements for graduation, move our tassels from right to left." The students behind him made the shift, as he transferred his.

Joining Shane at the podium, Principal Kyper spoke, "Please join me in congratulating this extraordinary class of 1997!"

The students stood, tossed their caps in the air, congratulated each other, and then searched chaotically for them on the floor. The band began to play the recessional as the scholars once again filed down the flower-covered arched aisle toward the exits.

The students met their friends and parents in the courtyard, where there were tables set with cake, water, and lemonade. The low afternoon sun reflected yellow orange against the red brick and grey concrete. Cameras flashed as groups got together to record precious moments and reunions of relatives. Young women, still in their gowns, received bouquets of flowers. There were handshakes, hugs, kisses, and high fives as people congratulated each other.

"Let me get a picture of the three of you," Mike said, orchestrating the pose. "Gina, now you join them." She wrapped her arm around Shane's, standing in her white gown, holding a bouquet of red and white roses.

"I'll remember this day forever" Suzanne said, wiping her eyes. "Mike, Lacy, now it is your turn. Come stand by the wall here. The sun will light up your faces nicely. Gina, get in the middle. Those flowers are beautiful, Mike. Smile. Okay, Shane, join them." Shane slid in next to Gina with her mother, and Mike stood next to Gina. "Everybody put your arms around each other. Nice."

"What time do the festivities start up at the Chateau?" Lacy asked, taking her camera back from Suzanne.

"Six, they start serving food at six," Shane said, removing his cap.

Chapter 8

Casually dressed, students started to arrive at the Chateau around a quarter to six. A few parents dropped off sons and daughters at the entrance with words for the evening, "Have fun, we'll see you at midnight." Most of those attending brought their own wheels. The sun slipped slowly behind the mountains coloring the sky in a powdery pink and orange.

A registrar sat at a table just inside the entrance. She asked their names and gave each individual the guidelines for the evening. "Once you have signed in, you would not be allowed to leave until twelve o'clock."

After signing in, other adults asked the young men and women to open their purses and empty pockets as they entered the foyer. Parents and teachers chaperoned the event making sure it was safe, drug and alcohol free.

Jake walked in confidently with his water bottle twirling around his finger.

"May I check your water, Jake?" Principal Kyper asked.

"Ah, what for? It's water. Says right here on the bottle," Jake said.

Mrs. Kyper unscrewed the lid and took a whiff to verify the contents. She poured a small amount on her hand and licked it.

"Tastes just like vodka. I didn't realize our Tahoe tap water had alcohol in it. I'll be happy to take care of this for you. Please step over to Mr. Kaczynski and he'll pat you down."

"Really, a frisk?" Jake asked.

"In the words of Fox Mulder from the *X-Files*, 'Trust no one.'" Mr. Kaczynski said as he walked over.

Nick watched the security check from back in the line and decided to get rid of the whiskey he'd stuffed in his underwear. He removed the brass and silver flask and hid it behind the garbage receptacle just outside the entry.

"Good thing we stashed the beer at JT's house," Chip said, watching Nick. "That fancy flask will be gone by the time we get out of here."

Mike pulled up and let Gina get out. She had on a pair of designer jeans, white glittered sandals, a white halter-top, and a light-green sweatshirt draped over her shoulder.

"I'll see you tomorrow. Have fun. Don't stay up all night. Maria's folks both have to work tomorrow," her father said, pulling away.

Gina went through security and checked her sweatshirt with Mrs. Davis at the cloakroom. She brought a small makeup bag with some overnight things that she fit into the large front pocket. Shane parked his Jetta outside, across from the entrance. He brought a sleeping bag, some snacks, a flashlight, and a small green tarp to lay their things out on. He perused the parking lot as he walked inside looking for familiar vehicles. He stretched his neck around Mr. Kaczynski, going through the obligatory pat down, looking for Gina.

The music coming out of the banquet room vibrated the glass doors and resonated up from the tile in the hallway. Shane met Jake coming out of the restroom at the far end of the hall, and they entered together feeling the pulsating beat of the music in their steps.

"Kyper took my water bottle full of vodka. I was going to spike the punch. No worries, though. There is no punch bowl, just a stack of refreshments. A bunch of us are going over to Chip's later. He scored a case of beer. What are you doing? Are you coming over to Chip's?" Jake asked.

"No, Gina and I are going to camp out at Whale Beach."

"No kidding. That sounds like fun. Well have a good time. Do her folks know?"

"She told them she's spending the night at Maria's," Shane responded, shrugging his shoulders.

Jake pulled the door open for Shane and followed him in. Music played, but no one was on the dance floor yet. People gathered in small groups at the tall cocktail tables while some wandered around aimlessly looking for things to do and people to talk to.

Ally Aldridge picked up the mike from the podium near the dance floor and tapped it against her hand to make sure it was on.

"Everyone. Hello. Class." They quieted down as all eyes focused on Ally. "Please help yourself to the food. The carving station will be open until eight. The buffet will close down at nine. Soft drinks and water, tea, and coffee are over in this corner next to the desert. This is Bryn." Bryn took a bow, standing behind his turntables and computer. "If you have any requests, write them down on these orange sticky notes." Also, please do not attempt to leave. If you have an emergency, please contact Mr. Kaczynski. There will be no smoking on the premises. That includes the bathrooms. You may not go down stairs for any reason or into the kitchen. Let's get things rockin'! Gina, Shane, Maria, Dusty, come out on the dance floor. Jake, where are you?" Ally asked, looking around the room.

"Come on, Dusty," Maria said, taking his hand.

Bryn shifted tunes; "That's the Way Love Goes" by Janet Jackson got their feet moving. One couple at a time joined the original few until the huge dance floor disappeared under several pairs of feet. The disco ball spun its prismatic light like glitter on their heads and shoulders. "Now, in honor of the class of 1997, *Queen!*" Bryn said booting up the tune.

> I've paid my dues
> Time after time
> I've done my sentence
> But committed no crime
> And bad mistakes
> I've made a few
> I've had my share of sand
> Kicked in my face
> But I've come through
> And we mean to go on and on and on and on
> We are the champions, my friends
> And we'll keep on fighting till the end
> We are the champions
> We are the champions
> No time for losers
> 'Cause we are the champions of the World...

A loud cheer went up at the conclusion of the song. People were dancing all over the room. Some couples and friends gathered in the hallway to cool off before resuming the rhythmic fervor. Ally summoned them all for the last dance.

"A reminder to all of you, we are planning to have a reunion every five years," Ally said. "If you can, please stay in touch...for the rest of your lives. The last dance of the evening is a going to be a slow one to the music of Mariah Carey singing "Forever.""

> As long as I shall live
> I'll hold you dear
> And I will reminisce
> Of our love all through the years
> From now until forever
> And ever, my darling, forever
> You will always be the only one

You will always be the only one
If you should ever need me
Unfailingly, I will return
To your arms
And unburden your heart
And if you should remember
That we belong together
Never be ashamed, call my name
Tell me I'm the one you treasure
Forever and ever,
I know that forever
You will always be the only one...

Hanging on to each other as they slowly moved around the room, Gina found Shane's lips in the colored darkness and tenderly held him. Shane gazed into her eyes, mouthing the words of the song when they broke for a breath. "You will always be the only one."

"Please, please be safe tonight. If you are drinking, make sure you have a designated driver or don't drive. I will miss you all," Mrs. Kyper said, putting down the microphone as the lights slowly came back on.

Parents lined up outside, engines running to pick up some of the students. Laughter and loud conversation greeted them as the young adults bolted for the exit and the fresh air outside. Chip and his friends found their cars, going back over the plans for the evening.

"Okay, my folks are cool with us drinking, but keep it together. You lose control, you will be kicked out, no drugs, no smoking in the house. If you have had too much to drink, we will get you a ride home or call you a cab. We've told the neighbors we are having a party. They are fine with it as long as we keep the noise down. No loitering outside. We don't want the police coming to the house. Got it?" Chip said, making eye contact with those who were following him.

Nick recovered his flask and took a swig. "Rrrrr, matey." He bellowed as he walked his friend Katherine to the car.

———⁊⁊⁊—

Shane and Gina arranged their things in the backseat of the Jetta. They put on their sweatshirts.

"I'm so excited to spend the night with you. You've been on my mind all day. Did you bring a warm sleeping bag?"

"Yes, but we won't need it because we have each other," Shane said, rubbing her shoulders.

"I want to snuggle naked with you until the sun comes up," Gina said, setting her head against his chest.

"What time did you tell your folks you'd be home?"

"I just said I'd see them in the morning, no specific time. I told them I'm staying at Maria's."

"I know, but I don't think you should have lied."

"It'll be okay. They would never let me spend the night with you otherwise. It will be our secret," Gina said as she got in the car.

Shane pushed the knobs on the radio until he found some music they liked. He turned it down low while they drove down the street and turned onto the highway.

"Give 'em the yellow," Gina suggested.

"What?"

Gina turned the volume down. "Stay away from the yellow center line. It's late at night. People are tired and have been drinking."

"Oh, sure, makes sense," he said, clicking the bright lights on.

The road snaked around the east shore in the darkness. The moon resembled a sugared lemon slice, giving off little light as it rose. The air was still. Not a breeze wrestled even the lightest leaves. They passed Sand Harbor, looking at the vacant brown buildings standing sentry in the faintest shadows of the moon. Michael Jackson sang low in the background as they looked at each other with shared anticipation. Gina put her hand on

Shane's leg, softly massaging his thigh as he drove. He pulled over and parked in the same spot they chose a few days earlier. He pulled his backpack out of the trunk and tucked the sleeping bag under his arm. Gina got her things off the backseat, took off her sandals, and put on socks and tennis shoes for the trek down to the beach. Shane pulled a pair of hikers from the floor in the backseat and took off his dress shoes. No cars came by as they collected themselves for the journey. Shane turned on the flashlight, shining a bright narrow beam of light on the trail. He led the way with Gina following close behind. Every rock, bush, clump of dirt looked dubious. Gina held tightly on to Shane's sweatshirt for balance just in case a bear jumped out of the woods. Her ears were searching the air for any signs of wild animals that might attack them. It was very quiet. Their feet slapped the powdery dirt, leaving billows of dust as they descended toward the water.

"Let's stop for a sec. I can't see real well even with the flashlight. How are you doing back there? I feel like an Indian guide," Shane said.

Gina opened a bottle of water and took a long drink before passing it back to Shane. "Want some?"

"Sure. The snacks at the dance made me thirsty."

Passing it back to Gina, "You ready?"

"I'm right behind you. What was that? Over there. Can you see anything?" Gina asked, grabbing Shane's arm.

They both stopped dead in their tracks to listen, looking, searching the darkness for movement, for animal eyes watching them. Gina pressed herself against Shane's back, frozen with fear.

"I don't see anything. Let's keep going," he said, prying away from her grasp.

"Are you sure it's safe? I'm sure I heard something," Gina said, shuffling behind him.

"Whatever it was is gone. We must have scared it," Shane said over his shoulder.

"Ah, okay, but I'm holding on to you just in case," Gina said, her mouth almost touching the back of his head.

Gina hung close behind looking side to side and reluctantly behind her. "Uh!"

"What?"

"Nothing," Gina replied, grabbing him by the shoulders and then letting go.

They made their way down the last man-made steps to the beach. The faint moonlight lay like gray fog on the lake. Shane flung out the tarp and unrolled the sleeping bag. Gina watched, still checking the darkness for orange eyes. Not shy this time, Shane peeled his shirt off, kicked off his hikers, socks, jeans, and slithered out of his boxers. Gina silently watched as his skin appeared bit by bit yellow gray, shadowless.

"Well, what are you doing? Better get inside the bag before the bears see you," Shane said, flagging it open.

"That's not funny, Shane," she replied, looking in all directions.

She unzipped her sweatshirt and dropped it on the tarp. She fought to pull her top off over her head catching some of her hair in the process. Shane watched closely as she took of her tennis shoes, socks, and jeans. She wore a lacy bra and panties. She stood, letting Shane take in the sexiness of her attire.

"I can barely see you in this light," Shane said, reaching up to feel her.

She reached behind and unhooked her bra, slowly letting it slip down her arms and away from her breasts. Shane struggled to focus.

"Feel my goose bumps," Gina said shivering.

She let the bra fall to the tarp. Shane's eyes remained on her skin as his attention began to lift against the flannel lining of the sleeping bag. She watched his eyes while she touched the folds in her panties with her index finger, spreading her legs ever so slightly. She peeled the panties off slowly and kicked them away.

"Come here," Shane said softly, extending his hand to help her into the bag. He opened his wallet to get the condom. Somehow, the foil package had punctured and lubricated a few of the dollar bills in the compartment. The latex was half dry and slightly torn as he pulled it out to inspect the damage. "I don't have a condom. This is ruined. What'll we do?" Shane asked, showing her the packet.

Counting the days in her head, "It's been long enough since my period that I should be okay," she said, looking down at him, silhouetted against the gray darkness.

With both hands, he reached around, gently grabbing her firm round cheeks and pulled her toward him. He kissed her tenderly as she stood.

"Ooooh, that tickles," she said, tilting her head back as he tasted her. Adding lubrication, he moved his lips against her open flesh. She held on to his shoulders, slightly bending her knees. Her figure danced in the shadows, moving up and down against his tongue. "Ahhhh, ahhhh," she trembled in a strong convulsion, letting her legs fold gently upon him. "I didn't know you knew how to do that. That was wonderful."

He smiled and pulled the sleeping bag cover back. He took her by the shoulders and gently rolled her on to her back.

"How does it feel?" He looked into her eyes but could only see the outline of her face.

"Sooo amazing." He was merely a shadow above her.

"You're so warm and wet inside," he said, searching her eyes.

He moved slowly up and then down her body as she lifted herself to meet each stroke. The rhythm increased in a gradual controlled crescendo until he groaned in a long pulsating release. She held him as he jerked spasmodically inside of her.

On his hands looking down, he said, "Are you okay? I feel euphoric."

"I was close to coming again. You felt so good inside of me," Gina said, whispering.

"Shall I continue then?" Shane asked, cocking his head.

"No, hold me...well, get off first. You're kind of heavy," she said with strained breathing.

"Oh, sorry," he said, carefully sliding to her side and cuddling her.

"I love you so much. I couldn't imagine life without you. You truly complete me," she said, pressing against his warm body as she arranged herself in the sleeping bag.

"Gina, I hope we are always this close. I will treasure this night forever," he said with a sleepy voice.

They lay staring at the water as it lapped at the sand, reaching for higher ground and then retreating in a small white hush. Soon, they were asleep, nestled serenely in the tired moonlight.

Chapter 9

An orange sun rose over the eastern Sierra through a spray of clouds as the faint slice of moon disappeared behind Crystal Bay. Shane and Gina slept coiled in each other's arms, cocooned in a forest green sleeping bag. The sound of approaching hikers startled them awake.

"Oh, excuse us. We didn't see you here. We're on our way down to Secret Harbor." The young couple quickly pulled the bag up around them to hide their exposed bodies. "Gina! Is that you? It's Jim and Dianne Bell from church. Have you been out here all night? My word, I don't know what to say."

Gina's jaw dropped open. She looked away and then back.

"Quite frankly, I'm shocked." Dianne placed her hand over her mouth and stood staring, not moving.

With difficulty, they put their underwear on inside the sleeping bag. Gina's mouth still hung open.

"You own the pharmacy in town," Shane said as he squirmed.

Gina let out a muffled "Damn!" under her breath as she wrestled with her clothes. She did not get up.

"Yes…" Jim replied.

"What are you staring at? Leave us alone. Go finish your hike…you…" Shane said, cutting him off.

"Well, you two should be ashamed of yourselves. Gina, you're the preacher's daughter, for crying out loud. You have been taught better. Your parents will be so ashamed of you," Dianne said, ignoring Shane's comments.

Gina kept her head down, averting their stern eyes. Jim Bell stood with his arms folded across his chest.

"We see you every week in church." Jim nodded his head as Dianne spoke.

Kicking the sleeping bag out of his way, Shane stood up and pulled on his jeans over his open boxers. "Leave us alone. We've done nothing!" Shane shouted.

"Don't you speak to us in that tone, young man. Let's go, Jim. We've seen enough." Jim nodded and followed his wife as they walked past the small camp, their hiking shoes squeaking in the sand.

Gina and Shane heard Diane discussing the event all the way around the large granite boulders at the point. Jim followed close behind.

"Help me up this rock," Dianne said.

"Yes, dear," Jim responded as he took her elbow, then they were gone.

Gina sat still with her head on her knees. Her eyes were full of tears as Shane kneeled down and wrapped his arms around her shaking shoulders.

"I know they are going to tell my mom and dad," she said sobbing, not lifting her head. "They'll be so upset. I don't know what to do. I shouldn't have—"

"Done what?" Shane asked. "We love each other. Who are they to judge us? We are good people," Shane said, stroking her hair and tenderly rubbing her head. "Gina, I don't know what else to say. I'm out of words. I—"

"Take me home. I want to go home. Can we leave now?" Gina asked, lifting her head to look at him.

"Yes, of course, but we need to talk about this. We need to have our story straight if they tell your parents...and—"

"Story straight! Are you kidding me? They saw us sleeping together, naked! Mom, Dad, we were doing a science experiment. It wasn't sex. Shane and me were studying body parts? How's that? Or someone stole our clothes so we had to sleep together to stay warm. I can't lie. They won't believe me!'"

"Yeah, well, I'm not real good at it either. Come on. I'll take you home. Maybe the Bells won't say anything," Shane said, gathering things together.

"Really, Shane? They just happened to stumble on to some of the juiciest news anywhere in northern Nevada and they'll just forget about it? I don't think so." Gina stood up, put her hands on her hips, and looked out over the lake. A cloud drifted by, blocking the morning sun.

With moisture streaming down her cheeks, she roughly picked up her clothes. Shane kept his distance, rolling up the sleeping bag, and stuffing his things back into the backpack. Perspiration ran down his back and dripped off his forehead. He hadn't put his shirt on and Gina was still in her bra and panties. With a huff, she pulled on her jeans and slid on her shirt.

The climb back up the trail was quiet except for the sound of their bare feet pounding the rock and dirt.

"Why can't people leave us alone?" Gina mumbled.

Shane raised his head to listen, but stayed a few steps behind. The sound of cars up on the highway began to get louder as they approached. The gurgle of an early morning boat bounced off the water in the background. Shane turned around to look, distracted by the noise. Gina kept going and arrived at the car by several steps. She put her stuff down at the edge of the path and pressed her fingers against the metal on the hood. With her head down, she shook her arms and legs.

"How am I going to face my parents? How?" she asked when Shane walked up and put the pack and sleeping bag down.

He gently laid his head on her back and slid his arms around her as she started weeping, drawing long deep breaths and exhaling tears. "I love you. That's all I can say. It's gonna be all right." She turned around and hugged him, tears running off his shoulder.

"Looks like it's going to be a warm day. There's supposed to be thunderstorms this afternoon."

"I heard that too," Gina responded, looking out her passenger window.

As Shane turned up Village, he passed his mother. She waved and looked excited to see them.

Suzanne called when she got to the store. "I'm glad you're both back safe and sound. Don't raid the refrigerator. Wait for me. I'm picking up food for breakfast. I shouldn't be long."

"I'm dropping Gina off, and then I'll be home. She needs to get back," Shane said as he carefully pulled up, parking one house down from Gina's. They both looked around. There was no sign of her parents.

He helped her get her few things out of the car and nervously walked her up to the front door. They hugged for several seconds. "I love you," Shane said, breaking the embrace.

"I love you too," Gina said as she opened the front door, taking a deep breath and going inside. "I'll call you later." After it closed, Shane quickly walked back to his car. He sat motionless for a while and then started the car and idled away. He arrived at home just after his mother got back from the market. He lifted two remaining bags of groceries out of her trunk and brought them in the house.

"Hi, honey," she said with a huge smile. "How was your night? You look miserable. What's wrong?" she asked. She walked over and held him close, looking into his glazed brown eyes. "Are you and Gina having problems? You seem so upset."

"Mom, the Bells, you know from the pharmacy, discovered us this morning sleeping together on Whale Beach."

"And what happened?" she asked, shrugging her shoulders and opening her hands.

"Well, we were naked in the sleeping bag when they walked up. I think they're going to tell her dad. You know, they go to her church and—"

"It's none of their business what you two were doing," Suzanne said, cutting him off.

"Yeah, but—"

"How dare they do such a thing!"

"Well, Gina is worried and crying, and, Mom, I don't know what to do."

"I've had conver—"

"You are so different from her mom and dad. They look at sex, if you're not married, as a sin. Gina won't even talk to her mom about it. And you actually bought me some condoms. Her mom and dad never had sex until they were married. They expect the same thing from their daughter. If the Bells tell her folks, the crap is going to hit the fan. I just know it. And….and…well, Gina is terrified."

"I've had conversations with Lacy and Mike about other issues. I know how they are. They have high aspirations for their daughter. They are planning to send her to medical school. They control as much of her life as they possibly can, and I think she suffers because of it. It upsets me to no end," Suzanne said, emptying the bags.

"She's not allowed to drive after dark. They have to approve her friends and they are strict about the way she dresses," Shane said, sitting down next to his mother.

"I know…"

"They always seemed to like you though."

"I know, Mom. I feel like I'm walking on egg shells around them."

"She's under their watch twenty-four-seven. Have Gina come over and I'll talk to her and I'll see if I can't help her," Suzanne said, starting to prepare breakfast.

"Thanks."

"They don't have any idea you two are having sex? I think they would know that or at least figure out that you might. You're young adults. Gina should be able to talk to her parents about that. Well, she can talk to me."

"Thanks, Mom. I'll let her know."

Suzanne took a medium-sized bowl out of the cupboard, poured some milk, and cracked three eggs in it. She added vanilla and cinnamon, turned the burners on under the griddle, and cut up some peaches, strawberries, and bananas. She opened a loaf of thick sliced bread and dipped two pieces into the batter. She kept looking at Shane as she flipped the toast over.

"What are you thinking, Mom?"

She didn't answer. He quietly finished his breakfast, mopping up the last of the syrup with his finger. His mother cleaned up the kitchen while he took a shower.

"Mom, I'm going to bed. Call me if you hear from Gina," Shane shouted back out as he came out of the bathroom and went to the bedroom.

She took the clothes out of the dryer and folded them. She stuffed another load in the washing machine and transferred the wet clothes to the dryer. She took a stack of Bill's dress shirts and began ironing them. She hung them up, looking for more clothes to iron. She made a pot of coffee. She took the last load of laundry out of the dryer and moved the other ones over from the washing machine. She ironed the shirts and pants. More coffee, she turned on the TV. She turned it off. Then she turned it back on. Finally, she went out on the deck, stretched, and hung her head over the railing. She looked down at the snapdragons and petunias. She inhaled and then exhaled a long sigh. "What's a mother to do?"

Gina went in the house, avoiding her mother's eyes while listening to her questions. "Was that Shane who dropped you off? How was the party last night? Did you have a good time? You look tired. Did you get any sleep at Maria's? Or we're you up all night dancing until the sun came up? Have you eaten breakfast yet? Honey, look at me. Are you all right? Why are you crying?" her mother asked, finally taking a breath.

Gina didn't look up. She wiped her eyes. "Everything is fine, Mom. I'm not crying. I'm just tired. Yes, that was Shane. We had a good time. Can I take a shower now?"

The lines in Lacy's forehead became prominent as Gina continued past on the way to her bedroom. "Honey, are you sure?"

"Yes! I need to go to bed. I'll talk to you later," Gina replied, closing the door.

Her mother watched her disappear. She heard the shower running and decided to go finish her morning workout. She went into the family room, turned on the news, and stepped on the treadmill. While into a slight jog, the phone rang. She paused, stepped off, and picked up the phone, wiping her hands and forehead before putting the receiver to her ear.

"Hello."

"Hello, Lacy, this is Dianne. Dianne Bell."

"Oh, hi, how are you? You know, I forget to RSVP you about the rummage sale. I've gathered glasses, dishes, and clothes and I was planning on dropping them off tomorrow morning. Gosh, my neighbor, two doors down, gave me a ton of kid's clothes and toys to sell now that her children are older. Do you still need baked goods or are we covered? I've been so busy I forgot to call you. How's Jim?"

"Jim's fine. That darn cold he had seemed to linger on for days, but he's fine now. Lacy, the reason I am calling is, well, I'm not sure how to put this, but Jim and I were out hiking early this morning. It's part of our daily routine, you know. Anyway, we had hiked down to Whale Beach and, well, when we got there. Jeez, I'm not sure how to put this…"

"What are you trying to say, Dianne?"

"Well, we found your daughter and her friend. I think his name is Shane, you know the Kaufmann boy, on the beach, naked together in a sleeping bag. And, well, I just thought you should know, That's all. Jim and I know how you and Mike, well, how much you love Gina and how inappropriate it was for her to be doing that. We just felt that it was our moral duty to let you know what we saw. That's all. I hope you understand how we feel," Dianne said, not taking a breath.

"What? What do you mean? I think you're mistaken. Gina spent the night at Maria's last night. She said so. I have no reason to think she'd lie to me. Shane is a nice young man. He'd never take advantage of my daughter," Lacy said. "I know…"

"I'm sorry, but it was definitely Gina on the beach," Dianne interrupted. "We didn't expect this from the preacher's daughter, of all people. Their—"

"Dianne, I've got to go." Lacy hung up the phone as though she was smashing a bug with the receiver, twisting it in its cradle.

Dianne looked at Jim, who had been standing a short distance away listening, and smiled faintly.

"I don't know if that was the right thing to do," Jim said, responding to his wife's smirk. "That was actually a miserable thing to do." He added, "I think we should keep this to ourselves now. The damage is done. You did your duty as you saw fit."

"Oh, I won't spread this around. But I think Lacy needed to know what her daughter was doing. We are just being concerned friends and Christians. If they were using drugs or drinking, I would let them know as well. How do you protect your children if someone doesn't speak up? We are just looking out for their best interests, Jim. Don't you see?"

Lacy's body was shaking. She felt nauseous. She stared at the phone for a long time. The shower stopped. Gina was probably asleep. *Or was she*, she thought. *I need to know now.* "Gina, damn it to hell!" *How could she do this to us. He has soiled our daughter. I knew that boy Shane was no good. Look at his folks. They let him do whatever he wants. There never has been any discipline in that family. His father is a mere carpenter with no upbringing. She'll not see that boy again.* She slammed her fist into the sofa pillow. "Gina!" *My daughter having sex? Maybe they were wrong? Oh, Mike is going to be so heartbroken.*

Lacy wiped her wet palms on her workout pants as she headed toward Gina's bedroom door. They were still wet when she twisted the knob and entered. Gina was in a fetal position on her bed with her head pressed against the wall. Her covers were pulled tight up over her shoulder. She did not turn to look at her mother. She kept her eyes closed.

"Gina. Gina! Look at me." Lacy touched her shoulder and rolled her back toward the edge of the bed. "I need to talk to you. I, I need to know something. Open your eyes and look at me." Her mother's pale complexion looked steel blue in the darkened room. "Gina!"

"What, Mom! I'm tired. Let me sleep. Can't it wait? What do you want?" Gina asked, turning back over.

"You watch your tone with me, young lady. I will not have you talk to me like that. Now open your eyes and talk to me. Now!"

Gina reluctantly opened her eyes. They twitched and blinked. Lacy drilled right into the black pupils in the center of her nervous brown eyes.

"Mrs. Bell just called me. And…"

Gina tried to swallow. "Mom, I…"

"She said she found you and Shane sleeping together on Whale Beach, naked! Naked! Gina! What were you doing? What have you done? You had sex with that boy. Didn't you? You have sinned against God. Do you understand? Your father and I will be held responsible for your blasphemy," Lacy said, shaking her head.

"Mom, we love each other."

"You, you lied to us. You've never lied. We can never trust you again. Never! We thought you were at Maria's. Is she in on this too? She must have been prepared to cover for you. Is she? Did she know you were spending the night at the beach? Everything we taught you. Everything that was good and holy has been thrown away by this act of sin. We always trusted you to do the right thing. What has happened to you?" her mother asked, shaking her finger.

"I can't even look at you." Lacy slammed the bedroom door. The pictures shook. One fell to the floor shattering the glass. It startled Gina, who covered her head. Peering out from under the covers, she broke into tears, staring at the fragments.

"Shane, are you awake? They know," she whispered as she sobbed. "This is going to be hell. Damn. Damn. Damn."

"Gina, hold on. What did they say? What happened? Talk to me."

"That Diane Bell lady called Mom and told her everything. I bet she's sitting at home right now smirking. Mom slammed the bedroom door and left. Dad's going to kill me when he gets home. I'm scared, Shane. I am so scared."

"I know. It'll be okay. I'll talk to your mom and dad and explain everything."

"I gotta go. I think Dad just pulled up. I love you, Shane."

Her father had been at church doing grief counseling, editing transcripts for a sermon, and meeting with a couple that was planning to get married. It was two o'clock when he arrived home. Mike parked in the driveway and used his remote to open the garage door. Lacy heard it going up and walked to the door to meet him. He saw her, set down his briefcase, and gave her a big hug.

Back in her room, Gina pulled the covers tight over her head with her phone still in her hand.

"Boy, is it a nice day or what? I am going to wash the car and then do some yard work—"

Lacy cut him off in midsentence as her eyes flooded with moisture. "I have something to tell you."

Holding her by the shoulders, "What, dear? What's wrong. Was there an accident? One of the kids last night? What happened?" His eyes were wide open, full of panic.

"It's about Gina," Lacy said, starting to shake

"What about Gina! Is she all right? Where is she?" Mike asked, still holding her.

"She's in her room," Lacy said, looking down at the floor and then back into his eyes. "She and Shane spent the night at Whale Beach last night and…"

"What happened? Why, why were they at Whale Beach? Is Maria—"

"Let me finish, please," Lacy said, taking a breath. "Jim and Dianne Bell were out hiking the East Shore this morning and found them, uh, sleeping together. They were naked together in a sleeping bag." "What are you trying to tell me? Were they having sex? Is that it? They were having sex." Mike walked around, pacing without direction. "Dianne and Jim saw them having sex!" He rubbed his lower lip with his hand.

"Dianne said she didn't want to tell me, but felt that it was her Christian duty as a friend," Lacy said, following him and then stopping when he turned around.

"She told us she was spending the night at Maria's. That was a lie? She spent the night at the beach with Shane having sex?"

Mike continued to pace, not knowing where to look. Lacy kept trying to meet his gaze, but it was elusive. He looked up at the ceiling, his hands heavy on his hips, shaking his head in bewilderment.

"She will not see Shane again. They are done. Done! I trusted that boy with our daughter. He has violated that faith, that confidence. Who else knows? Have they told anyone else? The Bells, I mean. I'm so angry. I want to pound my fists into his plain, innocent face. What a joke. That son of a… I'll kill him!"

Lacy grabbed him by the shoulders to get his attention. "Mike, Mike," she said. "Control yourself. You'll have a heart attack. We will deal with this, but calm down," Lacy said. "I feel the same way, but we have to deal with this rationally. We'll put a stop to the relationship. We'll get Gina back on the right path. I'll call Suzanne and—" Lacy said as he pulled away.

"No. I'll call her. No. I'll call Bill instead. He won't know what hit him. If he can't control his son, by God, I will," he said as he walked into the kitchen and picked up the wall phone. His index finger pounded the numbers as he dialed. "Why don't they answer?" he "Hello," Suzanne said, picking up the receiver.

"Where's Bill? Get Bill. I want to talk to your husband. Now!" Mike demanded.

Shane heard the phone and pressed his ear to the bedroom door.

"Who is this?"

"It's Mike Conrad and I want to speak to Bill. Put him on, damn it."

"I got that part," she said. "I'll get him, just a moment. Bill, it's Mike Conrad, Gina's father and he's upset."

Shane's heart started to beat faster. He sat on the floor, listening as best he could.

Bill was in the bathroom, washing his hands after doing some work on his car. "What's wrong? Mike is what? I couldn't hear what you were saying," he said, turning the water off and trying to rub the last remnants of grease off his fingers.

"Here, take the phone," she said, standing close as Bill spoke.

"Bill, I know wh—" Suzanne started to speak.

Bill took the receiver. "Hello, Mike. What is going on? I—"

"What's going on? I'll tell you what going on!" Bill held the phone away from his ear, looking at Suzanne with a puzzled look on his face. "Your son forced himself on my daughter!"

"What? What are you talking about? He did what?" Bill said staring into the receiver as though it was Mike's face. "You are mista—"

"Your son was found having sex with Gina. She has been brought up to disavow any desire of the flesh until well sealed in the sanctity of marriage. And your—"

"Now hold—"

"My daughter has been sexually violated by your son. That facade of an adolescent is responsible," Mike said, spitting on the other end of the phone.

Bill began a slow deliberate response. "Mike, have you talked to Gina? Suzanne spoke with Shane last week, and he said it was consensual."

Suzanne rolled her eyes, looking at Bill, she said, "No, it's about last night."

"Last week? They had sex last week? I'm talking about today on the beach. What the heck is going on here?"

"Shane shared with us that they went skinny dipping down at Whale Beach and that he and Gina had their first sexual experience and it was marvelous."

"Marvelous! You approved of them having sex? What kind of parents are you? You let your son have his way with—"

"He would never force your daughter...we love our son very much."

"With our daughter with, without asking for our consen— our approval?"

"Your approval? You can't control the kid's lives. We have open communication, dialogue about anything and everything.

Suzanne made sure Shane had protection just in case something happened. We talk about sex. About responsibility. About how to treat a girl."

"Suzanne gave Shane condoms? You condone this sort of thing, don't you?"

Shane walked out of his room and tried to get his mother's attention.

"Let me have the phone, Bill," Suzanne said, snatching the receiver out of his hand. "Let me tell you something, Mike. We trust our son one hundred and ten percent. He did not force himself on your daughter."

"What is going on h—" Shane said, trying to get a word in.

"She actually seduced Shane. Did you hear that? You're beautiful Gina suggested they skinny dip. It was one of those beautiful full moon nights at the lake! Maybe if you talked to your daughter without judging her, she would tell you these things."

"Your son will never see my daughter again. Do you understand? I will file a restraining order against him and you too, if necessary. Your son took advantage of our Gina, and as soon as I get her story, we are going to the police."

"What is he saying?" Shane asked, trying to listen.

"Mike, you are taking this way too far. They are two kids in love who have a sexual relationship. It's all part of the natural order of things."

"Let me talk to—" Shane struggled.

"Do not dishonor your Gina by labeling this as a filthy act. It was not. It was an act of love. The body is not dirty. It is beautiful. My parents raised me in a nudist camp. Yes, that's right, my parents were nudists. My sister and I were nudists. The human body is beautiful. There is nothing lewd or immoral about them having sex," Suzanne said.

"Are you kidding me? I won't listen to this diatribe any longer. Your son is to stay away from Gina. You are all white trash," Mike said and hung up.

Suzanne looked at Bill and Shane in disbelief. Neither of them moved or spoke. The air around them was still.

"What did he say, Mom? Tell me."

His mother didn't answer. She stared at Bill, shaken.

"Do you have any ideas?' Bill asked Suzanne, leaning on the kitchen counter with a glass of water. His mouth was dry. Suzanne took the glass from his hand and drank while looking into his eyes. Bill did not hear Mike's last comment.

"I will not let Shane be responsible for someone else's beliefs. This will hurt. Shane, you and Gina are so close, so beautiful together. It's sad. It's real sad," Suzanne said so softly that Bill and her son could barely hear her.

"What did he say?" Bill asked. Suzanne didn't reply.

Suzanne kept busy in the kitchen starting to prepare dinner. She was going to make ground turkey meatloaf, an array of steamed vegetables, and a Jell-O salad, but now she had no idea what she was doing. She emptied out the entire pantry and set it on the counter. She couldn't remember what she was looking for.

Bill went out in the garage and emptied a large jar of screws on the workbench. He separated them into different piles, one for Phillips, and one for slotted, another for machine screws, and another for bolts. Then he counted the number of screws in each group. When he was done, he mixed them all back together again and put them back in the jar. He looked around for something else to do. His hands were shaking as though he'd had too much caffeine. The refrigerator he kept beer and soda in was humming steadily in the background. *What an ass*, he thought.

Shane went back to his room. Rolled up in a fetal position, he stared at the wall. He fell asleep with his fists tucked under his chin. A few hours later, his mother opened the door and came in.

"Dinner is on the table. Get up and join us. We will all feel better after we eat." She left, leaving the door open. Shane was lying there in a daze. He slowly rolled over, got his feet on the floor, and stood up as though he had a hundred-pound sack of rocks on his back.

"What's for dinner?" he asked after her.

Suzanne, for a brief moment, couldn't recall. "Uh, turkey meat loaf," she said from the hallway.

Bill had already pulled his chair up to the table and was buttering a piece of french bread when Shane came in. "Evening, son, how are you feeling?"

"Ah, you know. What time is it?" he asked with his head down.

"Six-twenty. You were out a long time, almost eight hours. You must have had a lot of fun last night."

"Yeah, Pops, we did. We stayed at the graduation party until twelve o'clock. They had a great DJ. I ate so much food I could barely move. We danced until we were totally exhausted and covered in sweat. Chip had an after-party at his place and a lot of the people went over there. He had beer and a lot of the kids brought their own stuff too. Gina and I drove over to East Shore, like you heard earlier. We hiked back down to Whale Beach. It was so beautiful last night. The partial moon and the stars. Gina." Shane took a long breath, watching his parents. They became very quiet. Their eyes were steady and focused. "Pops, strangest morning, though. The Bells came hiking by our camp and woke us up. You know the Bells, right?" He nodded. "Well, they found Gina and me and starting giving us a bunch of crap about sleeping together. We, ah, we didn't have any clothes on…" Bill and Suzanne looked at each other. Shane noticed and went on. "They said we should be ashamed of ourselves. They just kept staring at us. It pissed me off. I finally told them to leave us alone. So Mrs. Bell called Gina's mom and told her everything. I guess that's what Mr. Conrad was raving about."

"Shane," Suzanne began. "You are not allowed to see her anymore—"

"What! What do you mean? Who says so? Mr. Conrad?"

"Yes, her father said you can't see her anymore," Suzanne said slowly and deliberately. "He said he will file a restraining order against you. Honey, I'm so sorry. They just don't understand. You heard us trying to talk to him, but it was no use. Maybe he'll cool off."

"Son, you are going to have to be calm, cool. We will try to work this out. I wouldn't call or go over to the house. They may come to their senses."

"Really, Pops? Are you serious? I—"

"But for now, you might just be pouring gas on their fire."

Shane leaped up, knocking the corner and shaking the dishes. He leaned on the table with both hands. "This is bull! They can't do this. It's not right!" He burst into tears and couldn't get the next sentence out as he choked with emotion. "What…what." Suzanne got up and hugged him.

They consoled each other. Bill buried his head in his hands. "I want to call Mike back up and tell him he's being a jerk about this whole thing." Bill got up and surrounded the two of them with his long arms. Moisture started to collect at the edges of his eyes from the anger. "He's trying to persecute you for something that…well, isn't a crime."

"Shane, let's take this one step at a time. Let the storm pass. When the sun comes out again, hopefully in a day or so, you, or we can have a talk with her folks. I believe that once they calm down, they'll be able to put this in perspective," Suzanne said sympathetically, but firmly. "Sit back down and we'll finish dinner. Okay?" Shane begrudgingly sat back down with his head dipped.

"Son, you're strong. You can deal with this. We will help," Bill said, adjusting his chair and moving his salad around on the plate. His free hand gripped his pants, white-knuckled under the table.

Chapter 10

Gina did not see Shane after that morning on the beach. She saw Maria and Ally occasionally. That next Saturday, they hiked up to Mt. Rose. The trail was moderate to strenuous, but the views were incredible. They stopped at the waterfall on the way up and on the way back down to soak their feet share a snack. Her mother and father called every few minutes to check on her. Sunday, she hiked the Tunnel Creek Trail by herself just to get out of the house. She left her phone at home.

Later that day after she returned home, Shane called. "Gina, how are you? Gosh, I miss you so much. It is so difficult for me. I just drove by your house. I could feel my heart pounding with fear, hoping your folks didn't see me. You need to get out of there and come and see me."

"They watch me like a couple of hawks. I just hiked Tunnel Creek. I should have had you meet me on the trail. Shane, I haven't been able to eat. I've been nauseous and I haven't slept in forever. Shane, what are we going to do? They were going to take my cell phone away, but luckily, Mom told Dad he should let me keep it for emergencies. They said they're going to the check my phone to see if I've been in touch with you. They'll find this call, I'm sure," she said, breaking down. "Oh, Shane."

"So what? Let them find my calls. You can't give up like this. I'm so pissed right now. Did he file that restraining order?"

"He called his attorney and I think he said it wasn't possible."

"So why can't we see each other then? Do something."

"I can't."

"Or you won't!" He hung up.

Shane sent her letters every few days. Unbeknown to Gina, her parents returned them unopened. He figured Gina had sent them back, not knowing the truth. He tried to call again, but her father changed Gina's cell number. As the weeks went by, the gravity, the hopelessness of the situation started to sink in. Discouraged, Shane took the boat out and hung out down at the beach, sometimes by himself. He tried to create a plan to rendezvous anywhere that was inconspicuous. But as much as he tried, he wasn't able to contact her.

On Friday toward the end of July, she called, "Shane, I'm over at Maria's. Can you come over and see me? I miss you so much. Her parents are gone. We could hang out for a little while. Can you, please?"

"I'm helping my pops build a deck. How long are you going to be there?" he asked, looking down at his father who was cutting railing cap and pickets. "Pops, how much longer do you need me?"

"Why, son, what's up?"

"Gina wants me to come over to Maria's for a while."

"I know how you feel, Shane, but don't do it. If her folks find out, it'll create a whole swarm of problems."

"They'll never know. I'm going over. This whole thing is bull."

"Son, listen to me. Let it go for now. They are still angry and upset. When they come to their senses, you two can get together," Bill said.

"Really? What if they don't, Pops? It's been weeks. What if this was you and Mom? What would you do? You wouldn't give up. Would you?"

"No, son, I wouldn't. But in this case, I think it is the best thing to do. He could file a criminal complaint or worse. That won't solve anything. Please be patient, and hopefully, at some point, they will change their minds," his father said, standing with his hands in his tool belt.

"All right. I get it," Shane said. "I get it, Pops."

"Gina, my dad doesn't think it's wise. I have to get back to work. I'm sorry."

"Oh, Shane, please. I haven't seen you in so long, I'm going crazy. Just for a little while, please. Don't do this."

"I gotta go. I love you." He hung up and threw his phone across the yard. "Damn!"

"Son."

"What, what do you want to tell me. This is bull." He picked up a picket and batted a screw across the deck.

Shane visited Arizona State University. Bill drove him out to Tempe in July. They crossed miles of barren desert, traveling down to Las Vegas through Kingman and on to Phoenix.

"Does it ever cool down here? What is that smell, low tide?"

"It's the stockyards, son. They water them in the evening to keep the dust down."

"This is a good-looking campus. Look at those buildings," Shane said, gazing down the center of promenade on the way to the administration building.

"This school is well-known for its architecture college. Frank Lloyd Wright, an internationally renowned architect, was on staff here," Bill informed him.

People waved as they passed them on the sidewalk. They met the head baseball coach wearing a Sun Devils cap and a counselor with black-rimmed glasses at the admissions office. They took them on an in-depth tour of the campus.

"I don't know, Pops. I'm just not feeling it."

"The school year is actually quite pleasant. September can be a bit warm. Then it cools down. It doesn't get hot until again until May. The students enjoy tubing down the Salt and Gila rivers on the weekends. It's a lot of fun," the counselor said, ignoring Shane's comment

"Wow, tubing." Shane rolled his eyes.

The hot sun ricocheted off the concrete as they walked down the promenade. Cactus and ice plant baked nearby. "The saguaro look like pin cushions with arms, Pops," Shane said, looking over at his dad. The barrel cacti stood covered in long curved fish-hook needles.

"Shane, we will definitely improve your game. I would imagine you'll be a starter by the time you're a junior, maybe sooner. In the meantime, we'll rotate you through all the positions to develop your strengths. Who knows, you may end up playing second or short. Mr. October, Reggie Jackson, played for us," the coach added, walking them through the locker room and then into the baseball stadium. "Whatever," Shane said, looking away.

"We have one of the top racked teams in the country. Several pro teams sponsor players here before going to the big leagues," the coach said. "The Brewers, the Giants, the A's, even the Yankees. We have our own bowl game. Perhaps you've heard of it, 'The Fiesta Bowl.' This is all new," he said, waving his hand around.

The counselor took over after leaving the stadium, finishing with the schools of architecture, law, and education, and a visit to the student union. "Most of the students and faculty ride bicycles or walk. All of our classrooms are air conditioned."

"How many students attend the university?" Bill asked.

"Oh, it's around thirty thousand. Any other questions?" the counselor asked as they returned to the admissions department. "Thanks for visiting our school. Let us know if we can help you with anything."

The coach gave Shane a baseball cap. They shook hands and left.

—◦✦◦—

A short time after returning home from Arizona, Bill and Suzanne drove Shane to Berkeley for a four-day weekend.

"I can't believe all this traffic. How do people do this every day? I'm already stressed out and I don't even live here."

"You'll get used to it. Everyone does. It just takes time to get adjusted," his mother said.

"We have to wait in a line for everything, at the toll plaza, at the restaurant, the movies. It's nuts, and everyone is shooting each other. What's with that?"

"Not everyone. Stop exaggerating," his father said.

"The news is like a live obituary, and look at this air, it's disgusting," Shane said, looking up through his window.

"What? What was that, Shane?" Bill asked, weaving through the cars.

"And it's noisy. Hey, that guy just flipped you off. Nice. I wonder if they provide Kevlar baseball uniforms."

The coaches were anxious to have him sign up, but they didn't make any promises about pitching.

"What happened to the pro teams that sent scouts to my games, Dad? I thought they'd at least contact me."

"I couldn't tell you, son. I thought they'd call and set up an interview after all the press you got."

"Maybe we should call them? It wouldn't hurt to inquire about what is really going on," Suzanne said.

Shane anticipated a four- or five-year stint at the university and then sign with a sponsoring major league organization. It was obviously not going to happen at this point.

"I don't know. I think they would have done something by now, Mom."

The coaches from both universities said they would play him as a freshman, and then redshirt him either his sophomore or junior year. He would have to prove himself beyond his current ability to achieve his dream. It was possible, but not likely. The scholarships got him into the ballpark, but not on the field. He wanted to focus on his academics as well. He couldn't do both.

He liked the Berkeley campus, however. They toured the classrooms, the different colleges, and the promenade. He noticed it was a little chilly even in August. At least, he wasn't frying like an egg, he thought. They showed them all of the sport facilities, the student union, and the dorms. However, he felt out of place even with the wide selection of amenities.

"Well, Shane, what do you think? A degree from here will take you a long ways. It is a nationally recognized university. They have a very strong baseball program. It'll take some patience and you would have to get used to life in the city though. I think it might be worth a shot," Bill said.

"Pops, Dad, I don't know. I feel frazzled here. A mountain boy goes to the city?" He shook his head. "I'll think about it."

"I think you're scared. I know I would be, this huge campus compared to Incline High and…"

"Bill, it's his decision…"

"Yeah, but, I think he may miss a great opportunity here with…"

"I don't agree. He's seen everything it has to offer and…"

"All right, that's enough. I got it. Whatever I'm going to do, I'll figure it out."

They drove back home up Interstate 80. They stopped in Auburn for a restroom break and burgers.

"Shane, I'm going into get some fresh fruit while we're here. Is there anything you'd like? The cherries look good."

"Nah, I'll just have a burger and fries," he said without looking up.

Bill followed Suzanne into the market while Shane waited outside for their meal to arrive. They ate their dinner in silence. It was dark when they got back home.

—⟨∘⟩∘⟩—

"Hey, get up. It's one o'clock in the afternoon. Do something instead of moping around. You didn't get out of bed until suppertime yesterday."

"Well, what's the big deal? All we've had for dinner these past few nights is leftovers. Dad just sits there drinking beer and watching TV until you go to bed. And all you do is read your stupid book."

"We've all been a little down lately. Your dad has been real tired after working on that roof all week..."

"Whatever, Mom. I drive by Gina's house every day now. Her car is gone. Her phone is blocked, and I don't know where to find her. My whole body feels so heavy. You know what I mean?"

"Yes, Shane, I do. I don't feel like cooking dinner. The salon cheers me up when I go into work, but coming home is depressing with everyone so despondent. This house sucks the life out of me."

"Well, I got some information on the University of Reno, Mom. I went online to check out some of their classes and I think I might just go there. I called their baseball coach and talked to him and his assistant about playing ball. They said I would probably be able to get a scholarship there too."

"Really? When did you do all this? You've been in bed all this time."

"No, not quite, but close. I guess I'll stay here for a while and commute."

"You're going to live here? I'm so glad, honey."

"Well, I'll be close to my friends and still get a little city life in Reno, if I want it. Gina is supposed to be going to med school there. Maybe we can hang out. Her folks can't do anything while we're in school," he said smiling.

Shane submitted his application the following week. After talking to the admissions office and sending in his scholarship forms, he was accepted. Classes started the second week of September.

—∿∿∿—

Gina did plan to attend the University of Nevada School of Medicine on her millennium scholarship with another National Honor Society scholarship from Incline High and a National Merit Scholarship to the University. It was near the end of July when Lacy went into Gina's bedroom to check on her. She hadn't come out for breakfast and didn't respond when she was called.

"Gina, breakfast is ready."

"I'm not hungry, Mom"

"You're not feeling well? Gina, have you been sick to your stomach?" There was a white bath towel lying next to her head on the bed. "Did you eat something that didn't agree with you?" Gina shook her head, looking very pale. "A virus is going around. Maybe you caught something. I'll call Dr. Smith and see if he can see you this morning."

"Mom, I'll be okay."

"You sure don't look okay."

"Mom, really, I'll be okay in a little while," Gina said, trying to avoid any more prying.

"All right then. I'll save your breakfast in case you get hungry later."

I can't believe I missed my period. It's been two weeks. When it rains, it pours. I don't even know who to talk to, Ally, Maria? Damn it. If I call Shane, I don't know what he'll do. He'll probably…I thought it would be okay. I counted the days since my last cycle. I feel like such a fool. I've really messed things up now.

Gina crawled out of bed a short time later. She got dressed and wandered out to the kitchen, looking tired and disheveled. Her mother put plastic wrap over a plate of scrambled eggs and bacon. She looked at the food and decided to try to eat it. Lacy came and sat with her as she took small bites of bacon.

"Would you like some milk or juice? There's a fresh pot of coffee."

"Milk. I'll have some milk, thanks. Do we have any Motrin?" Looking up at her mother, "Mom, I think..." Gina burst into tears. "Mom, I'm so sorry. I think I'm pregnant." She buried her head in her hands and sobbed.

"What. You're pregnant?" She pushed the words out. "I, ah, don't believe it. How could this happen? You told me he had a condom."

"He did. But it broke open in his wallet so we didn't use it. I checked and thought it'd be okay since enough days had passed since my last period..."

"You did what? What a stupid thing to do. You shouldn't have been sleeping together to begin with and then you take the chance of..."

"I'm sorry I'm stupid! I'm scared and I don't know what to do," Gina said, hardly able to look at her mother.

"We, your father and I will, will figure something out. I never pictured our daughter's life turning out like this. Is there anything else you haven't told us? How could you do this to us?"

"What about me?" she asked as her mother went into the living room and sat down in the chair next to the sofa.

"What about you?" she said with clenched teeth. Lacy dug her fingernails into the arms as she stared into the fireplace. *How humiliating this will be if anyone finds out*, she thought. *My God, the preacher's daughter is pregnant out of wedlock. We'll be the laughing stock of Incline Village. It's because of that family, those Kaufmanns. She was raised in a nudist camp. What would you expect from a mother like that? Bill's only a stupid carpenter. He doesn't know or care anything about social graces, that's obvious.* She didn't hear the phone until the third ring.

"Hello. Who is this? Oh, Mike, I didn't recognize your voice," she said, still thinking.

"Lacy, this guy named Chuck came by with a truck full of steaks, hamburger patties, and tri tips. They were a good buy so I picked a few up for dinner and barbecues later. I…"

"Mike, we need to talk." Lacy choked and was unable to finish.

"Lacy, what's wrong? Honey, are you crying?"

"Oh, Mike, it's Gina. She's pregnant," Lacy said, her garbled words almost inaudible.

"Oh, no, oh, no, no, no, no! I'll be right home." Mike hung up the phone, eyes and mouth wide open.

He took a handful of papers, pressed them into his briefcase, and left the sanctuary without saying good-bye. *What is happening here? My daughter is pregnant? Why? It's that no-good boy she was seeing. I'll get to bottom of this, and that boy is going to pay. The parents are just a couple of undisciplined hippies. They have no morals. I'm surprised they even have jobs. Well, they won't even be able to get food stamps when I'm done with them.* "White trash!" he yelled through the windshield. He wanted vengeance. His face was bursting bright red in his collar when he pulled up to the house. His heavy steps pounded the stone as he walked up to the front door and let himself in. He forgot about the meat on the backseat.

"Lacy? Lacy, where are you? Is Gina here?" Mike asked, entering the house.

"I'm in the kitchen," Lacy replied.

"Where's Gina?" Mike asked.

"She went out back. She's sitting in the lounge chair by the barbecue."

"Gina," he said, flinging the kitchen door open.

"Yes, Dad," she said, looking up with sad, apprehensive eyes.

"You're pregnant? Shane raped you, didn't he? Tell me the truth. Don't cover for that boy. He's no good. He needs to pay for what he's done to you," her father said.

"Mike, Gina said she consented. They planned this whole episode. Shane brought a condom, but the wrapper tore and they couldn't use it."

His eyes bulged and his mouth drooled. "What? You what?" He instantly wanted to slap her. He held his hand in check at his side. "You didn't have any protection and you had sex anyway? How could you? You committed a sin, and on top of that, you gambled that you wouldn't get pregnant? What were you thinking?" He threw his hands up in the air. "What did we teach you? This family has a set of convictions based on the teachings of Christ. Do you not love the Lord God our father and his son? Tell me about that night. No, don't. I don't want to know," he said, spitting the words out. "Lacy, talk to me. What is happening here?" he asked, his white hair standing on end.

Gina sat quietly, her head bowed, while they spoke about her. Mike turned and walked back inside. He made himself a vodka on the rocks and sat down at the counter. Lacy sat beside him. He wiped his hands down the sides of his hair, pulling his face back and hung his head. He took a drink. The taste was bitter.

"I don't want that boy to know anything about this. Has she told him?"

"I'll ask her, but I don't think so. I can call Millie in Tulsa. She has a small house she bought with her half of our folk's inheritance. Maybe Gina could go and stay there?"

"That's an idea," Mike said, taking a drink, finishing the glass, and pouring another.

Lacy hadn't talked to her sister in over a year. They were very different from one another and had never been close. Her shoulders hunched forward. She clasped her hands together and put them between her knees resting on her elbows.

"What do you think? Should I call her? Maybe we can get through this with no one here finding out. The university is there. We might be able to get her enrolled. I heard they have a nationally recognized medical program," Lacy said, looking over at her husband.

"Tell you what. I'll check on the university. You call your sister and we'll take it from there," Mike said, shaking the ice around.

Gina lay back and let herself drift out in the backyard while her parents determined the next stage of her life. She just wanted to be alone with her thoughts. She decided she would call Shane as soon as she was able.

"Mike, this is going to be difficult. You know, I dated Millie's boyfriend Roger in high school without her being aware of it. When Millie found out, she freaked out. She was devastated."

"Well, that was stupid, but she must be over that by now."

"Mike, it was her last romance. She never trusted men after that, or me, for that matter. She's been living alone since. I apologized, but she's never forgiven me."

"Really? The Lord says forgiveness cleanses the soul."

"Tell her that? We've hardly spoken in years. We've been married how long, and you've never seen her."

"It's a sham—it's a shame, I mean."

"Millie, it's Lacy. How are you, sis?"

"What do you want? You never call unless you need something. What is it?"

"Oh, Millie, I—"

"Tell me what you want. I'm busy."

"Gina is—"

"Who's Gina?"

"She's our daughter. She's pregnant."

"So what do you want me do about it?"

"Please let me talk, Millie," Lacy said calmly. "I know you bought a house with your half of our folk's inheritance. I was wondering if Gina might stay with you while she's going through the pregnancy. We are attempting to enroll her at the University of Oklahoma there in Tulsa in the medical college…"

"Oh, I don't know Lacy. This doesn't sound like…"

"Let me finish, please. We will pay a fair rent and give you money for her food and utilities."

"Well, I…I could use a little extra money. When is the baby due?"

"We don't know yet. We figure she's about six weeks along. I guess around the middle of March. We have medical insurance. Is there a Kaiser Hospital in Tulsa?"

"Yes, it's close, just across town. Does she drive?"

"Yes, Gina has a Toyota 4 Runner. It's good in the snow and ice."

"Good because I can't be driving her all over town and to school and such."

"Mike is checking with the University of Oklahoma to see if we can get Gina admitted into their medial program. Have you heard anything about it?"

"I've heard it's top-notch, but I can't tell you more than that. Lacy, I have rules here that Gina is going to have to follow. I don't want her bringing any boyfriends or even girl friends back to the house. She can have the guest room in the back. I'll have to move a couple things out, but there should be enough room. She'll have to share the bathroom with me and keep it clean, of course. There will be no smoking cigarettes or that other stuff, no alcohol, no drugs, no taking the Lord's name in vain and…" She got lost on a tangent. The list dangled in the air.

"Yes, Millie. She'll do whatever you ask."

"What are you doing? Who are you calling?" Gina asked with a trembling voice, as she walked in the living room

"We're trying to fix this mess you made. We'll fill you in later…" Lacy said, covering the receiver.

"Later, what later. I want to—"

"Go to your room. Get out of my face! I'll tell you when we get this figured out. Now, go!" Lucy yelled. "What is that? I couldn't hear what you said."

"I said. Do not call me Millie! I am Mildred, have been since high school."

Mildred. Where did that come from? "Mildred, I have to go."

Gina turned, ran down the hall, and slammed her door as Lacy hung up the phone.

Mike phoned the high school front office and had her transcripts sent to Tulsa. He contacted the Millennium scholarship department in Carson City. He made another call to the scholarship committee at Incline High School. He called the University of Nevada to get the National Merit Scholarship transferred. He contacted Kaiser Permanente to get the information on the hospital in Tulsa.

"Lacy, it's Mike. Gina has been accepted to the university."

"What about the scholarships?"

"They have all been transferred. I also talked to the nurse registrar at the hospital. Gina will need to fill out a few papers when she goes in for her first checkup. I'll be home at six."

"So what is going on?" Gina asked, walking out for breakfast. "It's been two weeks and someone has to tell me. You can't keep doing this."

Her father set his coffee cup down and leaned across the table. "Gina, we've enrolled you at the University of Oklahoma in Tulsa."

"What? What about UNR? What's in Tulsa?"

Mike took her hand and held it firm. "You're in Tulsa. Your aunt Mildred lives there. You'll be living with her. We've set things up with Kaiser, the hospital there, to take care of you during the pregnancy."

"And that's it?" she said, trying to pull away. "You're kicking me out of here? Really? I'm your daughter."

"Listen to us," Lacy said, blocking her exit. "You're pregnant. This could ruin your reputation, your future, our future. This is the best solution for all of us."

"No, you can't do this! What about my friends? What about my life, Mom? Don't I matter?"

Gina crumbled to the floor and buried her head in her hands as her folks looked on.

"Mike, we are doing the right thing, aren't we?" Lacy said softly.

Stepping around his daughter, he took Lacy's hand, "Yes, dear, we are."

——⟨∞⟩——

"Shane, I'm moving to Tulsa."

"Tulsa? What? What…" Shane asked as he drove.

"I miss you so much. I hope you are okay. I just ache for your touch, your embrace. There is so much I need to tell you, but I can't. I have been so lonely without you. My parents enrolled me in the University of Oklahoma medical school and I am leaving any day now. I can't believe this is happening. I will be living with my aunt. I have never even met her. I hope she's not a freak," Gina said, her voice breaking.

"It's been so hard not seeing you. I love you…I miss you too. You are leaving? For good? Why? Stand up for yourself. They can't make you move if you don't want to go."

"Shane, I'm so scared. I can't tell you how much I've messed things up. I have to go."

"It's all so unreal. I don't believe it." His voice trailed off into a whisper. "Gina…" She hung up.

God, I can't believe it's over. He pulled into the parking lot at Starbucks and sat staring through the windshield at the trees bending in the breeze.

Gina sat on her bed nostalgically looking at all the memories on her wall, pictures of friends, awards, posters, little mementos from good times past. She ran a brush slowly through her hair. Meanwhile, her father was busy loading the suitcases and bags into the back of the 4 Runner.

Gina called Ally. "Are you guys coming by? I need to see you before I leave."

"I'm picking up Maria, and then we'll be over. I can't believe your parents are moving you to Tulsa because you had sex with Shane. It's nuts."

"I don't want to talk about it…please hurry."

Ally pulled up. Gina heard the car doors open and came out of the house to meet them. Maria walked up and hugged her. Gina wept at her touch.

"Maria, I'm going to miss you." Ally joined them.

"I don't understand what your mom and dad are doing? Gina, it isn't that bad," Ally said.

"I know, but they don't want me around Shane. They say he has been a bad influence, and they don't want to tarnish our reputations any further. They are afraid of the rumors."

"But…Gina," Ally tried to speak.

"I'm not a whore. I know that," she said, stepping back, her arms still around the girls. "I love you two so much. I have to go. I need to finish packing." Their arms released like broken threads.

"Gina, your aunt Millie has a few rules for you to follow at her home. I'm sure she'll go over them again when you arrive," her mother said, packing a small bag of fruit, snacks, and drinks for their trip.

"Oh, great. Like what? Keep my elbows off the table. Always say plea—"

"Don't get smart with me. You'll be a guest in her house and you must respect her wishes. Like keeping your bedroom and the bathroom clean. She doesn't want you to bring anyone over, male or female."

"I can't wait. This sounds like so much fun, Mom. Are you sure you don't want to join me?"

"Mom, please, please don't make me go. I don't know anyone there. What about my friends? Are you going to visit? Dad, please."

"Of course, we'll come and visit. You just get settled in, concentrate on school and having a healthy child," Lacy said, struggling to look at her. "Get your things together. Here's a large suitcase, a duffel bag, and two smaller suitcases. Don't forget your toothbrush and your makeup. If you need any toiletries, make a list and we'll pick them up at Raley's."

As Mike and Gina pulled out of the driveway and headed up Eagle Drive, the tears dripped quietly down her cheeks. She held her pillow tight against her chest and did not attempt to hide her sadness. She didn't look back at the house or the lake. The mountains did not extend past the side of the road. Her father sat as cold as stone behind the wheel, not making any effort to comfort or console his only daughter. He looked straight ahead. He was on a mission. Her mother gave Gina a cursory hug, tapping her on the shoulder as though she was extended family. There was no kiss good-bye, no good-luck speech, no I'll miss you. The hurt that she felt slid like an ice cube down her throat, choking her with tears. Lacy and Mike lay shame in layer upon layer on Gina. She tried to fend off each insult, judgment, and accusation as best she could. She knew deep in her heart she was a good person. She knew God loved her. Jesus loved her. It still hurt.

I am going to get through this. I am strong. She filled her chest and blew the air out forcefully. *I am determined.* She let go of the pillow and grabbed the arm rest on the door with both hands and squeezed.

Her friends were gone. Her boyfriend, whom she loved with all her heart, was no longer accessible. Her family is casting her out. She would be living with a woman who denounced men and found life in general a drudgery. Everything looked out of focus as she stared out of the window, her jaw clenched.

The Nevada desert lay dirt brown, hot and foreboding. The winds swept the sage and weeds across the desolation in austere silence. Her father insisted on doing all the driving. Gina never said anything, even when Mike was obviously tired. He pulled over to stretch his legs and regain his energy every two hours or so. They drove all the way to Salt Lake City, arriving as the sun began to set, settling for less than a gourmet dinner at a fast-food restaurant. They spent that night in a motel, sharing a simple room with twin beds. Her father did not hold the door open for her or help her get her things out of the car. He grabbed what he needed for the evening and that was it. He showered and got ready for bed. Gina brought in a small overnight bag and spent as much time as she could in the bathroom. When she came out, her father was asleep. She lay on her side staring into the dark shadows, picturing herself with her new child running in tall purple, white, and yellow wildflowers, playing and laughing at the butterflies as they flew around them. Her father snored jaggedly in the background. She wondered how her folks slept together with him making so much noise, if they ever had sex, and what it looked like. She couldn't imagine as she drifted off to sleep.

The next day was a repeat of the first, more desert, mountains, and monotonous highway. She read a book, finding safety, solace, in her own little world.

"Let me know if you need to use the bathroom," her father said without turning his head.

"I will."

"We'll get lunch when we stop for gas," Mike added. Gina didn't answer.

Behind his sunglasses, he thought of the things that had gone wrong with his life and his daughter. He pounded the steering wheel with his hand. Gina looked over, stared and then back out her side window. They arrived in Denver, had a quiet dinner at Denny's, and found another inexpensive motel off the highway.

The next morning, they arrived in Tulsa. Mike got some of their things out of the car. He set his on the sidewalk. Mildred stood on the front porch.

"Hello, Mildred. I'm Mike. Nice to meet you after all this time," Mike said, shaking her hand. "And this is our daughter, Gina."

"Yes, Lacy said you'd be bringing her out," Mildred responded, looking over at the young girl.

"I need to call a cab to get to the airport. May I use your phone? My cell is dead."

She led him into the house. Gina followed with her suitcase and some of her belongings.

"Did you bring a check? Gina, your room is at the end of the hall," Mildred said, showing Mike the phone.

"Boy, you don't fool around, do you? I have cash," Mike said, pulling out his wallet.

The cab pulled up as Gina grabbed an armload of clothes from the back of her car. The cabby honked and her father jogged out, picked his suitcase up, tossed it in the trunk, and got in the front seat.

"Tulsa airport," Mike said to the driver. Gina turned her head to watch as they pulled away.

"There are no extra sheets for the bed, so you'll have to strip them off, wash, and put them back on the same day. I don't want any loud music. I believe your mom covered the rest of the rules, but I'll go over some of them again. Keep our bathroom clean. Pick up your dirty clothes. No smoking, no drugs, no alcohol, do not bring anyone back to the house. I do not like company, that means boyfriends, girlfriends, whatever. I keep the air conditioner set at 75 degrees and the heat at 65. Do not change it. You are to be home no later than ten o'clock. I'd like you to help me cook, and you are to clean up after each meal. Do you understand?" Mildred asked without blinking.

"Yes, ma'am, I do," she said closing the door behind Mildred and sitting on the bed. Her shoulders hunched over, her hands folded between her legs, she stared down at the grain in the oak floor.

The next several months were agony. Gina attended school faithfully, but her morning sickness caused her daily distress. The first and second semesters she took her prerequisites. She went to class and came right home. Mildred timed her to make sure she was on schedule pointing to her watch if she was late. When she arrived, Gina retreated to her bedroom to study. She came out for dinner and then went back to her room. She scheduled prenatal exams around her class schedule and was diligent about going. All the indications were positive. A sonogram revealed she was going to have a baby girl. She wanted an angelic name so she decided to name her Taylor. She talked to her on the other side of the fleshy wall.

"How's mommy's little girl? I love you," she said, gently rubbing her stomach.

Lacy flew out for Christmas and spent a week with her.

"Gina, there you are. I couldn't see you. You look so different."

"I've gained a ton of weight."

"You've highlighted your hair." She stepped back as Gina wrapped her arms around her. "Wow, I'm glad to see you too."

Lacy reserved a large double room at the Winchester Inn for them to stay in while she was in town. The next day, Lacy made them an appointment for a spa day at a local salon, getting a massage, their hair and nails done, and facials.

"I feel like a new woman," Gina said. "Mom, this is great."

"It's been a while since I've pampered myself. It does feel good," Lacy said as they left.

They ate their dinners out, and one night, they went to a movie. Gina was grateful for the chance to get out of the house and away from Mildred.

"Merry Christmas, what are you two up to today? Did you go to church this morning?" Mike asked.

"Yes, Mom and I went to church. Thanks so much for the down jacket. It has been really cold here, below zero some days. We are going to a—"

"Can I talk to your mother?"

Gina's mouth hung open as she passed the phone to her mother.

"Hi, Mike, Merry Christmas," Lacy said, adjusting the receiver in her ear.

"How's the weather?"

"It's been cold and gloomy. We had a girl's day Friday and went a movie last night. I'll see you on Wednesday." Lacy finished the conversation and hung up. "Gina, let's go to the movies again. *Something About Mary* is playing at the Century. I heard it's real funny. I think we both need to laugh." She smiled.

"I'd like that. Buttered popcorn?" Gina asked, raising her eyebrows.

Lacy laughed, "My treat. Let's go."

The week went by quickly. Gina and her mother got a lot closer. They talked late into the night.

"Gina, it's been difficult for me. The house is so empty. I can't bring your name up without having an argument with your father." She sighed. "Gina, I hope you understand why we sent you out here. Your dad is teaching morality through lessons in the Bible and would lose his credibility if your immorality were exposed. We miss you terribly. We'll figure out how to transition this whole nasty mess and make things right again, I assure you."

"Really, Mom. Are you kidding me? I'm good with who I am and what I have done. Dad is so nice to the people at church, but when it comes to me, he is such hypocrite and..."

"Don't talk about your father that way. He is..."

"He is what? He does grief counseling. He does marriage counseling. He teaches Bible classes. Then he throws me out of the house so he can continue to preach. Everyone is perfect in God's eyes. That is the reality. We are all God's children. Isn't that what he preaches? Why am I different?"

"Oh, Gina, you know he loves you and..."

"He only loves the idea of who I am, not who I am really. Do you understand? How long do I have to stay here?" she asked, spreading her arms.

After seven days, Gina felt a new empathy for her mother. She also realized that her mother was as lonely and confused as she was. Holding hands, Gina walked her to the gate and waited until the last person boarded. The deep groaning whoosh of the engines and the smell of diesel filled the terminal as her mother disappeared down the gangway. Gina watched the plane push away. It disappeared in a shimmering cloud of exhaust down the tarmac. She slowly turned around and left, her purse dragging on the carpet as she walked.

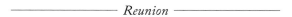

Lacy settled into her window seat and pressed her face against the glass as tears trickled slowly down her cheeks. They both waved good-bye without seeing each other. A curtain of sadness closed around them. *I miss her so much, and we've treated her terribly. I'm a horrible mother.*

Chapter 11

It was spring break at the university when Lacy flew out to help Gina during the birth of her new granddaughter. Gina was thankful to have her there. The last few weeks of school had been difficult going to and from class carrying the weight of child along with her books and schoolwork. Often, she parked two or three blocks from the building where the class was held. Her one evening class was a nightmare. She was so tired from the day's activities that it took all the initiative she could muster to get to school. She fell asleep during a lecture more than once. It was still cool and pleasant in Oklahoma when her mother arrived.

Gina met her at the baggage claim so she wouldn't have to walk all the way through the airport and down the terminal.

"Mom, I'm so glad you're here. I feel like I'm going to explode. The doctor said the baby is due anytime. He showed me the latest sonogram and she is so beautiful. I can't believe I have this little person living inside of me. I am so over my clothes though. Nothing fits, and I have altered them three or four times. Look at me, I'm huge. I hope I don't get stretch marks."

"You'll be fine. Don't worry about such things," Lacy said, squeezing her hand.

Gina cut her hair so it just touched her shoulders. She simplified her makeup by using very little eyeliner, blush, and lipstick.

Lacy pulled her hair back in a ponytail, wearing slacks with a pink shirt. The walk to the car was only a short distance, but Gina was dripping wet by the time they arrived. She leaned against the car, then slowly turned around and tenderly rubbed her stomach. She unbuttoned her shirt so her mother could see the baby move at the touch of her hand.

"That's is so amazing. I can see it pushing against your skin." She reached over and felt the undulations move across her belly. "Honey, do you want me to drive? I don't know my way around Tulsa very well, but you can relax and direct me. I reserved a room at the Marriot so I can be close by while you are in the hospital."

"We're going there now? What if my water breaks and I go into labor and you're not here?"

"Don't worry. I'll make sure that we have plans for every contingency. I'll stay with you until you give birth, and then, I'll be at the hotel. Don't be scared. God has given you a wonderful natural blessing. He will be watching over you the whole time. You know he is omnipresent."

———❦———

"I cleaned the sheets on the other bed in Gina's room," Mildred said as they came in.

"Thanks, I appreciate that," Lacy said, putting her bags down and looking around the house.

Mildred dressed in a charcoal apron over a denim dress and tennis shoes. Her salt-and-pepper hair was straight and firm. A stern expression, she barely moved her lips as she spoke. Her red lipstick was thick and glossy underneath the slits of her black eyes. She stepped to the side.

"Dinner is ready when you are." The steamy smell of sauerkraut and bratwurst drifted throughout the house, fogging the windows in the nearby rooms. Lacy picked her things back up and could not imagine what smelled so bad as she negotiated the narrow path down the hall with Gina to the back bedroom.

"What is that she's cooking? Smells like old shoes," Lacy said as they walked.

Gina ignored the poke. "It's German food. You'll like it. She makes it occasionally. She said your mom used to love to cook German food."

"She did, but it always stunk up the house. Dad would open all the windows and doors to air it out. She always used too much garlic. Dad hated garlic, but she added it anyway. They had a love-hate relationship with German food. It was funny, actually."

After she unpacked, Lacy helped Gina get dressed and groomed. She brushed her hair, rubbed her feet, and massaged her shoulders. She spread lotion on Gina's arms, legs, and stomach in a tender circular motion when she was done.

"Mom, thanks for taking care of me. It means a lot. I hope you can stay for a while after the baby is born. You know, Aunt Mildred doesn't like me. She's not very nice, and I need you here with me."

"Your dad is busy right now, so I don't think he'll miss me. I'll try to stay as long as I can. I know Millie was used to having the house to herself. It just takes time to get things worked out. Please have patience. I know she can be difficult."

"Patience? I've been here almost eight months, Mom. She is so mean to me. I try to do everything she asks. I anticipate what she needs, but she still scolds me like a little girl. Mom, I'm eighteen now. I am an adult. I can't seem to make her happy. If the TV doesn't work, she blames me. If her car won't start, it's my fault. If her feet hurt, it's because I've made her work too hard. I do her laundry, help cook, and clean the house. I do the bathroom. I keep my room immaculate. Still, she isn't happy."

Gina laid down on her bed, closed her eyes, and tenderly massaged her stomach. The birds were busy chirping away, leaping branch to branch in the bay tree outside the window. She wondered if they were mating or designing a nest. She marveled at what it would feel like to lay an egg. Her mother began to hum a lullaby as she fell asleep.

Lacy lay on the other twin bed, looking up at the ceiling. There was a plain white globe with two lightbulbs in it. They didn't seem to be very bright. She saw the remnants of a spider web hanging over by the closet. The light cast a shadow, making it look like a string on the wall. *Where's that 'ol spider now?* She tucked her hands behind her head and closed her eyes.

"Dinner's ready." The words sliced through the silence of their dreams. Gina sat up suddenly, startled at the interruption.

"Mom, you up? I was dreaming I was floating in the lake and the warm sun was breathing on my baby. And then, the rolling thunder of Aunt Mildred's voice overhead woke me up."

"Come on, dear. Let's go eat." *It reeks like a boy's high school locker room in here*, she thought. *I hope it tastes better than it smells.*

"I didn't put much garlic in," Mildred said, spooning the gray cabbage and meat onto their plates. They took their appropriate positions around the small kitchen table stuffed into the corner under a small window. Lacy checked around the nook, looking at all the boxes and things Mildred piled nearby, stacks of old newspapers, grocery bags, broken dishes.

"Why don't you get rid of all this junk? How can you move in here?" Lacy asked.

Mildred replied quietly disinterested, "I do just fine. It's none of your business."

"There are paths down the hall, through the living room, into the kitchen. You have boxes everywhere. I can help you get rid of…"

"You just never mind, miss nosy. Eat your dinner. This is my house."

Surprisingly to Lacy, the food tasted good. She had a small second helping.

"So you like the cabbage and bratwurst? I am a good cook, better than Mom."

———————

Gina saw Dr. Langton at Kaiser. She kept his number close by just in case she went into labor. He was kind, sensitive, and understanding. Fortunately, she was able to confide in him, and he had a great empathy for her situation. He gave her a strict diet to follow and instructions for caring for her baby as it grew in the womb. Up until the last few weeks, she went on long walks and swam at the pool at the recreation center where they offered additional classes in prenatal care. Lately, she did a few easy stretching and cardio exercises in her room, getting ready and remaining healthy for the delivery.

It was very early in the morning during the second week of March when Gina woke up suddenly feeling wetness in the sheets.

"Mom! Mom! I think my water broke," she said, sitting up, turning on the light on the end table and examining herself.

"Let me see, dear. Oh, we should get to the hospital. You get yourself up and I'll take care of the rest."

Gina's overnight bag was packed and already in the car. Her mother cleaned her off and helped her get on a clean nightgown. She waddled to the car, hanging on to Lacy's arm for support. Mildred poked her head out of the bedroom door as they traversed the hallway.

"What's going on? Is she in labor? I'll turn the porch light on. Can I help?" Lacy had a surprised look on her face.

"Wow, what's come over you, Mildred? Compassion?"

She ignored the comment and switched on the light in the hall and on the porch as she walked out in her loose cotton pajamas.

Lacy had a white-knuckled grip on the wheel with her face glued to the windshield as she drove. She pressed on and off the gas pedal, trying to go as fast as she could and still be safe as the car inhaled and exhaled down the surface streets. Gina sat on two towels in the passenger seat, feeling Taylor's movements with her hand, wincing in pain with each contraction. Lacy sat in the turn lane at one red signal light and decided to run it. "I just broke the law. I've never done that. I hope they understand," she said, looking around for a police car.

When they arrived at the hospital, the tires screeched, and they both jerked forward as Lacy dropped it into park while the car was still moving. Two nurses met them with a gurney as they stumbled through the sliding glass doors.

"Hon, you just lay yourself down here. Are you her mother?" the one nurse asked.

"Yes," Lacy replied.

"We will need you to fill out some paperwork over there," the nurse said, pointing to a receptionist sitting at a large brown desk with a computer monitor. "Mrs. Lunden will take care of you."

With a big smile, Mrs. Lunden waved Lacy over. "Have a seat. Isn't it just going to be a beautiful day?"

Lacy's face was a myriad of wrinkles as she nervously sat down. Gina remained on the gurney while the nurses covered her in a heated blanket to keep her warm. Lacy impatiently answered questions, signed release forms, registration forms, and insurance information forms and just in case forms.

"My daughter is in labor. Can't we hurry this along? Where is her doctor?" Lacy asked, squirming in her chair.

"Just a moment, Mrs. Conrad," Mrs. Lunden said, still smiling. "We are almost done here. Dr. Langton is on his way. He should be here any minute." She slid a final form across the desk for her signature.

Lacy quickly signed the document, slapped the pen down on the desk, and stretched backward rolling her eyes. She got up and went over to check on Gina as the doctor came around the corner from down the hall.

"Good morning. You must be Gina's mother. I am Dr. Langton and I'll be delivering Taylor. Do you have any questions at this time? We will be taking her up to the delivery room momentarily," he said, pointing across the lobby.

Lacy was a little tongue-tied but managed to ask, "Is she okay?"

"From what the nurses have told me, her contractions are still very far apart, so it may be a while before she's ready to actually deliver. We will monitor her very closely and make sure she has everything she needs. She going to experience a lot of pain, so we'll need you to help make her as comfortable as possible and help with her breathing. I'll have the nurse give you coaching instructions when we get up there," the doctor said, introducing the nurse that met them in the emergency entrance.

"Hi, nice to meet you, I'm Lisa and this is Ellen. We'll be taking turns, making sure Gina is as comfortable as possible."

"Owwww, arggggggg," Gina moaned as they moved into the elevator to the second floor. "Mom. It hurts."

"I know, sweetie. I'm right here. Squeeze my hand if you need to," she said, holding Gina's fingers.

The delivery room was nicotine yellow with watercolor poster prints by an artist named Depablo. They were paintings of large, calm Hispanic-looking women with smooth black hair flowing down their backs and sweeping colorful dresses posed around a fountain in a pueblo. Lacy looked at the prints suspiciously. Who was the interior designer that decided that something like these would be soothing in a delivery room? And the color of the wall paint? It made her anxious. She wondered how Gina would respond when she looked around.

Doctor Langton came in and took Gina's vitals. "Her heart rate is elevated but normal given the circumstances. Her blood pressure is good," he said, stepping to the front of the bed.

He inspected her birth canal, checking for dilation, and touched different pressure points to see how the baby was doing in the womb. He took his clipboard and left as the nurse came in. She showed them how to adjust the bed and how to use the emergency call button. She left water and straws on the tray table.

"Would you like the TV on?" Gina shook her head. "No. Well, I'll leave the changer right here in case you change your mind, dear. To make an outside call on the phone, you must dial 9 first. You can put your clothes and other things in the closet. They'll be secure in there. The light in the bathroom is on the wall to the left," the nurse said as she left the room.

The contractions got stronger and closer together over a period of eleven hours. Gina was thoroughly exhausted, and Lacy showed signs of fatigue as well.

"Okay, breathe. One, two, three, four," Lacy said, holding her hand as they processed through a painful contraction.

"Shane. You did this to me. Where are you? Argggggggg. Shane!" She screamed during a particularly violet episode. Lacy came to attention at the sound of his name.

Shane was left completely out of the picture. Gina did not want him to know about her unpleasant decision. Her father did not want him proposing to his daughter, and her mother didn't want him fighting for custody or anything relating to Taylor. The less he knew, the better for everyone concerned. Mike was addressing a pastoral convention for the Episcopal Church in Las Vegas, and he sure as heck didn't want anyone awakening the skeletons in his closet.

Shane settled into his schedule at the University of Nevada, Reno. It was baseball season, and he was aggressively competing for a starting pitcher's position on the team. They used him occasionally as a reliever, but there was quite a bit of talent ahead of him on the roster.

He committed his major to education. He took a variety of general education courses in case he still wanted to change. He wasn't sure what he wanted to do at this point. He considered teaching. He enjoyed kids. It may be the best course to pursue. He was on vacation in San Diego during spring break with Chip and a couple new friends from college at the time Taylor was being born.

—————

Nurses Lisa and Ellen assisted Dr. Langton as Taylor made her grand entrance into Gina's life. She had all of her digits, and everything appeared healthy and normal when the doctor inspected her. She had very little hair though. What she did have was curly brown and pasted to her head. Lacy was dripping wet with perspiration when she called Mike to give him the news.

"Mike, it's Lacy. We have a brand-new beautiful baby granddaughter." Tears flowed unexpectedly as she remembered the day she had Gina not so long ago. "She is so beautiful. You should see how she smiles. Gina is so happy."

"Is everything okay? I mean, is she…? How is Gina?" Mike asked in a low voice.

"It's reassuring to know that you care, Mike. She is doing just fine. They both are."

The nurse handed Taylor to Gina to hold for a little bit after they both were cleaned up.

"You did just great, Gina," the doctor said, filling in a couple things on her chart. "Now the real fun begins. The nurses will be here and give you instructions for the next few hours. You and Taylor should be able to go home tomorrow once we make sure everything is okay. Make sure you have a car seat," he said, looking over at Lacy.

The nurses took Taylor down to the nursery so Gina could rest and sleep for a while.

"Nurse, I'll be at the Marriot in case you need me," Lacy said, handing her the phone number for the hotel.

"I want my baby," Gina cried when she awoke. "Where's Taylor?"

The nurse calmed her down and brought in a wheel chair to take her down to the nursery.

Taylor, wrapped in a tiny pink blanket, was resting in a clear Plexiglas crib. Gina peered through the window as the nurse went to get her. She was softly sleeping, her little hands near her mouth. The nurse went over the breast-feeding procedures. She was not sure if Gina was physically ready to feed the infant or not. Using a breast pump, she expressed into a small feeding tube that Taylor could suck on. It took a while to get the fluid out of the nipple, but once it started, it flowed freely. There was an angelic glow from both as the nurse gave Taylor to Gina to hold. "She's so pretty," Gina said.

"You have a very beautiful little girl there," the nurse said in her sweetest voice.

"I know. She is so precious," Gina said, touching her cheek to hers.

"Make sure you support her head while you feed her," the nurse said demonstrating. Lacy watched undetected from a short distance away.

"Oh, hi, Mom. Isn't she lovely?" Gina said, looking up and seeing her.

Lacy smiled like a new mother as well. "Yes, she is an angel." She walked up and tenderly touched Taylor's head and tickled her palm with her finger.

"Heeeeee," Taylor let out a little sound and then sat quiet, her small brown eyes taking in all the new sights around her.

Chapter 12

Shane and a friend, Scott Swanson, from the University of Nevada, Reno baseball team found a small home to rent off Sentry Drive on Broken Arrow Court near campus. He got a part-time at Flood's restaurant busing tables to help pay for rent. Scott had come up from Las Vegas. Not bashful about his finances, he was on the parental aide program and came north to enjoy the mountains, ski, and play on the lake. Scott tried living in the dorms, but hated the rules and regulations. He obtained a waiver from the admissions department and his guidance counselor so he could live off campus. He and Shane were both pitchers down the roster. Shane still claimed that he lived at home so he was able to circumvent the requirement that freshmen were to live on campus their first year of school.

The house was in an older neighborhood nestled among tall cottonwoods and lilac bushes long overgrown. It was a three-bedroom, two-bath home with a large yard. The lawn was dead in the front and back, and the exterior was shedding its olive-green paint. Windblown shingles littered the ground leaving a checkerboard design of white and black on the roof.

Inside, dishes piled up in the sink, waiting for the boy's mothers to arrive. After a while, they discovered that the cleaning was actually going to have been done by themselves. The bathrooms became their personal petri dishes, a science project in the making. Shane used the floor of his bathroom as a clothes hamper until he saw movement under a pair of his shorts one morning. They weren't allowed to have exotic pets, so the mouse had to go.

Scott lived in the master's bedroom with an adjoining bath. He discovered a colony of big brown carpenter ants had set up shop behind the toilet next to the tub. The home had a small laundry room out in the garage where they could hide their dirty clothes until they ran out of clean ones. The kitchen was big enough for a table and chairs that also doubled as a desk for Shane. Scott studied at a table he set up in his room where his clothes and schoolwork constantly competed for space.

Scott was majoring in family law and had a rigorous schedule. Thanks to his folks, he didn't have to work. He concentrated on baseball and academics that fall. His arm got stronger while he dealt with prelaw and government classes. He and Shane got along well when it came to studying and focusing on schoolwork. They worked out together and kept each other motivated.

Scott's sister, Debbie, a sophomore at the University of Nevada, Las Vegas, had the same school breaks as her brother. Her initial visit was at Thanksgiving that first semester. She stood five feet tall with long wavy brown hair that reached all the way down her back. Her olive skin, soft round cheekbones, and sparkling brown eyes were mesmerizing. Shane was totally enthralled with her from the first time they met.

Shane invited Scott and Debbie up to the lake at his folk's house for a traditional turkey dinner. His mother loved to entertain and set a table fit for royalty in their small home. After that encounter, Shane and Debbie stayed in touch regularly. Shane went down to Vegas for Christmas with Scott and met the family. His dad was head of marketing for Flora Resorts and his mother volunteered at a hospice and other local charities. Debbie was majoring in child development, focusing on special needs children, and living at home.

During baseball season, Shane and Scott traveled all over the country. When they played UNLV, he stopped in to see Debbie for as much time as his schedule allowed.

"Shane's got a good head on his shoulders. Debbie seems to be quite happy when they're together," Debbie's father, Lou, said. "I'm glad he takes the time to stop by."

"He appears to be a mature young man, trustworthy. I like him," her mother added. "Scott has nice things to say about him as well. He studies hard, and Scott thinks he'll make a great teacher."

Shane didn't think that dating Debbie qualified as a serious relationship because of the distance between them and the infrequent times they actually got together. That all changed when Shane discovered that Debbie was coming up to the lake to spend the summer. She arrived with two girlfriends from her sorority Delta Gamma and rented a small condominium at Mountain Shadows.

This was the first time the girls were away from home and had a place of their own other than the sorority house. They were thrilled to get out of Las Vegas for the summer and hang out at Lake Tahoe. Their schedule had fun written all over it. With help from her dad, Debbie was referred through local hotels as a babysitter for vacationers, which left her a lot of time to hike, bike, and frolic at the beaches. She and Shane became the best of friends as their feelings for each other grew. Her roommates found jobs waitressing at a Mexican restaurant and as a host at health and wellness spa. The weather did not warm up until the end of June, but it was perfect for them. Las Vegas was already in triple digits by then.

Scott stayed in the house in Reno. Shane moved back home for the summer and crewed on the Sierra Cloud, a catamaran cruise ship that sailed from the Hyatt Regency two times a day providing meals, cocktails, and a narrated tour of the lake. There was a huge celebration planned for the Fourth of July at Incline Beach and on the Hyatt Regency pier.

"Debbie, I've got special passes to the Hyatt pier for the fireworks if you'd like to join me. Your roomies can come too, if they want. It's pretty cool out there. The fireworks barge is just off the beach about two hundred yards, so we'll be right underneath all the bursts when they go off. Incline Beach is way fun too. It's more crowded, but it's mostly people our age having a good time. If we hang at the Hyatt, we'll have to sneak in our own alcohol unless you have some fake ID we can use. What do you think?" Shane asked.

"We were planning on hanging out at Ski Beach anyway. I know you have to work. You said your last cruise was at six, right? Well, you can meet us over by the boat ramp. We'll have a place all set up and plenty of wine, beer, and food. My roommates invited some boys they met the day before from Sierra Nevada College to join us also."

"Yeah, that sounds cool. You're going to want to bring blankets or sleeping bags to wrap up in. It can get plenty cold when the sun goes down. Flashlights are a good idea too. I'll call you when I get off work. I'm sure I can find you easily enough," Shane said.

The girls went down to the beach to reserve a spot as soon as the sun came up. They grabbed a little yellow metal wagon from inside the gate to haul their stuff down to the beach. Canadian geese were standing sentry on the end of the boat ramp looking across the lake when they arrived.

"Hey, look at the huge ducks," Debbie's girlfriend Lisa said.

"They're geese, not ducks," Debbie said, rolling her eyes.

"No, don't feed them. They'll take your fingers off," Ginny, Debbie's other roommate, said.

"Let's spread our things out so we have plenty of space. Help me with this blanket. I brought a rubber mallet to pound in the bottom piece for the umbrella. Here, take this. I'll pound it in," Debbie said, directing the entourage around the campsite. "Set the cooler and beach chairs at the corners to hold the blanket down."

Boats, trailers, kayaks, families, and staff were all intermingled in choreographed chaos. For most participants, the day started out chilly. Folks warmed up with a cup of coffee or tea, a donut, or the annual pancake breakfast hosted by the Lions Club across the way at Aspen Grove. The boats were moored side by side and then staggered out toward the No Wake buoys. Trying to get in or out was a virtual obstacle course. The girls met their college friends mid-morning as the boat ramp movie began in earnest. People were bumping their trailers into the sides of the ramp. Boats wouldn't start, some floated away without their owners. Husbands, wives, friends, and lovers cheered each other on with various hand signals and expletives.

"I've never had so much fun. It's the Jerry Springer show live at Lake Tahoe. Did you see that one woman yell at her husband and pull the trailer away before the boat was all the way in the water? I laughed so hard my teeth hurt. They had to push the boat down the concrete ramp into the water. It must have torn up the hull something awful. And the prop. My God. It was all bent up," Debbie said, moving her arms animatedly to demonstrate the scene.

"Yep, I saw it all. Wait till they start drinking. Then it is really going to get good. Hey, by the way, anyone ready for a beer yet?" Lisa asked.

"Lisa, it's not even ten o'clock, girl. If you start too early, you'll be passed out before lunch," Ginny said.

"Okay, Ginny, I'll wait. It is a little early, but I feel so festive. Let's go play some volleyball. Ya game?" Lisa asked.

"Hey, guys, volleyball?" Debbie asked.

The boys nodded yes, grabbed the red, white, and blue ball, and headed over to the court. Debbie, Ginny, and Lisa followed, grabbing bottled water and a towel.

"We gotta keep an eye on our stuff," Debbie said as they left. They all looked over and then back to the court.

Sean, a lean tall blonde Norwegian student, sprayed the sand to keep the dust down. "Hey, watch it!" Ginny said, dodging the water as Sean decided to water everyone down as well.

As the sun got more intense, the crowd got thicker and louder. People passed around vodka, whiskey, beer, and wine. The music volume rose with the temperature. Rock 'n' roll, reggae, country, and hip-hop all competed decimally. After a few hours, the noise became a hush in the wind. Dip, sip, sleep, and then dip, sip, sleep again. The crowd became an undulating mass, moving in and out of the water. As the sun grew tired and started its steady retreat over the mountains, people started barbecuing. The smell of hot dogs, burgers, chicken, and beef drifted across the beaches and up into the park areas.

One of the college boys brought down a propane stove. They fired it up and grilled some burgers and hotdogs. The sky exploded with color as the last rays filtered orange, red, and purple through the clouds. The fireworks would have a tough act to follow.

Shane called just after nine o'clock. "How are you all doing? Are you staying warm and enjoying the cool mountain air?"

"We just made some hot chocolate with peppermint schnapps and are getting ready for the show. Hurry it up and get down here. I'm getting cold and need your body heat to keep me warm," Debbie said, shaking as she spoke.

"I'm on my way. I'll be the guy in the red shirt and white cap doing the fifty yard dash over people, blankets, and barbecues to get to you."

Debbie chuckled and looked down the beach toward the Hyatt. All she could see were black silhouettes and flashlights. She turned and grabbed her cup just as Shane arrived. "Hey!"

"Ah! You scared me! You were right here the whole time?"

"Well, almost. Did you miss me?" Shane said taking her mug and giving her a soft deliberate kiss.

"We had such a fun day, but boy, did I get burnt. Look at my shoulders. They're glowing even in the dark," Debbie said, exposing her back. Her skin went white at his touch. "Ouch. I just wanted you to look."

"Oh, sorry, when we're out on the boat, all we could see was a mass of people. It looked like a ball game just got over. Umbrellas and shade tents everywhere. Did you guys get trampled here?" Shane asked, looking around.

"No, it wasn't bad, actually. We were dancing earlier. I got a couple of glow sticks. Would you like one? Here, try my hot chocolate. It tastes so good," Debbie said.

"Thanks. That is good, smooth."

They sat down and wrapped a large blanket around their shoulders. "It feels wonderful to snuggle up against you. I'm getting warm now."

Shane recalled sitting on the beach with Gina, sharing feelings that he assumed he would never experience again. His mind was changing as he looked over at Debbie.

It was almost nine thirty when the first blast burst out in white flashes above them. As Debbie bent her head back to absorb the scattered colors amidst the reverberations, Shane leaned over, closed his eyes, and tenderly kissed her as though bathing a newborn infant in a whisper of love. Debbie slowly closed her eyes and let the sights and sounds float in through her closed lids. In that moment, they were alone on a beach exploding in a quiet celebration of their own.

Debbie left for school the second week of August. Before she left, Shane gave her a silver and amethyst ring to confirm his love and commitment. They travelled back and forth between Vegas and Reno on school breaks, holidays, and long weekends. While they dated, they didn't seriously discuss marriage or even living together.

Three years later, Debbie graduated with a degree in child development from UNLV. Her parents bought her a medium-sized house in West Las Vegas as a graduation present and a new Audi. She was thrilled to have a place of her own and a comfortable ride for the trips north. However, she was in no hurry to settle down. Shane had one year of school left before he got his general education degree and could begin teaching. After living in her new home for a week, she decided to head north. She showed up on Shane's doorstep and announced that she was moving in.

"Hey, stranger. Got a room for a lonely brunette?"

"What? Yeah, Sure. You mean now? I guess so. Ah, yea, come on in," Shane said, standing in the doorway.

"Well, if you don't want me, I'll go," Debbie said, pushing her bottom lip out.

"No. No. Sorry. You caught me off guard. I knew this next step might be coming and I, ah, I actually welcome it. So get your narrow ass in here and give me a hug, sweetheart," Shane said, stepping aside.

Shane was still living in the house on Windsor. Scott had moved out the previous year and he had been living alone ever since. He picked up a stray dog, Stella, a young energetic black lab. The yard was still a mess. He never replaced or watered the lawn, planted flowers, or did anything nice to it. Once a week, he cleaned up some of the beer and soda cans and the dog poop. Debbie saw a diamond in the rough. The first thing she did was have Shane fix the tired fence and build a dog run for Stella. Then she got the irrigation system fixed so they could have a nice lawn and flowers. It was another hot summer in Reno and the city was on water rationing. That did not affect Debbie's schedule in the slightest. She watered whenever and as long as she wanted until the water patrol stopped by to inform them that after paying the three hundred dollar fine, they would be on probation. The next time, they would shut the water off. Well, she retreated to the interior of the home and repainted the kitchen, living room, and the master bedroom. The place was getting a woman's touch.

Shane started working at the McCarran Academy, a charter school in central Reno, teaching high school English. It provided a meager income and covered his internship requirements for his degree. He enjoyed the curriculum and the classes. There were usually no more than eight or ten students in each class, and they all enjoyed being there. It made the endeavor fun and rewarding. Teaching and taking classes made a very long day. He was used to coming home, kicking his shoes off, grabbing a cold beer, and watching TV. That was all to change.

Debbie found an entry-level job at a childcare facility in Golden Valley. It started out part time with the prospect of longer hours. Intellectually, they had a lot in common, both loved to teach, and they both really enjoyed children. Debbie, being the more aggressive of the two, proposed to Shane in September, making wedding plans for the following June after his graduation.

"Shane, I reserved a banquet room at Treasure Island for the wedding. It was a gift from my dad. It'll hold two hundred and fifty people easily. He has a great chef and cooking staff, so they'll do the entire meal and custom design the wedding cake. Dad will take care of the photographer, florist, and music as well. Isn't that awesome?" she said, leaning back against the counter.

"What's this going to cost? My folks don't have much money, and well, I don't have much either. I thought we were going to hold the guest list to around one hundred. Do you know all these people?" Shane asked, poking his head in the refrigerator.

"For sure, it's all your friends, family, and my family and friends and some of their friends. It'll be so much fun. I've dreamt about this my whole life. We will have the best wedding photographer and a live band from the Mirage," she said, watching him.

"That does sound exciting. Who's paying for all this?" Shane asked, taking a bite of an apple.

"My dad is taking care of everything. He also told me we have a honeymoon suite at the Hotel de Paris, in Monaco for a week. It's right on the Mediterranean Sea. It's one of the finest hotels in the world. Oh, Shane, our life together is going to be wonderful," Debbie said, giving him a hug.

———

It was a bright, hot, sunny day on the commons at the University for the graduation ceremony. Several thousand people gathered to watch friends and family walk up and get their diplomas. Suzanne and Bill found a spot not too far from the stage under a large cottonwood tree. They beamed with obvious pride. Bill was in charge of picture taking while Suzanne enjoyed looking around at the throngs of people and experiencing the magnitude of the celebration.

"Bill, I am so proud of our son. He has worked so hard to get this. He is going to be the best teacher ever. I just know it." Bill put his arm around her shoulder as she leaned against him.

Debbie held Stella on a short leash, standing with Chip and JT, who had driven down from the lake for the special event. Chip and JT each had one more year left at Sierra Nevada College before graduating from the college of liberal arts. Debbie looked stunning in her high-heeled sandals and tight-fitting summer dress. Chip let his hair grow down to his shoulders and grew a goatee. JT let his hair grow long as well and had a patchy beard. They watched Shane sitting in the group of students near the stage in his black cap and gown. When he looked around, they'd wave, but he couldn't see them. It was more than an hour before his name was called. "I'm sure glad my name isn't Zelder," he said, leaning over talking to the graduate next to him. Perspiration dripped down his back and under his arms as he stood.

As Shane crossed the stage and took his diploma, Chip and JT let out war cries that deafened the ears of the people nearby. "Yeeeeeeeehawwwww! Atta boy, buddy. Whoooooooooooooooooahhhhhhhhhhhhhhh!" Debbie covered her ears and Stella howled. Bill and Suzanne clapped until their hands hurt.

When it was over, Shane went searching through the milling graduates and friends, looking for a familiar face among the crowd.

"Hey, did you hear us cheering for you? Even Stella howled in celebration," Chip said, grabbing Shane from the sea of people.

"I had to cover my ears they were yelling so loud. You did great, honey. I could see your mom and dad over there clapping with so much enthusiasm. It was cute," Debbie said.

"Honey, we're so proud of you!"

"Thanks, Mom."

"Son, son, I ah," Bill choked up as tears flowed down his cheek. He wiped his face with the back of his hand.

"I know, Dad," Shane replied as his father gave him a hug. After a few moments, Debbie squeezed in as well.

"Let's go back to the house and celebrate," Shane said, wiping his nose.

"We'll meet you there," Chip said, leaving with JT.

Debbie, Shane, Suzanne, and Bill all walked together back to her Audi and Suzanne's Sentra. "The traffic is nuts. We should have left our cars back at the house and taken a cab," Debbie said, staring at the line of cars in front of them.

"Isn't the grass nice and green? I planted mums, geraniums, and petunias and they are all doing so well. Smell the lilac?" Debbie said as they exited their cars and walked up to the house.

Shane held the door open as they entered. "It smells like fresh paint," Suzanne said, looking around at the different colors.

"I chose the hues from the plants outside and I painted the ceilings white for contrast," Debbie added.

"Wow, this is sure different. I like it," Suzanne said, wandering from room to room.

Debbie spread out a variety of food on the kitchen table and put a few bottles of champagne on ice in a metal bin. Friends, classmates, and family trickled in to congratulate the new teacher. Bill quietly took Shane aside and pulled a small box out of his coat pocket. Suzanne joined them.

"Son, this is for you, for all your hard work. We are so proud of you and we want you to have this," his father said, handing him the gift.

Shane opened the box and stood staring at a black diamond sport watch. The inscription on the back read, "*To Shane, congratulations, Love Mom and Dad*"

"Thanks, Pops, thanks, Mom. I love it." Shane gave them each a long hug.

Debbie joined them. "Oh, let me see. That is so sweet. It's beautiful."

They walked back into the kitchen for beer, wine, and cocktails. Suzanne baked a large sheet cake and decorated it with Wolf Pack souvenirs, Shane's name and date. She prepared a tray of meats and cheeses with several other finger foods scattered about.

Debbie poured each person some champagne. "I'd like to make a toast to our son. Shhhhh. Everyone." Bill raised his glass, clinking a fork against it to get the guests' attention. "To Shane, the best son ever. Here's to a glorious career and a bright future. We love you."

"Here, here," the group chanted.

"Thank you all very much for your support. It's been a long four years. It felt like six years actually. Thanks to Mom and Pops here and Debbie, I got through it."

Chapter 13

Finding an apartment or a house to rent as a single mother with a young daughter was tough. Tulsa is in the middle of the Bible Belt and folks looked down upon unwed mothers. It was easier to find a place that accepted pets. Mildred was anxious for them to move out, and they were beyond ready to leave. Taylor packed her small bag before they even started looking. She enjoyed sharing a room with her mother, but felt intimidated to be around Mildred.

"Honey, you are going to have to wear those clothes so you might as well leave them out," Gina said. "We will be out of here in no time."

They found a small home on Stewart Street near the Veteran's Administration Hospital where Gina was interning. It had clapboard siding and a shingle roof. She called it her eighty percent house because eighty percent of it was in need of repair or missing. The owner Daniel Morrison was glad to get it rented. The previous tenants used the apple trees in the front yard to dry their laundry, and there was a bathtub in the backyard by the storage shed where they bathed unashamed when the city turned the water off. The refrigerator looked like a science project for penicillin. Food rotted inside the warm box and had not been cleaned up by the owner after the tenants moved out. The cabinets, toilet, and carpet were just as bad. Gina and Taylor were literally as happy as pigs in slop when the two of them began the arduous process of cleaning. They bleached and painted the inside of the cabinets. They scrubbed the toilet and got a new cushioned seat. They cleaned the carpet, which showed stains from anything that walked, was spilled, or laid on it. They painted the walls blue, green, yellow, and pink pastels in Taylor's room. Daniel, their new landlord, replaced the refrigerator. The power company hauled off the old one.

"Thank heaven," Gina said.

"This looks like Chex mix," Gina said when they pulled the stove out to clean behind it. "And mouse poop, yuk. Cleaning the oil from the underside of my car would have been easier than getting this grease off the stovetop and out of the oven."

Taylor laughed. "You're funny, Mom."

It took them several weeks to get the place to the point where they could move in. Daniel occasionally brought over lunch while he trimmed the trees and cut off the dead branches. The previous tenants built a tree fort in the large maple in the backyard to live in.

"I can't believe people live like this," Daniel said, surveying the mess when he got it down on the ground. "Dirty sheets, blankets, mice," he said, holding up a pile of toilet tissue where they nested.

The lawn was a maze of dead circles where they urinated out of the windows. There was a twelve by fourteen foot storage shed in the backyard that he cleaned out. It had been full of construction junk, buckets of nails, screws, red traffic cones, plumbing parts, lights, wire, bugs, and more mice. He insulated, sheetrocked, and wired the structure so the girls had lights and electricity. There were more indications that people had been living in there as well, mattresses, a chest of drawers, a makeshift counter, and mirrors. "Pigs." He shook his head and mumbled.

147

Gina and Taylor gave him a friendly hug when they saw him stressing. "Thanks, Daniel." He turned red and smiled. "We love you, Daniel. Thanks so much for doing all this work," Gina said.

"So what brings you to Tulsa? I'm guessing you're not from around here," Daniel asked.

"I'm originally from Lake Tahoe."

"Wow, I heard that's beautiful. I haven't ever been there, but I'd like to see it," he said, adjusting the ceiling fan.

"It was a great place to grow up. We had the lake for boating, swimming, hiking, and camping. The Sierras go up thousands of feet above sea level so we skied and snowboarded in the winter. Yes, it was awesome. Then, I was accepted to the University of Oklahoma, here in Tulsa to study medicine. Taylor and I moved in with my aunt Mildred until I could get a place of my own. It was difficult to go to school and raise Taylor though."

"Oh, Mom, I was easy." Taylor chimed in.

"Yes, dear, you were," her mother replied. "Thankfully, my folks helped me out with my rent and food."

"That can be tough."

"My scholarship took care of most of my tuition and books."

"That helps too. You must be smart?" he asked, smiling.

"No, just a hard worker. I'm in graduate school now and interning at the VA. Next year, I start the doctorate program. I'm focusing on general medicine, and I eventually want to open a family practice."

"I'll come see you then," Daniel said, climbing down from the ladder.

"So tell me about you, Daniel."

"Well, there isn't a whole lot to tell. I have been here my whole life. I didn't care for high school, but I got through it. I like working on cars. Seems like me and Dad always had a project going on whether it was a motorcycle or a car. I have an older sister who is married and lives in Dallas. Mom and Dad still live in the house they raised me in, in north Tulsa. I went to an automotive school in Oklahoma City after I graduated high school for a few months and then went to work for the Ford dealership here in downtown Tulsa. I did a little wrenching, and then, they moved me to service where I am now. They said it was a promotion, but the pay is the same. I like it. It pays the bills. I picked up the place you're living in at an auction a while back. I didn't realize how much time it takes to be a landlord. Those last folks were horrible, but they paid their rent on time."

"We love your dog."

"Missy, she's a rescue. She loves to play Frisbee. Taylor, come on over here and I'll teach you to throw," Daniel said, picking up the disk. "Cock your wrist like this and flick it." Missy's tongue hung out as she hopped up and down, waiting for the release.

"Like this," Taylor said, tossing it sideways. Missy caught it on the roll and brought it back after Daniel coaxed her with a treat.

"That's great. Keep practicing. Missy will keep you busy," Daniel said, taking the Frisbee from her mouth and handing it back to Taylor.

The neighbors, Bob and Marianne, were delighted to have new people living next door and brought over food and simple house-warming gifts to welcome them. Marianne came over to watch Taylor while Gina was at school, interning or working. They confirmed that multiple families lived in the home together using every available space as bedrooms and storage. Bob shared stories of outdoor barbecues using whatever animal was available.

"I don't believe it," Gina said.

"Sure enough, they stuff the meat in pita bread with rice and veggies. We saw it. It's God's honest truth," Bob said. "It always smelled like low tide over there and it was particularly distasteful in the warm weather. As hot as it gets here in the summertime, we had to keep our windows shut on humid days to avoid the stench. So many children were living there that it wasn't possible to determine which ones belonged to whom. It was like living next to a schoolyard where all day long it was recess." They talked about the tree house and the couple that lived up there.

"They argued and fought until wee hours of the morning." Bob leaned over to Gina and whispered, "They were having sex up in there too. Could hear 'em. They weren't decent folk."

"You're too funny, Bob. Well, you won't have to worry about Taylor and me."

Bob came over and picked the apples in front yard that Gina couldn't reach. Marianne took them and baked apple pies with homemade crusts dusted with cinnamon. After a few weeks, the little house became a real home.

Gina made a large Crock-Pot of homemade chili one Saturday. Daniel stopped by with Missy to play with Taylor, and before he left, Gina offered to send a bowl home with him and an apple pie made from Marianne's now famous recipe. He quickly accepted and invited her to join him. Daniel and Missy lived across town just north of the university. Gina was a little reluctant at first, but after some cajoling, she agreed. She phoned Marianne and asked if she wouldn't mind watching Taylor for the evening.

"Daniel, let me clean up a little first. Give me your address and I'll meet you there," she said, cautiously excited.

"Sure, it's on Lewis, just off Apache Street." Daniel took the Crock-Pot and the pie and carefully put them on the floor of his truck. He turned on a country music channel and began to hum as he pulled away.

Gina felt anxious as she groomed herself and changed her clothes. Taylor watched her with interest each time she tried on something different. Finally, she decided on beige pants, a simple white shirt, and a puka shell necklace. Gina took a deep breath as she pulled the pants on. "Oooo, I'm a little nervous," she said as she exhaled.

"Mommy, can I come too? Daniel said he's going to teach me how to fish."

"No, sweetie. Mommy is going alone. This is an adult evening and you're only five. You'll have fun with Marianne. She said she is going to bake some cookies and you can help. How do I look?" She spun around slowly so Taylor could see.

"You look nice. Are you going to kiss?" Gina looked startled at the remark.

"No, honey. Your mom is just going over to visit for a while and then I'll be home." She smiled and decided on a thin canvas belt, pulling it out of drawer full of accessories.

Gina walked Taylor next door and dropped her off with Marianne. The cookie dough aroma was intoxicating when she opened the door.

"Well, hello, Taylor, are you ready to help me bake some cookies?" She stood in her red and white striped apron with her silver hair pulled back in a ponytail. Her brown eyes were bright with enthusiasm as she took Taylor by the hand and led her into the kitchen.

Gina thanked her and got into her Neon. She was apprehensive driving over. She liked Daniel, but hadn't been on a date since high school. He never asked about a husband or a boyfriend, so she didn't bring it up. Daniel's house was an unpretentious two-story home painted beige with coffee-colored trim. There was a large plum tree in the middle of a well-manicured lawn surrounded by rose bushes and a variety of flowers. He was in the living room when he saw her drive by looking for the house. He walked outside and waved.

"Gina, hey. Back here," he shouted from the front porch.

"Hi," Gina said timidly as she got out of her car. "Nice house."

"It's a great neighborhood. Lots of kids and friendly people," Daniel said, showing her to the front door.

"Whew, nice and cool in here," Gina said, looking around.

"Have a seat. What would like to drink? I'm having a beer."

"Beer's fine."

Daniel returned with an ice-cold bottle of Corona Light. "Glass or bottle?" he asked.

"Bottle," Gina replied, shyly taking it and setting it on the end table. "So you're not married. Tell me more about yourself."

"Well, I had a girlfriend for a couple years, but that didn't work out. I'm not real good with relationships, at least not so far. I'm not into the bar scene, and well, that online dating thing isn't for me either. Just been me and Missy," Daniel said, taking a drink.

"I had a boyfriend back in high school. I haven't dated since. Some boys I met on campus asked me out, but I never accepted. With Taylor and all, I didn't feel comfortable. My aunt Mildred didn't allow boys over anyhow," Gina said, shrugging her shoulders.

"Can I ask you about Taylor? Where is her father?" Daniel asked, looking at her for an answer.

"Well, her father was my high school boyfriend. My parents wouldn't allow us to see each other after they discovered we had sex. Then I discovered I was pregnant, and well, they moved me out here so no one would find out. Maybe we can talk about it some other time."

"Sure, I didn't mean to pry. I'm sorry," Daniel said, standing up.

Daniel finished his beer and started to set the dining room table and changed his mind. "Would you like to eat in the living room and watch a movie? I have a couple here I haven't seen yet." He showed Gina some DVDs. She picked through them and she pointed one out, taking a sip of her beer.

"I like *King Kong*. Let's watch this," she said, handing it to Daniel.

He loaded into the player and dished them each a small bowl of chili and set out some cheese and onions he chopped up while the movie loaded.

"The first time I saw it, I cried. It is so sad when he dies. He really loves her, you know," she said as he hit the *Play* button.

The sky was fading to purple as the film started. The small talked drifted to silence when the story began. The room grew dark, lit only by the large screen TV. Gina felt so comfortable just sitting there that a smile began to grow and then became obvious. "What are you laughing at?"

"I am so happy to be here. I haven't been away from Taylor in forever and I feel safe and comfortable." Daniel tenderly touched Gina's hand and smiled back. "You know, you're like family to me. I have had this void, this vacuum, for so long in my life and it feels good to be able to share time with you," Gina said as she gently put her hand on top of Daniel's.

They lay against each other, watching the men on the TV tranquilize the large beast. Daniel tenderly took her chin and raised it to his lips. She responded lightly, kissing him while watching his blue eyes.

"Thank you for all you've done for Taylor and me. You are a nice man, Daniel Morrison," she said, moving her head back to speak.

"It has been my pleasure to say the least. You deserve it." They continued to lie against one another until the movie was over. Daniel picked up the plates and empty bottles and carried them into the kitchen. "How about some coffee or desert? I have this wonderful apple pie that is dying to be eaten," he said, pointing at the tin with a knife.

"I really must be going." She slowly got up and hugged Missy who was lying asleep by the coffee table.

"I was hoping you'd stay longer."

"I need to get Taylor home and in bed. I'll see you soon. Thanks for inviting me over." She turned and gave Daniel a friendly hug and a kiss as she left.

I'll see you real soon, Daniel was thinking. *Wow, what a nice girl.* He began cleaning up the house before he called it a night, quietly whistling as he worked. Missy followed him as he moved from room to room.

The next day, Daniel called Gina. "Hey, I ah, I couldn't wait to call you. Is that weird or what? I had a good time last night, thanks for coming over. Missy and I haven't had company in a long time. I hope you don't think I'm being too forward. I just wanted to share that with you."

"No, not at all, thanks for calling. I was wondering when I would hear from you. I honestly didn't think it would be this soon. I had a great time last night too. It was nice to do something different. Taylor had so much fun with Marianne. I think she ate too much sugar because she was definitely wired when I went over to get her. Chatty, oh, my gosh. She stayed up way past her bedtime. She's still in bed this morning. She said you're going to take her fishing."

"Yes, I was."

"You know she adores you. Anyway, I'm glad we had a chance to get to know each other a little bit better. Oh, I hear Taylor calling. Well, I've got to go. Thanks again for everything."

"I'll be in touch. Talk to you later. Good-bye. See ya," Daniel said as Taylor asked her mother for the phone.

"Daniel, what are you and Missy doing this weekend? Can we go fishing again? That was so much fun."

"I just was thinking the same thing. The worms are slimy, aren't they? Taylor, you make the cutest faces when you're blowing them up and trying to get them on the hook."

"Taylor, tell Daniel I'll pack us a picnic lunch."

"Mom says she's making us lunch."

"How about Sunday? We should leave early in the morning when the fish are biting. How does that sound?"

"Mom, how about Sunday morning?" Taylor asked with her eyes wide open.

"Yes, honey, that'll be fine."

"Okay, tell Missy we're going Sunday morning."

"Sure thing, can I talk to your mom again? Bye," Daniel asked, waiting for Gina.

"Bye," she said, handing the phone to her mother. "Mom, do you guys kiss?"

"Yes, sometimes. I like him."

"Are you going to marry him?" Taylor asked, watching her mother.

"No, sweetie, we're just good friends," she said, taking the phone.

Daniel laughed on the other end. "So what are we having for dinner tomorrow night?"

"Oh, it's a surprise. That beef Wellington you prepared is going to be hard to beat, but I have something up my sleeve that'll knock your socks off."

"I can't wait."

"Daniel, thank you for being so kind to Taylor. You've been like a father to her."

"Well, Gina, she's been like a daughter to me. She's a special little girl. You both mean a lot to me."

"Taylor, let's finish these chocolate macadamia nut cookies and drop them off at Daniel's after breakfast."

Daniel, we came by, but you were gone. Enjoy. Gina and Taylor

He found the note and the cookies on the porch when he got home.

"Gina, hey, it's Daniel. If you two keep this up, I'm going to be so fat, I'll have to buy two tickets the next time I fly."

"You're welcome." Turning to Taylor, "He likes them." Taylor smiled

"Thank you, I am truly blessed."

"You'll never get fat. You're skin and bones. You're always able eat as much as you want. I'm jealous. By the way, my folks will be here next weekend and I'd like them to meet you."

"Sure, can I bring over a bottle of wine or something else? I could make a spinach and strawberry salad with sugar-coated pecans?"

"Yes, bring some wine. The salad sounds delicious. Thanks. Say around seven."

Mike and Lacy arrived in Tulsa mid-afternoon. An airport shuttle took them over to the Marriot where they reserved a king suite. They rented a compact car at the hotel and drove over to Gina's.

"If this car were any smaller, I could pick a lock with it," Mike said, squirming to get his legs under the steering wheel. "How come good gas mileage has to be so uncomfortable?" They pulled up to the house. "Nice place."

"Gramma, Gramma!" Taylor shouted.

"Say hello to Grandpa too, honey," Gina said, opening the door.

"Hi, Grandpa," she said reluctantly, slinking behind Gina's leg.

"Taylor, you're getting so big. How old are you now?" Lacy asked.

"I'm almost six," she said, holding up her fingers.

"Do you like school?" her grandfather asked.

"Um, I don't know. I guess."

"Dad, she loves it. Kindergarten is a half day."

"I wish it was longer 'cuz we play games, Grandpa."

"She has made so many new friends. A couple of them live just a few houses down. It's been so nice for her to have other children to play with. I have made some new friends too. We trade watching each other's children. It has been great. How are you? You look thinner."

"Oh, you know. Getting a little older. I've had the flu. It had me laid up for a week or so. Didn't your mother tell you?"

"She said you weren't feeling well was all. So you were really sick? Are you better now?" "Oh, yes, much better."

"Are you still giving the sermons?" Gina asked, getting them comfortable in the living room. "Have a seat, Dad, you too, Mom."

"Just on Sunday," her father said, sitting down. "Father John has taken over Friday night and Saturday afternoons. I am doing more marriage and grief counseling. We set up a hospice service that I run now. It all keeps me pretty busy. How is grad school? Is it tough? Are you working on cadavers?"

"It's coming along. I'm doing a lot of interning. We're doing more hands-on learning in class too. Yes, that means working on cadavers. I really enjoy it."

"Sounds morbid to me, I couldn't do it," her father said, squirming in his seat.

"Dad, are you sure you're okay? You look so pale. Have you had a checkup lately?" Gina asked, wrinkling her brow.

"Don't worry about me. I'm fine. Never felt better," her father responded, looking over at Lacy.

"Mike, that's not true. Honey, he's been weak and getting weaker these past couple of months. I can't get him to go in and get a blood test or a physical. Quite frankly, I'm worried about him," Lacy said, looking at Mike.

There was a knock on the door and then the doorbell rang. "Well, hello, don't you look handsome," Gina said, opening the door.

Smiling, Daniel stood there in beige slacks, a light-blue long-sleeve shirt open at the neck, and brown loafers. He held a bottle of wine and a large bowl of salad. Gina let him in with a quick kiss, taking the bowl and the wine and stepping aside to introduce him.

Lacy and Mike both stood up as Taylor started, "Gramma, this is my friend Daniel. He's Mommy's friend too," she said, looking around for his dog. "Where's Missy?"

"Honey, I left her at home today. Hello, I'm Daniel. You must be Lacy. Nice to meet you. And, Mike, is that right? Nice to meet you as well," Daniel said, extending his hand.

Mike looked him over before continuing the conversation. Daniel had a colorful tattoo on his neck. The top portion of a pair of eagle's wings showed just above the second button on his shirt. His eyes narrowed. "So what do you do, Daniel?"

"I am a service writer for the Ford dealership in Tulsa. I also own this home you're in. I bought it at an auction, fixed it up a little, actually a lot with the girls' help. I've been renting it to them. That's how I met Gina and Taylor."

"Well, it certainly is a cute little home," Lacy said, taking the conversation away from Mike. "Taylor told me you have a dog. Missy, is it?"

"Yes, she's a pit bull and sweet as can be. She and Taylor are great friends," he added, inching his way into the living room.

"Do you go to church?" Mike asked, looking at his tattoo.

"Not regularly. I was raised a Baptist. I used to sing in the choir as a young boy. I—"

"Are you a Republican or a Democrat?" Mike asked, cutting him off.

Daniel looked over at Gina and glanced at Lacy before answering. "I vote my mind rather than any party affiliation." Lacy looked away. "I believe in a woman's right to choose, gay marriage, and amnesty for immigrants," Daniel added, staring Mr. Conrad down.

"Alrighty then, let's have some dinner," Gina said, changing the subject. "Dad, you and Mom sit here. Daniel, you sit next to Taylor."

Gina passed the wine opener and the wine to Daniel to open. "This is a special reserve from Napa, California. I hope you like it," Daniel said, pulling the cork and passing it to Mike to smell.

Lacy helped Gina bring out the food and set it on the table. They all joined hands and bowed their heads in prayer before eating.

Mike spoke, "Bless this food and this family. Lord, watch over all those who serve and are in harm's way. Keep us in good health and spirits. In your name we pray, amen."

"Amen."

"Wow, this looks and smells so good," Lacy said, passing the meat.

"Thanks, Mom."

Daniel raised his glass. "Well, here's to a wonderful visit and to new friends." Taylor joined them, clinking with her glass of milk.

"What kind of tattoos are those?" Mike asked, finishing his sip.

"Mike, please, Daniel, you don't have to answer," Lacy said, passing the salad to Daniel.

"No, it's all right, Mrs. Conrad. I like body art. Each piece represents something special to me."

"Dad, they are beautiful. Someday, I hope you get a chance to see them all," Gina said, cutting up Taylor's meat.

"The tattoos, I remember, were on servicemen or convicts. You know, sailor types, gangs," Mike said, chewing.

"So, Gina, how's the internship going?" Lacy asked, looking away from her husband.

"It's interesting. I worked one day last week down at the coroner's department. I helped with two autopsies. Dr. Clark is the head medical examiner and she is very skilled. Holiday weekends are the busiest. Other than that," she said, "it's pretty dead around there."

Daniel laughed. "I like dark humor. I guess everyone has their way of dealing with a tough job."

Taylor left the table and came back with some picture she'd drawn at school. "Gramma, this is a horse, and this, this is a rainbow."

"Very nice, honey. You're quite the artist," Lacy said, passing them to Mike.

"Yes, nice job."

"You can keep them. They're for you." Taylor twisted as she spoke.

"Why thank you, my dear. They're lovely," Lacy said as Daniel pushed his chair back.

"Well, Gina, thanks for another fantastic meal. You've outdone me again," Daniel said, smiling.

"You're not going to stay for desert?" Gina asked surprised.

"No, maybe some other time," he said, standing up.

"Bye, Taylor. Mike, Lacy, it was very nice to meet you. Enjoy your stay," Daniel said, waiting for Gina as she got up.

Gina walked him out to his truck and kissed him good-bye. Daniel drove home wondering how someone so close-minded could have such a beautiful, free-spirited daughter. *I wonder what his sermons are like*, he thought. A redneck from California, how strange. Missy started yelping as soon as he opened the front door.

"Okay, daddy's home," he said, rubbing her belly. He got her a milk bone and freshwater.

The phone rang. "Daniel, it's Gina. Sorry about my dad."

"Nah, that's okay."

"No, really, I know he made you uncomfortable. It was embarrassing. I believe he wants the men in my life to be just like him," Gina said, sighing.

"What, a walking paradox. Sorry. I didn't…"

"No, it's okay. I understand. I've watched him. He preaches one thing and does another. The folks'll be gone in a few days. Remember, Taylor and I care about you very much and that's all that is important. I'll call you tomorrow," Gina said, taking a breath.

"I am here for you, if you need me. I'll see you after your parents leave."

"Okay, I'll be in touch. Bye," Gina said, hanging up.

Two weeks after her parents arrived back home, her mother called, "Hi, Gina, it's Mom. Your father finally went for a full physical and a blood test. He got a colonoscopy yesterday, and it revealed the first signs of prostate cancer."

"Prostate cancer, oh no, how bad is it?"

"He is going in for surgery to remove some polyps and part of his colon. The doctor believes we caught it early enough to eradicate the cancer, but it may leave him impotent," Lacy said, fading to a whisper.

"How's Dad taking all this?"

"He's a little depressed, angry. I think he's scared."

"Is he having laser surgery? If they are careful, all of his vital organs should be okay," Gina said in her doctor's voice.

"I believe he is. The doctor said he'll know more once they get inside."

Chapter 14

Gina and Taylor continued to live in the house on Stewart Street for the next several years. She and Daniel saw each other on weekends and occasionally took weekend trips when possible. Gina finished her internship at the Veterans Administration. She received her doctorate and began to practice medicine at Tulsa General Hospital.

Daniel was promoted to service manager at the Ford dealership. Taylor turned fourteen that March and was finishing her first year of high school.

Daniel called on Saturday. "I have just about got the rat rod finished. I'm going to drive down to Dallas for a car show. Would you like to join me? It starts on May 5 and goes through the twelfth. I reserved a room at the Hilton already. There's competitions, parties, and dances all week."

"Daniel, let me check. Taylor still has school that week, and I need to see if Marianne and Bob wouldn't mind watching her. I'll need to find someone to cover my shifts at the hospital too. What kind of car show is it?"

"It's garage-built cars and trucks similar to mine. People are coming in from all over the country to display them. My friend Jesse is driving down from Muskogee in his '38 Chevy pickup. It will be lot of fun. I've got two week's vacation coming from work, so I thought we'd do something together, if possible."

"I'm on call through May 18, and then, I have a light schedule until the second week of August. Can you move it around?"

"I'll see what I can do. The car show is what it is, but perhaps the second week, I can flip for someone else's."

Sunday morning, Gina phoned. "Hello, Marianne, it's Gina."

"Oh, how are you doing?"

"Fine, Taylor's enjoying school and I'm still busy at the hospital. Say, Daniel would like me to go to a car show with him down in Dallas around the fifth of May. Could you watch Taylor for a few days?"

"I'd love to, but Bob and I are going to a Lion's convention in Florida that week. I'm sorry."

"That's okay, I'll check and see what other alternatives I have. I know some parents in her class. I'll give them a call. I'll talk to you soon. I love your new flowers."

"Petunias and irises. The nursery is having a sale. You should pick some up," Marianne replied.

"I will. Give my best to Bob."

Gina called a week later. It was Saturday morning. "Oh, Daniel, I've tried, but my schedule and Taylor's are not going to work with yours. Bob and Marianne are going to be out of town and I wasn't able to find anyone else to watch Taylor or cover for me."

"Ah, that's too bad. I was hoping that…"

"I really want to go. I need a break too. You go to the car show. Have a good time with your friends. Take your second week and we'll go somewhere together. There is an art fair in Santa Fe the first of June, or we could take the train down to Amarillo for a weekend. We could do wine tasting, see the rodeo, and have a spa day. Or think of another place you'd like to go."

"I'm not much of an art buff. Amarillo sounds doable. I'll do some research and see what else is coming up. And I still need to schedule and exchange that time with someone at work. I'll figure something out, don't worry."

"So what are you doing today?"

"I ah…"

"Taylor is going over to Angie's for a birthday party and she's spending the night. I have to drop her off at two o'clock and then I'm free."

"I've got to fix my front door. It won't lock and do some yard work. I have to take Missy to the vet at one o'clock for a shot, and then, I'm open."

"There is a Red Hawk's game that starts at four. I think they are playing the Nashville Sounds. Do you want to go?"

"Sure, come by here after you drop off Taylor and we'll take my truck. That sounds like a great way to spend the afternoon," Daniel said.

Gina drove Taylor to Walmart and picked out a gift for the party. "What kind of music does she like? Choose a CD you can dance to."

"She'll really likes Alter Ego and Damian Cruz." She selected the albums and handed them to the clerk. "I'm hungry."

"You can have a healthy snack, but save room because you're going to have lunch at the party."

It was just after two when Gina pulled up to the house and parked in the driveway. Several kids were jumping on the trampoline on the front lawn. "Taylor, here's Angie's gift. Don't eat too much junk. You know how your stomach gets. I'll see you later. Call me if you need anything. Thank you, Martha. Have fun with all these girls. Here's my number if you need me," Gina said, kissing Taylor good-bye and handing her the birthday present.

Gina got out at Daniel's, wearing short, white jean cut-offs, a short sleeve t-shirt, and white tennis shoes. Daniel had on a ball cap and a faded Red Hawk's t-shirt. They headed down to Oklahoma City on Interstate 44. It was about an hour and half drive in the eighty-degree heat. They talked and sang their favorite country songs with the windows down. The air felt good blowing through their hair.

"I can't remember the last time I went to a Red Hawk's game. Some new guy is supposed to be unbeatable on the mound. Mark Brown. Have you heard of him? Anyway, both teams are having a great spring and are considered top ranked contenders," Daniel said, singing again.

"I'm excited. I'm hungry too. I want to get a hotdog when we get there. Oh, and some peanuts too," Gina said, humming.

"I'm ready for a beer. Gotta have a beer at the game," Daniel said, pulling into the parking lot.

"That'll be six bucks. Just follow that white car. There's plenty of parking up ahead on your right," the attendant said, pointing with his fist full of cash. It was almost four o'clock.

Daniel and Gina found their seats three rows back, in between home plate and first. They picked up their hotdogs and peanuts and carefully made their way down toward the field. The Red Hawks warmed up while a maintenance team made last-minute preparations for the game.

"Beer, beer here. Get your ice-cold beer," the beverage man yelled, carrying a blue plastic flat.

"We'll take two," Daniel said, standing up and getting his money out. The patrons carefully passed the cold frothy liquid down to Daniel as he passed bills the other direction. "Thanks, keep the change," Daniel shouted down the aisle " Whew, are we ready or what? Wow, what a day. Here's looking atcha," Daniel said, clicking cups. He pulled his hat down, shading his eyes. He glanced over at Gina who was sitting on the edge of her seat with a handful of peanuts and the beer focused on the pitcher while he warmed up. "That guy has got to be six four. What an arm. It's gonna be a great game," Daniel said, tossing a peanut in his mouth.

"He reminds me of someone I used to know," Gina said softly, noticing his sharp features, hair, and eyes. Her eyes watered. She wiped them with her forearm and continued to stare. "We should have brought a mitt. How are we going to catch the foul balls?"

"I'll bare hand 'em. No problem. I saw a man catch a ball in his beer cup once," Daniel said, reaching up with his cup.

"Really? No way."

"I saw it on TV a few weeks ago," he laughed, sipping his beer and cracking a nut. The shells crunched under foot as they both stood to let a man and his son pass.

Mark Brown took off his cap and wiped his forehead as he prepared to deliver another pitch. His resemblance was striking, short brown hair, brown eyes, and chiseled jaw.

"Gina, are you okay?" Daniel asked, noticing a few tears running down her cheeks.

"Oh, I'm a little emotional. I started my period today and it… no, I'm lying. That man pitching reminds me of Taylor's father… and I feel so sad. I am sorry, Daniel. So many memories and feelings are coming up for me right now. I…"

Daniel put his arm around her and pulled her close. She covered her face as she laid her head against his chest. He could feel the warm tears as they soaked threw his t-shirt. "Are you sure?"

She raised her head, looking at him with her swollen red eyes. "His name was Shane. I don't know what came over me. It has been years since I felt the grief I felt back then. Daniel, I am so sorry. I feel awful. Please forgive me."

"Gina, I understand. I definitely feel jealous though. I've haven't felt that with you before. I sense that you must really have been in love with him. Do you want to talk about it?" Daniel asked, pushing his cap back.

"No, not here, not now," she said, straightening up and wiping her eyes. "Let's just watch the game and have a good time, okay?"

Daniel released his arm from around her back. He leaned forward and grabbed his beer out of the seat pocket pulling his cap down over his eyes. He slumped back with his hands folded around the beer in his lap. He flipped his phone open and checked the time.

Gina opened her purse, found her lip gloss, and was applying it while checking her face in her small makeup mirror. The crowd jumped to its feet as a long fly ball went sailing over the right field wall. Daniel looked over at Gina. She sat unaffected, staring at herself in the mirror.

As the people returned to their seats, Daniel leaned over, "Would you like to leave?"

Gina looked at Daniel surprised, stared for a moment, and then nodded her head, yes. Daniel stood up and waited as Gina got her things. "Thank you. Daniel, I am so sorry. I…"

"It's okay. Here take my hand." He led her carefully down the row of seats, stepping on broken peanut shells and around discarded beer cups, up the stairs to the mezzanine and then to the exit to the parking lot. A slight breeze lifted Gina's hair as she tossed it back over her shoulders.

"I can't believe this weather. It's been over a hundred everyday this week. I'm drenched."

"I can put the windows up and turn on the AC if you'd like."

Silence. The hum of the tires on the pavement mimicked the drone in the cab. Daniel subconsciously started counting eighteen-wheelers as they passed on the other side of the highway. Twenty-one. *It's a dump truck. Should I count it, or not? It's not really like the rest. It only has twelve tires. I sure would hate to have to change one of those out here. God, it's hot.* He reached down to his left and slid the seat back a notch. Gina sat staring out the passenger window as the warm air blew her hair about her face. She moved a few strands away from her mouth.

"Daniel, I need to use the restroom. Could you pull into the next service station or restaurant you see?"

Without answering, he took the next exit, took a right turn, and pulled into a Chevron station. Gina hopped out as he brought the truck to a stop next to one of the pumps. Even in the shade of the canopy, it was hot and sticky. He ran his card, opened the gas door, and began filling up the tank.

Gina went inside, asked the attendant for the key to the restroom, and disappeared around the corner of the building. Daniel leaned back against the truck, listening to the gurgle of the gas. *I wonder what she is thinking. I knew she had never forgotten this guy, whoever he was. I hope we can get back on track. I feel so derailed. Railroad ties. Design ties that have locomotives on them. What a great idea.*

The pump clicked off and Daniel came back to reality. He looked around for Gina as he twisted the cap back on and closed the door. She came out of the mini market with two cold bottles of water.

"Thanks," he said, taking one and opening her door. She smiled queerly getting inside, not really looking at him. He flagged his shirt to get some air moving around before he sat down.

"Do you want to talk about anything?"

"Not right now. My chest hurts a little. I'd like to go home and lie down," Gina said, taking a drink.

"We are half way there," he said, starting the truck up.

She ignored the response. He turned the radio up and slid the back window all the way open for more ventilation.

She leaned against the door, remembering the last game that Shane pitched. The Rangers had a runner on second with the top of the order up. They hadn't been able to score. Shane looked in, nodded, looked back at second, and threw a fastball chest high that number 24 drilled past JT at third out towards the left field line. It landed just fair, bouncing on the warning path. Kyle played it off the wall and fired into JT who threw into Chip, covering the plate. The throw was late and the Rangers got their first run. 24 ran to second on the throw to home. Shane hung his head as Chip threw him a new ball from the umpire. He turned toward the outfield, rubbing the ball in his glove. She could see

Shane's face mixed with despair and determination under his cap. His hair stuck to his forehead with perspiration. Then that quick throw to second to pick the base runner off. His eyes. His face lit up from the earlier ashen gray to an exuberant glow.

She saw his face covered in shadow as he looked down at her the last time they made love. "How does it feel?" he had asked her in that sexy, raspy voice. "How does it feel?" She could hear and see his lips moving, but the rest of his face was hidden. The sound echoed in a distant chamber closed years ago. It haunted her now.

It was six-thirty when they arrived back in Tulsa.

"Do you think you can take a week off with me? My second week is floating, so all I need from you is the date," Daniel asked, looking over, hopeful.

"Daniel, I'm sorry, can we talk about this later?" Gina asked, opening her door.

He didn't reply. A shiver ran down his spine, and he jerked forward suddenly. Gina didn't notice as his eyes dilated.

Gina gave him a friendly kiss on the cheek good-bye, grabbed her purse, got in her car, and drove back to her house. She called Taylor to let her know she was home and that she would be by to pick her up in a little while.

"Mom, we're playing ping pong and dancing. I'm spending the night, remember?"

Gina sighed, "I'm sorry, but the plans have changed. I'll be by in an hour. I need you to come home."

"No, Mom. I hardly ever get to see my friends."

"That's not true, Taylor. I'm having a tough time right now and I need you."

Chapter 15

Bill and Suzanne drove their Sentra down to Vegas. Debbie's father reserved them a room at the Mirage Resort for the wedding. Travelling down Highway 395, they stopped in Bishop for the night.

"Suzanne, you know, I haven't said anything. But I don't know if Debbie is the right girl for Shane. Should we say something or just let it be?"

"After all this time, now you bring that up? Bill, she's a sweet girl. They'll be fine."

"I wonder sometimes. She seems so into herself. She's pretty and smart and very nice to us but..."

"She's nice to Shane too. She's young and still figuring life out. There is a learning curve that couples have to go through as they discover who they are, what is working, and what isn't. She comes from a good family and she has a great head on her shoulders. Shane seems to be happy. I know he would talk to me if there were problems."

"I've noticed Shane gets quiet when she starts nagging him. He doesn't speak his mind like you do." Bill said, "And I don't know about them living in Las Vegas. It's such a different environment compared to what he's used to."

"He showed me some pictures. They have a beautiful house there and it's paid for. It's good to push the boundaries of his comfort zone. That's how one grows intellectually," Suzanne said, watching Bill as he drove.

"I worry like a father, is all…"

"Honey, I love that about you. With our love and support, Shane and Debbie will have a good marriage."

"Mr. Swanson has quite a few contacts in Las Vegas. Whatever the kids may need there, he can help. Lou Swanson has been doing marketing for Flora Resorts all over the world. The way Shane described the wedding, it is going to be top notch. Shane said we have a suite with a pool and a private butler. That'll be different."

"We will definitely be stepping up. Lou said he would meet us at the registration area and give us a VIP tour when we arrive. It sounds exciting. You know, I sure like this drive. We don't get down this way very often. We used to come down here when Shane was on the ski team, competing at Mammoth. We stayed at the funky little motel in the center of town with the team. Gosh, there was very little heat and almost no hot water to shower in," Suzanne said, looking around at the landscape.

"Sleeping was tough too. The beds were so lumpy and the team was up all night talking. I miss those days."

"I think the last time we drove down this way was when we went out to Tempe to see the campus at Arizona State."

"It's been that long? Boy, we don't travel much, do we?" Bill asked.

"That Best Western over there looks nice. Let's check it out. Schotts Bakery is next door. Excellent," Suzanne said, seeing the vacancy sign.

The town speed limit dropped to 25 miles per hour as they arrived in Bishop. They spent a quiet evening and got on the road early. The sun was just coming up over the eastern Sierras. A shirt of clouds passed by, unbuttoning itself, stretched by the morning breeze. Bill and Suzanne sat in calm silence just enjoying the ride. They passed a few big rigs and some travelers, but the traffic remained light most of the way.

They arrived in Las Vegas just past noon. Driving slowly down the strip, they pulled into the Mirage and explained to the valet that Lou Swanson was meeting them inside. A bellman escorted them into the main lobby. Lou arrived with a small entourage of security personnel and introduced himself.

"Mr. and Mrs. Kaufmann, I am Lou Swanson, Debbie's father. Welcome to Las Vegas and the Mirage Hotel, anything you might need is at your fingertips. The kids are in room 1604, and you are just down the hall in 1612. All your room service is on the house, and if you need anything else, don't hesitate to ask. Here is my direct number." He showed them the vast array of amenities the hotel offered, taking them by the restaurants, spa, pool, fitness facility, and show room. Handing them each a business card, "Lillian and I are thrilled to have you as our guests. Dinner is at seven o'clock in the steak house on the first floor."

"Thank you for your generous hospitality. Everything is so grand here, the architecture, the furnishings, the spa, the stores," Suzanne said, looking around. "It's beautiful."

"After dinner, you can take in the pirate ship show at Treasure Island and the volcano here. It is spectacular after dark. Take some pictures," Lou said as he left.

The initial gathering at the restaurant was small.

"Well, everything is set for the ceremony," Lillian said. "Debbie and I have been busy, but it's been so much fun. How are things in Tahoe?"

"It's been beautiful. Bill has been busy finishing a construction project for a young couple in town," Suzanne said as Bill turned his head. "The drive down was enjoyable too. It's nice to take a break and get out of the basin."

"This wine is exquisite," Bill said, taking a sip.

"Chateau Laffite '89," Lou said as the waiter brought two more bottles to the table. "These are equally as fine, enjoy."

"I applied for a job at the Connections Academy, a charter school in town, and was accepted today," Shane shared with the family. "It's a year-round school, so I can start right away. I will be teaching AP English and literature. Starting salary is higher than they were paying in Reno and it's close to Summerset. I think it will be a good fit for me and…"

"Wow, Shane. That's great news…By the way, I'm teaching at Lotus, over near UNLV. The children there have learning disabilities and some emotional challenges. I've received two raises since I started They just love me. The kids are great too. My favorite is Victor. He's mildly autistic and I'm getting him ready for elementary school in the fall," Debbie said, looking around at her company.

"Debbie, how many children do you teach? What are the parents like?" Suzanne asked.

"There are four children in my class. I've only met the parents when they drop off their kids and pick them up. We've encouraged them to join us, but they work and don't have a lot of extra time to devote," Debbie said, taking a drink of wine.

"That's a shame," Suzanne said. "I believe parents are an important part of their child's education."

They finished the meal and watched the waiters remove the dinnerware.

"Wow, thanks for a wonderful dinner. I think we've had too much wine," Bill said, looking over at Suzanne who slumped in her chair. "We're pretty tired from the drive and need some rest. We will see you all tomorrow. We'll have to take a rain check on the pirate shit… ship show, sorry about that." Bill said, catching the slip. They excused themselves and went back to their room.

"How much are they going to pay you?" Debbie asked Shane.

"I think around forty thousand," Shane answered low, looking down.

"Well, I think your mother and I are going to retire as well. It's been a long day. Thank heaven tomorrow is Saturday. We can all sleep in." Lou stood up and helped Lillian with her chair. She was a little tipsy when she got to her feet.

"Whoa, I think I've had a little too much wine too. I am definitely ready for bed. We'll see you two in the morning?" Lillian said, holding on to her chair as she got her wrap and purse.

"I am so excited, I don't know if I can sleep," Debbie said, rubbing Shane's arm and tenderly kissing his neck.

"Good night, folks. Thanks again for dinner. It was great," Shane said, peeling Debbie's hand off. "We shouldn't discuss money at the table. I think it's inappropriate."

"Oh, it's okay. They don't mind," Debbie said, pushing her chair back.

"But I do," Shane said, standing up.

"Okay, okay. I won't do it again. Come on, let's go to bed. I'm so horny tonight. I can't wait to get naked," Debbie said, taking Shane by the arm and leading him to the elevators.

Shane woke up and the room was bathed in dark shadows. The clock by the bed read 2:06 in the morning. He stumbled to the bathroom, turned the light on, and checked himself in the mirror. The wedding was less than twelve hours away, and he couldn't place the feeling he had as he rubbed his chest. Was it pre-wedding jitters? He sat on the makeup stool in front of the mirror for a few moments, staring through his eyes into the distance. Something was missing. There was still a tangible thread attached to a past he could not rationalize. He wondered now if he ever could. Debbie lay sleeping just on the other side of the door, the girl he had decided to spend the rest of his life with, have children with, and grow old with. The hollowness felt like emotional indigestion gurgling behind his eyes. It'll all be good. *Let the past go*, he thought. *Just let it go.* He used the bathroom, crawled back into bed, and lay next to Debbie. He felt conflicted as he subconsciously caressed her breasts and thigh.

"Are you awake?" Debbie said in a sleepy voice.

"No, just getting comfortable," Shane said, staring into the darkness. *Is this love that I'm feeling or a need to love?* He drifted off.

The sun shouted through the window as soon as Debbie pulled back the drapes. "Wow, what time is it? Noon?" Shane asked.

"No, silly, it's seven o'clock. Time to get your lazy butt up and start the day. We have breakfast with everyone downstairs at nine. Let's go for a quick swim and then shower. You with me big guy?" Debbie asked, walking into the bathroom.

"Sure. Coffee?" Shane asked, his head resting on the pillow.

"I'll have some sent up. Get your suit on or we can skinny dip. I feel free as a bird," Debbie said, returning and stepping out into the sunshine, showing off her tan lines naked to the world.

Shane put his trunks on and slid into the pool. Debbie was doing a gentle breaststroke. Her white butt cheeks were in direct contrast to her tan back. Her hair floated on the surface of the water around her as she swam. She glided up to Shane seductively as he submerged himself. She reached up through his swim shorts and playfully touched him. He crossed his legs and swam away.

"Boy, you sure are playing hard to get these days," Debbie said, smiling.

"I'm saving myself for tonight," Shane said, as there was a knock on the door. He toweled off and let the butler in. The man set the tray down on the coffee table and left. Shane poured a cup and brought it outside.

"Deb, would you like some?"

"No, not right now. I'll have a cup when I get out," Debbie replied as she side stroked through the water.

Shane pulled a chair away from the outdoor table sat down and put his feet up on an adjacent chair. He watched the water bead off her smooth brown skin as she swam. She slowly exited the pool and spread out a large bath towel. Laying on her back facing Shane, she spread her wet legs in the warmth of the sun.

"How are you doin' over there? Sure you don't want some of this before breakfast?"

She closed her eyes. Shane slipped off his trunks and quietly snuck up on her. He took her passionately.

"Wow, where did that come from?"

"Breakfast?" he shrugged, breaking her grip. "Let's shower and eat. I'm starvin'."

He got up and dried off. Debbie rolled over and rested her head on her hands.

"I still wanna lay here for a while. Give me a half hour or so and then we'll go."

Shane walked back inside with his cup of coffee, sat down on the sofa, and clicked on the TV. He flipped through the channels until he found some cartoons. The phone rang. He reached over and answered on the second ring.

"Hey, you. How'd you sleep? Your dad and I slept like babies. I could get used to this. We had them bring up some coffee and we watched TV in bed. It's total luxury. How's Debbie? She must be excited. So I guess we're all supposed to meet for breakfast at nine, right?" His mother asked.

"Yes. We've been up for quite some time. We had a good night's sleep. Debbie is lying out by the pool relaxing. We're going to shower in a little bit and then we'll be down."

"What should we wear?" Suzanne asked.

"Hey, Deb, what should they wear to the breakfast?"

"Tell them to dress casual. Whatever they feel comfortable in."

"Debbie said to just wear anything you like, as long as you're comfortable. The whole wedding party is supposed to be there. You'll get to meet her side of the family."

"There's a final rehearsal afterward. Danielle is doing my hair, makeup, and nails at one thirty," Debbie shouted from out by the pool. "And Nina is doing the bridesmaids at two."

"Mom, we'll go over the schedule at breakfast, but everyone will be ready by four. You should see my tux. I look like a butler."

"I can't wait. This is going to be a wonderful day..."

"Chip has never worn a suit. He's stoked. I have been going over my vows so I can recite them without stumbling. You know how nervous I get in front of people. We'll see you in a few."

He hung up and started the shower. Debbie joined him as the steam filled the bedroom.

"I'm all wet and sticky," Debbie said, stepping in.

"Sorry," Shane replied, smiling and handing her the soap.

Debbie put on a pair of short shorts and sandals. She slipped on a revealing halter-top and large hoop earrings. Shane put on a pair of casual slacks with a button-down blue shirt and tennis shoes. Suzanne and Bill both had on off white slacks and Mirage souvenir shirts. They looked like twins standing next to each other.

"Your folks are so cute," Debbie said as they met them on the way into the buffet. The wedding party took up a long table near the back of the restaurant. Lillian sat next to Debbie at the head of the table. Lou joined them later as they finished eating.

After a full course of eggs, meat, French toast, fruit, pastries, and juice, the party kicked their chairs back, loosed their belts, and contemplated the situation.

"I can't move," Bill shared.

"Me either," Shane replied. "I could go back to bed right now."

"No, you don't," Maureen, the wedding coordinator, said as she gracefully entered and ushered the group into the ballroom. The chairs for the ceremony were set up in front of a wrought iron arch.. They timed the wedding song and the entrance of all the participants and went through the vow ceremony. Overall, it took about an hour for everyone to practice their parts and get comfortable with the choreography.

"Okay, everyone go get some rest. I want you all here no later than three thirty. We are going to start promptly at four," Maureen said, waving her arms around, doing a ballet exit.

Bill and Suzanne went and lay out by the pool. Shane joined them. Debbie, Lillian, and the bridesmaids made their scheduled appointments. They used Lillian's suite to dress in. Chip, Scott, and JT met up at Shane's room at three o'clock for a last hoorah. They opened a bottle of chilled Patron 1800 and each did a shot for old time's sake and to Shane's health and well-being, and to baseball, and to all the girls they'd known before.

At three o'clock, the photographer met the girls up at Lillian's. There were candid pictures of the girls putting on their makeup, garter belts, corsages, and jewelry. A photographer also chronicled the boys up at Shane's as they toasted to everything male. "Hoooooahhhhh!"

Bill and Suzanne each purchased new clothes for this special event. Bill bought a three-piece suit at Macy's and had it custom fit.

"I fell like a new man. I don't think I've ever looked this good," Bill confided. He bought a pair of black wing-tipped loafers and the loudest tie he could find. Suzanne persuaded him to tone it down a bit, but the tie he selected still shouted with color. Suzanne found an evening gown at Nordstrom's. It was a backless red silk formal with a sash across the front.

She dazzled Bill when she slipped into it. "Wow! I mean, wow! You look amazing. You will be the most beautiful woman there. I hope the others don't get jealous. Wow!"

"Oh, stop. Bill, I absolutely adore you," Suzanne said, admiring herself in the mirror.

Roses and carnations of every color adorned the ballroom. They draped white ribbon down the aisles and around the arch with large bouquets of white roses set on either side. The event coordinators covered the chairs in deep red and white satin. They set tables with similar ornamentation and centerpieces of crystal and carnations at the back of the ballroom. A guest check-in and gift area was set up just inside with wedding memorabilia wrapped in red chiffon. One of the photographers took pictures as friends and family were ushered to their seats by the groom's men. A litany of wedding songs played softly in the background. At four o'clock sharp, Maureen began the wedding march. Paired together, the wedding party entered and then split on each side of the arch. Shane entered with his mother and father. They took their seats in the front as Shane walked to the center of the arch

They each recited a poem they'd written to one another. "Shane Kaufmann, do you take Debbie Swanson to be your beloved bride, to have and to hold in sickness and in health," the minister continued. "in the presence of all who have come to share this moment, I now pronounce you, husband and wife. Shane, you may kiss the bride." A loud cheer erupted as they locked lips, turned, and walked back down the aisle.

The Wedding Bashers played popular tunes to get everyone out on the dance floor. Shane and Debbie started the festivities with a country waltz and finished with a slow wedding waltz. Ginny caught the bouquet and looked around expectantly for a beau.

"Bill, my feet are killing me. We haven't danced this much since I don't know when. I love you so much, Bill," Suzanne said, looking up, resting her chin on his chest.

Shane and Debbie retired to their suite thoroughly exhausted and a little inebriated. Debbie slipped off her long, white, embroidered dress and tossed it over the easy chair next to the bed. Shane had most of his tux off by the time he reached their room. She went into the bathroom and rinsed off, brushed her teeth, and put on a special teddy she'd bought just for the evening. Shane put on a pair of blue silk boxers and waited with the covers pulled back, obviously aroused.

"That was fantastic, honey," she said with her eyes closed. "You're such a stud when you want to be. Are you ready for bed? We need to get some sleep before we travel tomorrow. It's going to be a full day and more before we get there. I'm so excited to go to Monaco," Debbie said, pulling the sheets up.

"Where the heck is it again? I'm not real good with geography," Shane said, snuggling up next to her.

"It's on the Mediterranean Sea. The homes, town, and seascape are breathtaking. I'll show you on the map tomorrow before we leave. Give me a kiss."

"Good night, Mrs. Kaufmann."

———⟊⟊⟊———

The next morning, Shane and Debbie joined their parents for brunch. Despite the big event the night before, everyone looked well rested. Lou handed them their tickets and confirmation for the Hotel des Paris. Debbie brought out a world travel map that her mother had given her. "Shane, see this point of land right here, that's Monaco. And this is where we are."

"Okay, you don't need to show everyone how dense I am. I know that's Africa," Shane said as Lillian laughed.

"Thanks, Dad, you're wonderful. The wedding was fabulous. No one could ask for a nicer father."

"My family and friends have never been treated so well. Your hospitality and generosity were over the top. Thank you too, Mrs. Swanson," Shane said.

"Please call me Lillian. We are family now. I hope you two have a wonderful time in Monaco. Do you speak French?" He shook his head. "No, well, they speak several languages there as well as English, so you'll both get along great."

"Shoot, I wish we were going. We've never been outside of the United States," Suzanne said to Bill. "You two have the time of your lives. We're so excited for you. Shane, call us if you need anything. Debbie, we love you. Welcome to the family. Bill and I are so thrilled to have you as our daughter." Suzanne gave the kids each a hug and a kiss, and they worked their way down the line of family members.

Chapter 16

Their United Flight left at one in the afternoon. They flew into Los Angeles and then flew Royal Dutch into Nice, France. A driver met them at the airport and took them by limousine to the hotel. "I'm so excited. We're finally here, honey. Aren't you excited?" Debbie asked, squeezing his hand.

"Yes, dear, I'm a little tired after that seventeen-hour trip though," Shane responded, putting his hand on hers.

Their suite overlooked Monaco Bay and the city. The sun was just coming up when they arrived. The lights of the town were still on, as it transitioned from night to day. Debbie pulled back the curtains and walked out on the terrace.

"Shane, come here. Look at this," she said, spreading her arms at the panoramic view.

"Wow, this is awesome. What a beautiful place. Stay there, I'll get the camera," Shane said as he went back in and dug a small digital camera out of his duffel bag. He held it out in front of them and took several shots with the sea and the city in the background immersed in the morning sunrise.

"Let's go shopping. Come on, change your clothes and we'll go into town and see what's there."

"Really, I kind of need to rest for a bit. I have jet lag. Let's go down to the pool or the beach and relax. We can go into town later. We have all week."

"You go on down. I have a couple of calls to make and I'll meet you down by the pool," she said, looking over the railing.

"Okay, don't be long." Shane changed his clothes, got on his board shorts, grabbed a large towel from the bathroom, and headed downstairs. When he was gone, Debbie got on the phone and set up a massage, pedicure, manicure, and hair appointment for that afternoon. She tried on several string bikinis she brought before deciding on one that would suffice for the first day's pool attire. She met him in her high heels, strutting around the pool. The pool guests turned their heads and followed her to Shane's chez lounge.

"Wow, you look gorgeous," Shane said, watching the reaction.

"I picked this up in Vegas at the mall at Caesar's, nice, huh?" she said, showing off her suit.

"I talked to the concierge. You want to rent scooters and go for a cruise this afternoon? It's a great way to get around the city and see all the sights."

"Nah, I made an appointment at one thirty to get my hair and nails done and get a massage," Debbie replied, spreading out a towel.

"Really? You just had your hair and nails done for the wedding," Shane said, sitting up.

"Well, we're in Monaco now, and I want to have it done again," she said, sitting down.

"Okay. Got it," he said. "How about tomorrow? Here is a brochure on all the stuff to do around here. There is opera and a ballet right here at the hotel. The guy gave me a list of restaurants to check out in town too," he said, changing the tone.

"We'll see," she said, spreading oil on her arms.

Shane lay back down and closed his eyes. He slept for several hours. When he awoke, he was alone. Debbie left a note on the back of a postcard and went into the spa for her appointment. Claude, the masseuse, was rubbing her down with warm oil when Shane found her.

"Claude, this is Shane. Shane, come join me. His hands are amazing. You'll feel so much better," she said, talking through the bottom of the table.

He looked at Claude who shrugged his shoulders as he continued to work.

"Maybe, later. I think I'll…"

"Go out to the reception desk, and tell them you want a massage. Just bill it to the room," Debbie lifted her head up to talk.

"Yes, dear, I'll be back."

He talked to the hostess at the desk, but she couldn't get him in until late that same afternoon. He went back to the pool, closed his eyes, and slept. At around five o'clock, Shane wandered back up to the room and found Debbie disrobing.

"I'm hungry. How about some dinner?" Shane said, peeling his shorts off. "I need a shower. Are you going to take one?"

"Sure, I'll join you. I'm covered in oil and cream," Debbie replied, checking herself in the mirror.

"You smell wonderful," Shane said, walking up behind her.

"I feel wonderful. Life is going to be great. Shane, I'm so glad we're married," Debbie said, turning around, pressing her naked body up against his.

During dinner, they both started to nod off. "Honey, I'm tired. Are you ready to call it a day?" Debbie asked.

"Yes, let's go back," Shane replied, finishing his coffee.

The breeze spun softly through the drapes when they returned to the room. Debbie took a deep breath, twirled around, and held Shane close to her. "I love you so much."

"I love you too. Let's get some sleep. I hope that French press doesn't keep us up all night," Shane said, walking out of his clothes.

After a restless night, Debbie got up and found Shane out on the terrace reading a book. "Morning, honey, couldn't sleep? I felt you tossing and turning, coffee?"

"It was that coffee we had at dinner and I need to get used to the time change. Yeah, sure, I'll have a cup," Shane replied.

Debbie called room service and had a pot of coffee and some croissants sent up. She brought the tray out when it arrived.

"I'm going shopping this morning. You want to come along? Gabrielle is taking me down the Av des Beaux. They have the finest stores in the world," she said, pouring Shane a cup.

"Who's Gabrielle?"

"I met her yesterday while I was getting my nails done. She's like a concierge. So do you want to come with us?"

"Ah, no, I'll pass. How long will you be gone?"

"Don't really know. We'll be back this afternoon sometime, I guess," Debbie replied.

Debbie returned just before supper, loaded down with bags from Givenchy, Dior, Celine, Lanvin, and more.

"Look, Shane. I got a dress and a…" Debbie said as Shane rolled his eyes.

Debbie went through each bag, opening boxes and displaying all the purchases from the day's excursion.

"So you ready for dinner? I made a reservation for…" Shane said, trying to get Debbie's attention.

"You know, I had a late lunch with Gabrielle so I'm not real hungry. You go ahead. I'm going to take a shower and put this stuff away," Debbie said, holding up a sweater.

Chapter 17

They returned home to Las Vegas on a blistering hot summer day. Shane stepped off the plane. "My God, it's hot. How do people survive here?"

"Oh, you'll get used to it, dear," Debbie replied as she deplaned with her bundle of packages from the trip. "Grab that other bag? I…"

"Yes, dear."

Lillian met them at baggage claim area and drove them back to their house.

"How was the trip? You both look so refreshed and tan," Lillian asked.

"We had a wonderful time. It went by so fast. I can't believe we're back home already," Debbie replied.

"Shane, did you have a good time?" Lillian asked.

"Yes, ma'am, I…"

"Mom, please," Debbie said.

"Sorry, Lillian," Shane replied.

When they opened the front door, the house was cool. There were flowers and gifts stacked on the dining room table and in the living room. Shane looked around and took a deep breath, inhaling the confluence of fragrances. He set the suitcases down while Debbie and Lillian methodically went through all the treasures from Prada, Chanel, and Dior.

Shane walked over to the window and pulled the curtains back. The lawn outside was a deep green, despite the heat. The flowers resembled vegetables. Some looked like chard, others like heads of lettuce. The tile floors echoed as he went from room to room, looking around. He took his shoes off to muffle the sound. He fell back on the bed in the master suite and lay with his hands folded behind his head on the cool comforter.

"Come on, get up, lazy. We have suitcases to unpack and stuff to put away. Throw all the dirty clothes in the laundry, and Anna will do them when she gets here in the morning. There's no food here, so we need to go shopping too. I'll start a list. Come on, get up," Debbie beckoned.

Shane rolled off the bed and sat with his hands on his knees for moment. He got up, went back to the entry, and got their luggage. He set about the task at hand, dividing the clothes into piles of whites and colors. *I can't believe how many swimsuits she has*, he thought to himself. *I have two pairs of board shorts, one's wet and one's dry.* He laughed and continued separating.

Monday morning, Shane started teaching at Connections Academy full time. Back in his groove, he thoroughly enjoyed his students. He was very anxious to start a family of his own. As summer turned into fall, the students at school became an extended family. He was spending more and more time there volunteering to help troubled teens and students with academic problems. He went in early, often arriving before eight and leaving sometimes as late as six. He was instructing students from Hispanic backgrounds as well as eastern European children from Croatia and Romania. He invited them to the house occasionally to practice conversations in English and teach them American customs involving cooking, shopping, and other cultural life skills.

Debbie, on the other hand, took more time off to be with her mother. They spent a lot of time decorating the house, doing painting, pictures, window coverings, furniture and accessories. They enjoyed shopping together and working on other odd projects.

She had three students she worked with at Lotus. Victor was still one of her favorites and entered the first grade at the local elementary school only a year behind his actual grade level. She saw him in the afternoon once a week to help with basic communication skills as he progressed.

Kevin was another story. He had periodic violent episodes requiring a lot of attention and discipline. After three months, Debbie's tolerance level dropped. She deferred him to the other teachers as often as she could.

Little Ellen was a breeze compared to Kevin. She had Down syndrome, enjoyed coloring, and doing cut-and-paste projects. She was easily amused and laughed at the funniest things. Debbie giggled right along with her. She consolidated the three students, teaching only on Wednesdays and Thursdays so she could take longer periods of time off.

Anna came once a week to clean and Debbie began having her cook three days a week as well. She gave Debbie a list of groceries to pick up at the store for several days in advance. Anna cooked dinner and then prepared more food for breakfast and lunch, plastic containers of fruit, rice, beans, salad, and soup. All Shane and Debbie needed to do was pull them out of the fridge.

Debbie met Shane in the kitchen with a hot cup of coffee and a cup of fruit. Shane came out dressed for school as Debbie cornered him against the counter. "I'm in my cycle this week, so we need to have sex when you get home. Anna is changing the sheets today so the bed will be nice and fresh."

"I feel like a machine. The only thing that's missing is a stopwatch. We've been on this schedule for months. Maybe we should go back to the doctor and see what's up. I miss the spontaneity," Shane said, sipping the coffee and taking some fruit.

"Well, if we don't see results soon, Mom knows another pediatrician we can talk to. By the way, Scott and his girlfriend will be here for dinner. So come home right after class so we can make love before they arrive."

"Ya vol, Er commandant."

"Don't be smart. It's just something we have to do if I am going to get pregnant. You do want to have children, right?"

"Yes, of course. Okay, I'll see you tonight. What are you doing today?" Shane asked, gathering his things to leave.

"I'm getting a facial, and then Mom and I are going to the club for lunch," Debbie replied, rinsing his dishes.

"Awesome." Another tough day at the office, he thought as he closed the front door.

By December, it was evident that something was wrong with one or both of them. The ovulation periods came and went with no sign of fertilization. The third and final physician determined after a myriad of tests that Debbie was infertile and was not able to have children.

"We've done all we can do. What about adoption? A friend of mine at work told me about the kids that are in foster care. A lot of them are very easy to adopt, particularly the older ones. Once the parents have given the child up or have been disqualified, these children are available. What do you think?"

"Oh, Shane, I don't know. It is such an arduous process. I really don't want to go through it. What if we get a child with behavioral problems? Or fetal alcohol syndrome? It's difficult to know ahead of time."

"You seemed relieved that you can't have children. I don't get it. You love kids and yet you don't want one. Tell me what you're feeling. I thought you'd be heartbroken. I know I am. One of my greatest desires is to be a father."

"No, I am sad. Really. However, I am thankful that the drudgery of carrying an infant for nine months and childbirth will not disfigure my body. When Scott and Vanessa get married, we can help raise their kids. It'll all work out. You'll see."

"Really, I can't believe you just said that. We'll talk about it later. I've got to…"

"Shane, let it go. It's not going to happen," Debbie said as Shane walked away and sat down in the living room. He flicked on the TV.

Talking over his shoulder, "Mom and Dad are expecting us up at the Lake Friday. They got a foot and a half of fresh snow yesterday, so the skiing should be good. I'll give you another lesson, and soon, we will be cruising together down some fun intermediate slopes."

"You know I don't like the cold. I'll try it again if you want me to. I know, how about if you buy me a new ski outfit for Christmas. I want to look stylish if we go. By the way, I saw a white down jacket with a rabbit fur collar that looked very cute at Macy's when I was shopping with Mom. She can tell you what it looks like and where to find it."

"Great," he said. "I'll get right on it."

"I just love shopping at Macy's at Christmas. All the decorations and the sales. I feel just like a little girl in a candy store." Debbie walking up behind him and putting her hands on his shoulders.

They wanted to fly to Lake Tahoe, but the weather was not cooperating. The Reno airport closed for two days, stranding travelers going in all directions. McCarran Airport in Vegas was congested with travelers trying to leave for all parts of the country as well. They had no choice, but to drive. The California Highway Patrol closed the highway between Bishop and Bridgeport for hours at time. They let traffic through as the visibility and plows made it safe to pass. By the time Shane and Debbie reached Carson

City, they were ready to strangle each other. Debbie wanted to turn around, go home, and wait for the storm to subside. Shane, however, was adamant about getting home for Christmas. There was very little middle ground. The final stretch up Highway 50 and then around the East Shore was calming. Just seeing the lake again made a big difference in their attitudes. They began to reminisce about holidays past, funny family gatherings, the drunken uncle, trimming the tree, cooking, and baking. By the time they arrived, they were both punchy from exhaustion.

"Bill, the kids are here! Oh, come in. Let me take your coats. Bill," Suzanne called. She hugged and kissed them and then kissed and hugged them again.

"Hey, how was the drive. Must have been a nightmare. We figured you'd get stuck somewhere. That stretch between Bishop and Bridgeport gets so much wind and ice that they close it all the time. I hope it wasn't too bad. We're so glad you made it. Coffee. Something stronger? Name your poison," Bill said, getting in his share of kisses and hugs as well.

They had a robust fire going. Shane plopped down on the couch with his head on the arm. The smell from the pine logs burning in the fireplace and the fresh coffee in the kitchen made him feel right at home. He sat staring at the tree. Debbie fell next to him on the sofa, snuggled close, and kicked her Ugg boots off.

"Wow, your tree is beautiful. Where did you get it? Did you cut it down yourselves? It smells so piney and fresh," Debbie asked.

"It is a Noble fir. We got it from the Rotary Club lot over by Raley's. We used to hike up in the mountains and cut our own tree every year, but this helps the community and saves trees. You know, every time we travel somewhere, we pick up a souvenir ornament," Suzanne said, walking over to the tree. "This one here is from the Grand Canyon. This Mele Kalikimaka one is from Hawaii, and well, I don't want to bore you. Oh, Shane made this one in second grade, see his name on the back. He made this one out of a sea shell he found on the beach in Oceanside."

"Suzanne, that's great," Debbie said, getting up. "Excuse me. I need to use the bathroom."

"Shane, take your things and put them in your room. I've put fresh sheets and pillow cases on the bed."

"Thanks, Mom. I love you," he said, giving her another hug, wrapping his arms around her shoulders and holding her head against his chest.

"We're having tri-tip for dinner. You two clean up, take a nap, or relax and I'll call you when it's ready. Bill, would you like a snack or something?"

"I was going to make myself a ham and cheese sandwich. That'll hold me till dinner."

Bill took what he needed out of the fridge, made a sandwich, and grabbed a beer. He stopped by the sliding glass door and looked out at the falling snow, mesmerized by the flakes. They piled up against the bottom of the door, creating condensation on the bottom of the glass. Suzanne glanced over at Bill's reflection in the window. She sighed. It looks like a Norman Rockwell painting, she thought.

Shane and Debbie disappeared for a couple of hours while they showered and dozed off. Dinner was ready a little after seven. It was dark except for the Christmas lights outside when they sat down to the table.

"Bill, pass the salad around and then I'll set it up on the counter. So, Debbie, tell me what's going on these days," Suzanne asked.

"Mom and Dad took Scott and Vanessa to France for Christmas. They're spending a few days in Paris and then going to Nice and Monaco. I'm still working at Lotus a couple days a week. I have three children I'm working with. Victor, who's in the first grade is doing quite well, and Kevin, our little hellion, is my real challenge. Ellen is always so sweet and nice. She keeps me balanced. And Mom and I have been going to the club, playing tennis and some golf, depending on the weather," Debbie said, as she ate. "What's new up here? We miss seeing you."

"Well, let's see. Bill is working on a condo here in town, which he thoroughly enjoys because he doesn't have to drive to Reno, and I've been working at the salon and at the high school, helping out in the front office part-time. My business gets slow this time of year because most of my clients are second homeowners and have left for the winter. Other than that, not much."

"What's open? I heard Squaw and Alpine are running all of their lifts. It being Christmas week, I bet they're busy. On the way up, we passed a lot of cars with skis and snowboards on their racks," Shane said.

"You have to get there early and take a lot of patience with you. The whole basin is overflowing with vacationers and tourists. The snow is excellent everywhere, so there is plenty of terrain open. Debbie, are you going to ski?" Bill asked.

"We'll see. Shane said he would give me another lesson. Gosh, he is so patient with me, I feel guilty keeping him from skiing the more challenging slopes."

"I don't mind. Someday, we'll both be skiing the whole mountain together. You're so athletic. You'll get it down in no time," Shane said, reaching over and holding her hand.

Everyone was up early the next morning. Bill was out snow blowing the driveway in the dark. Shane stuck his head out the window at the shadowy figure and then grabbed a shovel to help.

"Hey, Pops," he said, shouting over the noise of the engine. "I'll move the cars. Are the keys inside?"

"I have 'em here in my pocket," Bill said, struggling to pull them out with his gloves on.

Shane carefully backed the cars out into the street while the snow continued to fall. Big fat flakes landed like wet kisses on their faces. The sunrise revealed a steel-gray dawn.

"Coffee?" Suzanne said, poking her head out the front door.

"Be right there," Shane said, propping his shovel against the house. "What time do the plows come by?"

"They should be here any time," Bill replied, turning the blower off, sweeping the snow off his arms and chest. He kicked the snow off his boots and came in the house.

Shane pulled the cars back in the driveway so the plows could get by. Debbie, dressed in black fleece long underwear, was in the kitchen with Suzanne helping her prepare breakfast. Shane came in, hung his wet jacket up, and grabbed a dishtowel to wipe his face. He walked up behind her and gave her big hug.

"Oooo, your hands are freezing," she said, pulling away. "Go get warmed up by the fire."

Even in long johns, she's good looking, he thought, taking his cup and sitting on the hearth. Bill came in and dried off. He took his cup of coffee and stood next to the fire, his free hand extended over the flames.

"You workin' today?" Shane asked.

"Nah, I took a few days off while you two are here. There's no rush. I've got to finish some texture and then paint the place, plenty of time. You know, as cold and as miserable as it can be outside, I still enjoy shoveling and snow blowing. And the real great part is having you here with me. I remember the two of us out there when you were barely big enough to carry a shovel. I miss those times," he said, hanging his head and looking away.

"Ya wanna go skiing with us?" Shane asked.

He looked up at Shane. "I'm going to get the rest of the lights up outside and help your mother around here today. Thanks for asking, though. I am out of shape anyway. I haven't skied since I can remember. I would just hold you two up."

Debbie was busy grooming while Shane loaded up the car. He kept telling himself to relax. It's just a lesson day, not a powder day. In the past, getting first chair had been a priority when the snow was fresh and deep. *With the crowds, the mountain is likely to be skied out early anyway*, he thought.

"Ya ready?" Shane asked, shouting down the hall.

"Almost. Be there in a sec," Debbie replied from the bathroom.

By the time she got in the car, he was fuming. *We're just going skiing, not to the Academy Awards.* They pulled onto Tahoe Boulevard into bumper-to-bumper traffic. *Perfect, just perfect, what a difference an hour makes.* He clenched his teeth.

"Well, how do I look?" Debbie said, pulling down the vanity mirror and glancing over at Shane.

"Beautiful, honey. I like your new jacket," he said, pushing the words out.

The interior windows started to fog up, and he didn't know if it was him or the cold air. He turned on the defroster as they inched forward.

"Let's go back to Diamond Peak, instead of Squaw. The traffic is too heavy. It'll literally take hours to get there."

Shane turned the car around and drove back to Incline Village. They parked at the Chateau and took the shuttle up to the ski area. It was almost eleven o'clock by the time they got their tickets and skis on. The lift lines stretched across the slopes, resembling a crowd at a ballgame.

"Hold my place in line. I have to go use the bathroom," Debbie said fidgeting.

"Just wait, there's a restroom at the top of the lift you can use. We'll be loading shortly."

"Shoot. Shane, I dropped my pole. This seat is freezing," she said as she loaded the lift.

Shane looked back as the man behind her grabbed the pole and waved. Several people had the same idea as Debbie. The line for the bathroom stretched out the door and around the building.

They propped their skis in the snow and waited. It was close to noon when they made their first run, and then they were back in the huge mass of people at the bottom, standing in line again. This is just like Disneyland. *Patience, patience,* he kept reminding himself.

Three ski runs later, they were at the bar waiting in line again. "The house cab and a Coors Light please," Shane said, pushing his shoulders in between two patrons, smiling apologetically.

They both arrived home exhausted. Bill was in his armchair watching football, and Suzanne was reading. Debbie came in, hung her jacket up, kicked off her Uggs, and went back to the bedroom without saying a word. Shane set the ski boots down and hung his coat up. He pulled off his shoes and set their wet ski gloves by the fireplace to dry out.

"How was it?" Bill asked nonchalantly.

"What a day. I can't believe how many people are in town. It was a mess. I'm glad to be home," he said, walking to the kitchen and opening the fridge. "Mind if I have one of your beers?"

"No, help yourself. Is Debbie all right?" Suzanne asked, looking up from her book.

"Mom, she's definitely not a mountain girl. She got wet and cold, and like I said, it was crowded, not a whole lot of fun. She'll be okay," he said, popping the beer open and taking a long swallow.

"How'd she do skiing?" Bill asked.

"Great. She's picking it right up. She'd like it better if it were blue skies and warmer, though. She really wanted us to go to France with her folks, so she's feeling a little resentment there."

Chip and JT stopped by Christmas Eve. "Hi ya, folks! Merry Christmas!" They stumbled in, kicking off the snow while trying to talk and hug.

"What a nice surprise!" Suzanne said, taking their coats. She brought out a variety of things she baked: nut rolls, almond raisin cookies, fruitcake, and other pastry covered in powdered sugar.

"Mrs. K, this is awesome. This is what I love about the holidays. The food is killer. Every holiday season, I gain about ten pounds," Chip said, grabbing a handful. "Shane, what have you been up to?"

"Teaching mostly, how about you?"

"Me and JT have been skiing, playing basketball down at the Rec. Got a lot of family in town for the holidays."

"Mom's had a tough year. We thought she had cancer," JT said, lowering his voice.

"Oh, no. And…" Suzanne said, leaning in.

"Well, it turned out to be a fibroid cyst. Anyway, she was laid up for a while. We definitely have a lot to be thankful for this Christmas," JT said.

"Hey, JT, you've got powdered sugar all over your nose," Shane said, pointing.

"You do too," Debbie added, looking at Shane.

"This wine is great. Thanks," Chip said, taking a drink.

"I love Rombauer. It's so buttery," Suzanne said, pouring them each another glass.

"It has been great seeing you all, but we have more stops to make, so we need to be going. Have a Merry Christmas. Shane, hit us up if you're going skiing again. Thanks for all the goodies, Mrs. K," Chip said, getting his boots back on. They got their jackets, gloves, and hats and left.

"Thanks, Suzanne, " JT said, following Chip out of the door. "Merry Christmas."

Suzanne picked up the plates and napkins. Debbie took the empty glasses to the sink and then went to the bathroom.

"Do you think they're doing okay? Shane hasn't said much. I asked him about not having children. He seemed resigned to the fact with very little emotion," Bill said to Suzanne as they were putting things away in the kitchen.

"Honey, I'm sure it bothers him. He said his students at the academy help fill the void. It'll take some time to adjust. Debbie doesn't seem bothered in the least, how strange. Have you noticed, she isn't very happy when she's around Shane? It's as though he's beneath her. That's what I think."

"No, really? Shane is there for her all the time. They're fine. It's just the weather, you know, all the snow and cold up here."

"She doesn't include him. It sounds like it's mostly her and her mother doing things together. He drops little hints when I talk to him, like he wants us to read between the lines. Oh, I don't know. It may all be in my head. They are still getting settled. It takes a while. We had our trials when we were first together. Remember? I made pasta six nights a week and then I'd make you oatmeal. We got through it though," Suzanne said, wiping her hands.

"You crack me up. You treated me like a king from day one. Even when we had very little food, the meals were still gourmet. Even when you made oatmeal, it was great."

When it came time to leave, Shane wasn't ready to go. It made him cranky. "The desert is such an ashtray. I wish we could stay here longer."

"Honey, you'll be able to come back sooner than you think," Suzanne said, giving him a hug.

"See ya, Pops. I love you guys," Shane said as he was leaving.

"Bye, Mom, Dad. Thanks for a wonderful Christmas," Debbie said, giving them each a hug.

The weather abated for the drive home. It had been a huge storm. The snowdrifts piled up as high as the eighteen-wheelers on the road. Sprinkled with dirt, the walls of snow looked ominous as they drove past. It was clear and bitter cold when they got back to Las Vegas. The desert was a dull brown with touches of sage green across its barren surface.

———✦———

"Debbie, I don't understand what you want, talk to me. Am I holding you back? I'm trying to support us on a teacher's salary, but it'll get better. We're doing okay, aren't we? I'll have my masters soon. I know—"

"Dad told me he could get you job in the marketing and sales department at one of the resorts like the Mirage or the Bellagio. You'll be making six figures in no time. Isn't that exciting news?" Debbie asked, raising her eyebrows.

"Debbie, I'm not a suit and tie sales type of guy. You know that. I'm a granola eatin', tea drinkin', tree huggin' mountain boy that loves kids and enjoys teaching. That's my calling. Yeah, sure, I wish it paid more, but I'm happy doing what I am doing. I thought teaching was your calling as well. What happened? You have these darling kids that love you, but you'd rather shop or play tennis. I feel like you're punishing me for staying on my path. Gosh, we never have sex anymore. It used to be you couldn't get enough. You're not having an affair, are you? I feel so insecure when I'm around you."

"No, I am definitely not having an affair. How dare you think that! It's just that I'm used to the finer things in life, that's all. I am bored. We live on such a tight budget that we can't do anything fun. Thankfully, Mom takes me shopping and lets me raise the bar. I enjoy going out for lunch and to the movies and buying shoes and new clothes. If it weren't for my parents, I don't know where we'd be living."

"Well, if we were both working full time, money wouldn't be a problem. You cut your schedule back so far that you're barely making anything. We have choices. You chose to live beyond our means. Living off your parents is parasitical. I feel the strain it's putting on our marriage. Life isn't just about you. It is about us, us as a couple, partners for life, common goals, common interests. All relationships take work, Deb. The path of least resistance can also be the least rewarding. I love you. Debbie, there is nothing that I wouldn't hesitate to sacrifice for you. You are amazingly beautiful, smart, athletic, but you need to bring that kind, loving person back to the surface. You've buried her beneath your shallow exterior. When—"

"Shallow? Go to hell, Shane! You're just jealous. You're insecure and boring. Boring. Get it!"

Debbie slammed the bedroom door and locked it. Shane stood staring at the six wooden panels like closed windows.

"Debbie, we need to talk about this," Shane said, leaning his head against the door. "Come on, open up. Be sensible. I'm sorry. I really am." *I'm not sorry, so why am I saying that? I just want her to open the door.*

He turned and walked down the hall, his feet tapping the tile like cats paws. He grabbed a beer out of the fridge and sat down in a dining chair, staring out the window at nothing in particular. *What did I get myself into? I know I can work this out. What am I not doing to resolve this? What?* He thought of Gina and that first night on Whale Beach, laying there next to her. *Gina, what are you doing? Where are you? Are you happy?*

Shane got up and sat down on the cool leather sofa in the living room, clicked on the TV, and watched the evening news update on Iraq as the sun set outside. *Well, this is going great.* He strangled his anger, crushing the empty beer can in his right hand. Some residual fluid dripped down his forearm as he watched it slowly migrate to his elbow. He got up, threw the can in the trash, and wiped his arm with a damp washcloth.

He took the towel, cleaned off the counter, and then dusted the dining room table, the chairs, the coffee table, and the end tables. He moved the books on the shelves and dusted those. He got out the mop and scrubbed the porcelain floor as though he was trying to remove the color from the tile. Stressed, the blood vessels popped out on his hands, his forehead, and his neck as he worked.

"Are you hungry? I am going to order a pizza. There is nothing here to eat. Pepperoni, mushrooms, and onion? Olives? What do you want on it?" Debbie said, entering the living room from the dark reaches of the hall as though nothing had happened.

"What? Can we talk first?" Shane asked, setting the mop aside.

"We can talk later. I'm hungry," she said, dialing the phone. "Tell me what you want on it. It's ringing." She had put on her pink cotton pajamas and slippers. Her hair was wrapped in a towel and there were pools of lotion on her face. "Do you want to have sex? The pizza will be here in thirty minutes. If you want to, do it now," she said, removing the towel and tossing her hair.

He looked at her and didn't say a thing.

"You say we never do it anymore, so let's do it." She pushed her bottoms off and lay spread legged on the sofa, her head turned to the side facing the fireplace.

Shane threw the dust rag in the laundry room, went to the fridge, and grabbed another beer as she lay there waiting. He ignored her, walked into the shadows down the hall, and closed the bedroom door. She got up, put her bottoms on, sat back down, and changed the channel.

"Well, I tried to do my wifely duties. That stupid jerk doesn't know what he wants. Men, it's all about them. What about me?" she said out loud. She picked up the phone and called her mother.

"Hi, Mom."

"When did you get back?"

"A few hours ago. What are you doing?"

"I'm reading a book, and your father is watching the golf channel."

"Oh, nice, I just ordered a pizza. There's nothing here to eat."

"I can bring over some food if you want. Make some tea and we can visit for a bit."

"No, that's okay. I'll go shopping tomorrow."

"Well, have a great evening and enjoy your pizza."

"Yeah, sure, okay, I'll call when I get back from the store and I'll meet you at the club for lunch."

"How was your trip up north? Did you have a good time?"

"Yes. It was great. We had a wonderful few days away, except for all the snow."

"I have to go. Your dad's calling me for something. I love you."

"Okay. Love you too. Talk to you tomorrow. Good night," Debbie said, hanging up.

Chapter 18

Gina woke up the next morning and called her mother. Taylor was still in bed.

"Mom, I'm struggling again. I've had anxiety attacks before, but this one is different. I want to move back to Tahoe. Oklahoma is not my home. I've tried so hard to adjust. Raising Taylor, finishing school, and becoming a doctor has not made me whole. There is a part of me that is missing."

"You need to take some time off. You've been pushing yourself too hard. You need to slow down."

"Mom, you're not listening to me. You never listen to me," Gina said, raising her voice.

"I most certainly do. I—"

"I've been seeing Daniel now for almost nine years. Nine years, Mom. Neither one of us can totally commit to a relationship. I'm not his ex-girlfriend, and he's not Shane. He has been like a father to Taylor, but he is not her father."

"What can you do about it if you come home? You're talking nonsense. Shane's gone. You left him years ago."

"I left him because I had to, because you and Dad wanted me to. I made a mistake."

"We only did—"

"Don't say that. I'm paying for a crime that was never committed," Gina said, raising her voice again.

"You sinned. You had sex. You got pregnant. I beg to differ."

"I have spent years burying the grief I felt when you moved me out to Tulsa to have Taylor and start school. It's back, Mom. It's never going to go away. Why, why did it have to be this way?"

"I just told you why. Now, who's not listening. This has been hard on your father and me. You never consider that. It's always about you and Taylor."

"Really, Mom! Really? I don't think so. I've had to live the life, not you."

"Your father, I'll—"

"Do you think I'm crazy? Do you understand what I am trying to tell you?" she said, breaking down and sobbing.

"You are not crazy. I love you. We did what was best for you at the time. Your father—"

"All this was for Dad! Not me! It is total hypocrisy." She gurgled out as she sobbed. "I miss Tahoe so much. I miss Shane. All my close friends. It has been fourteen years, and it still feels like yesterday."

"Honey, it'll be okay. I'll fly to Tulsa and we will figure this all out. Your father is delivering his final Sunday sermon, so I'll talk to him this afternoon when he gets home and set it up," Lacy said.

"I am...I've hurt Daniel. He is such a kind man. He's fun. He's smart. He is good-looking. He has been my rock and best friend, but he isn't Shane. I ah...I had an epiphany yesterday at the ballgame. The pitcher for the Red Hawks looked just like Shane. And I know Taylor knows something is up. She can see it my eyes. Up to this point, I have told her nothing but half-truths and lies. I sense she can see through the fabric I've draped over the past."

"Yes, she may have figured a few things out. She is old enough now to understand and appreciate the tough decisions that were made..."

"Really! Like they were good decisions. She will judge them for herself, if she has not done so already. I am certainly not going to tell her they were good or bad. They were what they were, Mom. To save Dad's reputation..."

"And to save yours as well."

"Mom, I totally disagree. We have been over this before. It was you and Dad that were humiliated that their daughter had gotten pregnant. Taylor is a gift from God, and God does not judge, right? *Judge not, lest ye be judged.* Isn't that what the Bible says?"

Daniel had not been able to sleep. At around three-thirty in the morning, he got up and stepped outside. The slice of moon hung like a yellow sliver over the cottonwoods in the yard. Daniel leaned on the railing and hung his head. This relationship was slipping through his hands like wet soap in the shower. The harder he tried to hold on, the more it slithered away. *The look in her eyes, I know she has feelings for this other guy, but she's living in a dream. After all of this time, he is probably married or off on some path half-way across the globe. I should commit now and ask her to marry me. I should have done it years ago. Heck, Taylor is like my daughter. I love them both so much.*

He walked back inside, Missy at his side. He made some coffee and sat down at the small breakfast table in the kitchen. The sky was just turning a gray dawn yellow. Missy lay across his feet. He could feel her ribs against his toes as she breathed. He looked down and sensing his gaze, she lifted her eyes up toward his. Daniel stood up, pressing against the surface of the table to lift his body. His insides ached with each beat of his heart. He scooted his chair back and slowly trudged down the hall. He took a hot shower, got his work clothes on, did some final grooming, and said good-bye to Missy. He got into his truck, changed the country station to classic rock, and headed down the road looking through the dew on the windshield. *Boy, I could use some breakfast. McDonald's, Nah. I'll stop at The Skillet and get some eggs, bacon, toast, some more coffee to clear my head and then I'll go to work.* Turning right and heading East on Triton Avenue, the new morning sun rose like a hot light in the distance. Lowering the visor, Daniel turned his head to let his eyes adjust. In the flash of a second, he swung too far left into the oncoming lane as the windshield exploded in front of him. His ribs cracked, absorbing the round-ribbed steering wheel. The flesh ripped from his face as his head lunged over the dash through the glass. Metal accordioned back, tearing away from itself, as the grumbling engine entered the cab crushing his legs against the seat. A hailstorm of chards descended like rain around him and then dripped slowly until all was quiet. Steam exhaled in the air like a final long breath. The torn frame lay strewn about in migrating puddles of gasoline, antifreeze, oil, and blood.

Gina left the kitchen and slowly got ready for work. Taylor lay on the bed watching her get into her smock, brush her hair, and put on her makeup. The phone rang.

"Dr. Conrad, this is Lupe in the ER at the hospital. Are you on our way in? We tried your pager but—"

"I was in the shower, sorry."

"Doctor, we have a vehicle accident and they are bringing in the victims right now. We are in the middle of a shift change and I need to know if you will be assisting."

"I am on my way. Be right there."

Gina leaned over and gave Taylor a long hug. "I love you."

"Mom, have a great day. Everything will be okay. You'll see."

—⟨⟩⟨⟩⟨⟩—

Thinking about her conversation with her mother, Gina wasn't focused on the present. She located her assigned parking spot, grabbed her things, and rushed to the emergency entrance. Halfway there, she realized she'd left her phone and ran back to get it. Two ambulances sat side by side with their lights on and rear doors open. When she returned, she could see commotion through the glass doors. The doors slid open as she entered. She was approached by one of the nurses.

"This patient is suffering from massive trauma to his head, chest, legs, and back. The other driver has several lacerations and compound fractures in both legs. We are trying to stabilize both victims. The first subject has a faint heartbeat. We are hooking him up to a ventilator—"

Gina recognized the tattoos on one of the injured and hurried over to the gurney. She wiped away the blood on his neck.

"Daniel! Daniel! Can you hear me?" No response. "Please be all right," she said to herself. "We need more gauze over here, Daniel," she whispered as her face went pale and her heart raced.

"We're losing him, Dr. Conrad," the nurse said, monitoring his vitals.

"Daniel, hang in there. I am right here. Oh, please don't die. Please. Two hundred cc's of adrenalin, now! Who's monitoring the ventilator? No, no, his ribs are broken. We can't use the paddles on him."

Blood continued to ooze as the nurses applied compresses to halt the bleeding on his forehead, face, and chest. She applied a tourniquet on his left leg above the knee and on his left arm above the elbow. His eyes were swollen shut. Tears mixed with terror fell on her trembling hands as she worked frantically to save him. The other victim was screaming in pain in the background as another doctor directed the nursing staff to work on his fractured legs and deep facial cuts. Gina kept a close eye on the beeping heart monitor as she gave Daniel an injection. He lay limp, an oxygen tube adding vital air to his collapsed lungs. All of a sudden, everything went quiet. There was no more noise, just the sight of the madness around her. It was as though she stepped out of the room and was looking down from a balcony above. She was screaming, but no sound was coming out. She looked around frantically for help. Suddenly, she felt someone grab her arm and then another person holding her. She struggled against the restraint, screaming, "Daniel! Daniel!" Subdued and disoriented, the nurses forced her onto a gurney. A nurse gave her a shot in her right shoulder. "Let me go! Daniel!" The monitor began a steady buzz. His heart stopped. His life evaporated with the last beat.

Gina reached desperately for his hand. Her body slowly relaxed, tranquilized by the strong sedative. Her eyes, dilated with fear, drug, and exhaustion, stared at the ceiling while her chest heaved with rapid shallow breathing. He can't be dead. We were just together yesterday. It unfolded before her scene by scene. The quiet tension during the drive home, his profile, his hands loose on the wheel. "Daniel, I'm sorry. I'm so sorry." Her hands reached for him, searching his blue eyes. The shadows grew darker.

"Nurse, call her daughter. The number is at the nurse's station. Take her down the hall to room 117 until she stabilizes." The controlled chaos spun around Gina like a whirlwind. Daniel lay still, now ignored, covered in bloody bandages, as the trauma staff worked on the second victim.

The funeral service took place at Southwood Chapel in Tulsa. Daniel's sister, her husband, and two daughters were there. His folks, cousins, classmates, coworkers, and anyone he had touched in his short life attended the memorial. Missy lay at the altar, her face on her front paws. She got up and wandered through the rows of chairs sniffing. Large vibrant sprays of flowers sat on both sides of the elevated stage in sharp contrast to the sadness that permeated the event. Father Bill led a prayer and then read a eulogy prepared by Daniel's mother and father.

His close friend and coworker, Joe, stepped up to the pulpit, "I was with Daniel when he got his first tattoo. It was my first one too. We decided it had to be something profound. I told him to put a Vargas calendar babe on his ribcage. He had a different idea. His close friend and mentor, Hans, had been killed recently in a motorcycle accident and he wanted to honor him with the words he used to live by. He had *Live at 9/10* inked in blue and black on his upper right chest. He said, you should always push the envelope, but save one tenth just in case. We rode together, partied together, and even dated the same girls. I took his one and only and he, well, he never really got over that. She dumped me like sour milk." Trembling, he took a deep breath. "I never apologized for that, and I'm sorry, Daniel. I didn't mean to hurt you. When she dropped me, I just blew the whole thing off, like it was nothing. I was just"—crying, he took another breath—"thinking about myself. I love you, buddy. I, I miss you."

Joe was escorted from the stage by two of his friends. Daniel's folks and his sister stood and shuffled up to the microphone, followed by Missy.

"D was our only son. Cindy wanted more children, but as Daniel grew, we were thankful we just had one. He was rambunctious, free spirited, and laughed in the face of danger. Even if he knew he would get hurt, he would do something just to experience it. Nothing scared him. We went camping when he was, I guess, around seven or eight. A bear had wandered into our campsite and was going through some food we had stored under the picnic table. Cindy was terrified. She told me to get rid of it. Before I could get out of my sleeping bag, Daniel was out of his tent with his Cub Scout bow and arrow, threatening to kill the beast if it didn't hightail it out of there." The congregation laughed. Trembling. "He and I used to work on cars and such. He had wrench in his hand before he could walk. He tore engines apart and put 'em back together, like it was nothing. He liked to figure out what made things tick." He started to choke up and Cindy held his arm to steady him. "He'd tell the dumbest jokes and laugh like it was the funniest thing in the world, even before he got to the punch line."

"He taught me how to swim," his sister Julie said, leaning in to the microphone. "Or should I say, he taught me how to stay alive in the water. Some of the bigger kids in our neighborhood used to pick on me, so he used to walk me to school so I wouldn't get scared or get hassled. We shared a bedroom until I was nine, then he told me I had become a big girl and needed to take care of myself. He took all my stuff and moved it into the closet under the stairs, even my twin mattress. Oh, he was tough on my boyfriends too. If he heard that any of them had mistreated me, yelled at me, or had not been a gentleman, they'd better look out. He took my friend Michael and tied him up with duct tape to the post in front of the garage because he was making fun of me." A little laughter.

Missy continued to wander. She went chair to chair, occasionally putting her chin in someone's lap and looking up with her sad eyes. At the conclusion of the service, people gathered outside the parlor in muffled conversation exchanging hugs and condolences before getting into their cars.

The funeral procession stretched as far as the eye could see. It wound through town, past the house he was born in, and the schools he attended before arriving at the cemetery. The mortuary set up a large tent over the grave with rows of white resin chairs for the mourners to sit in out of the intense heat.

The hearse stopped close to the gravesite and six men sequentially stepped up to carry the casket to its final destination. Once everyone was seated Julie recited a poem.

> My friends, when you feel a gentle breeze or the wind
> upon your face, that's me giving you a great big hug or just
> a soft embrace, and when it's time for you go from that

body to be free, remember you're not going, you are coming here to me.

Gina and Taylor sat arm in arm in the first row. Taylor leaned against her mother, avoiding looking at the casket. Gina held her chin against Taylor's head.

A boyhood friend played a Willie Nelson song on his guitar. He lightly strummed the strings while reaching out to share the lyrics and the music that Daniel knew so well. Father Bill offered a tender prayer of solace, "It is not for us to question the Lord's vision for us. It is for us to live and trust in him. Oh, Lord, take Daniel this day in your arms and hold him until we join him on our final journey. Friends and family, carry Daniel's spirit in your hearts and minds so that he may forever live among us. As we release Daniel from this earth, stand together to give each other the strength, the support we need as we grieve our loss. In the Lord thy God we pray. Amen." Gina and Taylor stood up and joined a single line of mourners. Each person gently laid a white carnation on the casket as each said their final good-bye. Blanketed in flowered grief, the casket was slowly lowered into eternity.

Holding her mother's hand, Taylor looked over the gravestones in the cemetery. Their eyes moist with sadness, they didn't move. Gina found it difficult to shuffle her feet. Taylor fell to her knees. Gina bent to console her. "Mom."

"It's okay, dear. He's in God's hands. It's okay."

"I don't want him to be dead. I…"

"It's okay," Gina said, her head against hers.

Daniel's folks took care of his estate. Deeply saddened by his death, they had a difficult time going through and dispersing his things. His sister came back up from Dallas for a few days to help them out, particularly with his personal items. She brought Missy by the house to see the girls.

"Would you like to take Missy? Daniel would have wanted her to be with you and I know how much she means to you," Julie asked.

"Mom, is it all right if we take her?" Taylor asked.

Gina reached down and rubbed her ears. "You're coming with us. Yes, we miss him too."

Missy looked up as though she understood.

"She gets up every time the door opens. She thinks it Daniel. It's so sad. I'm only here for a few more days. Call me if you need anything. Mom and Dad are a mess so I want to get back and help them while I'm still here," Julie said, her arms limp at her sides.

"Thanks, Julie, I know it must be hard on you too," Gina said, embracing her.

Gina sat in the living room with Daniel's jacket on, smelling his fragrance, staring out the window at the apple trees in the front yard. Since Daniel's passing, her small home had become dark and musty. Taylor was on summer break and slept until noon unless aroused by Missy. Lacy flew out to offer emotional support and to help them pack.

"Open the drapes, the windows, turn the fans on, get some air moving in here. My God, it's depressing in here," Lacy said when she arrived.

The sunlight and fresh air helped to lift their spirits. Gina turned the ceiling fans on in the kitchen and living room. Taylor walked groggily out from her room, followed by Missy.

There was a tapping at the front door. Lacy opened it apprehensively. "Hello, I'm Fred and this is Cindy. We're Daniel's parents. And you are?"

"I'm Lacy Conrad, Gina's mother."

"Nice to meet you. We are going to put the house on the market, however, we would like to offer it to you first," Mr. Morrison said softly, standing next to his wife on the stoop. "Daniel cared very much for Gina and Taylor and would have wanted to make sure they had the first opportunity to buy it." Lacy stepped aside. Gina stepped forward with Taylor just behind.

"Come in, please, water, coffee?" They shook their heads, stepping into the living room. "Thank you, but even before Daniel's, ah, before he died, we decided to move back to Nevada, to Tahoe, to be closer to our family," Gina said, touching her quivering lips with her fingers.

They looked at each other and then Fred spoke, "In that case, we will give our realtor the go-ahead. Her name is Carol and she will be coming by with an inspector. He will let us know what needs to be corrected and fixed before we list it, so there may be workmen coming by also. We'll make sure the contractor gives you at least a twenty-four hour notice beforehand. Will that be okay? Please let us know if you change your mind about buying the home. The proceeds." Mr. Morrison choked and cleared his throat. "The proceeds will go into an education endowment for Taylor and our grandchildren in Dallas." His wife held his hand tightly as his face trembled.

"Really? He set that up?" Gina said, fighting the joy and sadness that spread throughout her body.

"What little estate planning he did is in a document at our family's attorney's office. Mr. Logan is acting as the executor and he'll be in touch when everything is finalized"

Taylor covered her eyes, turned, and sat down on the sofa, crying.

"You had a beautiful son. I am so sorry for your loss. What a thoughtful thing this is," Lacy said, as Gina stood with tears streaming down her cheeks. "Thank you, Mr. Morrison, Mrs. Morrison."

"Lacy, please call me Fred, and my wife, Cindy. Now, I wish we had the time to become closer," he said as his wife wiped her swollen eyes. Looking at Gina, "We hoped you two would marry.

He mentioned it just the other day. He was not great at commitments as you know. He seemed so happy and finally ready to make a shift. He was a wild one, our Daniel. We used to work on cars together, build motorcycles, and…" Ben turned his head to hide his tears. Cindy put her arms around him, laying her head on his shoulder.

Looking at Gina and Lacy, Cindy spoke, "We should go. It's really hard. A mother should never have to bury her son. It's just not right. I, I ache all over." She heaved, trying to breathe under the weight of her grief.

Missy sat looking up. Fred escorted Cindy out to their car and they drove off. Lacy, Taylor, and Gina stood shaken, unable to move.

Chapter 19

Shane received his master's degree and continued to teach at the academy. He set up his schedule so he spent as little time as possible at home. He and Debbie each had their own bedrooms. Shane used the third bedroom as his study.

Debbie gave up teaching entirely. She joined the Women's Golf Association of Las Vegas and volunteered at a local charitable foundation. She traveled with her mother, often for weeks at a time.

Shane and Debbie went to counseling, but were unable to reconcile their differences. It was the spring of 2010.

"I don't need a man to take care of me," she told her mother. "Shane and I don't have anything in common. Men are so helpless. He thinks I should be more like a housewife than I am."

"Debbie, I don't get it. You don't like it when I cook. You'll dance with my friends but not with me. You don't like my friends."

"Well, they're stupid."

"Really? Thanks. I've worked so hard on this relationship, and you've done so little. You don't seem to care."

"Shane, when you cook, you stink up the kitchen and you can't dance. It's embarrassing to watch you. You just need to get over it. Frankly, I can't stand to be married to you anymore. I don't want you touching me. It's gross," Debbie said, wincing.

"Thanks for boosting my ego. I feel…"

"I met with Scott yesterday and I'm filing for divorce. I just want you away from me. He'll have papers for you to sign and then it's over. We can both get on with our lives. It should all be ready before Mom and I leave on our trip," Debbie said, closing the door and leaving.

Her brother called Shane into his office. "Sorry, bro," Scott said. "She's my sister so I gotta help her. You understand, right? I'll make it fast and as painless as possible for you. Sign these papers waiving all rights to the house, furnishings, her car, and her personal accounts."

"Don't worry about it. It's all good," Shane said, signing the documents. "I know you're just doing your job. I really don't have anything anyway."

"The Jetta is in your name?" Scott asked, confirming a statement on one of the pages.

"Yea, she wouldn't want it. It's eight years old and has a million miles on it. She refused to ride in it. Said it smelled," Shane said. "She's got a keen nose, can't stand my cooking either."

"Anything else?"

"No, like what? She's not asking for alimony?"

"No, she's not. Your income is so meager, those are her words, that it doesn't make sense. It's pretty simple, she takes her things, and you take yours and go your separate ways."

Debbie and her mother went to Scotland for two months, so he had the house to himself. He stayed there until the end of the school year. He put in his resignation at the Connections Academy. The faculty threw a small-going away party for him the last day of class.

"I ah, I want to ah, let you all know how much you mean to me. As difficult as it is, I believe it's an opportunity for me to shift directions. I'll miss all of you. We've been a team, a great team…" He couldn't finish and put his head down. No one spoke. He walked outside the school and took a deep breath. "Damn!"

The next day, Shane stuffed his car with clothes, a few pictures, and books. What wouldn't fit in the car, he took the thrift store.

"Would you like a receipt?" the clerk asked.

"No, thanks." He sat silently in the parking lot. Everything he owned was between eight small windows, a hood, and a tailgate.

Shane said a solemn good-bye to his friends, neighbors, and colleagues. Pulling out onto Interstate 95 in the early morning, he watched the gravestone towers of the casinos disappear in the rearview mirror. It was already in the mid-eighties. Outside of Las Vegas, an unfriendly landscape of charred rock, dead scrub brush, and sage lay silent on either side of the road interspersed with the occasional town and rest stop.

Reciting a Buddhist saying as he drove:

> Yesterday is a memory, tomorrow is a mystery and today is a gift, which is why it is called the present. What the caterpillar perceives is the end; to the butterfly is just the beginning. Everything that has a beginning has an ending.

This is an opportunity, he thought. *It must be. I've made some choices that didn't serve me. Here I am, thirty-three years old, divorced, no job, no children, moving back home with my folks.* "Damn it!" he shouted across the desert.

Weathered mile markers passed like wasted years on the side of the road. In contrast, he recalled Mile Post 1, just outside of Tahoe City, denoting the start of the seventy-two mile drive around the Lake. He pictured the lake, capped in white, the windswept waves braking from dark blue to gray brown as they landed on the granite sand and boats bobbing like salmon heading up stream, their heads diving beneath the waves, taking water down their spines. He recalled tall pines, their needles laughing with the wind, laying back and then standing straight again. He could see the sun pulling the color from the waves leaving their manes bright white and silver as they broke. He thought about the countless times he stroked through the translucent liquid as it glided passed his body. Absently, he took a deep breath, inhaling the scent of Doug fir and sugar pine.

The sound of jets from Nellis Air Force Base flying overhead broke his train of thought, ominously setting up for bombing practice. The thunder from the explosions shook him back to reality. Dirt and dust filled the air. Travelers, intrigued by the display, pulled off to the side of the road to watch. Some had cameras out, others watched with binoculars. *Rubberneckers*, Shane thought as he passed the haphazardly parked vehicles. He thought about these same people parked on the side of the road at Emerald Bay, picking up pinecones with all their car doors open, oblivious to the safety hazard they created. He laughed. The heat began to make the air shimmer ahead like someone waving clear plastic wrap over the terrain.

He stopped at Scotty's Junction to get some lunch, stretch his legs, and freshen up. Ralph's barbecued bison burgers caught his attention. "Where in the heck do they find buffalo out here?" he asked as he drove up. Ralph was the waiter, the cook, and the cashier. A swamp cooler spun noisily above the counter surrounded by three ceiling fans. It was cool and pleasant inside, a reprieve from the furnace outside.

"What'll have there, young man?" he asked, setting a glass of ice water down.

"Well, I'd like one of your bison burgers with Swiss. Say, where do you find bison around here? I've never seen one," Shane asked, taking a drink of water.

"The Delaney Ranch this side of Tonopah. They raise beef, bison, and chickens. Best meat anywhere. Fries?"

"Sure, and a Coke."

"Pepsi okay?"

"Fine, may I use your restroom to clean up?"

"It's just over there," Ralph said, pointing toward the hallway by the kitchen.

Returning to the counter, he opened a straw and drank half the glass of Pepsi.

"Thirsty, huh?"

"How do you folks live here? It seems as soon as you walk outside, you're cooked," Shane asked, twirling the ice cubes with his straw.

"I wouldn't have it any other way. It's a tough life, but there is a freedom out here you don't find in the city. I can do just as I please and it's peaceful, hardly anyone around to bother me."

"You married, kids?"

"Two boys, they live in Los Angeles. My wife passed on a few years back, so it's just me and my dog, Sadie, here, girl."

Sadie had been lying next to the refrigerator in the kitchen. A large Rottweiler, she lumbered over and stood next to Ralph. She lifted her head toward his hand, bumping it with her nose.

"Let me get back to cooking. How do you want your meat?" Ralph asked, not bothering to wipe his hand.

"Medium rare will be fine," Shane replied, noticing.

"So let me ask you. What is the difference between a bison and a buffalo?" Ralph asked as he cooked.

"I have no idea," Shane said. "What is it?"

"Well, you can't wash your hands in a buffalo," Ralph said, turning around. Shane heard him laughing to himself.

"Bet you tell that joke to everyone that comes in here," Shane said with a short laugh.

"Yep," Ralph said, his back still to Shane. "Gets a laugh every time."

After lunch, Shane reluctantly opened the door and stepped out into the heat. The car door handle was so hot, he had to wrap his hand in his t-shirt to open it. He turned the ignition on and started the air conditioning for a few minutes to let the interior cool before climbing in.

"Where are you?" Suzanne asked, calling him on his cell phone.

"Just outside of Carson. I should be there in about an hour or so."

"Have you had dinner?"

"No, I'm starving. I had a buffalo burger in Scotty's Junction a few hours ago. Got some gas and a snack in Tonopah and that's been it. Can't wait to see you, Mom."

"Your father and I'll have dinner ready for you when you get here. Chip called. He's in town."

"Oh, cool. It'll be good to see him. Okay, I'll see you in a little bit," Shane said, hanging up.

The temperature started to drop gradually as he made his assent up Highway 50 into the mountains. His back was stuck to the back of the car seat. He leaned forward to get some air circulating and cool off. Heading down the east shore, he noticed that the lake was tranquil, flat, the powder blue sky reflecting off the water. Now, he felt like he was home. He rolled down the windows and turned the air conditioner off. He stuck his head out and took a deep breath, feeling the wind through his hair. With his left hand, he pushed against the thin pine air, letting it massage his palm. He came upon the area where he and Gina parked to go to Whale Beach. Gina, her hands on the car, distraught. That morning came back, shaking him with stark recollection. *Her tears, I wonder where she is now? The dirt on her feet. I wonder if her parents are still in town. The redness around her eyes. Is her dad is still preaching?* The phone rang.

"Hey, dude, it's Chip. Where are you? How's it goin'? I'm in Tahoe."

"I heard that. Talked to my mom about an hour ago and she said you were here. What are you up to? Where are you staying?"

"I'm living in Sacramento. I'll fill you in when I see you, but I'm in town for the Fourth. Dang, it's good to hear your voice. Moving back from Vegas, yeah?"

"Yeah. It's been rough. I'll fill you in when I see ya. I'll call ya after I get to my mom's. Later."

"Yeah, later, bro."

Suzanne and Bill were sitting outside in the backyard when Shane pulled up. He opened the front door and could see them through the sliding door. He snuck through the house and surprised them.

"I'm here!" he shouted, stepping outside.

"You scared the poop out of me," Suzanne said, standing up and giving Shane a hug. Bill, startled as well, stood up and took his turn giving Shane a hug hello.

"How was the drive? Can I get you something to drink? Dinner is ready," her mother said.

"Boy, I sure would like a cold glass of water. The drive was so hot. That has got to be the bleakest part of the United States. No wonder they used it for a nuclear test site back in the day. Saw the air force doing bombing practice just after I got past Beatty. They missed me though, I had the pedal to metal."

"You sure that was safe? That car is on its last legs," Bill said.

"I'm kidding. My car couldn't do thirty going downhill with a tail wind. How are you doing, Pops? You look good."

"Work has been slow so I've been finishing up a few projects around her for your mother. Replaced the bathroom doors with solid cores and put a better steam vent in our shower. I like working at home because your mother is right here to make lunch, coffee, and be my helper. I'd be hard pressed to find a nicer client," his father said with his hands on his hips.

"How are things at the salon?" Shane asked, sitting down on the corner of the deck.

"It has been nice and steady. All of my second homeowners are back for the summer. I wish it would stay like this year-round. Ally and Maria came in to get their hair and nails done yesterday."

"They are still in town?"

"Maria is back for the Fourth of July celebration. Ally works at the Hyatt and is living in a home off upper Tyner with her boyfriend, Mitch," Suzanne replied.

"Nice. So, ah, what's for dinner?"

"Do you want to eat inside or out?"

"Whatever is easier, Mom."

"Let's eat out here. It is so nice out tonight. The wind has died down too. Bill grilled some steaks, and if you'll be so kind to help me, I've got a nice fruit salad and corn on the cob in the kitchen. The pine pollen is still a problem though. We just wiped the table off and it's covered again. I've been sneezing for days."

Shane followed her into the house and used tongs to load a platter with hot corn. Suzanne got the fruit salad out of the fridge while Bill brought the steaks to the table.

"Shane, grab some A-1 on your way out."

"Got it."

"Chip said he is town through the Fourth."

"Yeah, I talked to him too. I guess we're going to hang out tonight after dinner."

"After that long drive, are you sure you want to go out?"

"Oh, I'm fine. I still have a ton of energy left. It just feels so good to be back."

Shane finished his dinner, helped clean up the dishes, and took a cold shower. He came out, shaking the water from his hair. He had on clean shorts and a t-shirt. "Chip, where you at? Do you want to meet up at the Pub?"

"Yeah, meet you there in half an hour."

Shane pulled up to the bar. An older man stood outside smoking a cigarette. Shane nodded hello and walked in.

"Nick, what's up, buddy?" Shane said, pulling up a chair and reaching over the bar to shake his hand.

"Oh, hey, Shane, you back in town visiting? Sorry, my hands are wet. Just got done doing glasses," Nick said, reaching for a towel.

"No, actually I just moved back from Vegas. Staying with my folks until I get things settled. How are you doing? You running this place now?"

"Doing good. Yeah, Dad comes in every once in a while, but it's mostly me and Marcy running the business now. We see people from high school every so often. Glad to have you back in town. If you're still playin' ball, we have a coed softball team if you'd like to join with us. It's pretty low key. We usually come back here after the games for a few beers and pizza. What would like to drink?"

"I'll have a Coors Light, draft. Boy, ya know, I haven't played ball in years. That'd be fun. Who else is on the team?"

"Ally, her boyfriend Kyle, me and Marcy, Jake and a few other people I can introduce you to at the field. They remodeled Preston Field, got new dugouts, bleachers, and restrooms. The grass is in great shape too."

Chip walked in while they were talking and sat next to Shane. "Hey, Nick."

"How about you, Chip, would you like to bat some balls over the fence?" Nick asked.

"I would, but I'm living in Sacramento now. Just up here on the weekends. How often do you play?"

"We play Tuesday and Thursday evenings. Games usually last about an hour and a half. If you happen to be up here during the week, you are welcome to step in."

"Cool, I'll keep it in mind. I'll have what Shane is having."

"Coming right up."

"Pool, Shane?" Chip asked.

"Rack 'em up. So what's been going on? How are Marsha and the boys?" Shane said, setting his beer down, selecting a cue stick, and chalking it up.

"I hate to brag, but she gets prettier every year. You'd never know she delivered two ten-pound boys. Eric and Liam are eight and nine. They are a handful. When I get home, Marsha is usually ready for relief and a cocktail. They are playing soccer and base-ball. This summer they are going to a baseball camp in Stockton for a week. They are real excited to go and it'll give us a break. I'm still working at Siemens, pretty solid company. Get three weeks' paid vacation a year, health insurance, 401K, the usual bennies," he said, breaking the balls, sending them all over the table. "I'll take solids," he said, watching the five ball disappear in a cor-ner pocket.

"You sound happy."

"Things are great. Living in Sac took some getting used to, but we've adjusted pretty well. Folsom Lake is right there, and we can get out into the country in a few minutes. The heat and humidity are the hardest to deal with," Chip said, lining up the next shot.

"I sure am glad to get out of Vegas. Talk about heat, I can't believe I stayed there this long. I was teaching at the Connections Academy, which I really enjoyed. I really liked the kids."

"That's right, you're a teacher. So what are you going to do now?"

"Well, I've applied at the Regional Technical Institute in Reno. Did you take any classes there?"

"No, Mom and Dad talked to me about it, but I didn't want to do the commute," Chip replied. "I would have had to leave for school every morning at 6:30 and I wouldn't be home until 5, forget that."

"A couple of kids from Incline High took classes there their senior year to bring their grades up."

"Yeah, I remember. Didn't Jake go there?"

"Yeah, I think he might have. Anyway, it's a good fit for me, if they have an opening. I guess I'll stay with the folks until I find a place to rent, may have to live in Reno if I get the job."

"Divorced, huh. That sucks," Chip said, leaning against the wall.

"Debbie and I just couldn't make a go of it. Everything changed once we got married," Shane said, banking the eleven ball off the rail.

"Love is blind."

"Oh, that's profound," Shane said, watching Chip getting ready to shoot.

"No, I mean, she was probably not right for you from the beginning, and you didn't see it," Chip explained, leaning over the table.

"Yeah, I guess, maybe. Anyway, it's been real hard on me. I didn't know it at the time, but I just handed her my balls. I let her walk all over me. She didn't respect me and I didn't respect myself," Shane said, taking a breath and looking around.

"Whoa, dude, sounds like you've learned some hard lessons," Nick said from behind the bar.

"Everything I own is in my car. It's actually liberating to have so little. Chip, your turn, I scratched. Here's the cue ball," Shane said, pulling the ball back out of the side pocket.

"Did you get the invitation to the reunion?" Chip asked.

"What reunion?" Shane asked.

"Our high school class reunion. We have one every five years. You've missed the last two. They're pretty fun. It's great to see people we grew up with. At the last one, there were some people I knew since kindergarten. I can still see 'em covered in paint and paste," Chip said.

"When is it?" Shane asked.

"August 16. The committee rented the banquet room at the Chateau. I have the schedule of events at home. I'll e-mail them to you."

"Gosh, I don't know if I want to go. It's been so long. Where are you staying while you're in town?"

"I'm at my folk's house too. They bought a new home about five years back on Wedge Court. It's smaller than the house they had on Fairview, but it's on the golf course. They're on the fourth fairway, you know the par five, so they feel like they have this huge backyard. They go out and walk the cart paths in the evenings when the course closes. Marsha and the boys are there now. They all went to a movie tonight."

"Nice, what day is the Fourth on?"

"It's on Wednesday this year, so we came up for the full week. I'm like you. I miss the mountains. Thankfully, we are not that far away, two hours port to port. We should all play golf together. The boys and Marsha like the Mountain Course. Would you like to join us?"

"I don't have any clubs. I guess I could borrow a set. When were you thinking?"

"I don't know. I was just throwing it out there. I have to check with Marsha and see what her schedule is, although, we can easily walk on at twilight. We won't get eighteen holes in, but it is so peaceful and quiet that time of day it can be more fun to play. Shane, no kids, huh?"

"You know, I was all about adoption, but Debbie wasn't into it. She was relieved she didn't have to disfigure her body going through the pregnancy thing and then, well she didn't want to raise someone else's 'mistake' as she put it."

"Wow, sorry, dude. You sound pretty bummed."

"Yeah, I love kids. I was looking forward to becoming a father, and now, it's not going to happen. I'm thirty-three, not married, no job, no house. Sounds like a country song, doesn't it?"

"You left out, your dog died, and you have some incurable disease," Chip added, chuckling.

"I guess it could be worse. There was a side to Debbie I never saw while we were dating. She did a great job of hiding it and I was blind, as well. Blah, blah blah…sorry to carry on like this. Another beer?"

"Yeah, sure. How are your folks? They still living on Wendy Lane?"

"Yes. They're doing great. They are still so in love after thirty-five years of marriage, it's inspiring. Mom still sits on Dad's lap.

They go for long walks every morning, holding hands. I want that for myself. Dad is finishing some projects at home. He said work has been slow. Mom's salon is busy though. All of her second homeowners are back in town for the summer."

"Do you ever hear from Gina?" Chip asked, taking a sip.

"No, I tried to stay in touch, but her folks made sure she didn't see me. I sent her letters, but they were sent back. I called her a few times. You know she moved to Tulsa to go to med school. I guess she's still out there, probably married to some cowboy or oilman," Shane replied, leaning on his cue stick.

Chip's phone rang. "Hey, Marsha, how was the movie? Great, you heading home? We're shooting pool and hanging out. I'll be home in a few. Love you too," Chip said as he lined up a shot. "I should get going after this game."

The boys finished the game and their beers. They walked outside. "You drove back from Vegas like that? There is barely enough room for you to sit," Chip said, looking in Shane's window. Shane shrugged his shoulders and wedged into the car.

"I'll unpack all this stuff tomorrow. Hey, it was good seeing you. Call me tomorrow."

"Okay, but I think we're taking the boys to Virginia City for the day."

The morning of the Fourth, the Lions Club set up a canopy outside of Aspen Grove for their annual pancake breakfast. The line stretched most of the way down the parking lot. People started arriving at the beach as early as five thirty to set up their camps for the day. Traffic was backed up down Lakeshore Drive in both directions and up Village Boulevard to Starbucks. Shane, Bill, and Suzanne found a parking spot on street by the Recreation Center. They walked across Village Green and stood socializing in the warm morning sun waiting their turn for a plate of sausage, bacon, fruit, and pancakes. It appeared as though the whole town had shown up.

"I don't recognize anyone," Shane said, looking around.

"Well, you've been gone a long time," Suzanne said as Maria snuck up behind Shane and gave him a big hug.

"Oh, hey, where did you come from?"

"I'm here with Ally and her folks. Would you like to sit with us?"

"Shane, you go ahead. Bill and I'll sit over there with Steve and Marie."

"So what's going on?" he asked, stepping over the bench to sit down. "Hi, I'm Shane," he said, introducing himself to Mr. and Mrs. Aldridge. "It's been a long time."

He gave Ally a peck on her cheek.

"Yes it has, nice to see you again," they said.

"I came back for the summer. I am teaching at Arizona State and I leave and come back here during summer break to get out of the heat," Maria said.

"You look great, boyfriend, married, kids?" Shane asked.

"Married with a son and a daughter. My husband, Rob, is the Sun Devil's assistant baseball coach. He'll be coming out here for the reunion. He's stuck there for tryouts and screenings. I thought you were going to play for the Sun Devils. Did you get the notice for the reunion?"

"Actually, no. Chip told me about it the other night. It's going to be at the Chateau?"

"We reserved the same banquet room we had for graduation. Ally and I are putting it together."

"Chip said he was going to e-mail me the details."

"So you're going to come?" Ally asked.

"You know, I'm not sure. Are your kids here?"

"Yes, we're staying with Mom and Dad. They are across the street playing games. I'll introduce them to you after breakfast," Maria said.

"Ally, what have you been doing? I understand you're working at the Hyatt. Living up on the hill with your boyfriend, Mitch? How is that?"

"It's good, mellow. I was married for a few years. Caught my ex cheating on me. Learned a few things about men, life, you know," Ally replied.

"What about Mitch?"

"I met him at work. He's always happy. We enjoy doing things for each other and there's no pressure. I like him a lot."

"That's awesome."

"People say it's hard to meet guys here in Tahoe, but I guess I got lucky the second time around. Hyatt is a great company. They transferred me around a bit. I worked in Chicago, Atlanta, and San Francisco. I applied for Tahoe and they sent me back here. The new general manager, Jordon Ellis, is very community oriented and easy to work with."

"So what do you do?"

"I'm head of event planning. I set up weddings, business meetings, and conventions. It is fun and I meet a whole variety of people. Shane, I'm glad you're back," she said, smiling.

The smell of bacon, sausage, pancakes, and syrup filled the air. The warm morning sun gently massaged their faces and backs as they ate. The sound of rock-n-roll music from the sixties blared from across the street. The organizers set up games for the young children and concession stands selling food, cotton candy, and drinks. People lined up like refugees with coolers, chairs, umbrellas, and canopies to get into the parks. They wore hats, shirts, bathing suits, and face paint with stars, stripes, and mixtures of red, white, and blue. Bill and Suzanne drove back home after breakfast. Shane and Maria joined the mingling crowds, spreading out towels and beach chairs to claim a spot of sand. There was a confluence of activity going on, drinking, grilling, boating, games, music, dancing, volleyball, bocce ball, and more drinking. It got livelier every hour. An Air Force C-130 sea plane flew overhead.

Four soldiers dropped by parasail into the lake as people cheered and vied for a view from the beach. A helicopter appeared with its loud *wop-wop-wop* of the blades, and held steady just a few feet above the water. The spray cooled the hot crowd off as they watched. A line was lowered with a basket and then raised again with two soldiers lifting them safely back into the belly of the chopper. Once they were aboard, the helicopter flew off, circled back, and dropped the soldiers back into the water from a distance of about fifteen feet. The crew then lowered a rope ladder for the soldiers to climb back up on. The spectators went wild.

Maria said good-bye to her parents, dragged Shane over to Ski Beach, and got a volleyball game going with a few college students that were home for the summer. Chip called to say he was down at Burnt Cedar Beach with Marsha and the boys. Ally, escorted by Mitch, found Shane and Maria a short time later. Mitch, short and muscular with shaggy black hair, was wearing baggy cargo shorts and a tank shirt. He quietly introduced himself. Everyone else had stripped down to bikinis and board shorts.

"Shane, you are so white. I thought you'd be black from living in Vegas," Ally said

"It is so flippin' hot down there, no one goes outside until the sun goes down."

The sun set late. Around 9:30, the smaller barge holding the fireworks display started to fire off some practice rounds. The hush of the trees and lake meshed together in a pastel sunset. A breeze, laughter, children's voices, the smell of grilling played upon the air, drifting like clouds over the beach. The wind picked up as the sun folded its tired eyes sinking behind the distant peaks. Boats slowly motored by like toy ducks looking for a mooring to watch the anticipated display. Canopies snuggled up against each other, hiding the sand in disappearing shadows under towels, tarps, and blankets. Shoulder to shoulder, young bodies stood reflecting the warm sun off their bronze skin. The music got louder, the beat more defined as darkness changed the summer colors to grays, browns, deep shadowy blues, and blacks. A dog, irritated by the sound, scolded the absent musicians with its bark. A hush of yellow, followed by blue and green, spewed like boiling water out of funnels on a single barge. An explosion, then the burst of rocket after rocket delivering color sprayed across the ink dark sky. The blasts were so extensive that the show appeared to be a grand finale throughout the entire performance until the real finale arrived, color on color, green from blue, to white, trails of orange dripping on boats close to the floating beast. For more than thirty minutes, the show continued. Once the explosions ended, the crowd moved in a hush in the smoky darkness picking up their things, retreating to cars and exits.

Chapter 20

In the middle of the hot humid July, Gina rented a fourteen-foot moving van. They loaded it with every piece of furniture they owned. Placing the pieces was like playing Tetris with all sorts of odd shapes. The van was stuffed floor to ceiling when they finished. What they couldn't fit in they gave away or took to the Goodwill Store. It was not very comfortable, so she split driving the van with her mother. They took Interstate 35 out of Tulsa heading north, allowing roughly three days for the journey. The weather was cool and breezy. The box van had a governor on the throttle, so it was restricted to fifty-five miles per hour. Lacy drove Gina's late model Lexus the first day with Taylor as copilot while Gina took Missy as her personal assistant in the truck. The air conditioner didn't work very well, so she kept the windows down to circulate humid air.

"I don't think I have ever been north of Tulsa. How about you? If you haven't, you should keep your eyes open, Taylor. This is a part of our country that most people don't get a chance to see."

"It's Oklahoma and then Kansas. It's so flat you could play pool from one end of the two states to the other," Taylor said as Lacy chuckled. "Our soccer team went up to Wichita one year during a bad snowstorm. If it weren't for the overpasses, the bus driver wouldn't have known where the edges of the road were. It was a scary trip. The wind was blowing the bus all over the road," Taylor said, looking over. "Gramma, are you happy we're moving? It's a long ways, huh? Three days. Can I turn the radio on?"

"Why, of course. I mean that you're moving back to Nevada, and yes, you can turn the radio on. No hip-hop, though, that music is atrocious."

"Okay, Gramma. What kind of music do you like?"

"Oh, anything. Classic rock, Country, Christian."

Taylor fell asleep just a short distance from Wichita. Lacy turned the radio down and softly hummed to herself. *How strange, the way things turn out*, she thought. What a beautiful granddaughter. Her skin was perfect, her wide-set eyes, wavy brown hair, and even her nose is perfect. She reached over and gently caressed her leg as she slept.

Taylor woke up when they stopped in Colby for gas. The heat and humidity hit them like a hot wet towel when they opened the car doors. "Taylor, stretch your legs. We are going to try to make Denver today," Gina said, getting Missy a bowl of water.

Lacy went into the minimart to use the restroom while Gina filled the vehicles up. Taylor walked around the station absentmindedly. She followed her mother into the store as Lacy exited. "Mom, I feel a little weird. I have an ache in my neck and stomach."

Gina put her hand on Taylor's forehead to check for fever. "You feel a little warm. You may be a little dehydrated. Get a bottle of water or Gatorade and you should feel better. I have some ibuprofen in my purse. I'll get you a couple."

"Mom, Taylor is feeling a little under the weather. I gave her some Advil and some Gatorade to drink. Keep an eye on her and call me if she gets worse. Come along Missy. Atta girl," Gina said, helping her into the truck.

Taylor lay quietly against the window, looking out at the landscape, wheat, corn, more wheat, alfalfa, and cattle grazing, lounging, and watching the motorists that passed.

"How are you feeling?"

"Still a little achy, I'll be okay. You must be tired of driving, Gramma. How far is Denver?"

"We should be there in a couple of hours, maybe sooner. Google it on your phone and see."

"Gramma, did you know that Kansas is flatter than a pancake? We studied it in geography. Isn't that funny?"

"I see what you mean. I imagine that when this state is covered in snow it looks like a sheet cake," her grandmother said as Taylor laughed softly.

They arrived in Denver at bit past nine o'clock. Taylor lay in the car while Gina set up the lodging at the Hampton Inn. Gina took Missy for a walk and set out fresh water and a bowl of food in the bathroom. After a light dinner and a long cool shower, they were all ready for a good night's sleep. Missy snored on the floor. Taylor and Gina shared one of the queen beds while Lacy had a bed to herself. Taylor still felt ill and sore the next morning. Gina began to worry, figuring it may be a virus and she'd deal with it when they arrived in Reno. They had breakfast at Denny's before hitting the road for the second day. Gina gave Taylor more Advil and checked her temperature. She had a slight fever. Lacy took Missy for the second leg of the trip. They met strong headwinds as they merged onto Interstate 80 and then rain as they traversed Wyoming towards Salt Lake City. They ran out of washer fluid and stopped at a Circle K in Laramie to refuel and get more cleaner. Missy persistently marked the trail every time they stopped.

"That's what Lewis and Clarkson needed, a dog to mark the Northwest Passage," Gina said factiously, looking at her mother.

Taylor looked pale and disoriented. She appeared weaker as the day went on.

"Once we stop in Salt Lake City, I'll find a hospital or urgent care so I can have her checked out."

"That is your call. You are the doctor. I think she has the flu."

"That may be. I can get her a shot or some antibiotics at the clinic," Gina said, looking up the closest facility on her phone.

Utah unfolded in a mix of rowed farm land, green pastures dotted with cattle, and tall mountains reaching for the sky.

Lacy sat with Missy in the cab of the truck, trying to get her to sing. "You're not much of a companion. Can't talk, can't sing."

Missy looked up at her, as if to say, what?

"Mom, tell me more about Reno," Taylor said, trying to perk up.

"Well, Reno is a small version of Las Vegas. There is gambling and twenty-four hour entertainment. Have you heard of Burning Man?"

"It's that music and art festival out in the middle of the desert, isn't it?"

"Yes, and they have other events too, like balloon races and a weeklong car show called Hot August Nights, where people from all over the United States bring their classic cars to show off. The beautiful Truckee River runs right throughout the heart of town. And of course, Tahoe is just up in the mountains about forty-five minutes away. I haven't really checked things out for years, but there are lots of things to do."

"Where is Incline Village?"

"It is at the north shore of Tahoe, closest town on the lake to Reno. It's beautiful. You will love it, a lot different from Tulsa."

"Mom, can I drive for a while. I mean, we're out in the middle of nowhere. It should be okay, don't you think?"

"Honey, I'd love for you to take the wheel for a bit, but it's against the law and you don't look so good. If something should happen, God forbid, I'd be responsible. No, your time will come. Just be patient."

"Is that the Great Salt Lake? It looks like an ocean."

"Yes, the strong winds today are whipping the waves up."

"Do people swim in it?"

"You know, I don't know. I guess so. I heard the water is so salty, that you just float. Look, there are beaches over there. I couldn't imagine anyone would be in the water today though."

Gina pulled over to the side of the road to stretch her legs and give Taylor a chance to view the scenery. Lacy pulled up behind and let Missy out, who continued marking the trail.

"I'll get us checked in. There is a Howard Johnson's just up the road, and then I want to take you into the emergency room at Salt Lake General Hospital."

Gina left her mother in their room with Missy while she drove over to the hospital a short distance away with Taylor.

"My daughter has chills and feels achy and a fever hovering around a hundred and two."

"Please fill this out and have a seat over there. The doctor will be with you shortly," the nurse said, handing Gina a clipboard.

Taylor sat quietly with her arms wrapped around herself while Gina filled out the registration forms.

"Taylor Conrad." A tall female stood in a white smock, opening the door to the examination room.

"Please have a seat," she said, pointing to the table. A long sheet of paper had been unrolled for her to sit on. "So tell me what is going on," she asked, taking her blood pressure.

"Well, yesterday, she started feeling a little feverish and achy. She's gotten worse today. We are traveling from Tulsa to Reno. I thought it might have been the heat and the humidity. Her temperature has been around a hundred and two. I've given her some ibuprofen, but it hasn't helped much."

"Open your mouth and say ahhhh." She took a swab and checked her temperature again. "102. What else are you experiencing?"

"Hot and cold. My joints ache. I don't know. I feel real tired."

She checked her eyes and ears. She took her pulse.

"It appears she may have some flu symptoms, however, her throat is clear. Any trouble breathing, coughing, nausea?" She held her stethoscope to different areas of her back and listened.

"Definitely feeling nauseous."

"I'll prescribe cephalexin. Make sure you take all of it. That's three times a day for seven days. There is a pharmacy down the corridor that can fill this for you. Drink plenty of fluids and continue with ibuprofen two to three tablets twice a day as needed for fever and pain."

"Thank you."

"Anything else?" the doctor asked.

"No, this should be fine. Thank you for your help," Gina said. *I could have prescribed that myself*, she thought.

They picked up the medicine and went back to the room. Lacy was lying down, taking a nap when they arrived. Missy lay next to her on the bed.

"Missy, get down. You know better," Gina said, scolding the dog. Missy lethargically got up and jumped down to the floor.

"Taylor, go ahead and take a shower, and then Gramma and I will follow. Here take these now," she said, handing her one pill and two Advil.

Taylor came out and lay on the bed with the TV on while they showered. She was asleep by the time they were done.

"Maybe we should leave her here with Missy while we eat. She needs the rest. Where do you want to go? The lady at the front desk said there is an Olive Garden just down the block that we can walk to," Gina said.

"That sounds good. They have all you can eat soup and salad. We can bring back some soup for Taylor and a little salad. She hasn't had much of an appetite."

Taylor lay still as the shades of evening darkened the room. When they returned, Taylor hadn't moved.

"She looks so innocent lying there," Gina whispered. "Mom, I guess it's you and me together tonight. Which side do you want?"

"I am used to the right. Your father always sleeps on the left," her mother said, turning back the covers.

"Mom, what is Dad like?"

"Why, what do you mean?"

"You know, what kind of man is he? What is your relationship like? I'm curious," she asked as they both lay side by side staring at the ceiling.

"Well, I met him at San Francisco State. He was a theology major and very different from the other boys I dated. He was very good looking. He had blonde hair then and those blue eyes. I was intrigued the first time I saw him. He was kind, considerate, always a gentleman. I trusted him. I still do. After all these years, he still turns my head. He makes me laugh and he's full of energy," Lacy said, looking at Gina.

"How long did you date before you married?"

"Gosh, it must have been a couple of years. He wanted to finish college and…"

"So you waited to have sex until you were married?"

"Oh, yes, he wouldn't have it any other way. We kissed, sometimes passionately, but nothing else."

"Had you slept with anyone before Dad?" Gina asked, looking at her mother.

"Well," Lacy paused.

"Come on, Mom, tell me. It'll be just between us. I want to know," Gina said.

"There was this boy I met while I was working at Zims in the City. We sort of hit it off, nothing serious. I was probably around nineteen or twenty and he was a busboy, maybe sixteen at the time. He had never done it, and well, I hadn't either. It was pretty awkward. I think we both wanted so see what it was like. It was over almost before it started," she said, trying to suck the words back in as they came out.

"Does Dad know?"

"No, of course not, no reason to tell him. It didn't mean anything. After that summer, I never saw the boy again. We never went out again after that night. He was the only one," Lacy said, looking away.

"So did Dad ever have a fling?"

"No, he was saving himself. We talked about it. He wanted marriage in the purest sense of the word."

"Yeah, but you weren't a virgin anymore when you walked down the aisle," Gina said.

"To him, I was. I never let him know differently. I should not have told you all this," Lacy said, pulling the covers up to her chin.

Taylor turned over. "What are you guys talking about?"

"Nothing, honey, can I get you any water? How is your fever?" Lacy replied.

"I feel fine, just real tired."

"We brought back a cup of soup and a little salad for you if you are hungry."

"Can I have some water? What kind of soup?"

"Minestrone. It's good. You'll like it. Let me get you some," Gina said, crawling out from under the covers. She put the cup in the microwave for a few seconds to warm it up and got Taylor some cold water.

"Sit up. Let me put a couple pillows behind you. There you go. How'd you get that bruise on your arm? Did you hit it on something while you were asleep?"

"I don't know. I don't remember anything."

"Here, try this. Let me put a wash cloth down first in case you spill," Gina said, giving her the cup.

The wind subsided by the next morning. The rising sun exposed a grey white sky. Lacy and Gina got their things back into the vehicles while Taylor took one more shower.

"We should be in Incline by late afternoon," Lacy said.

Lacy drove the car with Taylor by her side. Pale and withdrawn, she curled up against her grandmother putting her head on her leg. Lacy stroked her hair and forehead as she lay there. The highway was desolate, almost ominous. She passed a Utah state trooper parked off to the side with her radar gun out. Lacy waved nervously even though she was twenty miles per hour below the speed limit. "That doesn't look like a fun job," she said to Taylor as she glanced back in the rearview mirror.

Gina drove with her elbow and hands on the wheel, wishing to get the drive over with as soon as possible. At fifty-five miles per hour, it was like watching the grass grow, she thought. She looked back at her mother in the side mirror. *She actually got laid before she was married to Dad. All these years, all these years, she's been living a lie. How dare they judge me.* Gina's hands slowly, deliberately, gripped the wheel harder and harder. Her body stiffened. Missy sensed the mood and watched from her side of the seat.

Gina picked up the phone and speed dialed her mother. "How is she doing?" Teeth clenched.

"She is lying on my lap. I'll let you know if anything changes. She is resting and comfortable."

"Mom, I, I ah, I can't believe you hooked up with some guy before you got married and treat me like a whore because I did the same thing. I am so pissed off right now. I…"

"Gina. Gina, listen to me. It was years ago. It didn't mean anything. I knew I shouldn't have said anything," Lacy said interrupting.

Gina hung up and threw the phone down on the floor. Missy sat up suddenly.

"Liar!" She pounded the steering wheel, took a deep breath, and reached for the water bottle.

In the car, her mother sat still. She looked over at Taylor and sighed. They reached Elko and stopped for lunch. Taylor was still pale and weak. They ordered sandwiches at the Subway and sat outside to eat in the mild desert air. Missy joined them with her bowl of water. Gina stared intently at her mother from behind her dark sunglasses. Lacy sensed the look and turned away.

"Mom, are you okay?" Taylor asked, noticing her posture.

"My back is stiff from driving."

"We all make mistakes," Lacy said, turning her head back.

"Sure we do, Mother. Sure we do."

"Mom, how much longer? I want to just crawl into bed," Taylor said softly.

"Well, I think we are about halfway. We should be in Incline by five or five-thirty. Did you take your antibiotic? Would you like some more aspirin? Try to eat something. It'll make you feel better. Have you been drinking your water? You need to drink lots of fluids, remember?" Gina replied, gently rubbing her shoulders.

"It's not time for the medicine, another two hours. I need to use the restroom." Taylor got up and hurried to the women's room. Lacy and Gina glanced up suddenly concerned. They waited for her return, listening over the muffled noises in the restaurant for signs of distress.

Gina walked up to the bathroom door and knocked. "Taylor, are you all right?"

"Mom, I'm getting sick. I'll…"

Her eyes got big, staring at the door, she tried the handle, but it was locked. Taylor reached up, opened it from the inside, and let her in. Taylor bent over, wiped her face with a paper towel. She flushed the toilet and looked at her mother.

"Are you still sick?" Gina asked, dabbing her forehead with a damp towel.

"I'm done, let's get out of here. I need to lie down," Taylor replied, pale and weak.

"You feel feverish. Have some water."

Gina held her as they exited the restroom and made their way back to the table. "I'm going to the car. Can I have the keys?" Taylor asked.

Lacy got up and joined them as they left the restaurant. "I'll take the truck. You and Taylor drive the car. Missy, come with Gramma. Atta girl," she said, opening the driver's door for Missy.

Taylor got in the backseat and curled up, using her hand for a pillow. Gina spread a small car blanket over her and found a sweatshirt and a large bath towel to use for a pillow. She lowered the passenger side window in the back a crack to let fresh air circulate.

"Drink this. Here are a couple of Advil. There's a towel on the floor by your hand if you feel sick again," Gina said, her face taut with concern. They pulled back on Highway 80 for the final leg of the trip. Gina tilted the rearview mirror so she could watch Taylor. With the radio almost inaudible, she lowered her sunglasses, set her phone by her leg on the seat, and stared absently at her mother's box van in front of her.

It was a little before five when they took the 267 exit off I-80 in Truckee towards Lake Tahoe. The tall pines stood like centurions at attention on the side of the road. *This is all new*, she thought, as she drove across the bridge bypass looking down on the Truckee River far below. She got a chill, thinking, *I'm finally home*. Her lip quivered with anticipation. She glanced back at Taylor who was sleeping soundly. *A Ritz Carlton at Northstar, wow, this place has really changed*, she noticed, passing the new stoplight and turn-off for the hotel. They crawled up the steep incline to the summit before making their descent into the basin. As they made their way down, Gina got her first glimpse of the lake stretched out steel blue against the deep forest green mountains. Snowless ski runs cut through the trees in the distance.

"Taylor, look, we're at the lake," Gina said enthusiastically.

Taylor lifted her head, grabbing the back of the passenger seat to straighten up, and peered at the unfolding landscape, her chin on the seatback. "Mom, it's beautiful," she said, taking a shallow breath.

A foursome was zigzagging their way down the first fairway at Old Brockway as they came up to the stoplight. "We're in Kings Beach, almost to Gramma's."

Driving down the main street, memories came back, the restaurants, the stores, and the powdery brown beach. "Looks like they fixed up the Crystal Bay Club," she said almost to herself as

Taylor gazed quietly next to her. Leaving state line, they wound slowly toward Incline Village, making a left on the Mount Rose Highway. Gina took a deep breath, knowing they were almost home. *Home, what a strange word,* she thought. Exiled to a new life, a different life in the center of the United States, she may as well have been coming home from a political prison. Her eyes watered as she made the final turn down Eagle. The house stood like a headstone in the distance to a memory buried long ago.

"Hi, Dad," Gina said, exiting the car and giving him a peck on the cheek. Taylor slowly came around the other side of the car.

"Hi, Grandpa," Taylor said.

Lacy turned the van around, parked in front of the house, and followed everyone up the stairs. The house was cool and inviting.

"How was the drive?"

"Exhausting," Lacy said, plopping down on the sofa.

Gina took Taylor into the guest room, helped her undress, and got her into bed. She was warm and pale. Her lips had turned a dark shade of blue.

"Gina," her father beckoned.

"Be right there, Dad. I'm getting Taylor into bed. She is not feeling well," she replied.

Mike stood with his arms crossed, waiting for Gina to reappear. All of the windows were open and a cool breeze shook the blinds against the screens. Gina smiled at her dad as she made her way into the kitchen and filled a glass with cold water to take to Taylor. Lacy slowly got up, looked around the house before going back to the master bedroom and taking a shower.

"What is wrong with Taylor?" her father asked.

"I think it is the flu. She needs some bed rest. I'm hoping she'll feel better tomorrow. When are we going down to the house?"

"Any time you wish. All of the papers are signed and I have a new set of keys since the locks were changed. Your room is ready for you, clean sheets and all. I put fresh towels in the bathrooms for you and Taylor. As soon as your mother is done, I suppose you'd like to shower as well." Gina shrugged her shoulders and walked downstairs to her old room. It was cool and coated in mid-afternoon darkness when she opened the door. The walls were bare, no evidence of the young girl that had called this her sanctuary for the first seventeen years of her life. There were cobwebs in the corners and on the ceiling fixture. She dropped her suitcase and lay down on the bed to remember. Her mother knocked on the door.

"I was going to order pizza for dinner. Why don't you take a shower and freshen up. By then, it should be here," she said as she turned back around and left.

"Mom, what's wrong? Is that guilt that's caught in your throat?" There was no reply. Gina peeled her clothes off and tossed them haphazardly on the floor. She walked naked across the cold travertine tile, oblivious to her surroundings. The hot water felt good as it massaged her tired back and neck. She washed her hair and stood for a moment before turning the faucet off. She toweled off and checked herself in the mirror. *It's been fifteen years since I've stood here. I look so much older now.* She rubbed the skin around her eyes, noticing the small wrinkles. She went back to her bedroom and spread lotion across her face, hands, arms, and legs. She pulled a pair of cotton pajamas and a robe out of the suitcase. There was a large combination pizza sitting on the counter when she went back upstairs. Her father had removed one slice and was trying to get the first bite into his mouth without dripping the hot cheese down his chin. He didn't succeed and removed the mess with the back of his hand.

"Wow, that's hot! Would you like a piece? There is fresh salad here too, if you want some?" he said, grabbing a napkin.

"Ah, okay," Gina said, staring out the window into the pines across the street. She looked up at the newly developing cones. "Looks like it may be a heavy winter this year."

"How can you tell?" her dad asked, bent over his plate.

"I think that when there are a whole bunch of new pine cones it means that there is going to be a lot of snow. It's like the forest is preparing the animals for a heavy winter with food," she said, still gazing outside. "Have the squirrels and chipmunks been busy gathering cones? That is a sign that there's going to be a lot of snow too," she added, walking to the window.

Gina woke up early the next day and went up stairs to check on her daughter. Taylor was in the kitchen making tea when she saw her mother walk by.

"Up here, Mom. I'm making tea. Would you like some?" Taylor asked.

"How are you this morning? How did you sleep? Are you feeling better? You look better."

"Yeah, I feel better, still a little achy." Gina touched her hand to her forehead.

"You don't feel hot. Is your fever gone?"

"I think so."

"Nauseous?"

"No. I haven't pooped since we left Tulsa though. I feel a little bloated," Taylor replied, pouring hot water into her cup.

"Sometimes, the medicine will do that. I have a laxative that may help."

They took their tea out onto the front deck and sat down, feeling the morning sun's warm fingers massage their bodies. A few people walked by, out for a morning stroll. They waved and said hello. *It's so peaceful here*, Gina thought. Taylor stood, trying to get a glimpse of the lake through the thick pines.

"Lake's flat."

"How can you tell, Mom?"

"By the color, if it's powder blue, the color of the sky, it's flat. If it's dark blue, that means there is texture or wind over the water. If you look up to your right, that mountain up there is Rifle Peak.

We used to hike up there and ski down the valley and traverse over to that ridge above the fire station," Gina said, pointing.

"It's so beautiful here, Mom. I can't believe you ever left."

"Me neither. That is how life unfolds sometimes. I am glad to be back. You'll like our new house."

"When can we go see it? Can we move in?"

"Well, maybe today, for sure tomorrow. All the paperwork is done so we can probably move right away. I have a job interview at Renown Hospital tomorrow afternoon."

Lacy and Mike came walking out of their bedroom about 9:30. Her mother looked refreshed, and her father was dressed and ready for work. Gina made egg sandwiches and sliced fruit for breakfast.

"Taylor, I've got to run to Raley's for a few things. Would you like to go?" Gina asked.

"Can I shower first?" Taylor asked

"Sure, I'll wait," Gina replied.

A breeze was coming off the lake as they made their way down Village toward the center of town. Subconsciously, she hoped she might run into someone she knew. She picked up a few things for Taylor, in case her flu symptoms didn't subside and a few toiletries for herself.

"Let's take a drive by the lake on the way home. It is such a beautiful morning." On Lakeshore Shore Drive, people prepared to launch their boats and set up for a day on the beach.

"Taylor, remind me to have Mom put us on their property list. We'll have to go to the rec center and get our picture passes so we can use the facilities. Not much has changed around here. It still looks the same."

People walked up and down the street with strollers, jogging, and bicycling. "It is so beautiful here, Mom," Taylor said, looking around.

"It feels so good to be back."

Lacy asked the girls to stay at the house another day for two reasons; it was nice to have them at home, and she was tired of driving. The next morning, they were anxious to get going. Gina and Taylor had their suitcases in the car and ready to go by eight o'clock.

"Mom, you just want to meet us down there?" Gina asked while her mother was dressing.

"Go on ahead. I want to eat some breakfast and have a cup of coffee first."

They bought a small house outside of Reno in the Virginia foothills. Mike and Lacy helped with a small part of the down payment and cosigned the mortgage. It was refreshing to get out into the suburbs where the air was clean and the neighborhoods safe to live in. The home had been in foreclosure and then gone back to the bank. It was on a half acre in an area zoned for horses and livestock. Several of the neighbors had horses, llamas, sheep, goats, or cattle. It was a single-level ranch style with views of the Eastern Sierras and Washoe Valley. A two-lane road behind it snaked up the hills to Virginia City. The house was a light gray with white trim. The front yard was a mix of pine trees, scrub oak, sage, and ice plant.

After they got situated, they put in a vegetable garden with tomatoes, peppers, spices, and squash facing the open field. She added a pen for chickens and dog run just outside of the garage for Missy to hang out in. Two cottontail rabbits visited regularly, eating the leaves and nibbling on the vegetables in the garden. There was no white picket fence, but it was her dream home. She got up early one morning with Taylor after a sleepless night and found eleven wild mustangs of all colors, feeding on the lawn up against the dining room window. Undaunted, the steam floated from their nostrils as they peered in at the strangers in the house while they pulled at the grass. Missy put her paws up on the windowsill and whined.

Leon and Sally from next door had a beautiful appaloosa and a couple of beagles. The horse would stick his head over the fence and watch Taylor and Gina as they planted and harvested their garden. The two small beagles barked incessantly at the horse's hoofs. Missy peered over at the noise and wondered what could be upsetting the dogs. The girls walked over and talked to them through the fence as they continued to yelp. A great population of quail squawked and chattered among the sage. When startled, they would lift like a huge sail into the wind drifting to a secure spot in the pines and oaks in the yard. When the wind blew and it was a strong southerly breeze, the dead sagebrush collected like great balls of straw against the cyclone fencing, like an audience of small children with their fingers wrapped around the gray wire looking into the yard.

Gina started working at the hospital, practicing family medicine from three to eleven, Tuesday through Saturday and on call the other two days. The shifts turned out to be ten to twelve hours long on average. She worked several of her days off as well. She was enjoying the commitment, but it was taking a toll on her.

"Mom, have you seen any of your friends?"

"Not yet, I guess I was hoping to run into them at church or at the store. I need to take the time and see who is still around."

It was the last week of July when Taylor had a relapse of flu-like symptoms. Gina took her into the hospital to run more tests when antibiotics didn't work. She was also concerned about a lump on her neck and the bruising on her arms.

Chapter 21

"Gina, I have some mail for you. I'll bring it down Wednesday, unless you're planning to come up between now and then. Any news from the doctor?" her mother asked.

"No, we're still waiting. No news is good news, they say. What sort of mail is it? Who knows I'm back?"

"I think it is from the high school. It has a Highlander logo on the envelope."

Lacy knocked on the door and then walked in. She opened up the entry closet and hung up her sweater. "Gina, Taylor, where are you?"

Gina walked out of the kitchen, drying her hands. Taylor was lying down outside on the deck reading a book.

"Hi, Mom," she said, taking the envelope.

"Coffee? A cold drink, water?" Gina asked.

"Water would be fine," she said, finding a spot on the sofa and sitting down. Gina got some water from the refrigerator and joined her in the living room.

She tore the letter open. "It's from Ally. There is a fifteen-year high school reunion for the class of 1997 on August 16 at the Chateau in Incline. It goes all day. It says here that there is a meet and greet for the kids and parents at Burnt Cedar Beach starting at twelve and going until three. There is a sit-down dinner with dancing starting at seven. I think I'm going to go! Wow, I'll get to see people I haven't seen in forever. Doesn't that sound like fun, Mom?" Gina asked.

"I suppose so. I never went to any of my reunions. Thought they were just a waste of time. But then again, I didn't have many friends in high school either, not like you did. Yes, I think you should go."

Rather than sending in the RSVP, she called. "Ally! It's Gina," Gina screamed. "I can't believe it's you. How are you? What are you doing? I just got the notice for the reunion with your phone and e-mail on it. I'm so excited to talk to you!" She screamed again.

"Well, I'm living here in town, up on Tyner with my boy-friend, Mitch. I'm working at the Hyatt. I can't wait to see you too!" Ally screamed back. "Where are you? Let's hang out. What are you doing?"

"I just moved back from Tulsa and am living in Reno with my daughter, Taylor."

"You are married?"

"No, I'm single. There was a great guy I was seeing for quite a while, but….. I'll fill you in later."

"Tell me about Taylor. I want to meet her. How old is she? What does she look like? We have so much to catch up on. Maria was in town for the Fourth of July. She'll be back for the reunion. And guess who I saw? Shane!" The phone went silent. "Gina, are you there?" Ally asked.

Gina lost her breath. "Shane, really? What, what did he look like?"

"He just moved back from Las Vegas. He went through a nasty divorce. He looks great though. He was staying at his folk's house here in Incline. I didn't get his cell number or anything. Come to think of it, I should have," Ally said. "So let's get together. What is your schedule?"

"I'm working the swing shift at Renown during the week and on call on the weekends."

"You're a nurse?"

"No, I am a doctor," she said with a chuckle. "I finished up my residency at the University of Oklahoma in Tulsa and worked at…well, I'll, I can't wait to see you. Where do you want to meet?"

"I'd like to see your new house. How about at your place this weekend. I'll call Maria too."

"Mom, I feel sick," Taylor said, coming out of her room.

"Okay, I'll be right there. Ally, I have to go. Let's plan on Saturday. I'll text you my address and directions. I love you, bye," Gina said, hanging up.

—⊷⊶—

Gina was referred to Dr. Lippert, an oncologist, after she described Taylor's illness to fellow doctors at the hospital. She made an appointment and brought her in.

"It may be nothing, but her symptoms are suspicious," he said, recommending an extensive examination. "The bruising and the lump on her neck have me concerned. A thorough diagnosis will answer a lot questions. I'd like to see her right away."

Dr. Lippert took samples of her blood and urine and sent them to a lab for analysis. He did a biopsy, removing a small amount of tissue. He also performed a full physical, checking her joints, heart, and blood pressure. He had an MRI done on her torso, back, spleen, liver, and neck. Two days later, Dr. Hansen, Dr. Lippert's assistant, called Gina into the office so Dr. Lippert could go over the results of the diagnosis.

It was Thursday morning. Taylor and Gina both had a sleepless night worrying about what the prognosis might be. Gina kept telling herself that the results would put her mind at ease. She arrived at Dr. Lippert's office at 9:30 for a 10:00 appointment. The new carpet had a residual smell from the installation a few days earlier. The air was stuffy, heavy. She took a wooden armchair in the corner and picked up a *Good Housekeeping* magazine off the end table.

"Ms. Conrad, I need you to sign in," the receptionist said, handing her a clipboard as she stood up. She signed the document and returned to her seat. She leafed through and read every magazine on the table before Dr. Hansen opened the door and escorted her back to Dr. Lippert's office.

"Dr. Conrad, may I call you Gina?" Dr. Lippert asked.

"Yes, of course."

"Please, sit down. Water?" She shook her head no. "Gina, Taylor's white blood cells have produced an aggressive type of cancer. This particular strain is called Non-Hodgkin's lymphoma. We have run several—"

Gina gasped and cupped her hands over her mouth. "What do you mean? How bad is it? Tell me!" Tears poured down her cheeks. "Doctor, what do we do? Do you have to operate?" Gina asked, staring into his eyes.

He waited a moment for Gina to collect herself. He sat with his hands folded on the desk. "This cancer is more common in adults than in children. The survival rate for children and young adults is very good. You may already know this, but I will cover it regardless. Lymphoma originates in the immune system cells called lymphocytes and cancer occurs when these cells are in a state of chaos. These out of control cells create tumors. Stage three..."

"She has stage three cancer? Oh, my God," she interrupted, leaving her mouth open.

"Yes, yes she does." He took a short breath and continued. "This is an advanced spread of the disease into two or more lymph nodes or an organ." He referred to the film from the MRI, pointing to the various tumors. "To get this into remission, we must do a few things to shrink and stabilize the lymphoma."

Gina did not move. She watched his lips move like a sock puppet speaking a foreign language. Beads of perspiration formed on her brows as his voice rebounded from ear to ear. "We must start immediately with chemotherapy and radiation. We will alternate the processes, but given that the lymphoma has metastasized, we will need to do a bone marrow transplant as well. I will also prescribe some oral medications. Taylor may experience a variety of side effects such as hair loss, nausea, weight loss, vomiting, and fatigue. I will spread these treatments out so that her body has a chance to recover and normalize. We must start now to find a possible bone marrow donor. This is critical for her survival. There is a pool that we can access once we have her DNA. Typically, family members are the first ones we screen for a match," Dr. Lippert said in a monotone. "I have scheduled treatment to begin tomorrow at eight o'clock. Do you have any questions, Gina?"

"Is she going to live? I need to know now," she said, pushing the words out between her teeth without moving her lips.

"She has a very good chance of survival. We must be aggressive with the therapies. Again, the transplant is critical and sometimes frustratingly difficult to find a genetic match if her platelets drop below a certain number. Dr. Hansen will provide you with the information you'll need to know regarding the chemo and the radiation. I have called in prescriptions to the pharmacy down on Wedge Parkway."

Gina could barely pry herself out of the chair. Dr. Lippert rolled his chair back and stood expressionless, watching her struggle.

"You seem so, so blasé about this whole thing. You must be used to giving people this kind of news, Doctor," she said, stepping back, staring at him.

"I'm sorry. I know how difficult this can be. Again, Dr. Hansen will give you the treatment information. Our office will be in contact with you to verify tomorrow's schedule," Dr. Lippert said.

"I don't think you do." She turned and left.

Gina drove home in the slow lane, unable to negotiate traffic at higher speeds. People honked and passed her. She didn't look over. She missed her turn-off, but recovered soon enough to avoid going all the way into Washoe Valley. The car drifted wide as she moved around the roundabout at the intersection of Highway 341 and Pinto Road. Turning onto Virginia Avenue, she felt trepidation at having to break the news to Taylor. She pulled over to the side of the rode and called.

"Mom…oh, Mom. Taylor…"

"Gina, what is it?"

"Taylor has cancer. Lymphoma," Gina replied, barely able to breathe.

"What?"

"It's bad, stage three. I am so afraid. She is so young, my baby!" she cried.

"Oh, my. What is it? I don't understand. I thought she had the flu. Isn't that what you and the doctor said in Salt Lake? Oh, my…" Lacy said, covering her mouth as she spoke.

"Yes, the symptoms are similar, but these don't get better. They want to start doing chemotherapy and radiation tomorrow. Mom, I'm so scared," she said, breaking down.

Lacy's voice choked on the phone. "I'll be right down. Is there anything I can get you?"

"Mike, it's Lacy. I'm going down to Reno. Gina just got the results back from Taylor's tests and she has some kind of cancer. Lymphoma, I think. She said it is pretty far advanced. They are going to start chemotherapy tomorrow morning."

"I knew something like this would happen."

"What do you mean, you knew?" Lacy asked, looking into the receiver.

"This is God's way of punishing us for Gina's transgressions," he said, rolling his fingers inside the palm of his free hand until they were red. "She should have…"

"Oh, please, Mike, this is not the time. Your granddaughter may be dying, for Pete's sake. I'll call you later," she hung up, shaking her head.

Gina sat in the car until she saw Leon from next door and felt conspicuous. She pulled into the driveway, stepped over the day's newspaper into the garage as the large double door came down. She quietly opened the door into the house, kicked her shoes off, and crossed the hardwood floor as silently as possible looking for Taylor. She was asleep on the sofa with the TV on and the shades drawn to keep the afternoon sun from baking the room. The two rabbits on the back lawn perked up when they saw Gina through the sliding door. Taylor lay wrapped in a thin blanket, her head on a pillow she had taken from her bed. Her skin appeared ashen in the shadows as Gina gently sat down beside her, leaned over, and put her face against her cheek.

"Mom, what, what did the doctor say? Am I going to be okay? What did they find out?" she asked as she woke up, her voiced muffled in the sofa.

Gina began to cry. Taylor could feel the warm tears wash down her skin. She rolled over propping herself up on her elbow. "Mom?"

"Honey, you have cancer," Gina replied, barely able to get the words out.

"I do, cancer. Are you sure? Cancer? Am I going to die?" she asked softly.

Taylor began to cry. Gina was unable to talk and held her in her arms until the tears subsided. Gina wiped their faces off with the blanket as they sat looking into each other's eyes. It took great effort to breathe. Their breaths got deeper and longer as they calmed down.

"Can I make you some soup?" Gina said, standing up, wiping her nose on her sleeve.

She walked into the kitchen, found some tissue, and blew her nose while Taylor stared into the fireplace.

"Taylor, they want to start chemo tomorrow. The cancer is fairly advanced, but they say you have a good chance of getting this into remission or even eliminating it. It will be painful, especially the radiation, but I will…" She broke down, bent over the counter, and cried into her hands. Taylor watched. "Honey, we will get through this together," she said, lifting her watery eyes to Taylor's. Taylor sat with her hands in her lap as more tears streamed down her reddened cheeks and fell on her shirt.

Gina called other doctors she knew and got similar responses regarding the treatments prescribed. She needed to start searching for bone marrow donors as soon as possible. Besides herself, her mother and father were her first candidates for the screening. When Lacy arrived late in the afternoon, Gina briefly described what she needed them to do. Hope hung like a beautiful fragrance behind each word, each thought. The next step would be accessing the national registry for transplant donors. If they needed to go down that path, the task would be daunting.

Later that day the phone rang. "Gina, hey, it's Ally. I talked to Maria. How about we hang out together Saturday night? Do you have other plans, or are you free? I got a real nice bottle of wine from the Hyatt as a gift, actually two. I will bring them down. Party!" Ally shouted.

"Ally, I, I have to tell you that now might not be a good time," Gina replied.

"What's up? Are you all right?"

Gina timidly told her about the diagnosis and what was going on. The mood changed as Ally pried out as much information as she could.

"We're coming down anyway. You need friends right now. Maria and I will be there midafternoon Saturday. We'll bring dinner too. What else can we bring? Your mom is there, yes? What about your dad?"

"I don't know about Dad. He has church Sunday and usually spends Saturday evenings preparing the final touches on his sermon."

"No big deal, we'll see you soon. I love you." Her voice choked with emotion as she hung up.

Gina prepared the guest room for her mother, who had arrived with a large suitcase, expecting to stay as long as she was needed. Taylor retreated to her bedroom and was sleeping comfortably when her grandmother arrived. Lacy set her things in the entry and held Gina in her arms until the shock and sadness began to dissipate.

"Where is Taylor?"

"In her room, sleeping. I gave her some soup and crackers and then she went back to bed."

Lacy carried her belongings back to the guest room, used the bathroom, and met Gina in the kitchen. She was watching a wild mustang feed on the other side of the fence.

"What a beautiful animal. I've never seen one up this close. Do they come around often?" her mother asked.

"They usually come by in small groups of three or four. Sally from next door said she doesn't like all of the mess they make, but it doesn't bother us at all," she said softly. "It makes good fertilizer…Mom, I need you and Dad to get screened as possible bone marrow donors," Gina said, looking at Lacy.

"I know, honey, you just told me," her mother said, holding her hands.

"Can you do that for me, for us? Taylor will need a transplant if she is to survive, according to Dr. Lippert and the other doctors I have talked to. Between the three of us, I think we can do it."

"Well, of course. I'll ask your Dad. We will do whatever we can," Lacy replied, pulling her closer.

"I need you to go in as soon as tomorrow. We have no time to waste."

Gina set up an appointment for the following day. "I don't know about this, Lacy. I heard it's painful. I may get an infection or something worse and it still might not work."

"Mike, you have the time and this is important."

"Oh, all right, I'll do it."

Arriving together, the initial test for genetic compatibility was a simple swab from the inside of their mouths. They drew three small blood samples, checked their type and platelet level.

"That wasn't bad at all," Mike said when the tests were done.

It would be a few days before they got the DNA results. Gina and her mother were optimistic. Their blood types were both B positive, matching Taylor's. Her father's blood was O positive.

Saturday, Ally and Maria arrived bearing gifts of food and libation. Their spirits were high and contagious. Gina cried and laughed at the same time. Lacy gave them each a hug as well. "Gina, Mrs. Conrad, you two just sit back and let us take care of you. Wine?" Ally asked.

"Oh, please call me Lacy."

"I'm ready," Gina said. "I'm so glad you're here."

"Where's Taylor? I want to meet this daughter of yours," Ally said, looking around. "By the way, you look adorable in short hair."

"I cut it and donated it to Locks of Love," she said shyly. "Taylor is lying down. She had radiation yesterday and is still feeling weak and nauseous. I'll get her up in another hour or so."

Lacy sat quietly watching the girls reconnect. She sipped her wine and listened.

Maria began with a brief summary of the past several years. "I went to Truckee Meadows Community College after high school and then transferred to Arizona State at the recommendation of my English professor. I met Rob there, my husband of nine years. He played baseball hoping to go pro. A pitcher like Shane, no less."

"How funny."

"He didn't make it professionally and became an assistant coach. I finished my degree in English with a minor in education. I decided to stay on as well and was hired as an English professor. We have a boy, eight, named Troy and a girl, six, named Alexis. We have a home in Scottsdale, not far from the university. Rob loves to golf and I play tennis."

"You used to be pretty good in high school. I couldn't beat you. Do you play a lot?" Gina asked.

"Just on the weekends. The kids keep us pretty busy with their sports and academics. There is a group of girls my age and we play singles and doubles. Sometimes, Rob and his buddies join us."

"So, Ally. I understand you are living back in Incline. What are you doing?"

"Well, I went to TMCC with Maria for a couple of years and then I met this guy, Ralph Jensen. We moved down to Sacramento and got married. We never had any children. I found him cheating on me just a few years after we tied the knot. He had been having an affair with a young girl he met at Hooters. He was a real piece of work. I understand now how Lorena Bobbitt felt. Anyway, we divorced and I came back here. I didn't like living in the valley anyway. I took a few courses in resort management at Sierra Nevada College and got a job at the Hyatt doing event sales and catering. My boyfriend, Mitch, is a real sweetheart. You'll like him. We met at the Hyatt. He is an assistant head chef. It isn't too serious yet, but we like hanging out and doing sports together. He's a great wake boarder. Okay, Gina, fill us in," Maria said, taking a drink of wine.

"I, ah…" Her lips started to quiver and her hands shook as she searched for the words to begin. Lacy squirmed in the armchair, staring at her wine. "Well, I got a scholarship to the University of Oklahoma in Tulsa to study medicine and left right after high school," Gina replied slowly.

"What about Taylor?" Ally asked, leaning forward to listen.

Gina took a deep breath and sighed. "Let me start over," she said, adjusting herself and taking a drink of wine. "Shane and I had sex." She looked at her mother, who had turned to look out the window. Maria and Ally didn't move. "It was after the graduation party. We spent the night at Whale Beach." Maria covered her mouth. Ally sat glued to each syllable as it left her lips.

"Shut the front door!" Maria screamed, embarrassing herself.

"I discovered a few weeks later that I was pregnant. I moved to Tulsa, so no one would know."

"Why didn't you tell us? We would have understood," Maria said, raising her voice. "What the heck?"

"I was scared." She looked at her mother. "It could have been embarrassing for the family. My folks thought it best if I leave."

"Really, that's unbelievable," Ally said, looking at Lacy. "That must have been so difficult for you."

"It was." Her lips started to quiver. "Well, I think you know, I was originally planning to attend UNR. We made new plans. I reapplied to the premed program at the University of Oklahoma in Tulsa. Taylor was born in March," Gina explained.

"You could have called us," Maria said, looking at Ally. "I'm actually pissed. Gina, I loved you like a sister. I still do." Ally nodded in agreement. "We could have been there for you…and Taylor," Maria said.

"I'm sorry. I just…"

"We thought it best that we deal with this inside the family," Lacy interrupted, sitting up straight.

"Really," Ally said. "I think it was a…"

Gina went on. "I lived with my mom's sister, Aunt Mildred, for four years while I went to school and raised Taylor. After I graduated, I began my advanced degree doctorate program." Gina noticed Ally rolling her eyes and looking at the ceiling. "I moved out of Aunt Mildred's and met this wonderful man who owned the house I was renting. Daniel was a great friend to me and he was like a father to Taylor. We were all very close." Her eyes drifted toward Maria. "He was killed a couple months ago in a tragic auto accident." She gagged with emotion, trying to push the words out. She put her head down for a moment, blew out a breath, then raised back up as she continued. "I decided to move back to Reno just before…" She broke down and sobbed. "I, I just didn't love him enough to marry…and Shane, I saw a young man that reminded me of Shane." Lacy wiped her eyes, still looking away as Gina continued to speak. "I have never loved anyone like I loved him. I've been lost all these years without him." Ally and Maria eyes were watering as she spoke.

"Oh, Gina," Ally, said holding her hand.

"I can't wait for you to meet Taylor. And now she may die, and…"

They grabbed each other and cried. "So much has happened, Gina. I am so sorry. Ah, more wine?" Ally asked, breaking away, trying to smile under her swollen eyes.

"Sure, why not?" Gina said, trying to cheer up as well.

Taylor came out of her room. "What's going on?" she said groggily. "Why are you all so sad?"

"Taylor, these are my old dear friends, Ally and Maria. We all went to high school together," Gina said, wiping her eyes.

Lacy stood up and met Taylor in the hall. Her pink cotton pajamas were misbuttoned. Lacy handed her a brown Indian blanket. She looked at the girls and sat on the sofa as she wrapped the blanket around her shoulders and tucked her feet up.

"Hi," Taylor said softly.

"She looks just like you. She's beautiful. So exotic looking. Taylor, tell us about yourself, school, boyfriends, sports," Ally said, leaning forward, her eyes exploring.

Taylor sat quietly composing a response. Her eyebrows twitched as she pulled the blanket tighter around her shoulders. A broad smile came out of nowhere and lit everyone up.

"Mom enrolled me at Galena. I'll be a sophomore next year. I, I like music and Mom and I enjoy cooking together," Taylor said, looking back.

"Awesome, what do you like to cook, Taylor?" Ally asked.

"Well, I like making pastries, but Mom won't eat them because she says they make her fat. But we cook all kinds of food like Mexican, Italian, and stuff like that. We went to Mexico last year and learned to make red snapper Vera Cruz and different kinds of rice and chicken dishes."

"Do you like to ski?" Maria asked.

"Well, there weren't any mountains where we used to live. I've tried it a couple times in Colorado. I mostly play tennis and I like to swim."

"I love to play tennis too. We'll have to play sometime. Now that you are here, we'll have to teach you to ski or snowboard and take you hiking as well. There are some great mountain bike trails here too," Maria added.

Taylor sat silent, looking side to side. "I'd like to become a doctor like Mom, a pediatrician, though."

"Oh, really," Ally said. "Impressive, I hope you're successful."

"I've met a few sick people, mostly kids, since my diagnosis and I feel drawn to help them." Lowering her voice a little further, "I left my friends back home. I hope they come to visit. I don't know anyone out here. We've had company, so I'm not too lonely, but I'd like some kids around my own age to hang out with."

"Galena is a large high school so I'm sure you'll meet people there," Maria said, smiling.

"I hope so," Taylor replied. "Anyway, I'm excited."

Maria made a three-layer lasagna dish with mild Italian sausage, ricotta, and mozzarella cheeses. Ally made a vegetable salad and garlic bread. After heating it up, they took the meal out on the back deck and ate in the warm evening breeze. Two wild horses, smelling the unusual food, strolled up to the fence from a neighboring pasture.

"Oh, my heavens, I need to get a picture of this," she said, pulling the iPhone out of her pocket. "Gina, this is amazing out here. Wow, look at that view. You can see Mount Rose and down Washoe Valley," Ally added, pointing west.

They finished dinner and the wine. Lacy made coffee and brought it out on the deck as the sunset exploded across the sky. The breeze had died down and there was only a hint of wind rattling the sage.

"This time of night reminds me of Tempe or Scottsdale when the crickets start to chirp. Ah, this is so nice. I am so glad we came down," Ally said. "How long will you be in treatment, Taylor?"

"I'm not sure."

"First, we have to find a donor and then we'll know depending on how her body accepts the transplanted cells," Gina said.

"Gina, Lacy, if you need anything…"

"I think we'll be fine. Thanks for offering. The meal was great."

"I'm sorry I didn't eat too much. It was very good, though."

"Taylor, you'll get your appetite back and things are going to be wonderful. I just know it. It was so nice to meet you. You truly are a beautiful girl. You can count on us to help any way we can," Maria said, helping to clear the table.

Taylor went in for chemo that following Wednesday. Gina decided to stop at Raley's before they went home from the hospital.

Chapter 22

"Morning, Mom," Shane said, coming down the stairs and walking into the kitchen. "Did Dad leave already?"

"He left around seven. Said he needed to replace a water heater and fix some framing over at a condo at Northwood Estates. What are you up to today?"

"I have an interview down at the Regional Technical Institute at eleven. If they hire me, I need to put a syllabus together by the third week in August. I guess school starts on Monday the twentieth."

"Would you like some eggs and toast? Coffee? Juice? What would you like?"

"You know, Mom, I may never leave here. I won't be able to find this kind of service anywhere," he said, walking up and squeezing her gently in his arms.

"You can stay here as long as you want. I love having you back home. By the way, this came in the mail for you yesterday," she said, handing him a beige envelope with the Highlander logo on it.

"This must be the notice for the high school reunion. Chip mentioned it the other day," he said, tearing it open. "It is going to be on August 16 at the Chateau."

"Well, are you going to go?"

"Sure, perfect, I don't think so. I am back in town, fifteen years down the road, divorced, no kids, unemployed, no house. Hey, yeah it's me, Shane, the picture of success. And what about that great baseball career that went nowhere," Shane said, looking away from his mother.

"Shane, you need to get off yourself. Where did all this negativity come from? Money, cars, houses, or what have you have never been a measure of success in this family. What is really bothering you?"

"I just told you."

"You're leaving something out and you need to figure out what it is. This is an exciting time. You're back where you've always wanted to be. You're single and can do as you please. You don't have any children, but life isn't over yet. If you are hired at RTI, which sounds like a certainty, you'll be teaching again. That's your passion. You're a fantastic educator and mentor," she said, looking him in the eyes.

"It says here that there is a pre-reunion gathering at Burnt Cedar for families, guess that leaves me out."

"Shane, for Pete's sake, it's very nice down there now. They put in a super water slide, fixed up the playground, and installed new barbecue pits. Just go down and visit anyway. Do you remember we used to take you and Nick swimming there? They still have the baby pool and the lap pool too. They took the diving board out though. Remember how much fun you had inventing dives and splashing everyone?"

"Mom, I don't have any kids."

"I heard you the first time. Well, here is your breakfast. Sit down and eat. The food will make you feel better. Bring your laundry down. I'm doing a load before I go into the salon," she said, setting the plate down.

"Shane, come in and sit down. I'm Dr. Williams. I've read your resume and have gone over the notes from your interview last week. We are a small school, but very similar to the Connections Academy in Las Vegas. I see here you have proficiencies in English, math, and science as well as vocational skills in construction and some auto mechanics. The class sizes are small, and we like to keep them that way. Like the Connections Academy, they may vary in size from six to ten, depending on the subject. Many students come from schools where they were falling off the radar. Most of these at-risk students were just a few days away from dropping out. Our job is to re-energize them, create drive and purpose. I have had students with D averages bring their grades up into the 3.0 range and higher. That is our reward. When they leave here, they have their diploma and the skills they'll need to lead a successful life. We also offer classes in nursing, the culinary arts, dental assistance, and social services. We will need to do a background check. Here are the numbers of two agencies that do fingerprinting. I believe they charge around $52. There is one off North McCarran and another over by COSTCO. This may sound like bureaucratic nonsense, but we are dealing with children here. I hope you understand. As soon as you are cleared for work, I will call you."

Shane stood up and shook Dr. Williams' hand. "I am very excited to work here. I had classmates that came down here from Incline High School their junior and senior years. They said it made a big difference. I enjoy kids, and I love to teach," Shane said as he shook his hand and left.

—◦◦◦—

"Hey, Shane, how did the interview go? You want to go bowling tonight? Kyle just flew in and wanted to hang out. You know, have a few beers, maybe play some pool, and get out of the house," Chip asked.

"It went great. I just need to get fingerprinted. Yeah, bowling'll be fun. Thirty-three years old and still looking for a job. Sounds weird, huh?"

"Well, at least, you're not wearing a name tag and schlepping burgers at McDonald's. You have a college degree. You'll be fine. Anyway, we'll meet you at Incline Bowl at seven. I'll try to get a hold of Nick and JT if they're around, later, bro," Chip said, hanging up.

—◦◦◦—

Several lanes were available when they arrived. Doug poured them each a draft and Janice got them fitted for shoes. Nick and Chip wore sandals so they had to borrow some socks before they could put their shoes on.

"That's strange. Socks. I guess we need them to protect our feet from the last person that wore the shoes," Nick said sarcastically.

"They're all sano, dude. They clean them out and spray 'em after each use," JT said.

They walked down the stairs to lane seven and each picked out a ball from the rack. "So are you guys going to the reunion?" Chip asked as he dried his hands off above the blower. He grabbed a dark green marbled ball and spun it toward the last pins standing. "Ally has been calling me so often, I feel like I'm being stalked." The ball entered the gutter on the right side just before the pins. "Hey, did I tell you I bowled three hundred once."

"Really, no way, you suck at bowling," Kyle lamented.

"No, really, I did. It took me four games, but I got there." They laughed.

"Yeah, I'm going to go. I hear it's not cool to bring your wife, though, in case you run into an old sweetheart," Kyle said, looking for confirmation.

"Not true. I'm bringing Marsha. We're going to go down to Burnt Cedar for the family get-together. You should bring Roberta, Kyle. She'll have a great time. You never had a steady girl in school anyway. Are you hoping to just get lucky or what?" Chip asked, raising a brow.

"No, you're right, Chip. What about you, Nick? Are you going?" Kyle asked.

"Alicia got her folks to watch the kids so we could go. She wants to dance. I can't remember the last time I shook a leg, could be very embarrassing. Ally said Bryn is DJing again. He must be close to fifty by now. He did spin some great music at the graduation party though. I guess about three quarters of the class has confirmed that they'll be there."

"Well, that's not a lot of people considering the class only had around eighty students in it," Shane added.

"By the time you add wives, husbands, girlfriends, and boyfriends, there may be quite a crowd. I wonder how everyone has aged. So, Shane, are you going? You're the only one that is still on the fence," Kyle asked.

"I haven't decided yet. I am still feeling the shock from the divorce. I mean, here I am back home living with my folks…"

Nick interrupted, "Blah, blah, blah. No one gives a crap, dude. You were one of the most popular people at school. You're still a great guy. Get over it."

"That's what my mom said."

"Well, she's right," Nick said, grabbing his ball and lining up the pins.

"Is this Taylor?" Adam asked.

"Ah, yes, yes, it is."

"Hey, it's Adam from Raley's. How are you feeling? I hope you don't mind, I called you. I got your number from an online parcel search when I looked up your address."

"How's that?"

"I used to do a little work for the county. Anyway, I thought you might like some company if you're up for it."

"Oh, hey, Adam, thanks for dropping off the groceries. I am always a mess after my treatments. I went straight to bed when I got home. I hate the sessions, but the doctor says the therapy kills the cancer cells. He says it makes them commit suicide. Sounds funny, huh?"

"Yeah, that sounds pretty strange…cancer is tough."

"I could just picture a cell trying to hang itself with a blood vessel around its neck swinging from an organ. Anyway, from Saturday afternoon until Wednesday, I get back close to normal. I'm feeling okay today. Would you like to come by for little bit? You can't stay too long because I tire easily. It's just me and Missy."

"Who is Missy?"

"Missy is our dog. She's a pit bull, but is as friendly as they get. You'll like her."

"I have to finish up a little yard work for my dad, and then I'll come by. Can I bring you anything, soda? Beer?" Adam said with a laugh.

"Oh, you're funny. No, no beer. I like Mountain Dew, though."

She hung up and rubbed her cheeks. Her face hurt from smiling. *I hardly remember him,* she thought. *I was looking up through my dirty hair and the rest of the time, I just wanted to get out of that store and go home to bed. He sure seems like a nice guy.*

Adam finished trimming the lawn and put the mower and edger away. He quickly hosed off his Mustang and vacuumed out the interior. He arrived at Taylor's midafternoon. She opened the door with Missy at her heel. "Hi, Adam. This is Missy."

"Hi, Missy," he said, reaching down to let her sniff his hand. "You look good," he said, extending his right hand.

Having met her approval, Missy trotted back to her favorite spot by the slider and lay down.

"Thank you. This is my feeling better time," she said smiling. "I'm not as nauseous or quite as achy. I start to get my color back little by little every day. Come in. Would you like to sit outside? It is nice and warm out on the deck. If it gets too hot, we can come back inside."

"Yeah, sure. Here, I brought you a Dew," he said, handing her a cold can. "This is a nice house. How long have you lived here?"

"We just got here from Tulsa a month or so ago," Taylor replied, opening the can.

"I live just over there," he said, pointing to the horizon. "I'm a, well, I'm going to be a junior at Galena High."

"Really, I'm going to be a sophomore there this year. That'll be nice. I'll have at least had one friend. It's okay if we're friends, right?" she said, taking a drink.

He laughed. "Yes, I'd love to be your friend," he said as he pulled up a couple of lounge chairs for him and Taylor and popped open his soda. Missy followed them out. "What do you like to do when you're not laid up?"

"I was on the tennis team my freshman year in Tulsa. I like to swim and read books." Missy nudged her as she spoke. "Not now, girl, I just fed you and you can't come up here. Go bug Adam. Maybe he'll let you up in his lap."

"She's a cool dog. Where'd you get her?"

"She belonged to a close friend of ours from Tulsa. He was killed in an automobile accident recently. We've been through a lot, me and Mom that is. It tends to space me out a little, sorry. So what do you like to do besides clean up messes at the grocery store? That was nice of you, by the way. I really felt terrible, in two ways, actually," Taylor said, watching Adam as he spoke.

"Don't worry about it. Stuff like that happens all the time. I have a horse. His name is Steve," he said as she laughed.

"Who calls their horse Steve? That's a funny name for a horse." She laughed again.

"I named him after my brother. He died a year and half ago from a rare flu virus…" he said, his voice dropping to a whisper.

"I am so sorry. I didn't mean to…"

"It's okay. You didn't know. Steve helped me get through some tough times. I rode off by myself into the forest and the hills for hours. It was hard on my folks and me. It still is. It's one of those things that time makes a little easier to handle."

"I kinda know how you feel," Taylor said, recalling Daniel's death.

"Do you know how to ride? There are some great trails all through here."

"I rode a little bit back in Oklahoma, but not much. We have wild mustangs that come and visit us here, though. They come right up to the fence there," she said, pointing. "They're beautiful."

"I've seen the horses. Yes, they are beautiful. Steve is gentle and easy to ride. I'll take you some time," he said, looking at Taylor.

She laid back and let the breeze and warm sun wash over her. Adam lay next to her with Missy licking his fingers.

"What did you have for lunch? Missy, stop that. You can just tell her no," Taylor said, scolding the dog.

"She's okay. I had some pizza and chicken wings. I guess I should have wiped my hands off better. They're clean now though," he said, turning and propping himself on his elbow to look at her. "I should let you rest. Can I see you again?"

"Oh, I'd like that. You need to call first though. It depends on how I feel," Taylor said, sitting up.

"So are you going to be okay? I mean you're not going to die or anything, right?"

"Gosh, I hope not. I need a bone marrow transplant, and in the mean time, I need to keep going to chemo and getting radiation. The medicine the doctor gave makes me sick too. It sucks. We're screening donors for possible matches."

"Can I be a donor? I mean, I'd like to help," Adam asked enthusiastically.

She caught her breath, stunned at the response. "Really? Yes... yes, you can, I think. You may need your parent's permission, though, because you're under eighteen. You can go to the Urgent

Care across from Raley's and do the tests there," she said, seeing Adam blush.

"I should get some rest. I hope you don't mind. Come on in the house and I'll write down what you need to know."

He said good-bye, opened the front door to leave, and then turned around abruptly and gave her a hug. She held on, stunned.

"I hope I see you soon," he said, breaking the embrace, flushing with embarrassment at his impulsive move.

"Me too."

The next day, with his parent's permission, Adam went to the clinic. His mother and father volunteered as well.

"I'm sixteen. Am I old enough?" he asked the attending physician.

"Yes, we take donors from teenagers all the way up to sixty, if you're healthy," she said.

She took DNA swabs and checked their vitals while checking their blood type.

"The most important thing at the beginning is to match the blood type. She is B positive," the nurse said. "I'll be back in a moment with the lab results before we continue."

What a great blood type, he thought. That fits her perfectly. They sat patiently in the waiting room, feeling a little uncomfortable.

"Thanks for doing this. I know she really appreciates it," Adam said to his father.

"Son, it's been a year of reflection. The most important things in life aren't things as we've found out. I'm glad we can do something to help." He squeezed Adam's and his wife's hand, recalling the trauma, watching his son slowly die. He took a deep breath and let the air out slowly between his lips, letting go of the emotion.

The nurse opened the door and stepped into the waiting room. "Unfortunately, not one of you is a match. Thank you for coming in. If it's okay with you, we'll keep your profile on file in case we need a donor for another bone marrow transplant. You'll be entered in a national registry. You never know."

"Well, yes, of course," he said, looking at Adam and his wife." We'd be glad to."

———*⟨⟩*———

"Shane, you can ride with Marsha and me. That way you won't be arriving alone, unless you prefer it that way. You are going, right? Don't say no," Chip said.

"Straight up, I'm depressed. I really don't think I'd be good company. A teacher friend of mine went to his ten-year reunion. This guy shows up and he's a funeral director. In ten years, he'd buried half of North Las Vegas. All he talked about were the classmates and the parents he'd embalmed. He said it was the most depressing thing he'd ever heard. I don't want to be the mortician," Shane said, raising his brows and stretching his smile.

"Come on. Ally and Maria are going to be there, Kyle, Tom, Dusty, Nick…Jake, all your old buddies from baseball and school. Dude, you gotta be there. We'll pick you up at seven. Hundred bucks says you'll have the time of your life," Chip pleaded.

"All right, already. I'll go. And you can keep your hundred bucks."

Shane spent the day trying on his limited wardrobe to see what he felt most comfortable in.

"You can wear your Dad's suit. It should fit you," his mother said.

"No thanks," he said, thinking about going down to the thrift store, if he exhausted his other options. "I have a nice golf shirt."

"You're not wearing a golf shirt."

"Son, check out my closet and see if you find anything you like," Bill said, listening to the conversation.

Shane selected a light blue shirt to go with his white jeans. *This will be okay*, he thought. *Who cares anyway?*

Chip and Marsha pulled up in the driveway. Chip jumped out to make sure if he had to, he'd drag Shane biting and scratching to the reunion. He knocked on the door and Shane opened it, casually walking out.

"All right, buddy!" Chip said, shaking him by the shoulders. "It's going to be a great night. Did you bring a toothbrush? You may not be coming home."

"You look great," Marsha said as he slid into the backseat. "I'm so glad you decided to come."

"Well, it was either this or watch the Giants game with Dad while he snores in his armchair."

Chip was wearing gray jeans with a plain white short-sleeve shirt. Marsha wore black jeans and an orange low-cut top. She had a design of Lake Tahoe in turquoise on a gold chain around her neck.

Ally and Maria, joined by other volunteers, decorated the ballroom to resemble graduation night 1997. They hung green and white ribbon and yellow balloons up. They set a disco ball up over the dance floor with colored floodlights shining on it. It was a true flashback. The only difference was they set round tables for a formal dinner instead of a buffet. The menu choices were fish, chicken, steak, or a vegetarian plate. Even though fifteen years had passed, Bryn looked the same. He set additional speakers throughout the ballroom. There was one in front of each bank of windows and in every corner. He was playing some Wiz Khalifa when people started to arrive. The whole room shook.

Gina styled her hair, put on some red lipstick, and did her eyes. She was stunning. She selected black pants, a loose black top, and black high-heeled shoes. She did her nails in a matching red. She draped a fox wrap, that her mother had given her, over her shoulders and grabbed a small, black, bejeweled handbag.

"Mom, you look amazing. I wish I was going," Taylor said as she lay across Gina's large sleigh bed, watching her get ready.

"Make sure you lock the doors when I leave. I'm not sure what time I'll be home, but call me if you need anything. You can call your Gramma as well. I told her you'd be home alone. How are you feeling?"

"Terrible. What's new? I'll be okay though. You know me. Missy and me'll watch a movie and fall asleep on the sofa." Missy looked up from the floor at the sound of her name.

"Make yourself some toast so you have something in your stomach. There is still some vegetable soup on the stove if you want something else. Oh, and crackers too. Don't forget to take your medicine before you go to bed."

"I know, Mom, sheesh. Don't worry. Go have a good time. You haven't done anything fun in forever. Tell Ally and Maria I said hi."

"I will, feel better."

The drive up Mount Rose was arduous. A large lumber truck overturned at the hairpin turn just above the Reindeer Lodge. Plywood, beams, and two-by-fours lay strewn over both lanes. The driver was uninjured, but it was taking forever to clean up the mess and get the truck towed out of the way. Traffic backed up for miles in both directions. Several motorists turned around and went back the direction they came from. Gina sat for more than a half hour before the cars started to inch forward. *Great*, she thought, *by the time I get there, it'll be over.* She checked herself in the mirror. The slow parade of vehicles gradually gained momentum and were up to speed when they reached the summit. The sun was beginning to set over a dark blue windswept lake. The clouds waited patiently to turn into the brilliant colors of dusk as Gina made her descent into Incline Village. She nervously changed tracks on her CDs as she hummed and sang along. Fear crept in slowly. *It's been so long. I won't even know or recognize most of these people.* Married, kids, fat, bald, saggy breasts, she checked herself again in the mirror. Her hands were wet on the wheel, her knuckles white.

—⟆⟆⟆—

Shane followed Chip and Marsha to an empty table. They marked their chairs with napkins and walked around reading nametags to identify old classmates. They introduced wives, husbands, and dates while they reminisced about the days gone by. Shane's eyes searched the ballroom for familiar faces, subconsciously looking for Gina among the crowd. When he spotted Jake, he wandered over to give Chip a break from his parasitic behavior.

"This is Joan, Joan, Shane," Jake said, stepping aside.

"Nice to meet you, where are you from? How did you two meet?" Shane asked.

"I'm from San Francisco. I came up here with my girl friends a few years back to get out of the city. They went back, but I meet this handsome man here and never left. I was hostessing at the Hacienda, and Jake came in after work and hung out with his buddies. He was pretty shy..."

"What, Jake? You have got to be kidding." Shane said with a laugh.

"Nope. I actually asked him out," Jake turned red at the revelation.

"Kids?" Shane asked.

"Two boys. They take after their father. Wild! I was raised with two sisters so I was not used to being around boys. They are full of mischief, energy. Wow, but I love 'em," Joan said, holding Jake's hand.

"I got them into motocross. It gives Joan a bit of break. She travels with us when we race out of town."

"It scares me to death. I hate it when they crash. Sometimes, I can't watch them ride. They have absolutely no fear. They're crazy. Just like their dad."

Ally picked up the microphone. "Everyone, please find a seat. Dinner will be served shortly. There is white and red wine on the tables. Please feel free to help yourselves. If you need more, let us know. If you did not fill out your RSVP, let your server know what you would like for your main dish. The choices again are steak, chicken, salmon, or vegetables if you are vegetarian. The bars at either end of the ballroom will be open all night."

Shane zigzagged his way through a maze of chairs, shaking hands, and saying hello until he found his spot at Chip's table. As everyone got seated, the noise began to get more subdued. Maria, her husband Rob, Kyle, and his wife joined the group. There were more introductions as the ice-breaking wine made its way around the table.

"Shane, what are you doing?" Kyle asked

"I'm a teacher. I interviewed for a position at the Regional Technical Institute in Reno. A couple students from our high school went there their senior year and really liked it," Shane replied.

"Married?" Kyle asked.

"I was. Didn't work out," Shane said, pouring some wine.

"Oh, sorry. Girl friend?" Kyle asked

"Nope," Shane replied, taking a sip.

"Okay then, hey, Marsha, could you pass me the bowl of bread," Kyle said, making an awkward exit from the conversation.

Gina arrived, flustered at being late. She parked the Lexus at the far end of the lot and hurried to the front door. She walked in and was surprised to see Mrs. Kyper handing out nametags.

"Gina. So nice to see you. Wow, you look beautiful this evening. I love your hair."

"Hi, Mrs. Kyper. It is nice to see you too. How's school?" Gina asked, pressing on her tag.

"It's been good. Hasn't been the same since your class left though. You were my favorite," Mrs. Kyper replied.

"I bet you say that to all your students," Gina said with a smile.

Gina hung up her shawl in the cloakroom. She could hear the sound of lively conversation as she walked down the hall, her high heels clicking on the porcelain tile. Entering the center of three double doors, she stood nervously and eyed the crowd looking for Ally and Maria. Shane had his back to the door. He was talking to Kyle when Maria stood up and waved. Rob glanced up and then back down, taking another sip of red wine. With her short hair, no one recognized her as she made her way through the ballroom. Heads turned, trying to place this stunning addition to the party.

"Maria! I'm sorry I'm late. There was this accident on Mount Rose that closed the road and..."

"Gina, I'd like you to meet..." Maria started to say.

Shane's mouth dropped open as Gina turned around. He stood up bumping the table, sending silver ware and wine glasses flying. "Gina?"

She stood motionless, her lips frozen. He stumbled around Chip and Marsha's chairs, trying to reach her.

"Easy, buddy, don't kill yourself," Chip said, ducking under Shane's elbow.

"I hoped I'd see you." His lips quivering as his eyes started to water. "Gina," he said softly.

"Hi," Gina said softly.

Maria dabbed her eyes watching the scene unfold. "They dated in high school," Maria whispered to Rob. "They haven't seen each other in years."

Shane reached for her hands and pulled her toward him. "You look beautiful, short hair. I wouldn't have recognized you," he said, almost whispering.

"You don't look bad yourself, stranger." She softly kissed his lips and then she held him. "Shane, I'm so sorry," she said, wiping her eyes.

"For what?" Shane asked, momentarily confused.

"I shouldn't have ever..."

"Kyle, why don't you and Roberta move over so Gina can sit next to Shane," Marsha said. Their eyes were on the couple. Shane took her hand and led her to a chair next to his.

"Gina, this is Rob, Marsha, and Roberta. Of course, you remember Kyle and Chip." Gina wiped her eyes again, shook hands, and made acquaintances. She took Shane's hand and pressed it into her lap.

"I am so glad to see you. I love your hair," he said, searching her eyes. "You shouldn't have ever, what?"

"Shane was the star pitcher on our baseball team," Maria said to the guests. "We thought he might go pro."

He turned his attention to the conversation at the mention of his name. "Nah. I ah, played some ball in college, UNR, but that was it."

"What are you doing now? "Roberta asked.

"He's a professional bowler," Kyle said, chiming in. Chip and Shane laughed at the inside joke.

"I'm a teacher, or I used to be. I'm interviewing for a job down at RTI." He looked back at Gina.

"What do you teach? Are these special-needs kids there?" Roberta asked.

"English, science, math, and I'll be teaching vocational subjects as well. They have classes in construction, nursing, things like that."

"I like your shirt, nice jeans, trendy," Gina said, making small talk. "We can talk later," she whispered.

"I want to tell you…" Shane began.

"Ah, food's here," Chip said, tucking his napkin into the neck of his shirt.

Leaning over, "I tried so hard to find you. No phone, no…" Shane continued.

"Okay, Shane, let the girl have some dinner," Kyle said as he cut into his steak.

Shane stared at Kyle and reluctantly pried his hand away so Gina could eat. Bryn played music softly in the background. When given the signal by Ally, he turned the music off and picked up the microphone.

"Everyone, please welcome Ally Aldridge, who with the help of several other classmates, put this event together." Applause.

"I would like to thank you all for coming. This is the largest turnout we've had. We have a photographer here. She's taking random pictures, and you can purchase them online. Before anyone leaves, we'd like to get a group shot of the class of '97. Danielle said we can do that as soon as the tables are cleared. Okay, who traveled the farthest to get here?"

Vanessa raised her hand and then stood. "My husband and I flew in from Maui."

"Anyone else?" Ally asked, looking around the room. Mona raised her hand. "Mona."

"New York City."

"Anyone else?" Ally asked, looking for another traveler.

"Okay, I don't know which is farther away, so I say it's a tie. I have a gift certificate to the Lone Eagle Grill at the Hyatt for each couple," Ally said, handing them each an envelope.

"All right, who has the most kids?"

From out in the audience, "Three," someone said.

"Do I hear four? Does anyone have four children?" Ally asked still checking. "Three it is. How many of you have three children, then?"

Two hands went up. "I have gift certificates for Jack Rabbit Moon. I'll have more prizes to give away later, so don't leave. It took a while for us to find him, but Bryn is back again and is going to be playing your favorite tunes. If you have a special request, please write it down on a piece of paper and bring it up," Ally said, setting down the mike.

"Gina, would you like to go outside and get some fresh air?" Shane asked when they finished their dinner.

She shook her head yes. "You don't smoke, do you?"

"No, no, I don't. Why?"

She grabbed his hand and led him out the back door unto the deck. "No reason. Just checking, didn't know if you needed a smoke break."

"So tell me what you are sor—" Shane started to say.

She put her arms around his neck and tenderly pulled his face to her lips, barely touching his skin with her eyes gently closed. She felt the slight stubble of his whiskers as she softly exhaled. She released him and laid her head against his chest, feeling his strong heart beat. "Shane, tell me about your life," she said, her lips against his shirt whispering.

"That summer, after you left Incline, I felt so lost. I tried to find you. Your parents wouldn't tell me anything."

"I hoped that somehow we'd be together again. I couldn't tell you all that was going on. I focused on school. I should have called."

"I don't understand. We could at least have been friends or something. You ripped my heart out," Shane said, pushing back and looking at her.

"Shane, I…" He looked at her closely.

He took a breath. "My folks and I went to Arizona State University in Tempe. If you remember, they had a baseball scholarship for me. I also had one to Berkeley too, but I just couldn't do it." He watched her eyes. "Do you understand how upset I was?" She didn't answer. "They both had great baseball programs, but it was clear it would be an uphill battle to get to where I wanted to be. Relative to the other players, I wasn't that good. I couldn't picture myself living in the desert or the big city, so I opted to go to the University of Nevada in Reno. It was close to home. I still got a scholarship. I got to play ball. I was close to Tahoe. I ended up really enjoying school and I got a bachelor's degree in education," he said in a monotone.

"And then what? I heard you were married," she said, stepping back a little.

He continued slowly, "Yes, I was. I fell for my roommate's sister. She had long brown hair, big brown eyes, soft round cheekbones. I fell for a girl that looked like you, go figure." He looked away. "She was a teacher as well. We moved down to Vegas where her parents live. We were together for about ten years or so. It didn't work out. She couldn't have kids. That caused the first fracture in our marriage. She was actually glad because she wouldn't mess up her body," he said, turning away, looking down the eighteenth fairway.

"That's odd," Gina said, surprised at the comment.

"Well, she didn't want to adopt either. Anyway, long story short, she was a city girl and I'm a mountain guy." Gina smiled. "I had a teaching job I liked, but I didn't care for Las Vegas. The divorce was final a few months ago, so I moved back home. I still drive a Jetta. Do you believe it?" Shane laughed. "Anyway, I'm living with my folks. They still have the same house over on Wendy. If I get this job in Reno, I'll move down there so I won't have to commute," Shane said, leaning aback against the wall.

He looks so handsome. He hasn't changed a bit, tall, strong, rugged looking, those deep brown eyes. "No girlfriend now?"

"No, haven't been looking. I've only been divorced a couple of months. Debbie, that was my wife, worked me pretty good. Her brother, my ex roommate is a lawyer, and he handled the divorce. I love being back in Tahoe though. The air is so clean and I can drink the tap water," he said, taking a deep breath. "Gina, I've thought about you all this time. Your face appeared before me, and I would stop in my tracks. I couldn't place the feeling. I guess, I never got over you." Looking into her eyes, "Tell me about your life Gina, you left so quickly. Are your folks still in town?"

"Yes, they're still here. Dad's still the pastor at the Episcopal Church. When I moved to Tulsa, I wanted to call you, but I couldn't. And my folks, well, they didn't help."

"I remember. They returned all my letters," Shane said concurring.

"You wrote? I never saw them," Gina replied, shocked.

"I tried to call, but…"

"I got a new cell number. I stayed with my Aunt Mildred while I went to school. That was rough. She didn't care for me, talk about walking on egg shells. But once I graduated, I moved out and got my own place while I went to grad school and got my doctorate."

"You're a doctor?"

"Yes, I practice family medicine. I worked at the Kaiser hospital in Tulsa where I did my internship."

"You are still there?" Are you married? Divorced?"

"Ah, no, I had a boyfriend for a number of years. We were very close, but never married. He owned the house I was renting. That's how we met…his, his name was Daniel. He was a very kind, sweet man, like you. Sadly, he was killed in an auto accident a few months ago. I moved back here a short time later. I bought a house down in South Reno with my folks help. I'm on staff at Renown Hospital. I hope to start my own practice some day. Shane, I have to tell you something." She took a long pause. "We have…"

The deck door flew open. "Hey, you guys, come back inside. The music is playing. You have all night to talk," Chip said, holding the door open. "You should have taken my bet." Shane smiled.

Gina took Shane's hand and he led her back inside. They walked back to their table shoulder to shoulder where two uneaten plates of chocolate cake draped with melted vanilla ice cream sat. "More wine?" Shane asked.

"No, let's dance," Gina said, pulling him toward the dance floor.

The music stopped just as they arrived. Ally held the microphone in her hand. "Okay, listen up everybody. I want to take a group picture. People, this is classmates only. Start lining up in the center of the dance floor and we'll move back and to the sides from there."

Danielle stepped among the students, arranging them by height. "Make sure I can see your face." It took several minutes to choreograph the photo. "Okay, everyone say, ninety-seven."

All together, "Ninety-seven." A few flashes and they were done.

"Okay, people, people, I have more prizes to give away. Shhhhsssh. Who here has been married the longest? Fifteen years?" No hands. "Fourteen, thirteen. Twelve. Twelve. We have a winner. Miles and Marissa Nelson." They walked up toward Ally to receive their envelope. "So what is your secret?" she asked.

They looked at each other. Miles shrugged his shoulders as Marissa leaned into the microphone." He's always a gentleman, and he does everything I tell him to do," she said, laughing. Miles shook his head.

"We have a request for Mariah Carey. It's the last song of the night so get out on the dance floor," Bryn said, booting up the tune, "Forever."

The lights dimmed as the song began. Shane cradled Gina in his arms. The melody took them back to that final dance fifteen years ago, when their hearts were young and their dreams were fresh and bold.

"I still care for you, Gina," he said tenderly in her ear, barely moving on the crowded floor.

"Oh, Shane. You feel so good. I feel so safe in your arms."

"It's like grad night all over again," he said, gently pushing away and looking into her eyes.

"Hey, you need a ride home?" Chip asked, poking his head in between them.

"Do you need a ride home, Shane?" Gina asked.

"Yeah, sure, if you don't mind. I came with Chip and Marsha."

"You okay then?" Chip asked rhetorically.

"I'll take him home," Gina said, grateful for the opportunity.

The lights came on. Everyone adjusted their eyes, gathered their belongings, and filed out into the parking lot. "Let me grab my wrap."

"Where's your car?" Shane asked.

"Way down there by that pile of sand by the Dumpster. There were no parking places left by the time I got here," Gina said, pulling her wrap around her.

"That's okay, the fresh air and exercise will do us good," Shane said as they walked down the parking lot hand in hand, disappearing into the darkness.

Gina clicked the key to unlock the car as Shane held her door for her. He slid in and gently pulled her chin toward him while she tried to start the car. "Gina, it is so good to see you." He kissed her gently massaging her lips with his.

"So I don't remember how to get to your house," she said, collecting herself.

"Well, it's about four hundred feet up that street over there," he said sarcastically. "I could have walked, but then again, I couldn't turn down a ride from such a beautiful lady. Would you like to go get a drink or something?"

"Sorry, but I need to get home. Tay, I mean my dog. I need to let my dog out. We, ah, I have this pit bull. Missy is her name," Gina said, covering her gaff.

Shane cocked his brow, looking at her. Perspiration gathered and dripped down the inside of her arms.

She spoke slowly. "Shane, I have...no, we have a daughter," she said, pushing the words out with no air in her lungs.

"What? We what? We have a daughter?" Shane asked, shocked by the revelation.

Chapter 23

ow voices, muffled by the breeze, conversed oblivious to the emptiness around them.

"I don't understand." He looked at her, his eyes pleading for information. "That night. Was it from that night? It was, wasn't it?" His hands gripped his knees.

"As soon as Dad found out, he freaked. Having sex before marriage was bad enough, but when he found out I was pregnant, well, he couldn't let anyone know," Gina said, meekly.

"And what, spoil his reputation as a pastor? I should have been told. I was the father. What kind of thinking is that?" Shane asked, raising his voice.

"Shane, this isn't easy. Please let me finish. We didn't want anyone to know. Dad drove me out to Tulsa. It was horrible."

"I had a daughter, and now years later, I find out. I've missed out on all that time with my daughter. Gina, you should have told me."

"I couldn't. Dad was tough on me. The drive out there was like..."

"Screw your dad..." Shane looked away as she went on.

"....being on prison bus."

"Really? You should have called me."

"Let me finish. Please. I lived with Mom's sister. Shane, she made the Wicked Witch of the West look like an angel, always had a scowl on her face. She wore thick red lipstick and her hair, it was crazy wild. I was stuffed into a back bedroom. She didn't like me and disliked our baby even more because she was a bastard child, born from sin. I delivered Taylor that March, March 18." She stopped for a moment. Breathing, "Her name is Taylor and she is so beautiful. She has your eyes, long curly brown hair, and olive skin. Her smile is soft and innocent." Shane didn't move. He watched Gina's eyes as she continued to speak almost in a whisper. "We lived with Aunt Mildred until I graduated, sharing the small room at the back of the house and the one tiny bathroom. The house was literally, swollen with junk. My aunt was and still is a hoarder of the worst degree. We could barely move. There were narrow paths from one room to the next. She and Mom did not get along either. That made things even worse, if you can believe it."

"I believe it. You're whole family is dysfunctional," Shane said exasperated.

"Will you please stop? Taylor was three and half when we finally got our own place. I felt so guilty having kept her there that long. We didn't have much money, even with Mom and Dad's help. After looking for what seemed an eternity, I found a beat-up old house on the east side of town by the hospital. As small and as young as Taylor was, she helped me paint and fix the place up. The owner, this man named Daniel, helped us too. Shane, you would have liked him. We dated until he was killed in a horrible traffic accident. He was like a father to Taylor," Gina said, catching her breath when she realized what she had just said.

"Like a father to her. She had a father. That should have been me. How could you do this?" Shane blurted back.

"Shane, I am so sorry. I tried to tell you, but Mom and Dad watched me like a pair of hawks."

"All the way out in Oklahoma? Yeah, right," Shane said sarcastically.

"Maria and Ally didn't even know. I was embarrassed, ashamed, as well. They laid so much guilt on me that I started to believe I was immoral, a sinner of the worst kind. I made up stories. Told people I had married and that it hadn't worked out. My husband left and I was a single mom struggling to survive with help from my folks. I kept you a secret from Taylor. She asked me all the time who her real father was, where did he live, what did he look like. Shane, you may not believe this, but you were always in my heart. I could not commit to Daniel, even after almost ten years of being together. There was always something missing." She choked as she related the rest of the story. "On our last date, Daniel and I went to a ballgame down in Oklahoma City. The pitcher reminded me of you. He was tall, same eyes and hair. The memories came back. The feelings washed over me as I realized I had to get back here and find you. It all happened so quickly, coming back here, going to the reunion and all. I didn't know if you were married, dead. I knew my relationship with Daniel was over. I discovered what I had been missing. I buried you because you could not exist in my reality."

"Gina, where is Taylor? Does she live with you? Can I see her?"

"Shane, she is very sick." Gina put her hand on Shane's. "She has been diagnosed with stage three lymphoma."

"What is that? Cancer? Some kind of cancer?" Shane asked, stiffening.

"Yes, it's a cancer of the lymph nodes. She has tumors we are treating with chemotherapy and radiation. She needs a bone marrow transplant if she is going to survive. We need to find a perfect genetic match. Mom and I are the same blood type, but our DNA doesn't match. Would you be willing to see if you're a match?"

"To save my daughter's life. Are you kidding? How much time do we have?"

A patrol car slowly, but deliberately, drove into the lower lot where they were parked. Unaware of its presence until the spot light startled them, the officer lowered his driver's side window and spoke, "This parking lot is closed. If you don't have business here or officially work for the Incline Village General Improvement District, you must leave."

"Yes, sir," Shane said respectfully.

"Have you been drinking?" the officer asked, shining his flashlight in the car, looking for contraband.

"No, sir, not a drop," Shane replied.

"Miss, may I see your license, insurance and registration."

Gina leaned over and opened the glove box, removing an insurance verification form and a registration receipt. She opened up her purse and handed him her license with the other documents. He got back in his car.

"You have any drugs in here?" Shane asked as quietly as possible.

"No, silly. It's me, Gina, remember? I'm a good girl."

"That's not what your dad says," Shane said sarcastically.

"You may have a point there," Gina said sighing.

"Okay, everything appears to be in order. You out here visiting from Oklahoma?" he asked.

"No, I just moved to Reno a short time ago," Gina replied, taking back her papers.

"Well, you'll need to get this car registered in Nevada and get a Nevada driver's license. If I see you again, I'll have to cite you," the officer said, leaning in the window.

"I understand. I will, thank you," Gina replied.

He got back in his car, waited for them to leave, and then followed them down to the corner of Fairway and Country Club.

"Where do you want to go?" Gina asked. "I really need to get home. Taylor is there by herself. Well, Missy is with her. But you know what I mean."

"Just take me home then. Can I call you tomorrow?"

"Taylor has radiation therapy at nine o'clock in the morning and I have to be at work at three. We should be home from the hospital around eleven. I'll give you a call when we get back. What is your number? Wait, I'll call your phone and then you'll have my number. I'll text you the info for the bone marrow screen," Gina said, checking her screen.

The lights were off when Shane arrived home. *I've been gone so long, they forgot to leave the porch light on.* He opened the screen door and slowly turned the knob for the front door. The weather stripping made a grating sound as it swept over the metal threshold. He took his shoes off and walked up the stairs in his socks. He walked stealthily past his parents' room, walking on the sides of the hall so the floor wouldn't squeak.

"Shane, how was the party?" Suzanne said, sticking her head through the door.

His heart skipped a beat. "You scared the heck out of me. I thought you were asleep." Collecting himself. "It was fun. Can I tell you about it in the morning?"

"Good night, I love you."

"I love you too, Mom."

———⚬⚬⚬———

The next morning:

"Hey, Shane, it's Dusty. Did I wake you? Chip gave me your number. I saw you last night dancing and stuff, but I didn't get a chance to talk to you? Who was the beautiful brunette you were hanging with?"

"That was Gina."

"Really, from before, Gina?"

"Yeah, she just moved back here from Tulsa."

"Tulsa, how'd she end up there?"

"She went to med school there. She's a doctor now."

"No kidding. Well, hey, would you like to hang out today? You want to meet me down at the Pub around, say noon, for lunch and a beer?"

"Sure, sounds good. Give me your cell while I have you on the phone."

—⟡—

Gina called around eleven. She just had gotten Taylor home and into bed to rest.

"Shane, would you like to come tomorrow afternoon to see us? Taylor should be feeling better by then. Maybe stay for dinner?"

His heart raced at the possibility of meeting his daughter. "I'd love that. Can I bring anything? Oh, what about the bone marrow screen?"

"I called Urgent Care and you can do the preliminary screening at the hospital there in Incline. Give them Taylor's name and my name. We're on file. If there's a problem, call me. The head nurse is Karen. I already told her you were coming by. I hope you don't mind. You can't imagine what this means to us."

—⟡—

"Shane, would you like some breakfast before I leave for work?"

"No, thanks, Mom. I have to go to the hospital to get checked to see if I am a possible donor."

"What? For who? For what?"

"We'll talk later. I gotta go."

"Is everything okay?"

"Mom, we'll talk later."

Karen was working the admittance window at the emergency entrance when Shane arrived. "Can I help you?"

"Yes, I believe Gina Conrad called regarding testing me to see if I am a possible donor for our, her daughter, Taylor."

"Yes, yes, she did. I have the paperwork right here. I need you to fill out these forms," she said, handing him a clipboard and a pen.

I hate sitting in the emergency area. Some ugly stuff comes in through here, he thought, hurrying down each page filling in blanks, signing, checking, and initialing. He handed the information back to the nurse and took a seat, tapping on the wooden arm of the chair in no particular rhythm.

Dr. Herman appeared through the double doors. "Please follow me. What have you eaten today?"

"Nothing yet."

"Are you taking any medications. Aspirin, supplements?"

"No."

"Do you have a fever, cold, or flu symptoms?"

"No. Nothing."

Dr. Herman put a clip on his finger and a thermometer under his tongue while he checked his blood pressure. "Ninety-five, good. Forty-five, are you an athlete? Your heart rate is very low. That is usually the sign of someone who works out regularly or has a heart problem."

"I take care of myself."

"And let's see. Your blood pressure is good, 110 over 70," the doctor said. "Have you given blood recently?"

"No."

"Have you traveled outside of the country in the last year?" he asked. "Have you given money or drugs for sex?"

"No."

"Have you had sex, even once, with another male?"

Shane chuckled, "No."

"Okay, you're going to feel a little sting," he said, slowly poking a needle into the large vein on his wrist. He filled three small syringes with blood and then covered the small hole with a Band-Aid after extracting the needle.

"Open your mouth and say ah." He took a swab and wiped the inside of his cheek to get a DNA sample.

"I understand that you are blood type, B-positive. Is that correct?" the doctor asked.

"I think so."

"We are done here for now. We will call you if need anything else."

"Thanks, Doc."

Shane walked out of the hospital feeling like a free man after serving a prison term. The warm morning sun hit his chest energizing him. *Wow, that feels good. It's always so cold in a hospital.* He walked down the eight wooden steps to his car in the lower lot and drove over to the Pub.

Marcy was behind the bar and her brother Nick was in the kitchen cooking. "Shane, what can I get you?" she asked as he appeared out of the sun and into the shadows of the restaurant. "I'm waiting for a buddy, but I'll take an iced tea while I'm waiting."

"Coming right up. Good game the other night," Marcy said, getting the drink.

"It was. I'm still getting used to slow pitch." Shane grabbed what was left of the daily news and sat down at a tall cocktail table a short distance away from the bar to read. Journey played from the digital jukebox hanging on the wall.

"Here ya go," she said, leaving a tall glass garnished with a lemon wedge and a straw on the table.

"Hey, Shane," Dusty said, emerging from the bright light outside.

"Hey, Dust," he said, shaking his hand. "Wow, you haven't changed, still wearing a bandana."

"You don't look much different either. What ya been doing?"

"Teaching. Just moved back here from Vegas. That was quite a party last night. I'm sure a lot of people are still in bed," Shane said. "So what about you? What are you doing? Girlfriend?"

"Nah, I live with a couple buddies out in North Reno. Golden Valley. Got a house on a about an acre. I'll have a New Castle," Dusty said, leaning over to get Marcy's attention.

"Okay, Dusty," Marcy responded.

"I'm doing some construction here in town, mostly just small stuff. The economy killed most of the new houses and big remodels we used to do."

"Who are you working with? Anyone from school?"

"Nah, it's just me and Bill. Sometimes, I work with my buddy Joe or Mike."

"So what else is going on?"

"Okay, what are you two having?" Marcy asked.

"Cheeseburger and fries," Shane said.

"Dust?" Marcy asked.

"Same."

"Well, I just got divorced. You been married?"

"Nah. I like living alone. The girls I've met are too needy. They want to know where I am all the time and are always making plans. After I work all day, I just want to come and relax."

"I know how you feel. I thought I might try to find a house in Reno. I applied for a teaching job down there and I really don't want to commute."

"Where are you staying now?"

"With my folks. I enjoy staying there, but it doesn't do much to boost my ego. It is what it is."

"You still playing ball?"

"A little. I started playing with Marcy, Kyle, Jake, Nick, and a couple of other people from town. The Pub sponsors a coed softball team. It's a lot of fun. You should play with us."

"I haven't thrown a ball since we graduated."

"It'll be fun. So what else you got going on? Maybe you'll meet a girl you can chill with."

"I'll see."

"That means no. Come on. I have an extra glove and you can play in your tennis shoes," Shane prodded.

"It's Monday and Wednesday nights, six o'clock, at Preston," Marcy said, chiming in.

"Dusty, ya gonna play some ball with us?" Nick asked as he brought out their food. "We come back here after, throw darts, drink, and wreck the place." Laughing. "Another beer, iced tea?"

"We're good, thanks," Shane said.

They finished their lunch and were blinded as they stepped out into the midday sun. "I'll see ya later, Dusty."

"You too. Later," Dusty said, getting in his car.

Shane drove home and assembled the rest of his paperwork for school. He dug out his taxes and character references from the Connections Academy. After he emptied his car, his bedroom became his filing cabinet and clothes closet. He said he had so little, but it sure took up a lot of space. He kept the door closed so his mother wouldn't have to see the mess. She did, though, when she came in once a week to get his laundry.

He was a neat-nick when he lived with Debbie and now he's overcompensating, she thought. "Hello, hello. Shane, I'm home."

"Up here, Mom."

Suzanne set her things on the dining room table, glanced through the small stack of mail, and walked upstairs. "How was your day?"

"Good. You're home early."

"I had a cancellation, so I moved my five o'clock to tomorrow. So tell me about this donor business. How was your reunion last night?"

"Well, let's see," he said, sitting down on his bed. Suzanne stepped over his lifestyle and sat down next to him. "Let me start with last night because that will answer some questions about today." He looked away from his mother and down at the papers in his hands. "They set up the Chateau just the way it was on grad night fifteen years ago. It was déjà vu. They had the same DJ, Bryn. Instead of a buffet, though, it was a sit-down dinner. It was good though." Suzanne leaned back on her hands to get more comfortable. "At our table, there was Chip and his wife Marsha, Kyle, and his wife Roberta, Maria, and her husband Rob, and then there was me and…Gina."

"Gina!"

"Yep," he said with a smile that told the whole story.

"Where did she come from? How is she? Oh, honey, you look so happy. So tell me what happened," she said, sitting back up, searching for eye contact.

He took a deep breath, preparing for a long explanation. "Well, she moved back from Tulsa and now she's living in Reno. She'd been living in Oklahoma since high school. She went to med school there and then became doctor."

"A doctor?" Suzanne said surprised.

"Family medicine. She's not married. I know you were going to ask me that. And…"

"And what?"

"And she has a daughter." He looked into his mother's eyes. "We have a daughter." Shane's lips crinkled as he spoke.

Suzanne's eyes watered immediately as she cupped her hands to her mouth. "A what? You have a daughter. How could that be?"

"She became pregnant after we had sex that last night at Whale Beach. The condom I had broke in my wallet, so we couldn't use it. She said it would be okay and not to worry. So in hindsight, we shouldn't have, but we had sex anyway. Her mother and father moved her out to Tulsa when they found out so no one would know. I guess, to save her reputation and protect her Dad's as well. They didn't tell anyone. Ally and Maria didn't even know."

"So she's got to be, what fourteen years old? Where is she?"

"Yeah, fourteen. They live in Reno. I'm planning on going to visit them tomorrow. Her name is Taylor, brown eyes, brown hair. Gina says she looks like me. I can't wait to see her," he said, choking with joy.

"I've always wanted to be a father, and I was and, I am. But, Mom, Gina said she has cancer."

"Who has cancer? Gina?"

"No, Taylor. She has lymphoma. She said it's stage three, whatever that is. I don't know anything about it. Do you?"

"Stage three sounds pretty advanced. I am not familiar with that type of cancer either."

"Gina says Taylor needs a bone marrow transplant if she is to survive, so I volunteered. That's why I went to the hospital today."

"You've already done it?"

"No, they just ran some preliminary tests to see if I'm compatible. They are going to check my DNA with hers and see if we match. The first thing they check is our blood types. If there is a match, they keep going."

"I'm a grandmother? I am a grandmother," Suzanne said, putting her hands on her chest.

"Yes, Mom, you are. I thought you'd be home late so I started dinner. Well, sort of, I have some chicken marinating and I cut up some veggies for a salad. What time do you think Dad will be home?"

"Shane, can I tell him everything? I am so excited. How about if your father and I get screened as well?"

"That would be awesome. If you're compatible, you may be able to help save your granddaughter's life. Anyway, first things first. I haven't even met Taylor yet."

Bill arrived home covered in dust. He took his shoes off outside and peeled his shirt off inside out. He leaned over the deck and brushed as much of the dirt out of his hair as he could. As he turned around, Suzanne grabbed him in a bear hug.

"We have a granddaughter!" she said, looking into his eyes as he tried to focus.

"What? That doesn't make any sense. What are you talking about?" he said, breaking the embrace.

"Bill, you're filthy. But I love you so much."

"I know. Let me take a shower and then we can talk," he said, taking his dirty jeans off and walking up the stairs in his boxers. He looked over at Shane who stood smiling as though he'd just won the lottery.

"Hurry."

Suzanne and Shane took turns relating the stories, past up to the present, while Bill sat in his armchair sipping a cold Coors Light.

"I'm a grandfather."

Chapter 24

Gina called just past eleven. Taylor and Missy were lounging out on the deck. Horses grazed in the distance as the morning shadows disappeared from the Virginia foothills. "Shane, hey, it's Gina."

"Hey. I, ah, so what's the plan?" he said, trying to contain his enthusiasm.

"Taylor is feeling great today. She's going down for her nap, so why don't you plan on around three o'clock. I'll text you the directions."

"Gina called. I'm going to head down around two thirty or so."

"Take a camera."

"Mom, I have my phone I can shoot with."

"Your camera takes better pictures, though."

"Got it," Shane said, running back up the stairs. *What am I going to do for the next three hours?* He grabbed some shorts and goggles, looking around his room for anything else that suggested an activity. "Mom, I'm going down to the rec center."

"You want some lunch first?"

"No, I'm okay. Bye."

Midday at the gym was busy. He checked the pool to see if any lanes were open. Three lanes were roped off with only one lap swimmer doing a backstroke. In the other half of the pool, an aquasize class for seniors was just starting. He went into the locker room, disrobed, got his swim shorts on, grabbed his goggles, and headed out to the pool. The room echoed with voices and music as the golden group swam and exercised. The eighty-two degree water felt cold to the touch as he slipped in, ducking below the surface and pulling his goggles on. Pushing of the side with his feet, he glided effortlessly forward and gradually began to stroke through the water, thinking about Gina. The past couple of days had been surreal. The fluid that surrounded him calmed his thoughts, breathing with each turn of his head. Four strokes, breathe, four strokes breathe, each flip turn was like the start of a new chapter, each lap a different page. Thirty-one, he counted, touching, turning, pushing, stroking, and looking down through the synthetic blue, striped in black tile. *I wonder if anyone has ever gotten a water rash from swimming too fast?*

He hopped out of the pool, pulled his goggles off, and headed carefully back into the locker room to shower. *Endless hot water, what a treat*, he thought. He toweled off and put on his gym shorts and t-shirt. Four elliptical machines sat empty. He stepped on, plugged in his headphones, and adjusted the resistance. He found a music-only channel and began a mellow cadence. He caught himself singing and looked around to see if anyone noticed him singing out of key. *I wonder how tall she is. I hope she likes me. What if she doesn't? Who was this other guy that was like a father to her?* He felt jealous.

He felt a tap on his shoulder. "Hey, if you're thinking about becoming a recording star, you'd better hang on to your day job," Kyle said, stepping onto the machine next to him.

"Oh, hey, Kyle, what's up?"

"How's Gina? Once you two hooked up, you tuned everyone else out."

"Sorry, we were just…" Shane stuttered.

"No, it's cool. You both were mesmerized. That's a good thing. It was nice to see you two together again. Have you seen her since?"

Shane pulled off the phones so he could hear. "I'm going down to her house this afternoon. Check this out. She has a daughter."

"And…" Kyle prodded.

"It's our daughter. I have a daughter. Do you believe it?"

"Really, how did that happen? You guys haven't seen each since high school, right?"

"Yep, she got pregnant that summer. Remember, her folks wouldn't let us see each other anymore? Well, that was part of the reason. The first reason being that we had sex," Shane said, lowering his voice to a whisper.

"No kidding? Wow, that's amazing. Have you seen her yet?"

"No, this afternoon. I'm so wound up I came down here to burn off some of whatever it is I'm feeling…. Anxious," Shane said, finding the word.

"I think that spot is clean," Bill said, walking up behind her and tapping her on the elbow. Suzanne turned the vacuum off.

"Oh my God, Bill, I'm so excited I don't know what to do with myself."

"You could repave the driveway."

"Oh, Bill, be serious. Something like this has never happened to us before. I feel like a new mother all over again." She grabbed Bill's arm and looked at him. "Remember bringing Shane home from the hospital that first day? I was so happy, and you were so proud. You installed a window shade for him that said 'Precious Cargo' and already a tiny mitt. You were so cute."

"His hair was plastered off the side of his head, what little he had. He smiled and laughed. He was such a happy baby. Do you think we'll get to meet her pretty soon?"

"Oh, Bill, I hope so. I hope she's not too sick."

Shane came bounding in the door, tossing his gym clothes in the laundry room. "Hey, guys, what ya doing?" he said, finding them staring at him.

They looked at each other. "Well, not much. Your father just suggested I repave the driveway, but I think he should reshingle the roof." Bill chuckled.

"We are both a little nervous, anxious for you and we were… when are you leaving?" Suzanne asked.

"Gina said three. So giving myself time for possible traffic, maybe around two-thirty."

Shane ran upstairs, skipping every other step. He showered again, found a clean pair of shorts, a golf shirt, and sandals.

"Well, how do I look? Would you call me Dad?" he said sarcastically, extending his arms for hugs.

"I hope everything goes well. Take it slow. I love you."

"Me too, son."

"Thanks, Pops."

Shane pulled his sunglasses down, checked himself in the mirror, and started the Jetta up. He felt like he was going on his first date. He wiped his teeth with his finger and checked for any food deposits. The afternoon wind was just beginning to pick up as he pulled out on to the highway. Two cyclists were making their way up to the summit and waved as he passed. *I wonder who that was*, he thought. He turned the music up. He set the cruise control to fifty-three, not wanting to drawn any attention from the Nevada Highway Patrol that tend to hide off to the side of the road, ready to cite spaced out unsuspecting motorists like himself. He took a deep breath. He thought of Debbie back in Vegas. She's probably playing tennis today. Or is today her shopping day. He shook his head. He thought of Scott sitting behind his desk doing *his job. Thank you for releasing me.* A young buck ran across the highway, its horns still covered with the fur of youth. *That was a brave and stupid thing to do,* he thought. *Young and dumb, where's your mother?* Thoughts swirled around him until he noticed he'd forgotten that he was driving and needed to pay attention. *The cops could pull me over for drunk driving*, as his tires thumped over the ridges next to the fog line. He checked his mirror for a red light. Another deep breath, he let the air out slow and steady as he took the hairpin turn at the summit. The parking lot was full. Lots of hikers out today. He brought his eyes back to the road. A cyclist came up on his left. *There's no real bike lane. I wouldn't be caught dead riding up that direction. Dead, that's what I'd be. Tagged by some guy's mirror or something. Oops, eyes back to what I'm doing. Maybe I should stop at Raley's and get some flowers for her, for them, a Barbie. She's too old to play with dolls. What do you get a girl you've never met before?* Braking late, the tires squealed around the turn. He checked his mirror, no red lights.

Twenty minutes later, he pulled into the Raley's parking lot, feeling like he'd had one cup too many of coffee. He shook his arms as he exited the car. Flowers. Which bouquet, though? A plant? Roses, ah, no. Hydrangeas. They're beautiful. A bouquet is better. Lots of color. He selected a medium bunch from the cooler, smelled them for no particular reason, and headed to the checkout stand. Back in the car, he took another deep breath, realizing this was the final stretch before he got to the house. He flipped down the mirror, checked his nose for hairs, eyes, teeth... still good.

His leg bones felt stiff as he walked up to the porch. *I look like a husband in retribution, standing here with these flowers.* He rang the bell. Gina approached in the shadows through the window. The perspiration came out of every pour as she opened the door.

"Hey, you. Those are so pretty, thank you," she said, giving him a tender kiss on the cheek. "Taylor, company." Missy walked up to Gina's ankles, her paws clicking on the hardwood.

"This is Missy."

"Hi, girl," he said stiffly. "Play fetch?" *That was dumb.*

Taylor had been in her bathroom putting the final touches on her eye makeup. She walked around the corner from the hall with her hand extended.

"Hello." Her eyes were bright and her smile charming and natural. She tossed her curly hair back over her shoulders.

Shane lost his composure. Lips quivering and watery eyes, "I'm Shane." Gina brought her free hand to her mouth as tears splashed off her fingers. "I'm your father." Taylor stood motionless, still shaking his hand as he put his other hand on top of hers and pulled her slowly to his chest. "You're beautiful."

"Shane, Taylor, let's go into the living room," she said, wiping her nose.

Gina opened the hutch in the dining room, located a cut glass vase, and went into the kitchen to arrange the flowers.

"So how do you like Nevada?" Shane said, staring at her and wiping his eyes. "Excuse me for staring. This is all very new to me." Missy quietly lay down next to his feet.

She looked down at Missy and then back up. "That's okay. I like Reno all right."

The phone rang. Gina took it in the kitchen. "Mom?"

"Your father and I have got to pick up a few things in Reno, and we thought we'd stop by if Taylor is feeling up to it. How about we fix you two dinner?"

"I have company."

Lacy was surprised. "Your girlfriends? We can pick up a little extra food. That's not a big deal."

"Mom, Shane's here."

Her face went pale as she looked at Mike to see if he heard what she said.

"What is it, Lacy?"

Speaking back into the phone, whispering, "What's he doing there? You told him about Taylor?" She covered the receiver. Mike came to attention.

"Mom, I don't want to talk about this right now. I'll call you later," she said, embarrassed at the intrusion. "Bye."

"She hung up. Shane is at the house."

"We need to start doing some damage control. At some point, the cat is going to get out of the bag. I don't think Gina realizes the consequences of what she is doing," Mike said, looking at his wife.

"Mike, this was inevitable. Gina shared with me, with us, that moving back here was partially motivated by the feelings she still had for Shane. Though we tried to snuff it, that candle never burned out."

"That was Mom. She and Dad were going to stop by. I told them you were here."

"I'm sorry. I didn't know. I guess, I hoped that they had changed," Shane said as Gina walked in with the flowers.

"I love all the color," taking a deep breath. "They smell so good."

"Shane," Taylor said, taking a deep breath of the fragrances as well. "Mom says you are a teacher. That's cool. What grade do you teach?"

He looked at Gina. It took a moment before he could speak. "I teach mostly senior level students, some juniors, English, math, science, subjects like that. What are your favorite subjects?"

"I like English. And I like poetry and reading. I write a little. I keep a journal, but I haven't been very good about writing in it. Since I got sick, I write more, though. I've noticed that I tend to write more when I'm sad, like songs, poetry, and stuff like that."

"That's true. It's a common theme. To go to the extreme, sometimes, it takes a tragedy to get people in touch with their deep feelings, values, and choices. Some of the best songs are blues tunes. A broken heart, your dog dies, you lose your job. Sounds like a country western song." He laughed, nervously.

"Would you like to read some things I've written?"

"I would be honored."

"Shane would you like something cold to drink? Beer, soda, water? How about you, Taylor?"

"Mom, can I have a Hansen's?" she asked, getting up and going to her bedroom.

"Shane?"

"A cold beer would be great," he said, looking at Gina, her short hair and dazzling eyes. "You look awesome."

"Thanks, you're sweet," she said shyly over her shoulder from the kitchen.

"My blood type matches," he volunteered. "I hope the rest is a match as well. How did your tests go?"

"I didn't tell Taylor yet, but Mom and I aren't compatible. I was close they said, but it has to be spot on. DNA is so complicated."

"Tell me what?" Taylor asked, reappearing in the hall. She had a small stack of papers and a notebook in her hand.

"Here," she said, handing the bundle to Shane.

"Can I take these home and read them?"

"Sure. Tell me what, Mom?"

Shane looked at Gina, suggesting with his eyes that she tell her the truth. "Gramma and I are the same blood type as you, but our DNA doesn't match so we can't be donors. I'm sorry, honey. We'll find someone, you'll see."

Taylor froze and became quiet.

Shane noticed her change and quickly spoke. "Taylor, I went in for a screening yesterday. So far, it looks good. Our blood types match. My Mom and Dad want to go in too."

"Really," Gina said, totally surprised and grateful. "I love your Mom and Dad."

"Mom was so excited to hear about Taylor. Dad too," he said, looking at Gina. "Taylor, you have to meet my parents. You'll like them."

Gina looked at Taylor and changed the subject, "Taylor and I love to cook together. Tonight, we have a pot roast, potatoes, and veggies. They've been cooking all day in the Crock-Pot."

"I was wondering what that smell was. Glade should make an air freshener that smells like home cooking."

Taylor chuckled. *Score one*, Shane thought. "Whenever you're hungry, we can eat. Taylor made an apricot pie for desert, so be prepared to get stuffed."

"Well,…ah, Gina, how do you like practicing family medicine?"

"I love it. It is so hands on. It's a wonderful blend of science and counseling. I'm new here, of course, but my clients are like family. It is such a great profession."

"I want to be a doctor too," Taylor said softly. "I enjoy children. They are so precious and innocent when they are sick."

"Nice, so you want to be a pediatrician?" Shane said as Gina leaned forward and gave her a hug.

"We just have to get through this. One step at a time. I am so grateful for the support so many people have given us," Gina said as Taylor withdrew and lowered her head.

"Gina, whatever you need. I'm here now," he said, reaching for her hand. Her lips started to quiver as she put her head on his chest. He lightly stroked her neck and rubbed her back.

"That feels so good," she said, sitting back up moments later. "We may come up for church tomorrow. I'll have to call Mom first. Dad'll probably ask us not to come now." Shane rolled his eyes and shook his head. "Dinner?" Gina asked.

"Let's eat outside, Mom."

"What can I do?" Shane asked, standing up.

Gina put her hands on her legs and stood up. She walked into the kitchen, followed by Taylor and Shane. She opened a cabinet, counted out three dinner plates, and handed them to Shane.

"Silverware?" Shane asked.

"In that drawer there, napkins are the next one down."

Taylor found a fat round candle, two wine glasses, filled a water glass, and left through the sliding door for the backyard. Shane watched her, leaned over, and gave Gina a soft kiss on her ear.

"Ooo, that tickles." She turned around, holding the clay Crock-Pot and kissed him back. "Let's go."

Shane followed her out. Taylor lit the candle and returned for the bottle of wine.

"Taylor, grab the bowl of bread. Thanks."

Gina went back for the salad and a wine opener. "Here's to family and friends," she said, raising her glass. A gaggle of quail lifted off unexpectedly, startling them.

"It's so peaceful out here." He watched a small group of horses wander through the sage a distance away. They raised their heads at the sound of the quail lifting off. A mare, her foal, and two other horses walked up to the cyclone fence. They snorted and stood watching them. "Amazing, I love this." The still air changed color from pastel blue to yellows and oranges as the sun slowly disappeared over the Mount Rose Ski area. Sally and Leon's horse next door hung his head over the wooden fence watching the mustangs. The beagles barked at its feet.

"Save some room for my pie," Taylor said.

"Maybe we should eat that first," Shane said, looking around for a consensus.

Gina scooped out the pot roast and passed the plates around, putting a small amount on Taylor's.

"Salad?" Shane took a portion and passed the bowl to Taylor. She took a small helping and set it down in front of Gina.

"Shane, what is your favorite kind of food?" Taylor asked, creating conversation in the midst of brief silence.

Shane sounds so, I don't know. I wish she'd call me dad...in due time. Two strangers meeting and I don't know, I...

"Shane, Taylor was talking to you."

"Sorry, oh, I like Italian, Mexican. You know, Taylor, I like everything but liver and lima beans." She laughed.

"He's funny, Mom," Taylor said. Shane smiled.

They finished their dinner and Shane helped Gina clear the dishes. Taylor sat watching the final rays of the day fade into gray blue shadows dotted with streetlights. The candle lit her face in orange and black. Gina watched her through the kitchen window while she dished out the pie. Shane tenderly turned Gina around and held her.

"Thanks for a wonderful dinner. Gina, I…" He couldn't finish.

"I know," she said, putting a finger to his lips. "Shsssh."

They each took a plate and joined Taylor at the table. "No pie?" Shane asked Gina.

"It makes her fat," Taylor said, interrupting.

"This is delicious. Bravo," Shane said.

"I love to bake," Taylor said.

"Well, I have a big sweet tooth, so we have something in common."

The warm air was so comfortable. Taylor slid back in her chair and surveyed Shane.

"We look like each other," Taylor said, looking at this new man. "I think your nose is bigger than mine, but same ears. I like your eyes." She looked at her mother. "Same eyes."

"What are you doing tomorrow?" Gina asked.

"Gosh, I don't know. Would you like to go for a bike ride or a hike?" Shane looked at Taylor. "How about you? What would you like to do?"

"Go to a movie."

"Really, which one?"

"Oh, it doesn't matter…*Brave, Batman*," Taylor responded.

He looked at Gina. She smiled. "We'll see. It's bedtime, my little darling."

"It was nice to meet you," Taylor said, standing up.

Shane started extending his hand and then brought both arms up to give her a hug. He held her and kissed the top of her head. "I am so grateful to know that you are in my life."

He released her.

"Come, Missy," Taylor said, walking down the hall.

Gina stood and took Shane's hand in hers. "She's a wonderful girl, Shane."

"She has a wonderful mother." The candlelight flickered off their faces under a half moon hanging in a cloudless sky.

"Would you like to go inside? The bugs are starting to attack," she said, brushing away a mosquito.

He took her hand and led her into the living room. He found a comfortable spot on the sofa while she searched for a program on the TV.

"Put on a music channel, so we can talk without a distraction."

She located a soft rock station, set the clicker on the coffee table, and lay back against him, pulling his arms around her.

Cheek to cheek, Shane asked her, "Gina, are your folks ever going to accept me?"

"We're thirty-two years old. It's not up to them. I can't change them and neither can you. You're a good man, Shane Kaufmann. I thought when Dad went through his prostate cancer scare he would be a different person, a nicer person. I think he's more bitter. He's lucky to be alive, but it left him impotent, according to Mother. She said it made him resentful."

"When was that?"

"It was about nine or ten years ago. When he met my friend Daniel, all he saw were the tattoos and not the man. Here he is preaching the Bible while he lives hypocritically. I can't put things in perspective with him. Mom sees it, but doesn't say anything. They won't talk to me and avoid anything to do with the subject." She clenched her jaw. "She loves him so much that she endures the paradox that is obvious to the rest of us. He appeared relieved at not being a match the other day during the screening. I believe he thinks that Taylor's cancer is God's way of punishing us for our sins! It's so messed up!... Excuse me."

"You have got to be kidding. If that is true, that is probably the reason he got cancer as well, right in the rear end where he deserved it."

"Please don't talk like that. He is a good man. Are you rolling your eyes? I know when you do that, you know."

"What can I do to help you now? I can tell how hard this has been on you. Taylor is amazing, her smile, her attitude, she seems so optimistic, happy."

"She has her moments as do I. We have been quite a team. She met a real nice boy from Raley's. He helped us through one of those moments while in the store. It's funny how things turn out."

"She takes after you. You have a positive outlook. You're independent, strong. Yet you're nourishing, kind, and compassionate. I admire that about you."

"Ah, thanks. I adore you, Shane." She turned her head and kissed him on his cheek. They sat quietly in the shadows, the room backlit from the light in the kitchen, staring out at the moon.

"I've thought about those nights at Whale Beach. They've been with me for years, your eyes reflecting the moonlight, the soft hush of the water on the sand."

"You're such a romantic. You are one of a kind. Have you done any writing?" Gina asked, pulling his arms tighter.

"A little, not much really. Not to blame Debbie, but our home life was not conducive to deep thought. At school, the students were my main priority, and the environment was a distraction. I wrote you a couple of poems in the letters I sent, that you never received. I should have kept them, but they were a bitter reminder of a loss I wasn't able to rationalize."

"You wrote me a poem? How sweet."

"Roses are red, violets are..."

"Oh, come on, be serious."

"I am. *Violets are purple, sugar is sweet and so is maple surple,*" he said, chuckling.

She playfully slapped his hand.

"I've got a bit of a drive. I'm going to call it an evening. I'll check with you tomorrow. Taylor said she may be up for movie."

"It will depend on how she feels, Shane. I know she's excited to spend time with you, but she needs to rest and stay as strong as possible."

Gina peeled herself off Shane and stood up, adjusting her shorts. Shane pressed himself up from the arm of the sofa and brushed off. Gina took his hand and led him to the front door. He turned and hugged her gently; tenderly, he touched her chin, bringing her lips to his. He shook his head in disbelief.

"Gina," he whispered. "Thanks for a wonderful evening."

She didn't speak. Tears slowly emerged as she closed the door on a beautiful night.

Shane followed the moon back over Mount Rose. The road wound through the dark shadows of the pine trees, lit only by the Jetta's headlights. If it weren't for the seat belt, he would have floated out of the car. Elation. His mind embraced every sent, every word, their smiles, their eyes. He didn't realize how big his smile was until he checked his rear-view mirror looking for approaching vehicles. The lake shimmered in white moonlight as he made his descent back into Incline. Glancing quickly into his headlights, a lone coyote crossed the highway up ahead, out for an evening hunt. Shane's mother and father were asleep when he got home. He turned off the lights and covertly made his way upstairs. Stepping over a folded pile of his cleanest dirty clothes, he rolled into bed and tucked his hands behind his head. Staring at the ceiling, he drifted off, still floating.

Chapter 25

he cotton-tailed rabbits nibbled at the lawn as the sun lifted its morning colors above the Virginia foothills. Gina watched through the kitchen window, washing out the coffeemaker, preparing to make a fresh pot. She cut up strawberries, cantaloupe, and grapes, added some raisins and granola and set the bowl on the counter. The rabbits froze, their ears at attention as she moved passed the window. Missy laid by the sliding door nonchalantly, watching a few quail with their sophisticated black headdresses forage for food. Gina walked over to the door, her bare feet sticking to the hardwood floor.

"Missy, do you want to go outside? Come on, let's go outside," she said, opening the garage door and then the side door to the dog run. She filled her bowl with water and poured some fresh kibble into another bowl. She closed the outside door with its doggie door and returned to the garage. As she reentered the house, she saw Taylor standing at the counter, eating a strawberry with her fingers.

"Good morning," Gina said, smiling.

"Hi, Mom. Did Gramma call? Are we going to church today?"

"No, I need to call her. Thanks for reminding me. Can I fix you something besides fruit?"

Missy started barking at the back fence when the neighbor's cat walked passed as though she owned the yard. The girls looked up to see the dog on her hind legs and front paws up against the cyclone fence.

"Good girl," Gina said almost to herself. "You get that mean 'ol cat out of here so he doesn't scare the birds and rabbits."

"Fruit is fine," Taylor said, taking a small bowl, walking into the living room, lifting her feet up on the coffee table, and searching the TV channels for something to watch.

Gina poured herself a cup of coffee, added a little cream, and sat down next to Taylor with the phone in her hand.

"There's nothing on but golf. Some tournament from England and another from Tahoe," Taylor said, setting the changer down.

"It's the celebrity event they hold every year. Isn't the lake beautiful? I heard Ray Romano is playing and the guy from *Fresh Prince of Bel Air*, Alfonso Ribiero, oh, and Michael Jordan. Not interested?"

"Not really. Golf and baseball on TV are boring. It's like watching grass grow. You know, I like Shane. He is a nice guy. He's my dad? That is so strange. I feel like I've known him my whole life."

"That's the kind of person he is. He appeared to be quite fond of you too. He's always wanted children. His first wife couldn't have any."

"Would you ever have any more?"

"Oh, I don't know. When I was around my girlfriends and their kids back in Tulsa, sometimes, I thought about it. I think I'm getting too old now."

"No, you're not. You are in great shape, perfect health."

"Thanks, honey, but let's change the subject."

The phone rang next to her leg. She picked it up setting her coffee down.

"Hi, Mom."

"Tell me about Shane."

"Well, good morning to you too," Gina said. "….He's been in town for a while. I'm surprised you haven't seen him. He moved back from Vegas around the middle or end of June."

"I don't know if I would recognize him now. How did he find you?"

"Oh, it was some great detective work, let me tell you," Gina said. "Ally and Maria ran into him over the Fourth of July at the Lion's pancake breakfast. He was with his folks. You remember his mom and dad, don't you?"

"Yes, we've seen each other now and again, but we haven't talked."

"What a shame. Anyway, after I called Ally about the invitation I received from her to the reunion, I found out that he was in town. We saw each other for the first time since that summer after high school at the reunion."

"Why was he in Las Vegas?"

"His wife was from there. He had a teaching job. He got divorced, quit his job, and came back here because he loves the mountains. It was fate that we found each other again."

"Yes, of course, fate," she said. "Your father is very upset. You know how he feels about him. Don't do anything you'll regret."

"What? Regret what? This has nothing to do with you. The only regret I have is letting you two run my life. That's over. I have a career, a beautiful daughter and, yes thanks to you, I was able to get this house," Gina said, raising her voice.

"Your father would like to speak to you," she said as Mike grabbed the phone out of her hand.

"Listen here."

"What, Dad. What are you going…"

"I did things for your own good. Don't forget that. All you think about is yourself and that daughter of yours."

"Excuse me. That's just not true. I have tried to talk to you and Mom, but you won't listen," Gina reminded him.

The sky rumbled as the trees shook their leaves. The rabbits took off for cover under the deck, anticipating the coming rain. Scared, Missy ran back in the garage, whimpering at the door. Taylor got up and let her in. The rain came down like a liquid fist, pounding the ground in torrents. Missy watched through the sliding door, grateful to be inside. Gina held the phone away. While the storm echoed outside, she contemplated a response.

"Dad, contrary to belief, God loves every one. I pray that you come to accept Shane, Taylor, and me for who we are. I am so sad when you are like this. It is so destructive." Crying. "I truly believe...I think that you must let your judgments go if we are to be a whole family. I wanted to come up for church today, I can't listen to you preach what you fail to follow. Good-bye."

"Let me talk to her again."

"She hung up."

"I wish you wouldn't be so hard on her. I hope we can resolve this. I am so upset," Lacy said, turning and going to their bedroom.

Taylor leaned over the back of the sofa and hugged her mother. "I love you so much," Gina said.

"I love you too, Mom. It'll be okay."

Taylor went back to her room to lie down. Gina busied herself cleaning the house. Missy found her favorite spot by the sliding door. Music played softly in the background.

"Gina, this is Dr. Hansen. We have the results of Shane Kaufmann's screen and he is a perfect match."

Gina's mouth dropped open and she tried to catch her breath. She put the phone to her chest. "Taylor, Shane is a match." Softer to herself, "Shane is a match."

Taylor came bolting out of her room as though the house were on fire. "Mom, really? I'm going to make it. I'm going to live. The phone hung limp in Gina's hand as the voice on the other end waited to provide them with more information.

"I'm sorry," she said, wiping her eyes and nose with the back of her hand. Taylor held on with both hands to Gina's free elbow, tears dripping down her cheeks and over her smile.

"Please bring Taylor in immediately," Dr. Hansen said.

Gina hung up and held Taylor in her arms. Overcome with joy and fear, they started packing a small suitcase.

"This may be worse than anything you've experienced so far, but you'll get through it. We'll focus on the light at the end of the tunnel."

Payton, the head nurse on duty, met them. They filled out a registration form and then were escorted down the hall. Dr. Lippert walked into Taylor's room, clipboard in hand, and went over what she was to expect.

Speaking to both of them, "This is an allogeneic bone marrow transplant, which means stem cells will be removed from the donor, Shane Kaufmann, and then injected into your blood, similar to a blood transfusion. The cells then travel through your blood to your marrow. First, we must, unfortunately, give you very high doses of radiation and chemotherapy to kill the cancer cells. This is the toughest part of the transplant procedure. You will experience nausea, chills, itching, vomiting, all the symptoms you've dealt with during your regular treatments, but worse. "

"Mom, I'm scared," she said with a frightened look on her face. "I hate being sick. It's going to hurt."

"I'll be right here," she said, squeezing her hand, holding her head to her breast.

The nurses began prepping Taylor for chemotherapy, a familiar ritual. Gina left the room and called her mother.

"Mom, I'm at Renown. Taylor is going in for the bone marrow transplant. They are preparing to give her chemo now."

"They found a donor?"

"Yes, it's Shane, her father," she said proudly, staring at the pictures on the wall. "Mom, I am so scared. The chemo and radiation are going to knock the heck out of her. Her recovery will be arduous. So many things could go wrong. Please pray for her," she said, weeping.

———❦———

"Shane Kaufmann?"

"No, this is Bill Kaufmann. Who is this?"

"This is Dr. Hansen from Dr. Lippert's office. Is Shane available?"

"Why, yes, just a moment." Bill knocked on Shane's door and carefully made his way into the bedroom. "Shane, it's some doctor on the phone for you," he said, handing him the receiver.

"Hello, this is Shane."

"Shane Kaufmann, this is Dr. Hansen from Dr. Lippert's office, Taylor Conrad's oncologist." Fear swept over his body making his skin crawl.

"What's wrong? Is Taylor okay?"

"We have completed your screening and you are a match. We need to get you down to Renown Hospital as soon as possible so we can begin the procedure. It's important to get this started before her platelets drop. How soon can you get here?" Dr. Hansen asked.

"Is an hour and half or two hours soon enough? I have to drive down from Incline."

"That will be fine. Check in at the emergency entrance and you'll be directed by the nurse on duty. Drive carefully. We don't want to lose you."

"Mom! Pops! I'm a match! They want to start right away," he said, flying up out of bed, almost doing a face plant into his pile of clothes.

Bill and Suzanne arrived at his door at the same time and tried to squeeze in at once. "That is wonderful news. I am so thankful. I was so worried," Suzanne said, pushing her way ahead of Bill.

"So what happens now?" Bill said over her shoulder.

Shane was having a leg fight with his pants while trying to pull his t-shirt on at the same time. "I don't know. I forgot to ask."

"I'll drive you down just in case you can't drive later. Bill, is that all right with you?"

"I wish I didn't have to work today, I'd go down with you."

"Shane, pack a toothbrush, deodorant, and a change of clothes. Bill, what else do you think he'll need?"

"Don't know," he said with a blank stare on his face.

Payton showed Shane and his mother to a room at the other end of the hall from Gina and Taylor. He got undressed and had Suzanne help him into the familiar hospital gown. "Oh, this is stylish. I feel so stupid with my butt hanging out."

"Nobody here but me, and believe me, I've seen it before."

Dr. Hansen came in with a nurse to go over the course of action before they started. "We are going to give you an anesthesia, which will put you to sleep while we draw marrow from your hip bone. You will not feel anything, but you may experience nausea, possibly vomiting when you awaken. Do you have any questions?"

"How long before we know Taylor is better?" Gina asked.

"It is a dangerous process. While Taylor's bone marrow is gone, she is susceptible to infections, and if her platelets get too low, it can cause dangerous bleeding. She may need several blood transfusions to combat these problems while the stem cells are growing. It may be a long process," Dr. Hansen replied

"Mike, I want to go down to the hospital and be with Gina. I'm a nervous wreck. I can't just sit here and wait for the phone to ring. She needs our support." Mike pulled her into his arms and held her, showing the first sign of concern.

"I understand. I think you should go too. I will pray for them," he said. "I ah…"

"Mike? I love you," she said, searching his eyes.

—◦◦◦—

Gina went down to the waiting room at the end of the hall. The *Jerry Springer Show* was on the TV. *What a great program to get one's mind off anything important*, she thought. A young woman on the show, expecting her boyfriend of several years was going to propose to her on national TV, discovered that he was coming out of the closet to profess his love for a male partner. Gina laughed and looked around at the other people waiting for news of their loved ones. "Some people will do anything for fifteen seconds of fame," she said.

After Shane was escorted out of his cubicle and into a surgery room, Suzanne slowly walked down the hall, entering the same waiting area as Gina. Gina was busy watching more nonsense unfold when Suzanne sat down a few chairs away.

"Gina? Gina, is that you?" Suzanne asked surprised.

"Suzanne!" She ran to her arms and wept uncontrollably. Suzanne's tears came as well.

"I didn't recognize you. You cut your hair. It's adorable. How are you?" she said, speaking nose to nose.

"Thank you so much for Shane. He's saving Taylor's life." Crying, she buried her head in her breast and sobbed.

"It's okay now. It's okay," she said, consoling her. "I've missed you, my dear. Everything is going to be okay." They stood for a long moment in each other's arms. Suzanne took Gina's hand and they sat down together. "How is Taylor doing? I've never seen her. Do you have a picture of her?"

"I've have several on my iPhone, just a sec here," she said, scrolling through her gallery. "Here's one."

It was a picture of her in Puerto Vallarta standing next to a statue on the Malacon. She flipped the screen sideways and enlarged the photo.

"My heavens, she's beautiful. Brown eyes, long brown curly hair, olive skin, she looks like both of you."

"I think she looks more like Shane."

"She has your wide-set eyes and smile. Lovely."

Gina slowly went through a collage of photographs, explaining where she was and what she was doing at the time. "We lived in the midwest all of her life. The lake and these beautiful mountains are all new to her."

"Shane said you're living here in Reno. How do you like that?"

"Mom and Dad cosigned for me on a house on Virginia Avenue, just off Toll Road. I like it. We like it a lot. It's on a half acre, almost an acre, zoned for horses. The air is so clean and there is very little traffic. Lots of wild animals, quail, rabbits, horses. You should see the horses. They come right up to our fence. One morning, there were eleven of them feeding just outside our window. Suzanne, they are so beautiful, and the young colts are adorable. There are so many quail. They are everywhere. They coo like chickens. When startled, they lift off like a huge air force. I dropped Shane off at your house after the reunion. It still looks the same."

"Some things never change. It's small, but Bill and I love it. We enjoy the simple life, always have. Are you hungry? Shall we go up to the cafeteria and get something to eat? The food in these vending machines doesn't look too appetizing."

"Taylor is going to be going through chemo for a while. Sure, it'll take my mind off things," Gina said, picking up her purse.

They took the elevator to the second floor. Turning right, the clatter of dishes and silverware led them to the dining area.

Meanwhile, Lacy parked and went through the main entrance to the information desk. "What room is Taylor Conrad in?"

"We show her in chemotherapy. You are not allowed in there. However, there is a waiting area right here," she said, pointing to the map. It was a long walk to that wing of the hospital. She passed a little gift shop and stopped in to get some flowers. *This is like walking down a terminal at the airport*, she thought. A few nervous-looking people sat in the waiting room. She imagined they must have loved ones in the emergency room. *I hate hospitals.*

She sat down wondering where Gina might be. *Maybe she's in the restroom.* Gina and Suzanne appeared just as she was about to call.

"Gina, how are you, honey?" she said, hugging her. As she released her embrace, she saw Suzanne who stood patiently waiting to say hello. "Hello, Suzanne. Thank you so much. It's been a long time," she said, extending her hand. Suzanne ignored her gesture and hugged her hello.

"You have a very special daughter. I know this is difficult for you, but together, we will get through this."

Payton interrupted them. "Taylor is out of chemo and on her way to radiation. We will begin the next series of treatments in about an hour."

"Can we see her?" Lacy asked.

"Yes, but she's pretty ill right now. She needs to get some rest before we start again. We will let you know when she's able to have company. It shouldn't be too long," Payton said.

"What about Shane?" Suzanne asked.

"I'll check with Dr. Hansen and get back to you. He is probably going to be out for another two hours or so."

"Lacy, you look good. How have you been?" Suzanne said.

"Very well, thanks. Suzanne, I want to apologize for the way I've acted." Her eyes tearing up. "All these years I've wasted trying to cover up something that…" Lacy said, her voice cracking.

"It's all water under the bridge. We're here now. We need to be strong for Taylor."

"I feel so stupid. You have a wonderful son." Gina held her mother's hand. "I just want you to know how grateful I am, we are, for what he is doing." Gina watched Suzanne. "I have been so blind. I am so sorry. Please forgive me." Suzanne's lips began to twist as she fought back her tears.

"I forgive you, Lacy. I forgive you. We need to move on," she whispered softly, leaning over and hugging her.

Dr. Hansen came in, looking for Suzanne. "Shane is resting comfortably. We'll let you know when he regains consciousness and then you can visit. We made a small incision on his left hip. He'll have to stay off that leg for a couple of days, but he'll be fine."

"Thank you, Doctor."

It was more than two and half hours before Shane was coherent enough to see his mother. All three of them joined him. He was sitting up in bed when they arrived. "Hi, honey, how are you feeling?" Gina said reaching him first. "I love you so much." He held her, his head resting on hers as she leaned over the bed. Lacy and Suzanne stood back. Suzanne held Lacy's hand. As Gina sat up, her mother inched forward, apprehensive, but determined.

She brought her face close to his and caressed his check with her hand. "Shane, I don't know what to say. Thank you so much." Tears. "You are such a good man." He wrapped his arms around her, looking at Gina and Suzanne. "I am so sorry for what we've put you through."

Tenderly. "It's okay. I am so thankful I could help."

"You, you saved her life. There is no greater gift."

"How are you feeling?" Suzanne asked.

"A little queasy. I feel like a piece of toast."

"How's that? All crispy and burnt?" Gina said, dabbing her eyes. He laughed.

"I'll have the nurse bring you something," Suzanne said

"Please, no Jell-o."

The nurse brought Shane some crackers and a ginger ale. He lay on the gurney for a short time longer before the nurse said he was okay to leave. He got dressed and met his mother, Lacy, and Gina down in the waiting room.

"How's Taylor doing? Have you heard anything?" Shane asked as he found a seat.

"She's done with the radiation. She will have to wait a couple of days before they can start the transfusion. They said they'd keep us posted. She's resting now," Gina said.

Gina and Lacy went into her room in the early evening. She was sitting up, sipping water from a straw. A light by her bed was on. "Hey, honey, how are you feeling?" Gina said, tenderly tapping her hand. She was gaunt and pale. There was a bowl by her pillow in case she felt sick to her stomach. Her eyes were a light green with red around the edges. Her ashen lips barely opened to admit the straw. Her sore nostrils matched her eyes. Gina pushed the fear back down her throat as Lacy walked to the other side of the bed, lowering the guardrail.

"Hi, Gramma," she said, mumbling, not removing the straw.

"Taylor," she said, gently caressing her face. "The doctor said you are doing fine. Because you are young and strong, you are in excellent shape for the rest of the procedure. Can we get you anything?"

She shook her head and then, "Cheeseburger, fries, and a large Coke," she said with a lisp. She smiled.

Gina and Lacy joined her bright-eyed. "That's my girl."

Shane wedged his way in followed by Suzanne. "Hi, how are you doing? This is your other grandmother, Suzanne."

I'm her grandmother. I forgot. She's just been Shane's daughter up until now, she thought. Her eyes watered as she met this frail figure for the first time. She held her hand as Gina moved to the side, hugging Shane.

"Hi there, I'm Suzanne. I am so thrilled to meet you." Taylor let a faint smile appear and signaled she was done with the water. Suzanne put it back on her tray and gently sat down next to her on the bed. Surrounded by her two grandmothers, her eyes went from right to left and back again.

"I'm sorry to disturb you, but she really must get some rest," the nurse said, softly interrupting. "You may come in to visit tomorrow morning after eight. We will continue to monitor her vitals. If anything changes, we will contact you immediately. Please leave your phone numbers at the nurse's station if you have not already done so."

Lacy and Suzanne each gave her a kiss on the cheek. Shane stepped between them as they left and held Taylor's hand. "I'll always be with you. Sleep tight," he said, leaning over and kissing her forehead.

Gina anguished over leaving her. She held Taylor until the nurse asked her to let her sleep. She kissed her lightly on the lips, smoothed her hair around her face, and hugged her good night. Taylor was fast asleep before she left the room.

—∿∿∿—

As Taylor recovered from her extensive treatments over the next two days, she began to spend more time with the family. It was difficult at first to keep any solid food down. The IV remained intact, feeding her slowly with nutritional fluids. Lacy kept Mike abreast of the situation by phone. She and Suzanne were becoming friends. They shared lunch together at Bertha Miranda's and talked over a couple of strong margaritas.

"I was doing hair at Caesar's when I met Bill. He used to come in on Fridays, cash his check, have dinner, and gamble or sit in the lounge listening to the music. We were both living in South Shore at the time. He had a construction job and going to school to get his licenses. I had just moved up from Carmel after finishing cosmetology school. It was so fun in those days. We got pretty wild. We eventually moved to the north shore to get away from the city atmosphere down there. Shane was born at Incline Hospital. We moved into our home when he was two. We were renting in Kings Beach, but Bill wanted to get out of California for tax reasons. We enjoyed all of the seasons, skiing, hiking, boating, biking, you name it, it kept us busy. Bill and I aren't as active as we used to be, but we still love living here."

"Well, Mike and I started dating in college. He loved to ski. We vacationed here as often as possible. When a position came up at the church, he took it. Gina was nine at the time. It is such a close-knit community, we felt right at home. We lived in an apartment across from Village Shopping center and gradually moved up until we found the house on Eagle. Due to some female problems, I was not able to have more children after Gina. She's been the angel of my life. Mike wanted a large family, but was very happy with our threesome. He took Gina everywhere. As she got older though, she and I became a tight duo. We'd shop and do girly things together. Mike was pretty much on his own after that. He and Gina still used to ski together, though. That was their together time while I read, cleaned the house, or cooked. After she moved to Tulsa, it was difficult for us."

"Shane said you moved her out there to your sister's place. That's when you found out she was pregnant, right? Shane went through a long depression. We went with him to Arizona State University and then to Cal Berkeley. Both schools offered him scholarships. His heart just wasn't in it. Bill and I felt it too. Shane opted to go to the University of Nevada in Reno and be closer to home. How did Gina adjust to living so far away from home?"

"Oh, you know. Young people are resilient. It took her a while, but she got used to it."

"It sounds like the American Calvary adage when they forced Indians off their native lands, '*We can send them to any godforsaken place in the United States and they'll learn to adapt.*' It sounds so cruel. She was pregnant, seventeen or eighteen, and alone except for her aunt. Is that right?"

"Well, not exactly. She had a nice place to live. We took care of her expenses. I visited as often as I could. She was going to medical school and with a new baby and class, she really didn't have time for socializing." Suzanne turned her head and rolled her eyes.

"So no one knew where she was except for you and Mike? I saw that Shane's letters were returned unopened."

"We felt it was the best thing to do at the time," Lacy said, defending herself.

"Really? It broke his heart. I can't imagine how Gina felt," Suzanne said pointedly.

As the margaritas evaporated, the conversation got less civil.

"We did the Christian thing when…"

"I'm sorry, but that's a bunch of crap. You can't tell me that…"

Their waitress came over and asked them to quiet down because they were disturbing some of the lunch guests.

Whispering nose to nose, "You can't tell me that ripping two lives apart, sending your daughter off to live with your sister and having her fend for…"

"Now, you're out of line. You don't know what it was like for us," Lacy said, getting more defensive.

"No, I guess I don't, I…"

The waitress appeared once again, "May we have more chips and salsa and some fresh water too? Thank you," Lacy said. She took a deep breath, looked away, and then back at Suzanne. "So Shane is a high school teacher. He seems like the perfect type…"

Cutting her off before she added the qualifying *but,* she said, "He enjoys children. He has a passion and a natural empathy for his students. The references he obtained from the Connections Academy in Las Vegas were outstanding. May we have the check?" Suzanne asked when the waitress returned.

Suzanne and Shane drove back up to Incline. Lacy stayed at Gina's. She was on watch, as she put it, while Gina was at work, even though Gina was short distance away in the same hospital.

Wednesday evening, after a thorough evaluation, they determined that Taylor was strong enough to start getting the stem cell injections. The doctors monitored her continuously for the next several days, checking for signs of infection, bleeding, nausea, and stomach problems. Dr. Lippert requested two blood transfusions to treat some of the bleeding problems related to low platelets. Shane, Gina, Lacy, and Suzanne nervously followed her recovery. Gina clicked the nurse call button as though she was changing channels on the TV. The nurses never objected. They understood the gravity of the situation. There was also the underlying fear of cell rejection. By the end of the week, it was evident that the cells had started to grow normally. Although not out of the woods yet, the forecast was optimistic.

Chapter 26

*L*acy let Taylor lean on her as they made their way from the car to the front door. She had been in the hospital for more than a week. Her eyes were bright once again, and her smile was the first thing Missy saw as she whined through the window. As she bent over petting the dog, Taylor looked around, reacquainting herself with the house. It felt good to be home. Gina was at work and wouldn't be home until close to midnight, possibly later if there was a critical case she had to take care of. Even though the windows were open, the house felt hot and stuffy. The shades were drawn down tight in her bedroom, keeping the room cool. Her grandmother put her things away while Taylor turned down the bed and got into her pajamas. Missy brushed up against her legs, begging for attention.

"Yes, yes, I know, girl. I missed you too." Excited, she wagged her tail hitting the furniture.

"Would you like some water or juice?" Lacy asked.

"Some apple juice would be good, Gramma. Missy, let me get changed and then I'll play with you, okay? Who put the TV up, Gramma?"

"Oh, Shane hooked that all up for you. He knew you would be in bed, recuperating for a while. The channel changer is on the end table. This one here is for the receiver. You have music with surround sound too," she said, pointing to the speakers in the ceiling.

"He bought the TV for me and the sound system? I won't ever have to leave my bedroom. That's so awesome. Gramma, do you like him?" Missy put her front paws on the bed and nudged her elbow with her head.

"Yes, yes, I do, very much. Over the past several days, I have gotten to know him like I've never know him before. Taylor, people are quick to judge, quick to spin stories to support their view of someone. I am learning what a devastating effect this can have, not only on the person it is focused on, but on the very person perpetrating the story. God teaches us to judge no man. He teaches us to love our adversaries as we love ourselves. The Ten Commandments are such simple rules to live by. I have found Shane to live his truth quietly without reservation. That is an admirable trait. Taylor, I respect Shane. Particularly, after all we have put him through. His mother, your grandmother, is a wonderful human being as well. She is a very loving person and not afraid to speak her mind. Something I envy."

"I love you, Gramma. I just wanted you to know that."

"I love you too. Now, you get some rest. Do you want your door open or closed? I'll be back with your juice."

Lacy left feeling reflective and very much alone. Would Mike ever acquiesce? She opened the fridge and poured a glass of juice. Besides a few condiments, it was empty. She needed to go shopping. By the time she returned to Taylor's room, she was fast asleep. She turned the TV off, gave her a light tender kiss. Missy lay on the floor at the foot of the bed and looked up. "No, I'm not going to kiss you," Lacy said as she left. Missy lowered her eyes.

After almost three months, Shane found living at home a bit stuffy. Suzanne and Bill were beginning to wonder when this thirty-something son of theirs was going to get his own place as well. They truly did enjoy having him there though. In the meantime, Shane received his acceptance notification from RTI. School was scheduled to start in another week. He drove down to Reno after searching craigslist and the *Reno Gazette Journal* for homes to rent. His first choice, of course, was something in Gina's neighborhood, but there was nothing available. He did find a few places by the school, which made more sense. The homes were nice, but not quite what he wanted. After checking out a few, he narrowed it down to three. Sitting in the living room at the folk's house, he leafed through the flyers he collected. He decided on a two-bedroom place with new appliances and hardwood floors.

Shane called the property owner and signed a six-month lease. The landlord only wanted a hundred dollar deposit. *Cool,* he thought. He borrowed Bill's truck and drove around to thrift stores looking for furniture. He found a queen bed, lamps, an oak veneer nightstand, a card table for a dining table, and miscellaneous chairs.

He stopped by to see Taylor and spend as much time as possible whenever he made a trip from Incline. Although her recovery was slow, he saw a little more progress with every visit. Lacy just about moved in. She stayed with Taylor during the week and went home on the weekends when Gina was off. Then, Shane came by and spent more family time with his two girls. He did not stay the night ever. He longed for Gina's touch and to share the intimacy that he had missed for so many years. However, he did not feel it was appropriate. Gina had a difficult time letting him go. They would talk quietly, play Scrabble or cards, and kiss like teenagers in love after Taylor had gone to bed. Gina buried her strong desires as well. *Take it slow,* she told herself, *all in due time.*

It was late October and the leaves were beginning to change. Shane grew to dislike his new place. There was no air conditioning and the ceiling fans did little more than move the hot air around. He put tin foil on the bedroom and living room windows to keep the heat out. It made the house dark and oppressive. The water pressure was so bad, he had to run around in the shower to get wet. He felt like he was back in college. He left the refrigerator door open to cool the kitchen until he got his first utility bill. *Things have got to change*, he thought. The bed was uncomfortable. He bought a new mattress, but it was lumpy and too firm. The upside was he really enjoyed his teaching position. The faculty was friendly and receptive to new ideas. They kept the students engaged, and they liked the way the subjects were taught. He had his English class keeping journals, writing poetry and short stories. He came up with creative themes, fun events, and impromptu debates. He made math and science interesting as well. With such small classes, he was able to take them in the school van on field trips. They went to art museums, the National Automobile Museum, and walked the downtown corridor studying the architecture. He tried to schedule an event every other week. The students were excited to come to class. *What a concept*, he thought. He helped Taylor with her subjects as well. The bonding was natural and smooth. Gina often was at work when he stopped by in the evenings. He would start with schoolwork and gradually relax with Taylor and her grandmother, talking or watching a movie on TV.

Taylor, although not fully recovered, had started back to school at Galena High. She and Adam became close friends. He picked Taylor up in his Mustang for school and dropped her off, sometimes coming in for a snack and a short visit. Her grandmother enjoyed watching them build their relationship, recalling Gina and Shane when they first dated. However, Taylor wasn't allowed out on school nights while she was recuperating and adjusting to her new schedule. On the weekends, she had a ten o'clock curfew, which still gave them enough time for dinner and a movie.

She saw Dr. Lippert or his assistant, Dr. Hansen, every two weeks, unless something changed. So far, there had been no significant setbacks. It appeared that the cancer had been arrested and with a bit of luck, eradicated. Every one kept their fingers crossed. Her color and weight were gradually coming back. Her hair was getting thicker. One thing that never left was her smile. It was getting bigger and brighter.

"I really wish you would make an attempt to get to know Shane. He is a very nice man. Whether you like it or not, we are family, well, sort of. He is so good with Taylor. He cares a great deal for Gina and treats them both like royalty. Men like him are rare. The more time I spend with him and get to know him, the more I like him. Suzanne is a very caring person also. Mike, you need to let go of this anger."

"It's not anger."

"Well then, what is it?"

"It's a lack of respect for our values, our beliefs. He has never apologized for what he did. He feels no remorse for what he put us through. He wants to go on as though nothing happened. Well, I can't sign off on that type of behavior. He has committed a sin and he must repent."

"He has done whatever he can for the girls without seeking appreciation or acceptance. He is being himself regardless of how he is judged. There is a calm innocence about him. He has been so good to Gina and for Taylor. He saved her life, for God's sake. Yes, for God's sake. He didn't do it for a reward or a slap on the back. He did it because he could. Because for him, it was the only thing to do. If you qualify a friend as anyone who would risk their life without hesitation to save yours, he is that man. We are lucky to have a person like that in our daughter and granddaughter's lives. Do you understand what I am trying to tell you? We need to heal these wounds that have festered for so long now. Mike, please. I know your prostate cancer has rendered you impotent. Has it made you self-righteous as well? You know how much I love and respect you. Do this for us. Do this for you."

"Lacy, we need to face God. If God is willing to forgive us, I can forgive Shane. I can forgive Gina."

"He is." Taking him her arms, looking up into his blue eyes, she continued, "He teaches us to forgive. Please, Mike. Dear God, please."

—⌖—

"Pops, can I talk to you for a minute, man to man?"

Chuckling, "Well, of course, son."

"No, seriously. I have something on my mind I want to discuss."

Bill sat down in his armchair, facing Shane. "What is it?" he said, putting the TV on mute.

"I want to ask Gina to marry me." Pause. "Do you think it's a wise decision? You know, because of her dad? I think he hates me."

"Whoa, easy, son. Hate's a strong word."

"I'm not sure what to say to him. I think he doesn't care that much for Taylor either."

"Suzanne, come down here."

"Pops, I just wanted to talk to you about it."

Suzanne turned the vacuum off, took four steps down the stairway, and leaned over the bannister. "What is it?"

"Shane wants to ask Gina to marry him."

"Really, that's…"

"Now hold on you two. I am asking for advice here. This is not a done deal."

"He's afraid Mike is gonna kill him."

"Bill, don't talk nonsense," Suzanne said, coming down the rest of the way into the living room.

"Well, he's afraid it might affect the marriage. What do you think? I think he should marry her and damn the consequences with her father. It's their life, not his."

"Oh, Shane, I agree. There has never been a more perfect relationship than you and Gina."

"I beg to differ, my love, I think ours is slightly better than perfect," Bill said smiling.

"Thanks, Bill, I just love you. You say the sweetest things. Shane, you have our blessing. I think it is the right move. What can we do to help?"

"Help me zip up my Kevlar."

———

Knocking on the front door, "Hello, Mr. Conrad, may I come in?"

"Mike, who is it?"

"It's the Kaufmann boy, Shane."

"Well, let him in. Hello, Shane, won't you come in?" she said, stepping around Mike and opening the door further.

"Yes, well, ah, may I talk to you for a moment?" Shane asked. "Yes, have a seat," she said, pointing to the sofa. Mike sat down on the love seat, facing Shane, and Lacy found a spot next to him on the sofa. "Something to drink? Coffee?" they asked curiously.

"Ah, no, thank you, ma'am."

"Ooh, ma'am, aren't we formal," she said, trying to break the ice.

"Mr. Conrad, Mike, Lacy, I'd like to ask your permission to marry your daughter." He held his breath, waiting for the earth to split and the lightning to strike.

"You know, Shane, it takes a lot of courage for a man to ask what you just did after what you did to our daughter. Lacy and I have tried to come to grips with the way it has affected our lives, including our granddaughter," he said, waving his wife off with his hand as he spoke. Lacy rolled her eyes, waiting for a chance to speak. "I've had to do a lot of soul searching and have made some terrible mistakes myself. My wife informs me that you are one special kind of man. Truthfully, I couldn't agree more." Lacy's eyes lit up as the epiphany hit her. "Shane, we would be thrilled, no, honored to have you as our son," he said, looking at Lacy for confirmation. "What you have done for our granddaughter and her mother is beyond wonderful. You have our blessing, son." Standing up, Mike pulled Shane up by the shoulders and hugged him. "I love you, son. I am so sorry. I have been a martyr and a fool," he whispered, choked with emotion.

Lacy was unable to move. Shane turned to her, bent over, and hugged her where she sat. She was unable to speak.

"Thank you. Thank you, I will always love her and take care of her. And Taylor too."

"We know you will, son. We know you will."

Lacy slowly got to her feet and walked over to her husband. "I love you so much," she said, hugging him, burying her head against his chest.

Chapter 27

touch of winter was in the air when Gina and Shane went out for a quiet dinner at Mario's Bistro Napoli. Gina wore an elegant white dress with a low-cut back. A halo of pearls adorned her neck and lay in subtle contrast to her olive skin. Shane dressed in designer jeans and a long-sleeved blue shirt. He combed his hair straight back, touching his collar. They selected a fine Napa Valley cabernet and an order of brochette to start. Shane watched carefully as the waiter uncorked a 1990 Mondavi Reserve California and poured just a taste into his glass. He swirled it around, watching it slide seductively down the sides. He took a long slow deep breath, smelling the aroma, and then sipped it curiously.

"Excellent."

"Very good." The waiter poured Gina a moderate amount and then poured Shane's glass.

"May I take your order?" the waiter asked.

"Gina would like the veal piccata."

"Excellent choice. Our soup tonight is minestrone or the house salad with gorgonzola?"

"Salad, please."

"And you, sir?"

"I'm hungry, so I'm going to have the eggplant parmesan. And I'll have your salad as well."

"Very good. Anything else?" he asked, picking up the menus, preparing to leave.

"No, I think we're good, thanks."

The appetizer arrived just as the conversation was turning to Taylor's new interest in fashion.

"She finds the cutest things to wear, and they are such a bargain. She sure knows where to shop. She always looks so ladylike, even when she goes to school."

"She is a stunning young woman, no doubt," Shane said, absently dropping his napkin on the floor. He bent down to get it, and on one knee, he looked up into Gina's eyes. She looked at him curiously. He pulled a small box out his coat pocket as he spoke softly, "I have loved you longer than I can remember. You have been my breath, my heart, and my soul. I, I thought I'd never see you again, and now, I never want to let you go. Will you marry me, Gina Conrad?" he said, opening the box, exposing a beautiful three-diamond ring. Explaining. "These two stones represent you and me. The smaller one snuggled between us here." Pointing. "Is Taylor," he said, slipping it on her finger as she sat speechless. She covered her quivering mouth as tears cascaded down her cheeks.

"Yes, oh, yes. Yes, yes, yes. I love you so much." Hands wet with tears, she reached down and kissed him affectionately. The restaurant was quiet. Every patron had their eyes on them as the scene unfolded, and then they erupted in a loud applause. Shane slowly got back in his seat, feeling very self-conscious. "Shane, it's beautiful." Crying with a huge smile on her face.

"Here, here." Came the toast. Shane held up his glass, and then Gina raised hers; they clinked and smiled at their kind audience, feeling a little embarrassed at the attention.

"Mom, it's Gina. Are you still awake? Guess what?"

Hiding what she already knew was coming. "What, is everything okay?"

"Shane asked me to marry him tonight. I am so happy."

"That's wonderful, dear."

"You don't sound excited for me."

"Well, to tell you the truth, your father and I already knew he was going to propose."

"You did? How? When?"

"He came by to ask your father's permission to marry you." Clearing the emotion out of her throat. "And he said yes. After all this time, he finally accepted him. It was a very special moment. I will never forget it."

"He did? Shane? What did Shane do?" Gina asked surprised.

"Your father picked him up and hugged him. It was precious. I know you two will be very happy. Have you decided on a date or where you'll have the ceremony?"

"Well, we'd like to keep it small, close friends, family. We'd like to do it soon too. And keep it a simple ceremony, perhaps at Sand Harbor."

"How soon? I'd like to invite a few of our friends. It'll take time to get the invitations out."

"Well, we were thinking, Saturday, December 10. We'd like to have it outdoors before it gets too cold."

Shane called the park service and reserved the gazebo between the boat ramp beach and a small inlet. It was a beautiful venue for the event, overlooking the lake from almost every angle. Inside the structure, there was a large gas cook top, counters, and a prep sink. The building was open on all sides and octagonal in design, the kitchen area being the center, and long rectangular tables fanning out from there. If the weather became adverse, they would be able to get out of the wind, rain, or worse case, the snow. Ally and Maria conspired to help decorate the interior posts, tables, and the walkway leading up to the gazebo from the parking area. Suzanne hired a local restaurateur and close friend to cater the event, setting up a buffet line along the northern perimeter. Ally called Bryn and asked if he would play DJ again and he gladly accepted. A sound system was already in place. All he had to do was set up a table for his computer and turntables to connect to it.

Just past the rotunda was a large open sandy area. Shane and Gina elected to create a circle of energy with everyone holding hands, surrounding the duo as they exchanged their vows.

A hint of wind hushed through the fading aspens and pines. Gray and white clouds slowly drifted by watching the wedding party set up. The boat ramp and adjacent beach were empty except for a few people out for a late autumn stroll. The sun blinked on the rocks and water, warming the day slightly and then disappearing again. Ally and Mitch were the first to arrive and starting draping white cloth. Maria and Rob joined them, adding white roses, accented with a red one here and there. They spread white and red linens on the tables and dropped rose petals along the paths, which shifted playfully with each faint gust. Arrangements of white and red carnations, roses, and black pebbles in small fish bowls were the centerpieces. Maria and Rob spread a variety of petals over the area where the circle would gather.

The caterers backed their van up as close as possible to unload pans of meat, platters of hors d' oeuvres, desserts, cases of wine and champagne. After lighting the stove, they prepared the main dishes. The aroma drifted out over the lake, attracting fowl, chipmunks and squirrels, standing at attention, waiting patiently for an opportunity to grab a morsel. They placed the champagne and white wine in large tubs of ice. They set a bottle of red wine on each table.

Taylor and Adam pulled up in his Mustang. She made a three-tiered cake topped with white frosting and a bride and groom. *My parents are getting married. How strange that sounds*, she thought.

She spread strawberry halves on top of the white icing with a few blueberries. She brought a few sheet cakes in case they needed them. They were expecting thirty people.

When Bryn arrived and hooked up the stereo components, the forest was suddenly alive with the soulful sounds of Frank Tarantino and Jack Johnson as everyone went about their tasks.

Shane parked his Jetta in a spot reserved for the bride and groom. He dressed in a white linen suit with a light blue shirt and dark blue tie. Suzanne and Bill parked next to him. She wore a beige lace dress over a satin slip joined by Bill in gray slacks and a rose-colored shirt. Bill hung a camera over his shoulder. Holding hands, they walked cautiously out to the point overlooking the lake. With their backs to the shifting sun, they held hands, retracing the steps of their lives.

"Suzanne, as my bride, my life partner, you have brought me the greatest joy a simple man could ever hope for." Looking into her eyes, "I will love you from now until forever."

Softly smiling, "I adore you. You have given me magic, laughter, the best son ever, all the beauty and love a girl like me could ever want and need, my dear husband, thank you. This is such a precious day and standing here alone with you by my side, I feel so grateful that we have each other," Suzanne said, gently kissing and hugging, oblivious to the preparations going on behind them.

Guests arrived and signed in, leaving inspirational messages and small tokens of their friendship. Linda, Suzanne's sister, drove up from Reno with her husband Kevin. She would minister the intimate ceremony. Kevin set up a microphone stand and two chairs where he and Suzanne's brother Russell would play. Russell, tall and distinguished, shoulder length gray hair with streaks of black and a mustache, brought his favorite guitar. Kevin, tall and gray haired, a jazz singer, added a deep velvet soulful voice to the duo. Bryn continued to play his style of music until the ceremony began.

Dusty arrived with his date Katie, followed by Kyle and Roberta, Jake and Joan, JT, Tom, Chip and Marsha, and Nick with his sister Marcy.

Mike and Lacy pulled up in their Escalade with Gina sitting majestically in the back. Seeing them nearing the gazebo, Adam and Taylor opened the door for her and helped her out. Everyone stopped what he or she was doing as she made her entrance. Her short silky hair was smartly styled. Soft pink lipstick, a long white satin dress, and a bouquet of white roses in her hand, she looked stunning.

Shane took her hand and led her out to the sandy area beyond the rotunda. Russell played softly in the background as Kevin sang a love song he had written.

Linda coordinated the circle. "Everyone, please gather around Shane and Gina and hold hands." Linda stood eloquently, her long gray hair streaked with black, feathered around her in the breeze. Standing between Gina and Shane, holding their hands, she began as soon as the circle was complete.

"Everyone, I invite you to close your eyes and take a long deep breath. Feel the ground beneath you. Feel the energy that flows through your hands around the circle. Feel your feet on the earth, the air that moves around you. We are standing here today upon the shoulders of our ancestors that have passed before us. Our fathers, our mothers, welcome their spirit here today to join us. Feel the life that surrounds us, growing, breathing, the trees, the leaves, the animals, the water. Breathe, the mountain air, feel the clouds as they float by. Tilting her head back, breathe. Slowly open your eyes bringing all that energy, all the spirit, and love to this circle, to this moment, to Gina and Shane." She moved Gina, Shane, and herself so they stood back to back facing the circle. Slowly turning counterclockwise, "As we turn, look into our eyes, sharing all that is beautiful, feel the love, the energy, breathe." Eye to eye, they nodded. They smiled. They felt the energy flowing through their hands. The circle became one heartbeat, one breath. The bond was strong as Linda turned Gina and Shane to face each other and recite their vows.

"My dearest Gina, since we were teenagers, young and foolish, I have loved you. I have suffered grief, despair, loneliness, but like a light in the distance, your love was out there guiding me back to you. You and our daughter Taylor are the greatest gifts any man could hope for. I have always and will always love and cherish you. Marriage is but a sign of the commitment I made to you years ago." In the background, Bryn plays Mariah Carey's "Forever." *"Forever and ever, I know that forever, you will always be the only one."* Shane slipped the ring back on her finger. "This unbroken silver band represents my eternal love. I love you." Taylor let go of Adam's hand to wipe her face. A few others did the same.

Standing together again, Gina spoke, "Shane Kaufmann, you have been in my dreams forever. Your strength, your unconditional love, I always knew you were there with me in my darkest days. You saved our daughter's life. There is no greater gift a mother can receive. I will always love you. We will always love you. There is no greater, kinder man on earth. As we grow old together, I will adore you, cherish you until my heart beats no more." Slipping on his ring. "This symbol of my love, our love, is just that, a symbol. We truly don't need rings, my love is deeper and stronger than any symbol I may give you. I will always love you."

Linda said, "Please step forward as tightly as possible and welcome Gina and Shane Kaufmann." Russell played softly in the background as each member of the circle hugged and kissed the newlyweds.

Ally choreographed the wedding pictures with Mitch's help. They walked out to the point where Suzanne and Bill had stood earlier, taking a picture of the couple, then with Taylor and introducing each set of parents, shooting a final set of group shots down by the water.

Returning to the gazebo, Bryn, Russell, and Kevin had opened the champagne, poured the guests each a glass, and asked for a toast.

Mike stepped forward, surprising Lacy and offered the first words. Clearing his throat, "You people have known me most of your lives. I almost made the greatest mistake a person, a parent can make. In fact, I have made grievous errors in judgment. I am thankful and proud to welcome Shane to our family. My wife, my daughter, my granddaughter are the most precious"—choking with emotion—"things in my life. I am honored to add my new son-in-law Shane to this cherished set." Tears ran down Lacy's face as she held his hand and arm. "May they live long, laugh often, and love always."

"Here. Here."